"YOU ARE SO BEAUTIFUL WHEN YOU'RE MAD."

Camille blinked in confusion, and then did something she'd never done in her life. She slapped Seth's face with a resounding smack. "There! Do you find that amusing?"

His eyebrows rose as one hand came up slowly to rub the spot that was turning red. "You're quite a little hellcat, aren't you?" he said softly, surprise and a hint of admiration mingling in his dark gaze.

Realizing what she'd done, Camille promptly burst into tears, dropping her face into her hands and sobbing, "Just go away."

Seth ignored her command and wrapped his arms around her shaking form. He held her fast until she stopped struggling, whispering soothing words in her hair and stroking her back. That he'd caused her this much unhappiness flooded him with more guilt. He couldn't leave her behind when he returned to Oregon. His conscience wouldn't allow it. Extracting a handkerchief from his coat pocket, he pressed it into her hands and said gruffly, "I'm not taking this lightly, I assure you. Everything's going to be fine, Camille. Please stop crying. I think I should marry you. It will solve both our problems."

BOOK YOUR PLACE ON OUR WEBSITE AND MAKE THE READING CONNECTION!

We've created a customized website just for our very special readers, where you can get the inside scoop on everything that's going on with Zebra, Pinnacle and Kensington books.

When you come online, you'll have the exciting opportunity to:

- View covers of upcoming books

- Read sample chapters

- Learn about our future publishing schedule (listed by publication month *and author*)

- Find out when your favorite authors will be visiting a city near you

- Search for and order backlist books from our online catalog

- Check out author bios and background information

- Send e-mail to your favorite authors

- Meet the Kensington staff online

- Join us in weekly chats with authors, readers and other guests

- Get writing guidelines

- AND MUCH MORE!

**Visit our website at
http://www.zebrabooks.com**

MAIL-ORDER BRIDE

Sandra Donovan

Zebra Books
Kensington Publishing Corp.

http://www.zebrabooks.com

TO MY STAUNCHEST SUPPORTERS:
AMY, MOM, BEV AND BONI—
AND MY TWO LITTLEST DARLINGS,
MOLLY AND HOPE.

SPECIAL THANKS TO MY FRIENDS AT
NUTRACEUTICS—
YOU ALL LIGHT UP MY DAYS.

Chapter 1

San Francisco, California
August, 1860

Seth Braden's dark head nestled comfortably on Sally's shoulder as they slept peacefully in her room above the Red Door Saloon.

Cooper Maxwell moved down the dingy hallway and tapped lightly on the door. When he got no answer, he opened the door a crack and peered in. Crossing the room, he shook the sleeping man. "Wake up, partner. Today's a big day . . . come on."

The man in the bed groaned and tried to snuggle closer to the soft warmth of the woman next to him, but Cooper shook him again. The iron bed frame creaked loudly, and Sally opened one bloodshot eye and mumbled, "You'll have to wait yer turn, I'm busy . . ."

Seth turned his head to stare, bleary-eyed, up at the intruder. "Who the hell do you think you are—my mother? Go away," he growled.

"Your mother would yank a knot in your tail if she had to pull you out of a situation like this every morning," Cooper said, grinning.

Seth sat up with a groan, running a hand through his dark brown hair. "Dammit, Cooper, what do you want?"

Cooper moved to the end of the bed and leaned against the post. "I promised you a surprise today, and you said you'd get slicked up for the occasion, remember?"

Sally wrapped her arms around Seth's middle and cooed in a voice still raspy from sleep, "We had plans for this morning, sugar."

Seth patted her arm absently as he scowled at his partner. "I don't want a surprise—I want some sleep."

Cooper grinned again. "Since you're awake, you might as well get up."

"Boy, you clamp your teeth in and hang on just like a mean bulldog, don't you?" Seth shoved the blanket away and stood up, his head swimming for a moment. "I don't know how you can drink half the night and be so cursed cheerful in the morning."

"A strong constitution and a clear conscience," Cooper said without hesitation. He stepped over to a straight-backed chair and sat down, crossing his legs.

Seth snorted and began picking up his clothes from the floor. He knew from experience that Cooper wouldn't give up.

When Seth finished dressing, he leaned down and dropped a light kiss on top of Sally's head and discreetly pressed some money into her hand. "Thanks for puttin' up with me, Sal," he said, giving her a disarming smile.

"Anytime, sugar . . . anytime," she murmured.

As the two men walked through the saloon, Seth felt his queazy stomach rumble at the smell of mixed odors in the barroom. Stale cigar smoke, unwashed bodies, raw liquor and cheap perfume. He grimaced. It was funny, he thought, how differently he viewed a saloon at night. It was exciting—the cigar smoke was aromatic, the prostitutes were beautiful and alluring. The cold light of day effectively took the sparkle off the place, leaving a dingy residue in its place.

The only inhabitant this morning was a skinny, balding man wearing a wide apron who stood at the end of the bar polishing glasses. He nodded as they passed. Once they were on the street, Seth's head began to throb with a vengeance. The bright sunlight pierced his skull by way of his squinting eyes. Damn Cooper Maxwell—he'd been playing mother hen for the last month since they'd arrived in San Francisco. Coop had been pulling him out of bar fights, crooked poker games and whorehouses, and Seth was tired of it. After ten months at their isolated logging camp in Oregon, he needed to let off some steam.

Cooper led him to a fancy hack where a young driver waited patiently on the high seat. Seth's eyebrows rose. "I hired it for the day," Cooper said. "We'll need it for the surprise I promised you."

They climbed into the roomy carriage and Cooper nodded to the driver. "O'Leary's Boarding House," he instructed. "Unless you'd rather go for eggs and gravy at the El Dorado first?" he asked, glancing at his friend with a mischievous twinkle in his eyes.

Seth scowled. His stomach revolted at the thought. He swallowed heavily as the vehicle bounced over the uneven plank street. "You're enjoying yourself too much, Coop. What have I done to deserve this torture?"

Cooper's brow furrowed as if in deep thought. "Well, for the last six months I've had to listen to your complaints about fickle women and endure your sour moods—not to mention occasional fits of temper."

"Dammit, Coop, that's a lie. I'm easier to get along with than a hound under the supper table," Seth protested.

Cooper fixed him with a level look. "Not since Patience Underwood jilted you."

With a warning frown creasing his brow, Seth pointed out, "She wouldn't even cross my mind if you didn't mention her all the time."

Cooper sighed. "The only thing wrong with you is your male pride has been trampled. Hell, Seth, if I was a woman, I wouldn't wait six years for a wedding ring either."

As the carriage left the saloons and houses of prostitution in the Cat Alley district, the driver maneuvered the vehicle skillfully through the bustling central business area. Seth gazed disinterestedly at a passing iron foundry and grumbled, "Whose side are you on anyway?" He wondered if Coop was right, not that he would admit it. Perhaps he had been more angry than hurt at her defection. It was the first time in his life a woman had walked away from him.

"Starting today you can put all that behind you. It'll be a new beginning." Cooper slapped him on the shoulder and settled back in his seat.

"I can hardly wait," Seth murmured, closing his eyes against the glare of the sun. All he really cared about was arriving at Mrs. O'Leary's without losing the contents of his stomach. A stiff shot of whiskey, a bath and clean clothes were the things he needed before he could think about any harebrained scheme of Cooper's.

Mrs. O'Leary's Boarding House was located in the north part of town fronting the cove. The area was a mixture of residences and businesses in retail and manufacturing. It was a homey neighborhood, well-tended and safe. Seth and Cooper always stayed at Mrs. O'Leary's when they came to San Francisco, and they'd grown quite fond of her . . . and she of them.

When the carriage stopped outside the two-story red-brick house, the wiry little gray-haired woman was vigorously sweeping the front porch. She stopped and leaned on the broom handle as the two young men came up the steps. "Top of the mornin' to ya now, Mr. Braden. It's glad I am that Mr. Maxwell found your darlin' self, though I'll not be askin' where.'' Her faded blue eyes twinkled mischievously.

Seth gave Cooper a sour look. "It seems there isn't a place in this whole blessed city where he can't find me."

"You young rips need to sow a few wild oats, and I'm not too old to be understandin' that, but it's about time you thought of settlin' down. Now, I have two darlin' nieces, Bridget and Nola—strong, hard-workin' girls—they work for the Rooneys up on Rincon Hill—"

Cooper coughed. "Excuse me for interrupting, Mrs. O'Leary, but Seth is looking a little green around the gills. Do you have any of your wonderful coffee brewing? I think he could use a cup as well as a bath. We have an appointment at one this afternoon."

At the mention of Mrs. O'Leary's nieces, Seth grew paler. The last thing he needed, he thought grimly, was an entanglement with a "nice" girl who had marriage on her mind.

The ruddy-faced little woman frowned. "Dear me, I'm just blatherin' on and here you are feelin' sick. Take him on up, Mr. Maxwell, and I'll send Finnigan with the hot water."

Relieved, Seth followed Cooper across the immaculate foyer and up a flight of oak stairs. Cooper turned to Seth as they reached their adjoining doors. "I'll take a short nap, then join you for lunch. I had a pretty late night myself."

"Don't oversleep, Coop. I'd hate like hell to miss this 'event' you have planned for me," Seth advised.

Cooper grinned. "Go ahead and make fun, but you'll be sorry you did before the afternoon is over."

"I'm sure I will," Seth muttered.

At one-thirty, Seth and Cooper sat in the rented carriage across the street from the stage depot on Montgomery Street. Both men were dressed in their best black broadcloth suits and white shirts. Seth had combed his thick brown hair, but a stray lock fell forward on his wide forehead, giving him a rakish look. He lounged against the padded cushion with one black boot resting on the seat across from him and was smoking a cheroot. "Just how long do we have to wait—and what are we waiting for?" he asked, boredom edging his tone. Two women approached on the boardwalk that fronted the stores. The younger one, probably the other woman's daughter, Seth guessed, caught his eye. A slow smile curved her lips as she boldly looked him over. Seth tipped his head in acknowledgment and returned her perusal with lazy interest. The older woman caught his look and gave a sharp yank on the girl's arm.

Cooper chuckled when the two were past. "Better watch it, Seth. You've been flogged by more than one mother hen."

"She smiled at me first, and I don't like to be rude," Seth said, defending himself, blowing a smoke ring into the air and watching it drift away.

"That's the damnedest part of it; all these females are drawn to you like bees to a hive. If we could bottle and sell it, we could give up logging and live a life of ease," Cooper teased.

"If you're trying to flatter me into forgetting that we've been sitting here for hours with nothing to do, it won't work. I could have won a fortune by now at the faro table at the El Dorado." Seth pulled his watch from his coat pocket and glanced pointedly at it.

Appearing undaunted by his friend's testy attitude, Cooper smiled. "All right, I'll give you a hint. Your surprise will be on the next stage, but it's a little late. It's something that you've been needing and will keep you warm on cold nights."

Seth was curious, in spite of himself. He discarded the idea of a woolen union suit. He already owned three. No, it had to be something that wasn't normally shipped in. The only thing he could come up with was the special wool socks his mother knitted. The supply he'd brought with him six years ago had long since worn out. Seth's brow furrowed. Even if Cooper had asked his mother to send some, why would he create such a tempest in a teapot over something as trivial as socks? Well, Seth thought, Cooper's sense of humor was a bit strange at times.

Before he could speculate further, the stage turned the corner and came barreling down the street. Cooper climbed out of the carriage and Seth followed, dropping his cheroot on the planked road and crushing it under his heel. "When we pick up whatever it is, Coop, I say we retire to the El Dorado for a drink and some pretty companions—I'm buying."

Cooper threw him an amused glance as they crossed the street. "Your surprise may not appreciate that," he said.

Seth rolled his eyes heavenward. Could ten months in the deep woods of the logging camp have addled Coop's brain?

The stage door opened, and a man dropped the folding steps and descended. He turned to assist the female passengers. Cooper and Seth stood back and watched. Cooper's eyes lit up as a pretty young woman stepped down, but his face fell when she turned and plucked a toddler from the doorway of the coach. Next came a heavyset matron and then a young boy. The driver jumped down and closed the coach door. "Damn," Cooper swore under his breath. "Her wire from El Paso said she'd be on this stage."

Seth frowned at Cooper. "What are you muttering about?"

"I need to talk to the driver. You wait here," Coop said, following the man inside the building. Seth ignored the command and went after them.

Camille stood talking to the older woman. At the same time, she glanced at the people who milled around the stage. Some were just curious, but others had a purpose. It was someone in this last group that Camille was looking for.

"Good luck finding your brother." Mrs. Porter smiled. "It's been a pleasure knowing you."

Camille smiled. "The same to you, Mrs. Porter. I hope we meet again someday." Camille's gaze settled on the two handsome young men entering the stage office. The dark-haired one looked exactly like the description in the letter. With a pounding heart, she moved to the window of the building for a better look. He was tall, broad-shouldered and lean of hip and carried himself with confidence. The dark scowl on his face, however, sent an unexpected shiver of apprehension down her spine. He's the one . . . he had to be Seth. His companion was blond, the right age, and just as he had been described in the letter. I must have been moonstruck, Camille thought suddenly, turning from the window. It was too late to get away, however, for they were on their way out the door with Hadden, the stage driver.

"This young lad's name is Sinclair, Mr. Maxwell. That's the best I can do for ya," Hadden said.

Cooper looked mildly confused, while Seth's frown deepened. "What the hell is going on, Coop? You didn't tell me it was a woman you were expecting. And what has she got to do with a surprise for me?" Seth asked, his voice bristling with suspicion.

Cooper ignored Seth, and shook his head as if to clear his thoughts. Stepping forward, he asked, "Your name is Sinclair?"

Camille's mouth felt as dry as a wad of cotton. "Well . . . yes, I'm Camille Sinclair." Reluctantly, she reached up and took the hat off, exposing a mass of auburn hair in a bun on top of her head. She thrust her hand out. "You must be Cooper."

Still confused, Seth watched this exchange, taking note of her huge cornflower blue eyes, wide with anxiety as she stood her ground. She reminded him of a colt, brazen, yet unsure of itself.

A slow smile curved Cooper's mouth as he muttered, "Well, I'll be damned . . . it's a her instead of a him."

Seth found nothing amusing about the situation. He demanded, "What are you up to, Cooper?"

Cooper smiled serenely and reached for the girl's hand.

"This is Camille Sinclair, Seth . . . your mail-order bride."

Chapter 2

"My what?" Seth exploded.

Camille might have found Seth's ferocious expression comical had it not struck a note of dismay in her. The man she had traveled thousands of miles to marry, Seth Braden, knew nothing of her coming. It was clearly written across his face along with the revulsion he felt at the very idea. Obviously, it had been his friend's doing. That much she gleaned from their exchange. Camille wished the ground would open up and swallow her.

Cooper squeezed her hand. "Now, now, Seth, calm down. When you have time to think about this you'll be pleased. I'm sure he will, Miss Sinclair." Cooper smiled and nodded.

Seth looked at Camille as if she had two heads, even as his mind registered the fact that she had the face of an angel. It was heart-shaped, with a delicate bone structure. Her blue eyes were framed by thick, dark lashes and her lips were full and sensuous. All he could think about at the moment, though, was the outrageous trick Cooper had played on him. "What would please me, Cooper, is if you would stay of my business. If I want a wife, I'll damn well get one myself!" Seth turned abruptly and strode away.

A strange feeling of relief washed over Camille as he disappeared around the corner. She couldn't explain it, but the moment she'd laid eyes on him, warning bells had begun to go off inside her head. He was so big and masculine . . . he exuded power and strength . . . he caused her insides to tremble. Taking a shaky breath, she said, "I suppose I can safely look forward to spinsterhood now."

Still holding her cold hand, Cooper chuckled and gave it another squeeze. "Horse feathers! Let's get your bags and I'll take you to meet Mrs. O'Leary. We'll talk on the way."

When the carriage headed toward the north part of town, Camille recovered enough to ask, "If Seth doesn't want a wife, why did you send for me?"

Cooper grinned. "He does want a wife. He just won't admit it. We've been close friends since we were boys and I know him pretty well."

Camille looked dubious. "Now that I've met him, I can't say I'm sorry he's against the idea. His disposition is rather bad, and I've no wish to be tied to a snarling beast for life."

Cooper laughed outright. "His bark is worse than his bite, I assure you. As a matter of fact, before Patience . . . uh, what I mean is, he's normally very pleasant. Now, I have a question if you don't mind?"

Bemused by this tame description of his friend, Camille nodded.

"Why are you dressed like a boy?"

She smiled. "For protection on the journey. Big Amos thought I should hide the fact I'm a woman. All sorts of men would take advantage of a female alone, he said. Although I hardly think anyone would bother me, and I told him so, but he made me promise. Plain girls have no need to fear that sort of thing," she said matter-of-factly.

Cooper's expression registered surprise. "I don't know who told you you're plain, but they're wrong. I think you're pretty, and when we get you cleaned up and into a proper dress, I'll bet you'll be downright irresistible." He frowned suddenly. "Who's Big Amos?"

Camille decided he was just being kind. He seemed to be the sort, like Big Amos, who was tough on the outside and all soft on the inside. She was fairly sure Seth Braden didn't share such an opinion of her. He'd taken one look at her and run the other way. Letting the compliment slide, she answered his question. "My best friend. He owns a tavern on the Charleston docks. It was Big Amos who pointed out your advertisement in the newspaper. If it hadn't been for him, I would be married to old Josiah Hall by now. He's eighty if he's a day, and hasn't got a tooth in his head." Camille sighed. "We didn't have much in common."

His eyes danced merrily. "Your best friend is the proprietor of a tavern, and you were betrothed to a man old enough to be your grandfather? You've lived a colorful life, little Camille. No wonder you weren't concerned about traveling clear across the country by yourself to marry a man you'd never met."

Camille shrugged. "I figured he couldn't be as bad as toothless old Josiah."

Cooper threw his head back and laughed. "If my pigheaded friend holds out against this marriage, I'll marry you myself."

Camille gave him a sidelong glance "So you're not married either? Why, pray tell? You're much nicer than Seth."

Cooper grinned. "Well, I suppose I've been too busy with the work at the sawmill. Seth and I started this business three years ago and each year our output has doubled. We've barely had time to breathe, much less court possible wives. Besides, we're pretty isolated up in Oregon for most of the year."

"You found time to send for me," Camille pointed out.

Cooper's gaze slid away. "I was worried about Seth," he said, and hastily added, "Ah, here we are."

Camille looked up as the carriage rolled to a stop. The redbrick house with the wide porch was neat, clean, and looked wonderfully inviting after her long journey. Later, after she'd rested, she would question Cooper more on his last enigmatic remark about Seth Braden. At the moment, though, she was exhausted.

Camille awoke with a start in a dim room. She was lying on a soft bed, covered to her chin with a warm blanket. It was a luxury she hadn't known in weeks.

A feeling of euphoria surrounded her until she remembered where she was and the events of the afternoon. When the stage arrived, she'd felt both relief and anxiety. It hadn't helped matters to discover that Seth Braden was not the man who had asked her to travel out here to be his bride, but his friend, Cooper. And what was worse was the fact that neither man wanted a wife.

Loud voices from the next room caught her attention, and she sat up, recognizing the deep, angry tones of Seth Braden. It wasn't polite to eavesdrop, she thought, but then again, they shouldn't be shouting if they didn't want everyone in San Francisco to hear their conversation.

"At least stay for supper, Seth. You're going to hurt her feelings if you don't!" Cooper's voice sounded exasperated and coaxing at the same time.

"Dammit, Cooper, she looks like a boy! I like my women soft and feminine. This is the craziest scheme you've ever had and you can damn well get out of this little scrape on your own."

Camille's face burned as she listened. Self-consciously, she touched her plump breasts. She knew her curves had been hidden beneath loose boy's clothing, but his tone was less than complimentary. She heard a door slam and the sound of heavy, booted feet stomping down the hall. "Mr.

Arrogant Seth Braden, I am not a 'scrape' to be gotten out of!'' she muttered. He needn't worry about her any longer, she decided with a stiffening of her spine. She'd been taking care of herself since she was nine years old—ever since her brother, Forrest, had sailed away. She would find work and make her own way in this vast, sprawling city.

With that resolve firmly in place, she rose and lit the lamp that stood on the dresser. After washing her face in the porcelain bowl, she shed her nightgown and took a light blue silk dress from the armoire, along with her hoop. She grimaced at her lack of wardrobe. The blue silk and one other of forest green were the only two nice dresses she owned—and they had been hand-me-downs from her cousin Prudence, along with the brown wool shawl that the girl had deemed not pretty enough to wear. The white lawn nightgown she had just removed was threadbare. Two gingham day dresses, and two sets of boys' clothing—which had been her brother's, a pair of black kid slippers and, of course, her boots.

It hadn't mattered before, she thought. Finding Forrest had been the only important thing. Now, however, she would need to find work.

Stepping into the hoop, she tied it around her waist. She slipped the blue dress over her head and fastened the tiny buttons down the front of the bodice. She blushed when she noticed the outline of her nipples under the smooth material. Her only chemise had gone threadbare and she'd thrown it away. Aunt Lavinia was miserly. Camille still remembered the dozens of pretty dresses she'd owned before her parents died and their plantation had been sold. There had been plenty of everything then, especially love. Pushing these thoughts from her mind, Camille donned her slippers and brushed her shiny auburn curls. Before leaving the room, she sat down and wrote a brief letter to Forrest. She prayed he would answer soon.

* * *

Evening shadows gathered in the parlor as Camille passed through. Light streamed from the kitchen doorway, as well as the wonderful aroma of hot food. Her mouth watered. She'd already had a sample of Mrs. O'Leary's cooking when she first arrived. The ruddy-faced little woman had been more than hospitable, feeding her, helping her wash her hair and take a warm bath.

When she reached the doorway, she saw, to her dismay, Seth talking to the older woman. Camille thought he'd gone out. Mrs. O'Leary looked up just then and caught sight of her. "There's the sweet colleen now, Mr. Braden, up from her nap. Did you get enough rest, dearie?"

Camille avoided looking at Seth as she advanced into the room. "Yes, thank you. I slept very well," she said, and then gestured. "Is something wrong with your hand?"

"Oh, dear, just a silly accident. I was blatherin' to Mr. Braden here and spilled some hot soup on it," Mrs. O'Leary said, making light of it.

Camille walked over and gasped at the sight of the angry red patch of skin. A nasty blister was already forming. "That must hurt terribly."

"Not so much," the woman said with a strained smile. "With all the work to be done around here, I can't be takin' to me bed for something like this."

"Well, you can't put it in hot dishwater or it'll get infected," Seth warned, affection and concern lighting his dark eyes.

His kindness surprised Camille. Briskly, she said to the older woman, "I'll be glad to finish the dinner and wash up afterward. You stay put. I have some wonderful ointment to spread on that burn. It'll take all the pain out of it." Without waiting for a reply, she went back to her room and retrieved a small tin.

When she returned, Seth was leaning casually against the sink with a cup of coffee in his hand.

For the second time that day, his presence overwhelmed Camille. He was so big and masculine . . . his wide shoulders seemed to fill the kitchen. He was dressed in snug black trousers and a white lawn shirt, open at the throat, revealing dark, curling chest hair. Abruptly, she dropped her eyes and moved past him to kneel down next to Mrs. O'Leary. "This won't hurt at all. I got it from a sea captain in Charleston who sailed regularly to Mexico. It comes from a plant down there. He said the Indians use it for all sorts of things."

She spread a thin layer of the salve on the burn and tried to concentrate on the task instead of the man who watched her.

Mrs. O'Leary looked from the young woman kneeling beside her to the frowning man nearby. "That does feel ever so nice, dearie, and I do believe I'll lay down in the parlor for a few minutes. Supper's all done except for taking the cornbread from the oven. Mr. Braden, would you be a good lad and get it out? And I would be ever so grateful if you would help Miss Sinclair here to carry the food to the dining room."

Seth's gaze narrowed for a moment at the innocent look the old lady bestowed on him. He'd never known her to ask for help of any kind, and usually made a great fuss if anyone even suggested she needed assistance. Short of looking like a jackass, however, he had to acquiesce. "Of course," he said.

Camille looked up at him. Their eyes locked for a moment, and she felt a frisson of excitement pass through her as if the contact had been physical. He turned away and picked up some pot holders. Camille helped Mrs. O'Leary rise, and walked with her into the parlor to see her settled.

When she returned to the kitchen, Seth's back was to her as he looked into one of the pots on the stove. That's good, she thought. She found it much easier to speak to his back. "I think we should discuss our situation, don't you? It's awkward, I realize, but it's not our fault, and I don't expect you to honor the bargain, especially since you didn't make it in the first place. We could, however, be civil to each other. And if we put our heads together, we could come up with a suitable punishment for Cooper.''

He turned after she started speaking, and the small frown on his face eased until she actually detected a twinkle of amusement in his dark eyes. ''I've already thought of quite a few ways to inflict pain on his person, but unfortunately they're all against the law.''

Camille moved to the built-in wall shelves and took down several serving bowls. ''From what I can gather, he thought he was doing you a favor, so I suppose his heart was in the right place. But it does leave me with a dilemma. Cooper hinted he would marry me, but I think I should look for employment instead.''

Seth took the pot of soup from the stove and dipped some into one of the bowls she placed on the table. Her close proximity, along with the musical sound of her soft Southern drawl, sent his pulse racing. She looked so different tonight. The silk dress displayed the curve of her generous breasts and matched the color of her incredible eyes. He had to fight an urge to span her tiny waist with his hands. She hardly looked like a boy now, he thought ruefully. Annoyed with his weakness, he moved away to the stove to get another pot.

''At the risk of repeating myself, I can choose my own wife if I decide to marry, but I don't see that possibility in my future,'' he said. ''And as to your situation, I'll see that Cooper finds a solution.'' He filled a bowl with boiled potatoes and carried it toward the dining room. Her comment about Cooper's offer of marriage had a disquieting effect on him. Why, he didn't know, for Cooper could do anything he damn well pleased with his own life. Seth placed the bowl on a hot pad in the center of the long mahogany table, and then lit the wall lamps around the room.

Camille's brow wrinkled in confusion. For a moment there,

she'd thought he was going to be friendly. She dropped a ladle in the soup bowl and started for the dining room. They met in the doorway, and he reached to take the bowl from her, brushing her fingers in the process. A current of excitement raced between the two of them and Camille's eyes flew up to his. Seth felt it too, but disguised his feelings more quickly. "We'd better hurry. I hear the boarders coming down," he said, his tone clipped.

Without another word, and avoiding any chance of touching, the two of them filled the table with food. Camille fixed a plate and took it to Mrs. O'Leary in the parlor. "How's the burn?" she asked.

The older lady smiled. "There's not a bit of pain now, dearie. It's a miracle!"

"Good. I left the tin of medicine in the kitchen for you. If it starts to hurt, just put more on. I'll be doing the dishes tonight, so don't worry about that." Camille's tone brooked no argument.

"You're just the kindest lass, and I thank you for all your help," Mrs. O'Leary said, and then added, "Why don't you ask that darlin' Mr. Braden to help you? I'm sure he wouldn't mind."

A slow flush crept over Camille's cheeks. She protested, "Oh, no, I can manage it fine by myself. Besides, he probably has plans for the evening."

"All right, dearie. You'd better run along and eat now, or there'll be nothin' left," the old woman advised.

When Camille returned to the table, Cooper rose quickly and held out the chair next to his. "Everyone, this is Miss Sinclair. Camille, meet Mr. Weston, Mr. Brown, Mr. and Mrs. Callen, and Miss Grainger." The people around the table nodded and spoke politely. Camille returned their greetings. She noticed Seth avoided looking at her, concentrating instead on his food.

Everyone obliged by passing the bowls to Camille and when she had her plate full, the young lady introduced as Miss

Grainger spoke up, "What brings you to San Francisco, Miss Sinclair?"

Seth's fork halted halfway to his mouth. The piece of potato wobbled and fell back to his plate as he glanced swiftly across the table.

A devilish gleam lit Camille's eyes as she opened her mouth to reply. She was stopped by Cooper's hand on hers. "Forgive me, Miss Grainger, for speaking out of turn, but Miss Sinclair has had a tragedy and finds it hard to talk about," Cooper explained with a note of concern in his voice.

"Oh, dear, I'm sorry! I wasn't trying to pry," Miss Grainger said, distress marking her expression.

Camille gave her a comforting smile. "Please don't be upset. It was an innocent question." She turned reproachful eyes on Cooper as everyone began to talk at once to cover the moment. "Shame on you," she hissed.

He leaned close and whispered, "I just wanted to save you and Seth some embarrassment."

Camille glanced over at Seth. His stare drilled into her as she gave him a sweet, innocent smile.

They finished the meal without further mishaps. When Camille offered the apple pie dessert, everyone declined but Cooper. Camille had a feeling they were anxious to leave the strained atmosphere of the dining room, which they did posthaste.

Camille, Seth and Cooper were left at the table with their coffee. Cooper dug into his piece of apple pie as if he hadn't eaten in a week. Seth glared at him. "If we hadn't been friends since we were boys, Cooper Maxwell, I would beat you sense-less. And I still might!" Seth's furious gaze swung to Camille. "And you! You were going to tell them the whole sorry story, weren't you? Admit it—I saw it in those big blue eyes of yours!"

"I was just going to tell them the truth," she protested, and rose to scrape the plates.

"Aw, Seth, don't get mad again," Cooper wheedled. "I

saved the day, didn't I? And you don't even have to thank me.''

Seth stood and threw his napkin on the table. ''The two of you deserve each other,'' he growled, and stalked out of the house, slamming the front door behind him.

Mrs. O'Leary appeared in the doorway, empty plate in hand, with a grin on her face. ''That darlin' Mr. Braden reminds me of me own dear Paddy, God rest his soul. He could raise hell with the best of 'em.''

Chapter 3

After breakfast the next morning, Camille took her sketch pad and charcoal to the front porch and sat on a wicker chair. She looked out over the bay at hundreds of tall-masted schooners as they bobbed in the water, vying for space. The terraced streets that ran parallel to Mrs. O'Leary's sloped gently down the hill toward the beach, the rooftops of the neat brick houses looking like stepping-stones for a giant.

As Camille sketched, some of the tension left her slim shoulders. An unconscious smile curved her lips. "A beautiful view, a sketchbook and a sunny day," she murmured. "What more could I ask for?" As she worked in broad, sure strokes, she took stock of her abilities. She could clean house—she'd certainly done enough of that at Aunt Lavinia's. Even if her cooking was a disaster, she could serve food at a restaurant. Being a seamstress was out of the question, for she couldn't so much as stitch a handkerchief. Perhaps a factory position, she thought. However, she'd had no experience with that type of thing either. Maybe in a city of this size, she could find a post as a governess.

After all, she liked children, could teach reading, writing and anything else with the proper books. With an emphatic nod of her head, she muttered, "Take care of the small details in life, Camille. The big ones will take care of themselves."

Seth felt like death warmed over as his hired carriage stopped on the corner of Mrs. O'Leary's street to let him out. He climbed down and dug in his pocket for some money. He looked up, shading his bloodshot eyes. "Remember one thing, partner. Drinking and gambling all night at the El Dorado will not make your problems go away . . . I know."

The driver took the fare with hardly a glance at Seth. "Yes, sir. I'll remember that."

As Seth neared the boardinghouse, he saw Camille on the front porch looking as fresh as a spring morning. He slowed his steps and watched as she glanced out toward the bay and then back down at something in her lap. Her profile was as delicate as a fine cameo, and the sun turned her thick cap of hair to molten copper. What was he going to do with her? he wondered irritably. It was one thing to tell Cooper that she was his problem, but quite another to turn his back on her. Something happened to his insides when she turned those big, innocent eyes on him. All his protective male instincts rose to the fore. "Dammit," he swore softly. He didn't need any more problems—the ones he'd had at the logging camp this past year were enough.

When Camille caught sight of him coming up the front walk, she nodded. "My, my! You're an early riser. How was your morning stroll?"

Seth rubbed the dark stubble on his chin and frowned. "You know very well I'm just getting home. And I don't find your wit very amusing." He climbed the steps and moved to her side.

"You weren't amused at dinner last night either. Does anything tickle your fancy?"

His dark eyes held hers for a moment before he shrugged. He didn't feel like arguing. "What's that you're doing?"

Something indefinable in his gaze sent her pulse skittering as her eyes dropped to her lap. She caught the faint scent of bay rum and tobacco as he leaned near to see her sketch. They were familiar masculine smells, ones she remembered from all the hours she'd spent on the Charleston docks talking to sea captains, sailors and the dockside tavern owners. They were all men, those friends of hers—young and old, big and small, all muscular and virile. None, however, had ever made her feel as this man did. With one look from those dark eyes or one word from him in that deep, velvety voice, she trembled inside with a strange excitement. She pushed these disquieting thoughts away and handed him her sketchbook. "I do a bit of drawing." Her voice was not quite steady.

Seth looked at the half-finished picture. "I'd say it's more than 'a bit.' This is very good. Do you have more?"

She nodded. "In my room. I have some scenes from home, and then I did a few of the passengers on the stagecoach."

He handed the book back. "I'd like to see them." Seth was careful not to touch her. It was hard enough being this close, where he could see the swell of her breasts and the faint outline of the darker crests of her nipples through her gingham dress.

"Sometime, perhaps," she said, guessing that he was only making polite conversation.

"Is Coop around?"

"He went out directly after breakfast and didn't tell me where."

Seth nodded. "How is Mrs. O'Leary's hand this morning?"

Camille smiled. "Much better. She cooked breakfast and I did the washing up. There's a pot of coffee on the stove if you'd like some."

The even whiteness of her smile was dazzling, and abruptly, he turned away. "Thanks, I could use a cup."

When he left her, Camille continued with her sketch and mentally calculated what she owed Cooper. She fully intended to reimburse him for her travel expenses, which he'd paid for as part of the bargain they'd made. Now there was the room and board here at Mrs. O'Leary's. Since she was not going to marry Seth, she couldn't allow Cooper to pay her way. She had a small amount of money put aside from selling her sketches on the docks.

When she figured Seth had had time to get his coffee and retire to his room, Camille rose and went in search of Mrs. O'Leary. She found her in the kitchen slicing meat from a large smoked ham. "You helped enough already this mornin', dearie. I can manage the cookin' of the noon meal," she said, putting the ham into a large pot of beans on the stove.

Camille smiled at the woman's brisk but kindly tone. "Although I'd be glad to help, I actually came in to ask your advice. I need to find employment and thought you might have some ideas." She put her sketchbook on the table and poured a cup of coffee before she sat down.

Mrs. O'Leary's brows rose as she wiped her hands on her white apron. "But dearie, Mr. Maxwell told me you came out here to be Mr. Braden's bride. What would you be needin' with work?"

"The whole thing was Cooper's doing and Seth is not too happy with the situation. He doesn't want a wife," Camille explained, a flush warming her cheeks.

"Heavens above! You mean you traveled all this way for nothin'? You must be heartbroken." The older woman looked outraged at the thought.

Camille had to smile at her dramatic response. "To tell you the truth, I'm not heartbroken at all. I answered the advertisement in desperation. My aunt was going to force me to marry an old man. And too, there's my brother, Forrest. I received a letter from him several months ago saying he was on his way to work at a logging camp in Oregon. I haven't seen him in nine years. So you see, coming out here was a godsend for me. All I have to do now is earn enough to pay my debts and my fare to Oregon.''

Mrs. O'Leary had been gathering ingredients to make pie crust as Camille talked. She stopped a moment and placed her hands on her hips. ''That may be so, lass, but those young rips should pay for misleading a darlin' girl like you!''

Camille sipped her coffee and waved away the older woman's objections. ''I'd rather take care of myself.'' She plunged on, outlining her abilities, and then asked, ''If you know of anyone needing help, I would appreciate a recommendation. Or, perhaps, I could find something in the newspaper.''

''I expect ya know yer own mind.'' Taking a basket from the pantry, she handed it to Camille. ''Be a good lass and fetch some peaches from the tree in the backyard while I give it some thought.''

After lunch, Camille set off on foot down the hill toward the docks. It was several blocks, but she didn't mind. She had a purpose. With her hair combed back sedately and her brown shawl wrapped around her shoulders, she hoped she looked older and more reserved for the coming interview. Patting her pocket, she was reassured her letter of introduction from Mrs. O'Leary was still there. Her letter to Forrest was tucked in there also, ready to send.

She passed several manufacturing businesses and two fish markets before coming to Kelly's Tavern, one street away from the docks. She wrinkled her nose at the fish smell in the air, and looked dubiously at the exterior of the plain brick building. Wide windows in front afforded little view of the interior since they were grimy. Mrs. O'Leary had, however, assured her it was a respectable place.

Sandra Donovan

Squaring her shoulders, she opened the door and walked in. It took a moment for her vision to adjust to the dim room, but when it did, she saw several pairs of male eyes staring at her from various tables. She swallowed nervously and glanced toward the bar, where a large man was serving a customer. His faded red hair was streaked with gray. Plucking up her courage, she headed toward him, fishing the letter from her pocket. ''Mr. Kelly?'' she asked.

He looked up and surprise flickered briefly in his eyes. ''That I am. Now what might I do for a pretty colleen like yourself?''

Camille relaxed a measure at his friendly tone. ''Mrs. O'Leary sent me. I'm looking for a position.'' She handed the letter to him, and waited while he took his time reading the missive. Finally, he folded the paper and stuffed it into the pocket of his apron. His shrewd green eyes assessed her for a moment, giving away nothing of his thoughts. ''Paddy O'Leary was a dear friend of mine for fifty years. We grew up together in Dublin and sailed on the same hellhole of a ship to New York back in '23. That's where he met Kathleen. They married the next year, and when the two of them set sail ten years ago for the gold fields here in California, I packed up and came with 'em. Now if Kathleen vouches for ye, yer hired.''

A slow smile lifted the corners of her mouth. ''So the waitress position is still open?''

Kelly gave her a reassuring smile. ''Aye. You'll be waitin' tables, lassy. Lots of sailors come in here to eat supper every night—and drink—but yer job would be to feed 'em. I'll pay you five dollars a week, six nights. And a pretty lass like you will be makin' half that in tips. This ain't a fancy place, but it's respectable. And I don't allow no trouble.''

She could believe that. He seemed amiable enough, but there was a no-nonsense tone in his voice, and he was big—big enough to back up his word. She smiled and held out her hand. ''I'll take it, and thank you, Mr. Kelly.''

He took her small hand in his meaty fist and returned the

smile. "It's just Kelly. Can you start tonight? My other girl quit a week ago and I'm shorthanded."

She nodded, feeling slightly dazed. As she was leaving, he called out, "Give Kathleen me regards. See you at four o'clock."

After stopping at the general store to mail her letter to Forrest, she headed back up the hill to the boardinghouse. Her head was spinning. What with a regular salary every week, plus the tips, it wouldn't take long to repay Cooper and save enough to go to Oregon. And the best thing of all, she wouldn't have to marry a man she didn't even know and be dependent on him for her needs. Aunt Lavinia had treated her and Forrest like charity cases after their parents died, and they'd hated it. It was the reason Forrest had run away to sea. Unfortunately, Camille had been too young to follow him.

Hurrying through the house, Camille found Mrs. O'Leary in the kitchen making preparations for supper. She gave the older woman a hug. "Kelly hired me! Thanks to you."

Mrs. O'Leary chuckled at her enthusiasm. "Don't thank me yet, dearie. Wait till you work night after night waitin' on hungry, impatient men. Then we'll see how grateful you are."

"I'm used to hard work. I'm not afraid," she said firmly.

"You're not afraid of what?" Cooper asked from the doorway.

Both women turned and Camille smiled. "I'm going to work. Isn't that wonderful? Now I can repay you for all my expenses, and Seth will be pleased that I'm no longer a problem."

His brows drew downward in a frown as he crossed the room to take her hands in his. "I don't want that money back, and you are not a problem," he chided her gently. "I brought you out here, and I'll take care of you, Camille."

She gave his hands a squeeze. "I know you mean well, Cooper, but I can't let you. I'm a grown woman, perfectly capable of working. No, you mustn't give it another thought, for I've made up my mind."

Cooper turned an accusing look on the older woman. "You gave her a job, didn't you?"

Mrs. O'Leary chuckled at his outraged tone. "I did no such thing, Mr. Maxwell. But I did recommend the lassie to a dear friend of mine, and he gave her a job. Kelly's Tavern down near the docks. I think you know the place."

Cooper's mouth dropped open and his eyes bulged. "She can't . . . it's not a proper . . . Mrs. O'Leary!"

"Calm down, Cooper," Camille urged. "Mr. Kelly is a very nice man—"

"Nice? Nice has nothing to do with it," he all but shouted. "Do you know what kind of men frequent a place like that? They'll gobble you up for a tasty morsel before you know what's happening! Are the two of you daft?"

Camille felt her patience slip a notch, and yanked her hands free of Cooper's grip. A stubborn light flickered in her eyes as her voice rose to match his. "You apologize to Mrs. O'Leary at once, Cooper Maxwell! Just where are your manners? She's done me a great kindness and I won't have you slander her. And another thing—I'll do as I please, and you won't stop me."

"I'm not daft or deaf, Mr. Maxwell, but I am busy," Mrs. O'Leary pointed out. "I have a boardinghouse to run and a meal to cook, so be a good lad and take your argument into the parlor."

Before Cooper could open his mouth to reply, a bellow came from the doorway. "What's all the damned yelling about?"

The three of them looked up. Seth stood there in his bare feet, his shirt flapping open. His dark hair was tousled, his face puffy from sleep. Camille stared, fascinated at the thick mat of dark hair visible on his muscular chest. Her eyes followed the line of it down to the waistband of his trousers, where it disappeared from view. She gave a guilty start when he growled, "A man could get some sleep if people had a little consideration around here."

Camille didn't much like his tone, and snapped, "If you didn't stay out all night, you wouldn't have to worry about sleeping through normal household noises."

"She has a point," Cooper chimed in.

Seth ignored him and glared at Camille. "In case you've forgotten, we are not married, Miss Sinclair. And since you're not my wife, I don't have to account to you how I spend my nights. And just to set the record straight, this shouting match is not what I would call normal."

Camille saw his point, but wasn't about to admit it. What he did was none of her business, nor did she want it to be. Still, there was something about him that sent her emotions into a turmoil. Since she'd arrived, he'd done nothing but point out the fact that he did not want to marry her. It was humiliating, and Camille was appalled to realize her eyes were filling with tears. "You're the most hateful man," she gasped, and fled from the room.

Mrs. O'Leary glared at Seth, hands on her hips, while Cooper said accusingly, "Now see what you've done! And it'll be your fault if something happens to her at that wicked tavern!"

Raking his fingers through his hair, he growled, "Granted, I upset her, and I feel lower than a snake's belly. But what the devil are you accusing me of besides that?"

"I told you I didn't need an escort," Camille said as Seth fell into step beside her. She gave him a sidelong glance and ground her teeth when she caught him smiling.

"Kelly's Tavern has the best beefsteak this side of the bay. That's why I'm going there. It has nothing to do with you," he assured her.

"After our little talk this afternoon, you're not fooling me, mister."

"I apologized for making you cry and you forgave me. I thought the whole thing was forgotten."

"In a pig's eye," she said. "You may have been sorry for that, but if I remember right, you lectured me as if I was a half-wit because I wouldn't give up my new position."

His mouth dropped open. "That's not true! I merely pointed out a few facts, but you wouldn't listen to reason."

"Ha!" she said as they reached Kelly's. She swept through the door as he opened it, her chin up.

Seth took a seat at the bar and settled in for the evening. Out of the corner of his eye, he watched her having a conference with Kelly. Then they disappeared into the kitchen. When she returned, she was wearing a large bib apron. Seth ordered a shot of blended whiskey and struck up a casual conversation with Kelly while he waited for his steak.

Camille dropped a plate in her nervousness. She didn't know which was worse, having to wait on all these strange men, or Seth watching her every move like a hawk scouting its prey. After sweeping up the broken crockery, she fetched another plate of stew. The sailor who'd ordered it was sitting alone beside the window. "I'm sorry for the delay," Camille apologized. "Would you like anything else?"

The man was unkempt, his once-white shirt dingy with dark spots staining the front. There was several days' growth of stubble on his face, and a jagged scar marred his left cheek. He removed his flat-topped hat and grinned, showing a gap in his smile. "I sure would like some company later, ducky . . . your company," he said, his eyes raking her boldly.

His oily tone made Camille's skin crawl, but she knew she couldn't show any fear or dismay. "Sorry, but I'm busy," she said briskly. When she turned away, he grabbed her hand.

"Think you're too good for the likes of me?" he asked.

Camille stared pointedly at him, her eyes never wavering. "What I think is that you'd better let go. I have work to do, and Kelly will be mad if I get behind."

The man glanced over at the bar, catching the eye of the

big, burly owner. He shrugged and dropped her hand. "I wouldn't wanna get you in trouble with your boss."

Camille walked away, her tense muscles relaxing. He had backed down when she'd threatened him with Kelly, but she felt his eyes boring into her back. Having roamed the Charleston docks since she was nine, she'd met a few mean and lascivious sailors, but then she'd had more than one champion to look out for her. All that stood between her and the strangers who came in here was Kelly. And, of course, Seth was here tonight, but she'd rather die than admit she needed him.

The rest of the evening was uneventful, and when she finally pulled off her apron and wrapped her brown shawl around her shoulders, Seth slid off his stool and followed her out the door.

"This is no place for a woman like you, Camille," were his first words as they walked up the quiet street in the moonlight. "Kelly's a good, decent sort, but you still have to get to work and get back home every night."

Camille bristled at his censorious tone. "I may look fragile and helpless, Seth, but I'm not. I've been looking out for myself since I was nine. And the fact is, I need to work."

Seth flinched. Even though bringing her out to San Francisco had been Coop's doing, Seth felt some responsibility for her. "What about the scurvy bastard who bothered you tonight? You're hardly a match for someone like him," he growled.

"What do you want from me?" Camille asked in an exasperated voice.

"I've been giving this a lot of thought—why couldn't you work as a seamstress, or a cook? There are lots of respectable restaurants in San Francisco. Then you wouldn't have to associate with a bunch of rough men."

They reached the boardinghouse, and Camille paused beside the porch rail to face him. "Those would be good suggestions if I knew how to sew or cook, which I don't."

"You don't?" Seth asked, an incredulous note in his voice.

"But Coop said you could out-cook, out-sew, and out-scrub any woman west of the Mississippi."

"Cooper Maxwell is the master of exaggeration, I'm learning. I assure you, I didn't tell him any such thing when I answered his advertisement. All I said was if called upon, I could perform any domestic chore. I didn't say how well." Camille looked up at him, her eyes wide and innocent.

"Don't you think that was a little misleading?" he asked. "Some poor fellow—namely me—might have married you expecting a good meal at the end of the day and a shirt to cover his bare back."

Camille's chin came up. "I would have done my best. Besides, I was desperate." Turning away, she walked to one of the wicker chairs and sat down. There was no use going up to bed. She was so upset she'd never get to sleep.

Seth followed after a moment and lowered his large frame into the chair beside hers. "I'm confused. Your speech and manners give the impression of a refined, educated lady, yet you said you've been looking out for yourself since you were nine. And now you tell me you were desperate to become a stranger's bride. Perhaps you'd better tell me the whole story."

Camille pulled her shawl a little tighter around her shoulders and looked out at the swirls of fog above the bay. "Until I was eight, I lived with my parents and brother on a cotton plantation outside of Charleston. After the harvest that year, Papa decided to go to New York to take care of some business and took Mama with him. Their ship went down in a storm. My father's stepsister took my brother and me in, but she didn't really want to. If she hadn't worried so much about how it would look to her friends, she would have sent us to an orphanage." Camille paused, thinking that might have been preferable. "Aunt Lavinia and Cousin Prudence treated us like charity cases. After a year, Forrest, my brother, went to sea on a merchant ship. He promised he'd write, and return for me when he'd made his fortune. For nine years I didn't hear a word, and then a few months ago, a sailor brought a letter from him."

Seth felt a twinge of pity for the child who'd been deprived of a loving family. He thought of his younger sister, Phoebe, and knew he could never have left her when she needed him. "Why didn't he at least write?" Seth asked.

"He did, but I never received the letters. Aunt Lavinia took them. I confronted her with the letter my brother's friend gave me, and she told me without a bit of shame she'd destroyed all the others. She said he was a wastrel and a bad influence on me."

Camille's matter-of-fact tone told Seth more than an emotional outburst would have. He wanted to take her in his arms, but sensed she didn't want his pity. Reaching over, he took her hand and squeezed gently. "I shouldn't have jumped to conclusions about your brother. What happened then?"

Camille was sharply aware of the strength and warmth of his hand. Her pulse skittered alarmingly as she fought the feeling. "The sailor told me Forrest was heading up to Oregon to work at a logging camp. He wanted me to know his whereabouts even though I never answered his letters."

Seth no longer felt angry with her deception, but a new and more disturbing emotion was taking its place, "So that's why you answered Cooper's advertisement? You were trying to reach your brother?"

She nodded. "I know it was wrong, but I didn't have enough money for the trip, I would have waited and saved, except that Aunt Lavinia was going to force me to marry Josiah Hall."

"And who is Josiah Hall?" he asked, part of his attention drifting to the feel of her soft hand in his.

"A friend of my aunt's, a widower. He took a liking to me and promised Aunt Lavinia a large sum of money if she'd persuade me to be his bride." Camille shuddered involuntarily at the memory. She could still remember how his lascivious gaze followed her everywhere when he came to visit.

Seth was beginning to get a clear idea of Camille's life with her aunt. It wasn't a pretty picture. Absently, he caressed the back of her hand with his thumb. He could see why any man would want Camille for his bride—if a man had marriage in mind, he added hastily in his mind. She was beautiful and spirited. "I take it you objected to Mr. Hall as a husband?"

Camille wished he would take his hand away. When he touched her, she had trouble keeping her thoughts straight. "The man was eighty years old. I would rather have been tortured than submit to him," she said with a voice that trembled a little.

"Didn't you worry about what sort of man you were coming out here to marry?"

"I had some anxious moments, but the letter I received from you—or I should say, Cooper—was really very sweet. He gave me the choice of backing out if I wasn't entirely happy once I got here."

Seth chuckled and released her hand. Standing up, he gazed down at her. "That's the Coop I know—generous to a fault."

Camille smiled, thinking about the outrageous situation Cooper had landed them in. And then she began to laugh. Soon, they were both laughing, the sound interrupting the silence of the night. The more they tried to stifle their mirth, the harder they laughed.

"Quiet down! Folks are tryin' to sleep," came a raspy shout from the house across the street.

Camille saw a man leaning out an upstairs window shaking his fist. She gasped as Seth caught her hand and propelled her out of the chair, pulling her toward the front door. "That's Old Man Jenkins. He'll get his gun out next."

Once inside the house, they closed the door quietly and leaned against it, catching their breath. "What time is it?" Camille whispered, her heart beating a rapid tattoo against her ribs.

"Close to midnight, I think," he replied. "Why?"

"Let's roll Cooper out of bed and make him apologize for interfering in our lives," she suggested, feeling the laughter bubble up within her once more.

His mouth twitched with amusement. "Excellent idea, but I doubt he's home yet. He was joining some men for a big poker game tonight at the El Dorado."

"Oh, well, it was a satisfying thought," she said, bringing her hand up to stifle more giggles.

The house was dark and quiet, and suddenly, Seth became aware of how warm her body felt pressed close to his side. Her hand remained in his, and the womanly scent of her tantalized him as he breathed deeply. An overwhelming urge came over him to take her in his arms . . . to touch her . . . to kiss her sensuous mouth. Pushing away from the door, he whispered tightly, "We'd better go to bed before we wake the household."

Chapter 4

Camille felt the change in him and reacted to the disturbing quality in his voice. She too felt the pull of something between them. Although she didn't quite understand the feeling, she trembled with the need to explore it. "Yes . . . we should," she murmured, fearing he would take her in his arms and yet afraid he wouldn't.

"Dammit," he swore under his breath as she swayed toward him. If he had any sense, he'd run like hell. Nice young ladies were nothing but trouble, an inner voice warned. But he was already drawing her close, one hand cupping the back of her head as his mouth found hers.

Camille felt the blood surge from her fingertips to her toes. With a moan, her lips parted as he boldly pushed for entry with his tongue. A hot curl of desire formed in her stomach, making its way down to the juncture of her thighs. As the kiss deepened, she grew brave enough to invade his mouth with her tongue, and was rewarded with an answering groan from Seth.

Damn, he wanted her . . . wanted to see her naked in the

moonlight, wanted to caress the silky skin of her thighs, wanted to bury himself in her and hear her whisper his name with passion. It was madness, he knew, but even as the thought crossed his mind, his hand moved up to her breast. He cupped the weight of it, and found the pebble-hard crest ready for his touch.

Camille shivered with pleasure and uncertainty. She hadn't known a man could make a woman feel this way. Her bones turned to liquid and an intensely delicious ache started between her legs. He tasted of whiskey and smelled of bay rum and tobacco. His chest felt hard and muscled beneath her restless fingertips. She delighted in the warmth of his hand on her breast.

Seth broke the kiss to bury his face in her sweet-scented hair. He whispered hoarsely, "You're so sweet . . . and beautiful . . ."

Camille's breathing was ragged, her emotions spinning wildly. "Oh, Seth . . . we shouldn't, but it feels . . . so good."

Her breathless words penetrated his fog of desire, as did the realization of how innocent she really was. She'd never been with a man—hell, she'd never even been kissed properly before now. The reality hit him like a sluice of cold water. He couldn't take advantage of her naivete. It was one thing to charm a worldly woman like Sally with his lovemaking, but quite another to use his experience on an innocent like Camille. He sensed she could be his for the taking. All he needed to do was rouse her passions a little further with his hands, his body. But he couldn't do it. Gaining control of himself, he dropped his hand away from her breast. He gripped her shoulders. "Look at me, Camille," he ordered hoarsely.

Through heavy-lidded eyes, she let her head fall back to gaze up at him. His dark eyes glittered in the semidarkness of the room, and Camille felt her pulse quicken at their intensity. "You can kiss me again, Seth," she offered, her voice low with passion.

He almost ground his teeth in frustration. The most desirable woman he'd ever met was offering herself to him and he was refusing. Hot desire tricked him into visualizing how passionate and pliable she would be if he lifted her skirt to touch her in that hot, wet, womanly place between her legs.

He gave her a gentle shake. "Stop it—you don't know what you're asking for," he whispered fiercely. "I want you to go to your room and forget this happened. Understand?"

Camille swallowed tightly, hurt by his words and attitude. As reason began to assert itself and her passion ebbed, she felt ashamed of letting him take such liberties. She'd even encouraged it. Hadn't Aunt Lavinia always preached against the weakness of the flesh? Until now, Camille hadn't understood. Pride straightened her shoulders as she stepped away from his grasp. "Don't worry, it won't happen again. You've made it clear you're not interested."

Seth reached out, but she backed up a step. "Camille, honey, it's not what you think, believe me—"

She held her hand up. "You don't have to explain," she said with a tight smile. "Like you said, it's best forgotten." She forced herself to walk sedately up the stairs.

Seth watched her go with regret gnawing at him. It was he who had made the first move, and therefore, his fault. He had known where it would lead. And now, she was angry and hurt. He didn't know how to change that. He sighed. Perhaps it was for the best. Getting involved with her would only lead to more trouble. However, he couldn't stop the erotic dreams of her later as he slept.

Very early the following morning, Camille was awakened by unusual sounds coming from outside. She rose sleepily and padded to the window, throwing it open. She leaned out and saw a steady stream of wagons and Mexican *carretas* moving down the hill toward the bay area. When she descended for breakfast, Mrs. O'Leary explained that the farmers and *rancheros* brought their produce, meat and goods to trade and sell in the open-air market every Saturday. "Would ya be interested in goin' with me when I do me marketin' after breakfast?" she asked, placing two loaf pans of bread into the oven.

"I'd love to. I haven't seen much of the city since I've been here." Camille got clean plates and cups off the shelf.

Mrs. O'Leary took a side of smoked bacon and began cutting strips with a butcher knife, placing it in an iron skillet on the stove. "And how was your first night at Kelly's?"

Placing a handful of silverware on a tray, Camille looked up and smiled. "I was exhausted, but it went well, I think. I only dropped one plate of food."

Mrs. O'Leary chuckled. "I remember when me darlin' Paddy was workin' a claim in Dry Diggin's Gulch and I was cookin' for the miners. Ah, those were happy days, but full of back-breakin' work from dawn to dusk. I cooked two meals a day and did the cleanin' up meself. Many's the night I was so tired I couldn't remember me own name. What with Paddy's earnin's and mine, though, we were able to start the blacksmith business and build this house." Her smile lingered and her faded blue eyes had a far-away look in them.

"How long has Mr. O'Leary been gone?" Camille asked gently.

"Three years come November. His heart gave out. He was a fine man, strong and gentle," the older woman said, turning to busy herself with the bowl of eggs on the wooden counter. "When he passed away, I turned our home into a boardin'house and sold the smithy. I don't like bein' alone and it gives me a tidy income."

"It's so very hard to lose those we love," Camille sympathized. "Both my parents were lost at sea when I was eight. I still miss them. Did I mention how much I appreciate the recommendation you gave me?"

The older woman turned to smile at her. "Several times, dearie. And you're as welcome as the flowers in May. Now, get along with ya and set the table so I can finish up here."

As Camille worked in the dining room, she wondered what it would be like to share a life with a man she loved deeply and who loved her above all else. With her parents dead and Forrest gone since she was nine, she'd had no one to love her. There were her friends on the docks—and they were dear to her—but it wasn't the same. Aunt Lavinia and Cousin Prudence had never shown her any affection; rather, their dislike had come through quite clearly. Her aunt had made her work in the house while the two of them lived the genteel life of ladies, telling her she was nothing but a poor relation and must earn her keep. The one thing she could thank her aunt for was her education, and it had been a dubious gift on her aunt's part. "I'll not have you embarrassing me with your ignorance and bad manners," Lavinia had said when she allowed Camille to go to school. She had been rigid about her daughter's and niece's social training as well. Camille sighed. It hadn't cost the woman anything—public school was free, and the social graces Lavinia had taught herself.

She realized suddenly that she was being summoned by a voice outside her thoughts, and glanced up. Seth was standing in the doorway, a brooding look on his face. Camille's cheeks flushed a becoming pink as she experienced a gamut of perplexing emotions.

"I know you're angry with me—and with good reason. What happened was my fault, Camille, and I'm sorry. Could we put this aside? After all, I won't be here much longer and then you'll never have to see me again," he said in a gentle tone.

Camille had spent the better part of the night reliving the scene in the foyer with him. She'd felt breathless with newfound desire, and then hot with anger and embarrassment at his abrupt rejection. Over and over, her mind had replayed it. As he stood just a few feet away in the cold light of day, however, she realized the attraction was still there between them, strong and vital—more so now after what had occurred between them the night before. Although she'd fiercely vowed to forget what happened, she was shocked to find he could make her tremble with a mere look. With a calm she didn't feel, Camille said, "You're quite wrong, Seth. I'm not angry in the least. It was a silly incident and best forgotten, which I've already done."

Her soft-spoken reply stung him. The fact that she no longer seemed disturbed perversely made him angry. He had been prepared to soothe her ruffled feathers this morning, but found her serene instead. "Good . . . I'm glad to hear it," he said, his voice faintly hostile. He strode past and into the kitchen.

Camille stared after him for a moment, confused by his swiftly changing attitudes. She'd given him the answer he wanted and he still wasn't happy! The more she learned about men, the less she knew. By the time she finished setting the table, the other boarders were drifting in to take their seats. Mr. Weston, a salesman for a mining equipment company back East, stopped beside her. "Good morning, Miss Sinclair. You look like a ray of sunshine in that yellow and white gingham."

Camille returned his smile, but felt uncomfortable as his gaze flickered over her. Middle-aged with a slight paunch and thinning brown hair streaked with gray, he was a successful businessman and quite eligible, he'd told her, though not in those exact words. He was nice enough, but Camille was not interested in being more than casual friends. "Why, thank you, Mr. Weston," she said lightly.

He cleared his throat. "I was wondering if you might be interested in accompanying me for a ride this morning. That is, if you're not busy?"

Giving him a contrite look, she said, "Oh, dear, I'm sorry, but I've already promised Mrs. O'Leary I'd go to the vegetable market with her. Her hand is not quite healed and she needs me to carry her purchases."

"How kind of you," he said in a solicitous tone. "What about this afternoon? I'm free all day."

Before Camille could formulate another excuse, Miss Grainger, just sitting down nearby, interrupted, "She's already spoken for this afternoon, Mr. Weston. Camille promised to help me choose a new hat."

Giving her rescuer a grateful smile, Camille agreed, "That's true, Mr. Weston, but there's no reason you shouldn't enjoy this glorious weather. It's a perfect day for a ride." With that, Camille made her escape into the kitchen. She was just in time to hear Seth saying to Mrs. O'Leary, ". . . it's true! I told Kelly just last night that you're the prettiest colleen in all of San Francisco. And do you know what? He agreed with me."

The older woman swatted at him with a dish towel and giggled like a young girl. "Oh, go on with ya. 'Tis just your silver tongue flatterin' me again. I know what ya want, Mr. Braden. You're wantin' me to make some of me famous Irish stew for dinner."

Camille watched them unnoticed for a few moments, seeing a different Seth from the one who snapped and snarled at her. He could be gentle when he wanted. It forced her to see him in a different light. Careful to avoid Seth's gaze, she advanced into the room and picked up the platter of fried eggs and a basket of warm, sliced bread. "Everyone's down but Cooper," she informed Mrs. O'Leary.

"I'll go see if he's up," Seth offered, his manner having suddenly grown serious.

He passed Camille without looking at her. Mrs. O'Leary watched the two young people, her eyes twinkling. Picking up the platter of bacon, she said, "Well, dearie, let's feed this hungry bunch so we can get to market before everything is gone."

When breakfast was over, Miss Grainger picked up her plate and followed Camille into the kitchen. Once the door was closed, Camille turned. "Oh, I was hoping I'd have a chance to thank you for your help. I was fresh out of excuses and truly didn't want to hurt Mr. Weston's feelings.''

The young woman smiled as she put her plate on the table. ''I'm relieved to hear you say that because I wasn't sure I was reading the situation correctly. After watching him pursue you for the last couple of days, however, I felt you were not interested in him.''

Mrs. O'Leary clucked her tongue as she primed the pump at the sink. ''Dear me, no. Mr. Weston is not Miss Sinclair's type at all. Now Mr. Braden—that's another cup of tea.''

''Mrs. O'Leary!'' Camille exclaimed, her face coloring. ''I'm not interested in him either, and he can barely stand the sight of me.''

Taking Camille's plate from her hand, Miss Grainger proceeded to scrape it into the pan on the table reserved for garbage. ''I wouldn't be too sure of that,'' she said with a smile. ''He seems to watch every move you make. I'm an avid student of human behavior.''

''Could we please change the subject?'' Camille said. She escaped to the dining room to fetch more dishes, and when she returned, Miss Grainger gave her a shy smile.

''I apologize for getting too personal, and promise not to do it again if you'll go with me this afternoon to choose that new hat? I would love the pleasure of your company.''

Camille made a face at her. ''It's my duty, I suppose. I can't have you telling a lie on my account.''

''Did you sleep through breakfast and lunch, Cooper? We missed your smiling face,'' Camille said, finding him in a chair on the front porch.

''Must you shout?'' he grumbled, rubbing his temples with his fingertips.

''Oh, dear. That's why you didn't come down to eat,'' she sympathized, sitting in the chair next to his.

He turned his bloodshot eyes on her. "Too many hands of poker," he said.

"More like too many shots of whiskey," she corrected, adjusting her straw bonnet.

"Hmmmm. Where are you going so early?"

"Early? I've already been to the market with Mrs. O'Leary and now I'm going to shop on Montgomery Street with Miss Grainger. Want to come along?"

Closing his eyes, he leaned back in the chair. "No, no, I don't think so. By the way, what time will you be leaving for Kelly's tonight?"

"Around three-thirty, why?"

"I just wondered," he said. "How did it go last night?"

Camille's eyes narrowed. "Did Seth say anything to you?"

Cooper grunted. "About what?"

Camille relaxed. "Never mind. Everything was fine at Kelly's. I made a dollar and a quarter in tips."

"That's great. Do you work on Sunday nights? Tomorrow night in particular?"

"That's my night off every week."

"Good. I ran into my uncle at the El Dorado, and he invited me to his house for dinner tomorrow night. He said I could bring anybody I wanted. Would you go?"

As exasperating as he was, she couldn't stay mad at Cooper. If it hadn't been for him, she'd probably be married to Josiah Hall by now. And besides, Cooper was like a naughty little boy with the best of intentions. "I don't have any formal dresses," she warned him.

He smiled. "That blue dress you had on the other night would be fine. As a matter of fact, you looked absolutely gorgeous in it."

"You don't have to flatter me, Cooper, I'll go," she said, making a face at him.

"It's not flattery, it's the truth," he insisted. "Don't you ever look at yourself in the mirror? A man could drown in those big blue eyes of yours.''

Camille frowned, ''You're in worse shape than I thought. I advise you to stop drinking so much and get more rest.''

''With my head pounding the way it is, I don't have the energy to argue with you, but I'm serious, Camille. You're every bit as pretty as Seth's sister, Phoebe, and that's the highest compliment I can pay you. She was the prettiest girl in all of Maine.''

''Was? She didn't die, did she?''

Cooper glanced away. ''Naw, but almost as bad. She married the banker's prissy son two years ago.''

So that's it, Camille thought. He's in love with Seth's sister. ''Did she know how you felt about her?''

Cooper nodded. ''Yes. She even asked me to marry her, but I had nothing. She deserved more.''

''You had love, and that's something special,'' she pointed out gently.

Cooper shrugged. ''It's too late now anyway. About this dinner at my uncle's, I think you'll enjoy it. They always invite interesting people.''

Camille took the hint and dropped the subject of Phoebe. ''You don't have another friend lined up to marry me, do you?'' she asked, a suspicious gleam in her eyes.

His gaze widened in mock dismay. ''You cut me to the heart, Camille.''

The front door opened and Miss Grainger stepped out. Camille waved to her and stood up. ''Try not to bleed too much on Mrs. O'Leary's clean porch,'' she said with a laugh.

Montgomery Street was lined with various shops designed to entice and delight a woman's heart. There were several milliners, and Camille and Miss Grainger visited each one before the schoolteacher decided on a white silk creation with pink flowers. The French proprietress gave Camille's plain straw hat a cursory glance and urged her to try on some, but Camille declined. She'd purchased her plain straw with some of her earnings at the market earlier. She couldn't afford the ones in this shop. "Thank you, but not today. Lucy, however, looks lovely in that one."

Lucy Grainger turned from the mirror and quirked her eyebrow questioningly. "You don't think it's too frivolous for a schoolteacher?"

"Absolutely not," Camille assured her. "Besides, you'll have a life outside your schoolhouse, won't you?"

Lucy chuckled. "I hope so." She took off the hat and handed it to the Frenchwoman. "I'll take it."

As they left the store, Camille thought how pretty Lucy was when she smiled. When she'd first met her, Camille had thought the young woman plain, almost nondescript, with her prim attitude and conservative dress. Today, though, she'd seen a new side of Lucy—a smiling, warm and sensitive young woman. She gauged Lucy's age to be about twenty-five, and wondered why she didn't have a beau, what with all the eligible men in San Francisco. "What made you leave Boston, Lucy?" she asked as they walked down the boardwalk. "If you don't mind my asking, that is."

"My two older sisters," Lucy answered, laughing at Camille's confused expression. "They're beautiful, smart and made excellent marriages. I was always plain and a trial to my dear mother. She wanted me to marry like my sisters, and I wanted to be a schoolteacher. Since there were no eligible young men begging for my hand, Mother finally relented and allowed me to attend university. When I finished and began teaching near home, my sisters were constantly inviting me to dinner, along with some bachelor friend of their husbands'. It got to be embarrassing after a while. Either I didn't like their choices or they weren't interested in me. Finally, I saw an advertisement asking for teachers in San Francisco and decided to take a chance."

They strolled past dress shops, shoemakers and a general store as they talked. Camille felt a definite kinship with Lucy in one sense—she also felt plain. "I think you were very brave to leave your family and come to a place you knew nothing about," Camille said. "And if you want to know my honest opinion, I think you're very pretty, especially when you smile."

Lucy chuckled. "That's exactly what my mother used to say, only I was offended when she said it. I thought it was her duty to say something nice because I was her child."

Camille gave her a stern look. "Well, I wouldn't dream of telling you anything but the truth. What I think is you don't smile and flirt enough. From what I've seen, men are attracted to simpering females who bat their eyelashes and ply them with flattering speeches. My cousin Prudence was an awful flirt, but she had dozens of beaus, while I, on the other hand, had none. Except Josiah Hall."

Lucy pointed to a restaurant just ahead. "Let's have a cup of tea and rest a bit. You can tell me more about this Josiah Hall."

When they were settled at a table next to the window and a waitress had taken their order, Lucy gave Camille a skeptical look. "I can't believe you were not besieged by beaus, as pretty as you are. Did you say that just to make me feel better?"

Camille blinked and shook her head. "No, really. My aunt always said with no dowry and the fact that I was so plain, she'd probably never be able to marry me off."

Lucy's shocked look was almost comical. "But it's not true—the part about you being plain, I mean. What an awful thing for her to say! Excuse me for speaking my mind, but she sounds like a nasty person."

Camille smiled. "She does have a mean streak, and she

didn't like me very much, I'm afraid. She seemed to take great pleasure in arranging my marriage to Josiah Hall. I just couldn't go through with it, however. And that brings me to my explanation as to how I came to San Francisco.''

Lucy leaned forward, her eyes sparkling. ''Did you murder your aunt or Josiah in a fit of rage? Or both? When Mr. Maxwell introduced you, he mentioned some sort of tragedy. I've been dying of curiosity.''

Camille couldn't control her burst of laughter. She glanced around the dining room, her hand pressed to her mouth. At midafternoon there was only one couple seated across the room, and they didn't even look her way. Turning back to her companion, she said, ''No, I'm sure they're still breathing and making someone's life miserable at this very moment.'' She paused as the waitress brought their tea. When the woman left, Camille continued. ''I must apologize to you for Cooper's fib. You see, he was trying to spare my feelings and those of Mr. Braden when he said what he did.'' Camille reached over and touched Lucy's hand. ''I believe I can trust you with my secret.''

Lucy nodded and said earnestly, ''Of course you can, but you don't have to tell me, you know.''

''I want to. To begin with, Josiah Hall is eighty and quite lecherous. That should give you some idea of why I was desperate to get away from Charleston. I answered an advertisement from the newspaper for a mail-order bride, and was accepted by the gentleman who sent money for my fare. When I arrived, I found it was Cooper who had sent for me, but not for himself— no, he'd pretended to be Seth in the letter. He thought he was doing Seth a favor by sending for a bride. However, Seth didn't see it that way.'' Camille stopped to take a sip of her tea.

Lucy's eyes were nearly popping out. ''What a fantastic story. It sounds like something out of a penny dreadful! But when you found this out, what did you do?''

"Well, of course, I didn't blame Seth for not wanting to marry me. And I was truly relieved to have escaped from Charleston, so I wasn't too angry with Cooper for what he did. They've both tried to be helpful, but I don't expect charity, which is why I found employment," Camille said, shrugging.

"So that's why you blanched this morning when I said something about Mr. Braden. But I still don't understand why you think he dislikes you," Lucy said, refilling her cup from the china pot on the table.

"When he first found out what Cooper had done, he made quite a scene, and now I think he's embarrassed. Rejecting me as he did face to face made him feel, well, ungentlemanly," Camille explained.

Lucy's brows rose. "No matter what you say, that's not the impression I get. He's smitten with you. I'd wager a month's salary on it."

The waitress reappeared and asked if they wanted anything else. When they declined, she left their bill on the table. The interruption saved Camille from having to reply to Lucy's last comment, but the memory of Seth's kiss came unbidden to her mind. Having had no experience with lovemaking, Camille was on shaky ground. However, he had seemed to enjoy it as much as she. And he had called her beautiful. It was just something a man said to a woman, she told herself sternly, remembering how the sailors who came into Big Amos's tavern used to flatter her. They didn't mean it, she was sure.

Lucy reached for the bill, snapping Camille from her reverie. "It's my treat. I owe you for saving me this morning," Camille said. She paid as they left.

Outside on the boardwalk, Lucy asked, "Is it all right with you if we visit Madame Riva's dress shop?"

"I have plenty of time before I have to go to work," Camille assured her.

As they made their way across the planked street, avoiding

carriages and men on horseback, Lucy told her, "Madame Riva is French, and her creations are divine. I hear she has a cousin in Paris who sends her the newest designs almost as soon as they're sketched. She's a wonderful seamstress; all the ladies on Rincon and Russian Hill use her."

Camille's heart sank. She had always loved beautiful clothes, but could never afford them. The only pretty things she had owned over the years were cast-off dresses from Prudence. Still, she didn't want to disappoint Lucy. She would just have to be satisfied with looking.

A little bell tinkled as they opened the door and entered the quaint shop. Camille could hardly take her eyes off the jade-green dress displayed on a dress form in the window. "Oh, Lucy, isn't it exquisite? Look at the workmanship."

"It would look wonderful on you with your coloring," Lucy commented.

A thin, bird-like woman came from a back room into the shop, smiling. *"Bonjour, mademoiselles.* May I help you?"

Lucy asked about some day dresses, and the Frenchwoman led her to a selection in a mahogany cabinet against the wall.

Camille wandered over to a table where several silk chemises were displayed. They were white, pale blue or shocking red. All were lace-trimmed and delicately made. She thought they were beautiful, and longed to own one.

"I'll be right out, Camille. I'm going to try on some things," Lucy called over her shoulder as she disappeared through a curtained doorway.

Madame Riva joined Camille. "These are lovely, are they not? My sister sews them for the shop. She worked for a talented designer in Paris, but the woman treated her like a peasant. Colette was unhappy, so I sent for her and now she lives with me."

Camille smiled. "They certainly are exquisite. Did she also

make the green dress in the window? I noticed it when we came in.''

The little Frenchwoman rolled her eyes heavenward. *"Oui,* for the daughter of a rich banker. Alas, the chit eloped with a sea captain and her poor mama never returned for it.'' She shrugged. ''I 'ave tried to sell it, but not every woman can wear that color.'' Looking Camille over critically, she tapped her finger against her cheek. ''You, *cherie,* would look divine in it.''

Camille blushed. ''Thank you, Madame Riva, but I'm afraid . . .''

''A little to let in the pockets at the moment?'' the woman asked, her eyes sympathetic. ''If you should decide you want it, *cherie,* I will sell it for a good price. You would be doing me a favor, *oui?''*

Camille could almost imagine herself in the dress. She wondered what Seth would think of her. Perhaps he would truly think her beautiful in something that lovely. Giving herself a mental shake, she turned back to the chemises. ''You're very kind, and I'll think about it. For now, though, I could use a chemise. Do you have any cotton ones?''

"Oui, but these are just a little more in cost. Why not take the blue one. It will match your eyes.'' Madame Riva named a price.

Camille touched the pale blue silk and decided to throw caution to the wind. It would cost all her tips from the night before, but it was worth it. ''I believe I will.''

Lucy came out of the back room as Camille took her package and paid for the purchase. ''Did they work out?'' she asked her friend.

''Yes. Both dresses fit nicely. Since school will open in a couple of weeks, I thought I'd better get ready.'' Lucy paid for her things, and the two left the shop with promises to return. Camille couldn't resist one last look at the green dress.

* * *

That afternoon as Camille was leaving the house, Cooper was sitting on the front porch. "Going to work?" he asked when she paused to say hello.

"You know very well I am. You asked me already, remember?" She draped her shawl across her shoulders.

Cooper rose, walked over and took her arm. "I think I'll just walk along with you. The exercise will do me good."

Camille gave him a sidelong glance. "Do you plan to sit at the bar all evening and watch me like Seth did last night?"

Cooper urged her down the steps. "Of course not. I just want to see you safely there. But I will be back later to walk you home," he said in a soothing tone.

"I suppose you mean well, but what happens when you go back to Oregon? Are you going to hire a bodyguard to stay with me?" Her voice was edged with exasperation. It was better, she reasoned, if he didn't guess how sad she would be when that time came.

"I've thought it over, and there's nothing to worry about," was his enigmatic reply.

Camille tried to pry his plans from him, but he refused to say more, so she changed the subject. "I've been meaning to ask you, have you heard of Hansen's Logging Camp?"

Cooper frowned. "Sure. It's a big operation in the Northwest. Why?"

"It's where Forrest was headed when he wrote his last letter." She sighed. "I wrote him before I left Charleston and sent it there, but there was no letter from him when I got here. I mailed another one yesterday."

Cooper slipped a comforting arm across her shoulders. "If you don't hear soon, write to the owner. Maybe Forrest left there or went to work at another camp before he got there. We have men who come and go every year."

A flicker of apprehension coursed through her. "If he didn't work there, how will I ever pick up his trail?"

"Don't fret, honey. We have a detective working on something for us, and if you can't get a lead on Forrest, we'll put our man on it."

When they reached Kelly's, he gave her a reassuring smile and turned back toward the boardinghouse.

Seth sat at a table in the Red Door Saloon as darkness fell over the city. Sally finished lighting the lamps around the room and came over to sit on his lap. She nuzzled his ear and whispered a risque suggestion to him. Seth sighed. Even after several shots of whiskey, her offer was unappealing.

"Not now, Sal," he said, reaching around her voluptuous form to fill his glass. The piano player pounded out an out-of-tune rendition of "Clementine," which grated on his nerves.

Sally moved her bottom in a provocative way and giggled. "We could take the bottle with us to my room, sugar."

"Maybe later," he said, tossing the drink down in one swallow.

Sally studied his handsome face for a moment. "You haven't been to see me in days, and now all you wanna do is drink. If I'm not keepin' you happy and satisfied, sugar, just tell me, and I'll fix it," she said, her red lips forming a seductive pout.

A vision of Camille floated through his mind. It was her fault he was preoccupied. When he was with her, all he wanted to do was get away. And when he was away from her, all he could think about was how sweet her kisses had been. He wondered how she was faring at Kelly's tonight. What if that scurvy sailor returned and bothered her? "Dammit," he muttered, resenting Camille's intrusion in his thoughts.

Sally wrapped her arms around his neck. "What's wrong?

Tell Sal about it. She'll cure what's ailing you,'' she coaxed in a honeyed tone.

Abruptly, he stood up, scooping Sally into his arms. ''Grab that bottle,'' he ordered. Catching her breath, Sally gave a whoop and hung on as Seth strode purposefully toward the stairs.

Chapter 5

Cooper and Camille were just a short distance from the boardinghouse when they saw a carriage coming down the street. They could hear a deep voice singing lustily about "Sweet Betsey from Pike." Cooper groaned. He took Camille's hand. "He'll wake the whole street with his caterwauling. Mrs. O'Leary warned him once about coming home drunk—well, noisy drunk." They began to run, and caught up with the vehicle as it stopped in front of the house.

Cooper caught Seth when he stumbled getting out. "Coop! Where'd you come from . . . ol' friend, ol' pardner? Uh . . . Mavish was looking for you," Seth said as he tried to stand upright.

"Be quiet, Seth, or Mrs. O'Leary will yank a knot in your tail," Cooper warned. He turned to Camille. "Hold him up while I pay the driver and then we'll get him to bed."

Camille slipped her arm around Seth's waist and wrinkled her nose in disgust. He reeked of cheap perfume. Having observed life on the Charleston docks, she knew what that meant. "Who's Mavis?" she asked tartly.

"Just a girl we know," Cooper explained as he returned to take Seth's other arm. They started up the steps. "Sh-h-h, no more singing, Seth!"

". . . for I come from Alabama with a banjo on—don't you like 'Oh, Sushanna,' Coop?"

Cooper paused at the door and whispered, "I do, really, Seth, I do, but Mrs. O'Leary doesn't. We wouldn't wanna wake her up now, would we?"

Seth frowned for a moment, and then rested his head on Camille's. "You smell so nice," he said, breathing deeply. "Camille smells like that . . . jus' like the woods after a rain."

Camille glanced at Cooper, her eyebrows raised. He shook his head. "He's pretty drunk. Pay him no mind," he urged.

Opening the door, they maneuvered Seth inside and up the steps. Fortunately, he fell to mumbling in a low tone. When they reached Seth's room and had him safely inside, Cooper breathed a sigh of relief. "Help me get him on the bed."

When they accomplished that feat, Camille stepped back, breathing heavily from the exertion. Seth was a big man and had been as limp as a rag doll. "I can't believe you wanted me to marry this big oaf," she hissed. "Just what kind of a husband would he make drinking all the time?"

Cooper glanced over his shoulder at her as he quietly discarded one of Seth's boots and reached for the other. "He's not usually like this, Camille. It's just been the past few months—"

"Camille?" Seth called, coming back to life and half rising from the bed.

Cooper pushed him down. "Everything's all right, Seth. Go to sleep now."

He settled back and closed his eyes, mumbling, "Why won't she leave me alone?"

Camille stiffened. What in creation did he mean? she fumed

to herself. She didn't care if he left for the Oregon woods this very minute! "I'm going to bed," she said.

Cooper tugged off Seth's other boot and dropped it on the floor. "Wait, Camille. He doesn't know what he's saying—" But she was already out the door and gone.

After a restless night, Camille rose with the first light of day and left the boardinghouse. She hugged her shawl around her as she followed the street all the way down to the beach. A friendly black and tan collie was the only living thing she met at this early hour. She stopped for a moment to pet him. "Good morning, fellow. You're up mighty early." He wagged his tail vigorously and pushed his head up against her hand. When she walked on, he ran along at her side.

The planked street gave way to a grassy knoll before it dipped down to the sandy beach. The cool salty breeze off the water caressed her skin in an achingly familiar way. Camille stopped to take off her boots, carrying them as her bare feet sank into the cool sand. As a rule, few ships anchored at this end of the cove, most preferring the closer proximity of the wharves and business district farther around the half-moon-shaped bay. However, the wispy morning fog shrouded the water, making it seem as if she were all alone in the world. Even the dog raced down the beach, chasing a seagull.

She sat on a rock, well away from the lapping waves, and stared at the water's edge. From one ocean to the other, she'd crossed this vast country to begin a new life, but the journey had ended in disappointment. She didn't know why she felt that way, for she'd been unsure about what kind of man she had blindly agreed to marry. But Seth's attitude hurt.

Digging her toes into the sand, she kicked up a spray. "Why am I attracted to that arrogant devil?" she muttered. Falling in love would be dangerous. Every time she loved someone, they left her.

She closed her eyes, remembering the long-ago days at Sweetwater, her family's plantation. A picture surfaced of her father riding his white stallion up the lane. He laughed a lot and teased her, making her laugh too. She and her mother spent a lot of time sitting on the veranda, waiting for her father and Forrest to return from the fields. Camille could still feel the love that surrounded the small family group each time they were reunited. Two scalding tears escaped her tightly closed eyes, and a painful lump formed in her throat. Swallowing tightly, she wiped away the wetness from her cheeks. "Stop it," she chided herself aloud. "Count your blessings, not your losses."

The collie set up a rapid barking nearby, and Camille gave a start, looking over her shoulder. While she'd been day-dreaming, the sun had risen over the grassy knoll. She shaded her eyes with her hand, catching sight of a tall, broad-shouldered form. The sun glinted off his sable brown hair, giving it golden highlights. Her heart beat a little faster as he made his way down the hill toward her.

Halfway, he stopped and bent to make friends with the dog. Sniffing cautiously, the collie finally began wagging his tail as if deciding Seth was all right.

Camille turned back to stare at the bay, her shoulders stiff.

"Nice morning for a walk," he said casually, stooping down beside her.

"Uh-huh," she said.

"Cooper woke me to tell me how obnoxious I was last night." Seth glanced at her rigid profile, trying to gauge her mood. He caught a whiff of her scent on the breeze. She always smelled fresh, like flowers and rain and soap. He fought the overwhelming need to be close to her . . . to touch her.

"Do you want me to say it isn't true?" she asked, refusing to look at him.

"No. I came to ask you to forgive me. Coop told me I said some stupid things," he declared with quiet emphasis.

His deep voice sent ripples of awareness through her. She'd never been at ease with him, and especially after the night he'd kissed her. "You're always saying stupid things to me, and then apologizing. And I'm sure this was Cooper's idea, so don't bother," she said as she got to her feet. Turning, she started toward the knoll.

Seth blinked in surprise at her outburst. Recovering his wits, he ran after her and caught her hand in his. "I beg your pardon! Apologizing was my idea. Why are you so mad?"

Camille trembled at his touch and jerked her hand free. "I don't have to explain anything to you, Seth Braden. Stay away from me and we'll get along just fine!" Picking up her skirts, she continued toward the boardinghouse.

Seth stood watching her. He still didn't understand why she was so angry. True, he always seemed to say the wrong things to her, but Hell's fire, he'd apologized to her more than he'd ever apologized to anyone in his life! Jamming his hands into his pockets, he started up the hill. Maybe it was the kiss, he thought irritably. Maybe she was a prudish little miss, horrified by any simple act of intimacy with a man. Then he remembered how soft and willing she'd been in his arms . . . how eagerly she'd followed his touch with caresses of her own. He felt an unwelcome surge of excitement. If anyone should be mad, it should be him! He'd been unable to make love to Sally the night before, even though she'd enticed him with erotic promises. But it was no use. Every time he touched Sally, Camille's face swam before his eyes, cooling his ardor. What the blazes was wrong with him?

After Mrs. O'Leary returned from Mass at St. Mary's, Camille spent most of the day helping her in the kitchen. She broke string beans, peeled apples for pies, and kneaded a mountain of bread dough. She stayed busy to avoid thinking of Seth, but errant thoughts of him intruded anyway. He pretended to be disinterested, but she knew he'd coerced Cooper into escorting her to work and back home the night before. Cooper was as transparent as glass. The fact that he didn't want her bothering him, yet he stuck his nose in her business, infuriated her.

Camille put a large kettle of water on the stove to heat. "I'd better start getting ready. Cooper wants to leave at six."

Mrs. O'Leary was right behind her with two pies to put into the oven. Camille took a pot holder and opened the door for her. Both women were perspiring and pink-cheeked from the exertion and heat in the kitchen. "Aye, that you should. I'm obliged for all your help today, lass. You go on up and I'll send Finnigan with your water and the tub."

Later, Camille sank gratefully into the brass tub of warm water. Mrs. O'Leary had sent up some lavender bath salts, and the fragrant scent wafted under her nose. Despite the fact that she'd worked hard all day, Camille was excited about the prospect of an evening out. Aunt Lavinia had rarely included her when she took Prudence to social functions.

When Camille finished, she toweled her hair until it was nearly dry. Then she slipped into her new chemise. The silk felt deliciously smooth and cool against her skin. She almost hated to hide it beneath her dress, it was so pretty. Gazing into the mirror, she was surprised to see she actually looked attractive. The blue of the chemise brought out the blue of her eyes, and they sparkled with excitement. Her hair framed her face in soft curls and her cheeks were pink from the warm bath. Would Seth think she was pretty if he could see her now? she wondered, her heart thumping. "You're a shameless hussy, Camille Sinclair!" she whispered.

Turning away, she busied herself with dressing. She didn't care what that arrogant man thought about anything! Until he left for Oregon, she intended to avoid him.

When she left her room, she met Lucy in the hallway. "How beautiful you look! If I had your eyes, I'd wear blue all the time," the schoolteacher said.

"Oh, Lucy! You do carry on," Camille scolded her. "I'm going to dinner with Cooper at his uncle's."

Lucy grinned and linked her arm with Camille's. "I hope you have a wonderful evening." They made their way toward the stairs, and Lucy added, "And speaking of dinner, the most heavenly smells have been drifting up the stairs all afternoon. I'm starved."

"Mrs. O'Leary has outdone herself tonight. She's made potatoes and string beans, a ham, and apple pie," Camille told her, and laughed. "I've almost decided to stay here."

They reached the bottom of the steps and made their way into the parlor. "So you have a night off already?" Lucy asked.

"Every Sunday ni—" Camille broke off when she saw Seth standing next to Cooper beside the fireplace. It would be silly to run, but she had the strongest urge to do so. Seth's expression was guarded when he caught her eye.

"Good evening, ladies," Cooper said, smiling broadly.

Camille swallowed tightly and attempted a smile. "Good evening," she parroted as Lucy urged her toward the sofa.

Seth moved to the table in front of the bay window and refilled his glass from a crystal decanter. Turning, he inquired, "Would either of you care for some sherry? It's not quite time for dinner."

His deep-timbred voice did disturbing things to Camille's composure. Lucy accepted with a smile, and Camille nodded woodenly. When Seth passed a glass to her, his fingers brushed hers, sending a current racing up her arm. She managed to murmur her thanks.

Cooper drew Lucy into a conversation about her work at the small school nearby. Seth moved back to the window and stared out. It gave Camille an opportunity to study him. He was dressed in elegant pinstriped gray pants with a darker gray coat and waistcoat. His white ruffle-fronted shirt contrasted sharply with the bronze of his skin. The broad outlines of his shoulders strained against the fabric of his coat, while his stance emphasized the force of his thighs and the slimness of his hips. He must be going someplace special tonight, she thought suddenly, for he never dressed this formally for dinner at the boarding-house. It surprised her to realize how curious she was about where and with whom. When he turned and caught her staring, his left eyebrow rose a fraction.

Camille averted her gaze and felt her cheeks grow warm. She sipped her sherry and turned her attention to Lucy and Cooper.

"I hate to leave good company, but it's time for us to leave," Cooper said. "My uncle insists on sitting down to dinner on time." Cooper rose and nodded to Lucy. "I hope you have a pleasant evening, Miss Grainger."

Camille stood up, relieved to be going. "I'll just get my shawl."

When she came down and let herself out the front door, she found Cooper and Seth waiting on the porch. She glanced from one to the other questioningly.

"I didn't know you were going with Coop tonight, and obviously you didn't know I was going," Seth said. "He tricked us . . . again." Seth's expression was grim.

Camille gave Cooper an accusing look. "Well, I can just stay here," she said tartly.

Cooper looked sheepish. "It wasn't a trick. I just wanted my two good friends to spend the evening with me. Please, Camille, don't back out now. I already sent a note around to Uncle John saying you'd be there."

Camille ignored his wheedling tone and glanced sharply at Seth. He shrugged. "I suppose we can stand each other's company for one evening. If Camille's willing?"

He made it sound as if she were being childish. It was a challenge she couldn't refuse. "I can stand anything for a few hours," she said. Without another word, they descended the steps to where Finnigan waited with the carriage.

* * *

The houses on Rincon Hill were large, well maintained, and spoke of wealth. Ten years ago, before the Gold Rush had made millionaires out of simple farmers, merchants and vagabonds, this area had been considered worthless. With the explosion in population and businesses crowding the bay, folks with money had moved up and away from the press of humanity to build wood and brick monuments befitting their new station in life.

Camille gazed out of the open carriage at the variety of mansions they passed. One of them reminded her of Sweetwater, with its white columns marching across the front of the wide veranda. Finnigan, the older man who worked for Mrs. O'Leary, nodded toward the next estate, which was reminiscent of a turreted stone castle. "That one belongs to Timothy Rooney. He came from County Kerry early in '51 and struck it rich before the year was done. 'Tis a fine place he built for 'imself. Bridget and Nola, they be Mrs. O'Leary's nieces, work for 'im as maids."

"Is Kerry where you're from, Mr. Finnigan?" Camille asked.

"Nay, me home was in County Galway, and we were farmers, one and all. Until the famine of the forties, that is. 'Twas a black time in Ireland, those years." He shook his head and began mumbling to himself, as if he'd forgotten his passengers' existence.

"Uncle John struck it rich in the gold fields too," Cooper explained. "He was a logger in Maine, just like my father and me, before he came to California. We were never a close family, though. I wouldn't have known he was still in California if I hadn't run into him at the El Dorado a couple of years ago. Now, when Seth and I are in San Francisco on business or a vacation, I usually look him up."

"Does your uncle have a family?" Camille asked.

"No, but he's married. Annabelle is her name. They've been

married for three years. Uncle John has never said anything, but I get the feeling their union is not blissful. She used to be an actress, and is quite beautiful.''

Finnigan turned the carriage into a driveway leading up to a Victorian-style mansion. The shrubs and flower beds on the front lawn of the ornate house were carefully tended.

As they alighted, Cooper urged Finnigan to get some dinner in the kitchen. ''Thank ye, Mr. Maxwell. I'll be ready and waitin' whenever ye folks are.'' The old Irishman clicked his tongue and slapped the reins on the horses' rumps, guiding them around the house.

Cooper preceded them up the steps and onto the wide porch, which stretched across the front of the house and continued around one side. Camille ignored Seth as they followed. It was still daylight, but she could see the soft glow of lamplight coming from a bay window. She wondered what Cooper's uncle and aunt would be like. Never having met an actress, she was extremely curious about Annabelle Maxwell.

The front door swung open a few seconds after Cooper rapped with the elegant brass knocker. A butler in formal black and white stood aside with a distinct air of disapproval as the three of them entered. ''Good evening, Mr. Maxwell,'' he said in a frigid tone.

Cooper handed the servant his hat, and gave Seth a surreptitious wink as the man reached for Camille's shawl. ''Evenin', Thorpe. I hope dinner's ready. I'm starved!''

The English butler, short of stature but regal in bearing, had a pained look on his austere face. ''Your uncle and his guests are in the drawing room. You may join him there.''

Camille glanced at the beautiful mahogany staircase they passed, and the seascape paintings hanging on the papered walls. Ornate brass wall lamps lit the hallway they traversed. Carved wooden tables were spaced along the passage, and held either vases of fresh-cut flowers or porcelain Oriental figurines. Cooper's Uncle John must have panned a ton of gold dust, she thought wryly. As they approached a double door, Camille heard the murmur of voices within, and smoothed her skirt with cold hands, not knowing what to expect.

Cooper opened the door and Seth took her arm, escorting her inside. Camille tried to ignore the fact that his touch felt so good. A swift glance around the room revealed a score of people, elegant ladies in silks and jewels and men in frock coats and narrow striped trousers. All ages seemed to be represented. Cooper moved to her other side just as a middle-aged gentleman broke away from a group of people and came forward to meet them. He had blond hair streaked with gray, a husky build and a face weathered by many years in the sun.

"I'm glad you could come." The older version of Cooper held out his hand formally to his nephew. He then turned a cordial smile on Camille and Seth. "And also your friends."

Cooper made the introductions as his uncle shook Seth's hand and nodded politely to Camille.

"Thank you for the invitation, Mr. Maxwell. You certainly have a lovely home," Camille said.

For a moment, a ghost of a smile curved his lips. "I'll be happy to show you the rest of it before the evening's over if you'd like. I bought this place from a sea captain in Bangor, had it dismantled and reconstructed here. Most the furnishings I bought with the house. It reminds me of Maine." Cooper's uncle motioned to a servant, and the young maid brought a tray of glasses. "Champagne? If you'd rather have sherry, Carmen will get you some." He looked questioningly at Camille.

She shook her head. "Champagne will be fine." The three of them accepted glasses, but John declined with a brief shake of his head. He turned to Cooper. "I want you and Seth to meet the new owner of the South Bay Sawmill. I told him about your business and he seemed interested."

"We appreciate that, sir," Seth said.

Camille smiled and nodded as they stopped at each little

group to be introduced. She couldn't remember many names, but the beautiful gowns, diamonds and elegant coiffures made a vivid impression on her. Next to them, she felt excruciatingly plain in her simple blue silk dress. Aunt Lavinia had hosted dinner parties and soirees, but nothing like this.

"Sven Lang, I'd like you to meet my nephew, Cooper, and his partner, Seth Braden. I was telling you about them earlier." John stepped back to allow Camille to join the circle. "And this is Miss Camille Sinclair, a friend of my nephew's."

He was a tall, rawboned young man with an ingenuously appealing face. "I'm pleased to meet all of you," he said with a thick Swedish accent.

They made the proper responses, and then the talk turned to the lumber business. Camille sipped her drink and looked around the room, wondering where her hostess was. Mr. Maxwell had made no mention of her. Camille gave the furnishings a cursory glance. There were green silk-covered sofas and rose brocade chairs. A beautiful walnut chiffonier stood near the open French doors, and Camille could see delicate Oriental figurines, richly painted plates and lacquered boxes gracing the shelves. The sea captain from Maine had obviously traveled to the Orient a great deal. Camille wondered why he had sold his house and his treasures.

Before she could come up with an imaginative reason, she saw two women enter the hallway. One was petite with raven-black hair, olive complexion and large, dark eyes. She was wearing a deep-red satin gown with a lace ruffle that draped low across the front, showing off delicate shoulders and quite an expanse of swelling bosom. It tapered down to a waistline that was positively minute, and then gently swelled over her hips, falling in graceful folds over a modest hoop. She was easily the most beautiful woman Camille had ever seen. By rights, the woman should have been in the chiffonier with the other exquisite treasures. Her companion was a perfect foil, being tall, statuesque, and blond. Her expressive face was open and friendly, while the dark woman had a look of mystery in her eyes.

In just moments, the two had made their way over to Camille's group. John Maxwell looked up, nodding politely to the blond lady. Sven broke off his conversation to say, "Catrina, my dear, your pretty nose looks no different than before you powdered it."

An affectionate smile lit her face as she turned her gaze on the newcomers. "Sven loves to tease me. Pay him no mind." She extended her hand to Camille and introduced herself as Sven's wife. Cooper, in turn, introduced Camille.

The dark woman stepped forward and kissed Cooper's cheek and then Seth's, murmuring a greeting to each. Finally, she turned to Camille. "I'm Annabelle Maxwell, Miss Sinclair. I'm pleased you could attend tonight."

Camille nodded and smiled, but she felt a definite chill as the beautiful Annabelle gazed at her. The woman's words had been cordial, but Camille had a distinct feeling she hadn't meant them in the least.

The group had barely begun a new conversation when Thorpe entered and announced dinner. John Maxwell offered his arm to Camille, and she noticed that his wife had already taken Seth's arm. Camille felt a prick of annoyance when she saw the dark beauty favor Seth with a seductive smile.

Seated midway down the long, lace-covered table, Camille found herself sandwiched between two older gentlemen. On her left, Mr. Thaddeus Skaggs, president of the Miner's Exchange Bank, kept falling asleep between courses. This gave Camille the dubious pleasure of conversing exclusively with Monsieur Jacques Bonat, a jeweler. By the time the meal was half over, she was blushing with the extravagant, and sometimes risque, compliments he insisted on bestowing upon her. "Your accent, *ma petite,* is truly delightful. If I could but listen to you speak all night, I would be a 'appy man," he gushed, his tone low and intimate.

His eyes were sending messages she would rather not receive. Trying to ignore his meaning, she concentrated on the roasted chicken on her plate. "Tell me about your business, M'sieur Bonat," she said. "It must be exciting to work with precious gems every day."

The short, balding man swiped distractedly at a grease stain on his fancy embroidered vest straining over his protruding stomach. Dropping the linen napkin onto his knees, he gave a Gallic shrug. "They are cold, *cherie,* not like a beautiful woman. Now you, *ma petite,* are more exciting than any stone I have ever possessed. Your eyes remind me of the bluest of sapphires, while the color of your hair outshines the deepest ruby."

As he waxed poetic, his stubby little fingers found her leg under the table and gave it a squeeze. Camille was so shocked for a moment, she nearly dropped her wineglass. Collecting her wits, she reached under the table and pinched his hand. "Stop that this instant, or I'll tell your wife!" she whispered fiercely.

"Mon Dieu! What fire . . . what spirit you have, *ma petite!"* he breathed, his eyes glowing with admiration.

"M'sieur Bonat," she warned, her brows rising ominously.

He lifted his hands in a gesture of surrender, but his eyes sparkled. "I will be good, *mademoiselle*—but that is no fun."

"Madame Bonat's wrath would not be too pleasant either," she reminded him. For the rest of the meal, he behaved himself, much to Camille's relief. His unwanted overtures had nothing to do with her sinking mood, however. That was caused by her frequent glances toward the far end of the table where Seth sat next to Annabelle Maxwell. The two of them seemed to be enjoying each other's company immensely.

Chapter 6

When dinner was over, the guests returned to the drawing room, where Annabelle continued to monopolize Seth. Camille talked for a short time with Catrina Lang, but when Monsieur Bonat joined them, Camille excused herself, looking around for an escape.

"Do you mind if I sit with you for a while?" Camille whispered to a gentleman seated on a green settee.

He smiled and patted the space beside him. "I've been saving this place just for you."

Sitting down, Camille looked to make sure the Frenchman hadn't followed. Once she assured herself he was still attached to poor Catrina, she turned a warm smile on the man beside her. "It's Dr. Jarvis, isn't it? You've done me a great favor."

"Quite the contrary. You've just rescued me from a lonely, boring evening. My undying gratitude, Miss Sinclair."

Camille laughed. "Oh, dear, not another silver-tongued devil. I just escaped from M'sieur Bonat." She rolled her eyes heavenward.

His mouth twitched with amusement. "Ah, yes. I saw you sitting next to the lascivious jeweler at dinner. What a mean trick for Annabelle to play on you, an innocent newcomer to our fair city."

Camille's brow rose. "How did you know I'm a newcomer?"

"I heard John's nephew, Cooper, telling Mrs. Stanton at dinner."

"Do you always eavesdrop on other people's conversations, Dr. Jarvis?" Camille asked, a teasing tone in her voice.

He winked at her. "Always. I hear the most shocking and delicious bits of gossip that way."

Camille laughed. "I thought doctors took an oath to be discreet."

"Only about a patient's ailments, not about his—or her—social escapades," he replied with a wicked smile.

A servant stopped beside them and offered a tray of champagne. Both reached for a glass, and their gazes fell simultaneously on Seth and Annabelle, who were standing across the room beside the grand piano, talking quietly. Camille felt a twinge of annoyance. Didn't the woman's husband care if she spent most of the evening with another man? It didn't help to remember that Cooper had said their marriage was not a happy one.

Camille was quiet on the ride home. Cooper and Seth carried on a desultory conversation, mostly about the new business they might obtain from Sven Lang's sawmill. Whenever the breeze shifted a certain way, she got a whiff of the exotic perfume Annabelle Maxwell wore. The scent clung to Seth like a second skin.

Seth noticed Camille's silence, and wondered if her thoughts were on Dr. Jarvis. He'd seen the two of them talking and laughing like old friends. Had he been able to extricate himself from Annabelle's tenacious hold, he'd have . . . he'd have what?

The sudden question jolted him. What Camille did was no business of his, was it?

When they reached the boardinghouse, the three of them parted in the upstairs hall at their respective doors.

Hours later, Seth lay on top of his rumpled covers, unable to sleep. Thoughts of Camille, and how beautiful she looked at the party, kept intruding. She was so innocent, she didn't even realize the interest she'd stirred among the men there. That was part of the allure, he supposed irritably. Her appeal was quite different from Annabelle Maxwell's, which was exotic and overpowering. Camille exuded an aura of seductive innocence that was nearly irresistible.

A low moaning interrupted his tortured musings, and he sat up, cocking his head to listen. When the sound came again, it was more like the whimper of a small child. He got up and moved to the wall on his right, where he heard soft weeping from Camille's room. He stood for a moment, undecided as to what to do. She wouldn't want him to intrude. She didn't even like him. Yet the pitiful sound wrenched his heart. Deciding he had to leave her alone to deal with whatever grief she was experiencing, he turned back to his bed. Then he heard her sobbing softly, "Mama . . . Papa . . . don't leave us . . . don't die . . ."

Pulling on his trousers, he left the room barefoot and shirtless. She was obviously in the throes of a nightmare, and sounded as if she was in pain. He tried her door and found it unlocked. Stepping inside, he closed it behind him and made his way to her bed. The faint moonlight from the window showed the disheveled state of her covers and her small form curled in a fetal position. "Camille," he whispered, gently brushing the hair back from her face. She moaned softly before she opened her eyes. Giving a small gasp, she jerked away.

"It's Seth, Camille. Don't be afraid," he said, stooping down to her eye level.

A ragged sigh escaped her lips as she visibly relaxed. "You

scared me . . . what are you doing in here?'' She raised herself
to a sitting position, her sleepy gaze cautious.

Seth reached out and took her hand. He was trying not to
notice how thin her nightgown was, or how her breasts were
clearly outlined against the white material. ''You were having
a bad dream. I heard you and came to see if I could help.''

The touch of his hand on hers was hot. The deep sound of
his voice was hypnotic. Her heart jolted and her pulse pounded
as she tried to come to grips with the fact that Seth was in her
bedroom in the middle of the night . . . and she wanted him
there, desperately. ''I . . . I don't remember dreaming . . .''

Seth heard the tremor in her voice, and saw something in
her luminous eyes that caused the blood to pound in his brain.
Reaching out, he gently brushed a stray tear from her cheek.
''You were calling for your mother and father, love.'' He moved
to sit beside her on the bed. Silently, she watched him, and
offered no resistance as he took her in his arms.

Camille drew in a long breath as her hands came in contact
with the rough hair that matted his chest. He was so warm and
hard and muscled. She knew this was dangerous. He was merely
giving her comfort, but she ached for more. She let her fingers
play over his chest in a light caress. ''I'll be fine now . . . thank
you,'' she whispered.

His rough breathing accelerated. He captured her hand to
stop its roaming, but then carried it to his lips. ''God, Camille,
you're so soft and sweet.'' Her heartbeat quickened at the husky
quality of his deep voice, while the touch of his lips on her
fingers set her to trembling. She wanted this moment to last
forever.

Turning his head, he nuzzled her temple, acutely aware of
the way her body trembled. ''You were so beautiful at the
party . . .''

Camille closed her eyes with a long sigh. ''I didn't realize
you'd even noticed me considering the amount of time you
spent with our hostess.''

Seth drew back and tipped her chin up. "It wasn't my choice, I assure you." Even as he acknowledged with satisfaction that her comment sounded like one a jealous woman would make, his eyes narrowed as he whispered, "You didn't lack for company, especially the new doctor's."

The absurdity of their exchange caused her to smile suddenly. "He saved me from Monsieur Bonat. He had a terrible time keeping his hands off me."

Seth frowned. "Dr. Jarvis?"

Camille's smile broadened. "No, silly, the jeweler. I swear, the man had ten hands."

At one and the same time, Seth wanted to laugh with her and strangle Bonat, even knowing nobody took the little man seriously. "I should beat him to a pulp," he murmured, his lips twitching.

Camille leaned forward and kissed his cheek. "It's not necessary, but thank you."

Seth's arms tightened around her as the light moment changed to something entirely different. Groaning, he lifted her effortlessly to straddle his lap, crushing her closer. "This is crazy, Camille . . . we shouldn't," he breathed in a hoarse voice.

Little waves of shock rippled through her when she realized her nightgown was up around her waist—and the swollen thickness bulging in his trousers was pressing intimately between her legs. The only thing separating them was the taut material of his pants.

When Seth's calloused hands cupped the soft rounded flesh of her buttocks and pulled her hard against his need, Camille's dry lips parted as she sucked in air in ragged, gasping pants. "I know," she agreed, but didn't pull away. Common sense told her to, but her body refused to obey the command. Quickening passion washed over her in a fierce tide. Being with him this way was like nothing she had ever imagined. Her body burned for this man she barely knew.

Seth dipped his head and captured her mouth in a hungry kiss. His tongue explored the sweet recesses and challenged hers with erotic jabs. When she began to whimper with need, he pulled back and asked hoarsely, "Tell me what you want, Camille. The choice is yours . . . tell me no and I'll stop."

His smoldering dark eyes met hers squarely, the heat of his passion burning there. Camille trembled. "I don't know anything about . . . what happens between a man and a woman."

Seth's hands moved from the soft flesh of her hips under her gown to her bare breasts. His glittering eyes held hers as he murmured, "This is what happens, Camille." He cupped the tender weight of the rosy globes while he grew harder still and throbbed with unbearable yearning. If she pushed him away, he didn't think he could stop, even though he'd given her the choice. He would have to make her want him as much as he wanted her, he decided. Lifting the gown up, he slipped it over her head, leaving her naked to his hot gaze. Immediately, his hands returned to her creamy breasts, and his mouth followed. Drawing one pink nipple into his mouth, he sucked gently while his hands kneaded the warm flesh.

Camille's head dropped back and she gripped his shoulders with tense fingers. "Oh, God," she rasped deep in her throat, quivering with intense pleasure.

"And this," he murmured, moving to the other nipple to suck gently. One of his arms went around her back to support her, while he trailed kisses up her neck and back to her parted lips. As he kissed her deeply, his other hand found the soft skin of her inner thigh and began to stroke. When his fingers moved to caress the crisp curls between her legs, she arched against his hand, wanting more. "Yes or no?" he whispered against her mouth.

"Oh, yes, Seth . . . oh, yes," she gasped.

A twinge of guilt pricked him even as he slid a long finger inside the hot, wet darkness of her body and felt her meet his strokes with greedy need.

A funny little moan escaped her lips as he abruptly shifted her off his lap and onto the bed. She instinctively struggled up on one elbow to protest, "Don't go . . ."

"Sh-h-h, love. Lie back. I'm just undressing," he said softly, his eyes caressing her beautiful body. Her skin glowed like cream-colored satin in the moonlight, her hard, pink nipples and the auburn triangle of hair at the juncture of her thighs the only contrast.

His words reached her ears, but she was past the point of resistance now. It was going to happen, and with her full consent. Her mind clouded with passion and her body quaked with the force of her need. Camille's big blue eyes grew even wider as he shed his trousers and the bulge sprang to life. She'd never seen a naked man before, and the sight both frightened and fascinated her. He looked huge standing at the edge of the bed. His wide shoulders and thickly muscled thighs looked hard and unyielding. The dark mat of hair on his chest tapered to a thin line that snaked down his flat belly to widen once again around the thick organ that throbbed with pulsing life in his hand. Her eyes flew up to his face and saw hot, glittering desire in his gaze.

"Are you sure, Camille?" he asked, his voice raspy and low. Bending one knee on the mattress, he leaned over, placing his hands on either side of her body without touching her.

"Yes." Her lips barely moved, but he heard her.

His mouth came down on hers with exquisite gentleness, his lips brushing hers lightly, his tongue tracing her full, lower lip. "I've dreamed of making love to you, sweet Camille . . . every night since I met you. I'm going to taste every inch of your body before we're done," he whispered hoarsely. "And then I want to start over and do it again."

Camille's arms circled his neck and she threaded her fingers through his hair, pulling his teasing mouth hard against hers for a deep kiss. The weight of him crushed her into the soft mattress while one of his hands stroked her satiny hip. There was a hot excitement building between her legs and she arched against him instinctively.

Seth pulled away before her erotic movements caused him to lose control. He kissed and suckled her nipples until they grew pebble-hard. Then he moved to her flat belly, laving the little indention there with his tongue. Camille's whimper of desire sent him lower still to the cleft hidden by the soft hair. He closed his mouth over it.

Camille gasped suddenly when she realized what he was doing. Struggling to sit up, she whispered, "No, Seth . . . oh-h-h, please." Her protest died on a moan of quickening pleasure as he continued the exquisite torture. His tongue flicked over the soft folds and the nub at the top. When she thought she'd die from the wonderful sensations, he put his tongue inside her and stroked until uncontrollable tremors wracked her body.

He moved up to nuzzle her breasts once again, and then kissed her mouth, her sweet, wet scent lingering between them. "Oh, God, Seth, is that what making love is about? I didn't know it felt so good . . ." she said, breathless and clinging to his shoulders weakly.

He straddled her, gazing at her pale face in the moonlit room. Her eyes were closed and her swollen lips parted as her breath came in short gasps. "That's not all of it, my love," he told her, a smile in his voice as he watched her eyes fly open. "There's so much more," he promised.

Her expression was dreamy. "If there's more, I'll surely die of the pleasure."

"No, you won't. You'll want it to happen again and again." He pushed one knee between her legs.

Camille glanced down at his manhood, still hard and huge, and she swallowed tightly. "Will it hurt very much?" she whispered. Memory flashed back to the one and only time she had ever discussed sex with anyone. It had been Dulcie, the prostitute who worked in Big Amos's tavern. Dulcie had told her it hurt the first time a woman made love. Since what he'd done to her with his mouth had not hurt, she reasoned, it must be this. She caught her lower lip between her teeth.

Seth's gaze was warm and tender. "I won't lie to you, Camille. There will be a small amount of pain, but it passes quickly and then there's so much pleasure, you'll forget the pain. And I promise to be gentle."

She looked into his eyes for a moment, and then nodded. "I trust you."

Seth caught his breath. He wanted to make love to her more than anything in the world, but her innocence and simple faith gave him pause.

Noticing his hesitation, Camille slid her hands along his chest and down his hips in a caressing gesture. "I'm ready," she whispered.

Seth pushed aside his guilt and bent to cover her mouth with his, lowering his body to hers at the same time. He groaned as her tongue warred with his. Caressing her with one hand, he leaned most of his weight on his other arm. He wanted her desire at a fever pitch. It had to be good for her, he thought fiercely. He wanted her to experience pleasure at their joining.

Camille felt as if she were being pulled down into a whirlpool of passion as Seth sucked gently at her nipples and slid a hand between her legs. His finger found the very core of her, and thrust in and out until she felt shameless with the need for release. There was more, and she wanted it with all her being. Her hands roamed his body of their own volition, and the only thing that stilled her cries was his mouth on hers. When she thought she could stand it no more, he moved between her legs and parted the swollen lips with his throbbing erection. "Hold on, love, we're going for the ride of our lives," he said hoarsely, lifting her hips to take the first gentle thrust.

Camille wanted him, all of him, but she closed her eyes tightly as the pain sliced through her. Gasping, she sank her nails into his back, and he stilled for a moment. He whispered sweet, comforting words in her ear and stroked her hips. Then he began to kiss her again, and moved slowly in and out until she responded to the rhythm.

The pain passed and Camille whimpered as passion enveloped her again. He was huge and hard and filled her nearly to bursting. The hunger of her kisses matched his and she wrapped her legs around his back, riding the tidal wave of desire, crying out his name on a tortured breath as they found their release together.

Seth rolled over onto his back and reached for her hand. As his breathing slowed, he kissed her fingertips and murmured, "Sweet Camille . . . it was better than I dreamed."

She turned on her side, facing him, and asked softly, "Was I . . . did I do the right things?" A picture of Annabelle Maxwell flashed through her mind, and she knew now why the exotic woman had clung to Seth all evening. Annabelle would never feel unsure; she would know how to please a man like Seth. Unreasonable jealousy gripped her, and she felt the sting of tears. What had happened between them was special for her, but how did he feel about it? Perhaps this was no more than he shared with other women—even Annabelle.

Seth leaned closer and kissed her cheek gently. He raised up suddenly on one elbow and tipped her chin up. "Are you crying, love? Of course you did the right things," he assured her in a gentle tone, and then asked, "Was there much pain? I'm sorry if I hurt you."

Camille sniffed, wiping at the moisture on her cheeks. "It's not that, Seth," she murmured, gazing up into his dark eyes. "It was wonderful, but I always thought I would give myself to my husband on my wedding night."

Her words were like a cold dash of water in the face. He should have listened to his conscience earlier, but he'd been carried away by passion. Now he had taken something from her he couldn't replace. Marriage? Just how did he feel about marriage? When Cooper had sprung this mail-order bride on him, he'd been livid, but not because he found any fault with

Camille. He still had deep feelings for Patience. But now, after what had just happened, what was he to do about Camille?

"I'm sorry. This was my fault," he said finally. He enfolded her in his arms and tried to explain his feelings, "We hardly know each other, and I think we should spend some time together. I was engaged to a girl back home in Maine and before that, I had known her for years. But looking back now, I realize I didn't know her at all. She up and married someone else and wrote to me afterward. Marriage is a big decision. One we should think about carefully . . . don't you agree?" He felt as if he was floundering.

The answer she'd been waiting for was not the one he gave, and she felt let down once again by life. This time, however, it was her own fault. He was trying to extricate himself from this situation as gently as possible, but she felt his reluctance. She should have said no, should have sent him away. Breathing deeply of his masculine scent, she kissed his cheek. "I wasn't hinting that you should marry me, Seth. I'm as much to blame as you for this . . . more really. It was a mistake, and I think we should forget it happened."

A mistake? Her quiet words cut through him like the slice of a knife. Of course he wasn't sure if he wanted a permanent commitment, but did he want it to end here? He'd never felt so confused in his life. He sat up, pulling her with him, and was surprised when she grasped the sheet and covered herself modestly. "We should give it some thought, at least," he suggested in a guarded tone.

Camille refused to look at him, drawing herself up against the headboard, gripping the sheet at her chin. "Why? You've never wanted to become involved with me. It's better if we end it now."

The moonlight streaked her hair with silver threads. Seth's eyes drank in her beauty as if for the last time. What she'd said was true. He hadn't wanted to get involved, but he didn't want to say good-bye either. He gazed at the stubborn angle of her chin, and decided tomorrow might be a better time to discuss it. He reached for his pants and pulled them on. "Let's see how we feel in the morning." With that, he left the room. He had to have time to think.

Camille felt fresh tears welling in her eyes as the door clicked shut. Angrily, she dashed them away when they fell on her cheeks. "Stop it!" she whispered fiercely. For years she had endured loneliness, near-poverty and verbal abuse from her aunt. She'd grown strong and hadn't allowed anyone to make her cry. And here she was weeping like a baby over a pigheaded man who wasn't worth one of her tears.

Picking up a pillow, she buried her face in it, willing her mind and body to forget him. His male scent clung to it, however, reminding her of their lovemaking. Vibrant pictures of the two of them tangled in the sheets flashed through her mind and she blushed. She had been wanton, absolutely shameless. His body was beautiful and her gaze had caressed it brazenly. He had kissed and touched her in her most intimate places, and she had gloried in it. Just thinking about it made the heat rise in her body once again.

And the worst thing of all—it was no more than sex to him. She had made an absolute fool of herself by crying, by mentioning marriage when marriage had been the last thing on her mind. She hadn't even realized she harbored these silly romantic notions before it popped out of her mouth. How could she ever look him in the eye again, or herself for that matter? In frustration, she threw her pillow across the room. It landed on the chest, knocking the porcelain bowl off. The shattering of the bowl gave her momentary pleasure.

Chapter 7

Lewis's General Store on Montgomery Street carried a wide assortment of everything a household needed. Camille chose a plain white porcelain bowl and had the shopkeeper wrap it for her. Her small store of money was dwindling instead of growing, she thought as she paid for the purchase. It was a replacement for the one she'd broken the night before. From now on, she reprimanded herself, she would be careful and save. When she located Forrest, she wanted to have enough money to go to him. That reminded her of her other mission. "Could you see if there's any mail for me, Mr. Lewis? And also for Mr. Maxwell and Mr. Braden?" She watched the bent little man make his way to the mail window. He knew her by name since she'd been in everyday looking for a letter from Forrest.

He shuffled back to the counter and handed an envelope to her. Camille's heart raced until she saw the name on the front. It was for Seth. "Thank you," she murmured.

Handing her the package, Mr. Lewis said, "Take heart, Miss Sinclair. Your brother will answer soon."

"I surely hope so," she said, and turned to leave. The little bell above the door tinkled as another customer came in.

"Why, Miss Sinclair, what a pleasant surprise." Dr. Jarvis removed his wide-brimmed hat and smiled. He was dressed almost as formally as he had been the night before, in striped trousers, a silk vest and a brown frock coat.

Seeing him brought Camille's thoughts back to Seth and the dinner party. She held out her hand and managed a small smile. "What a coincidence meeting again so soon."

In Southern style, he bent over her hand and briefly touched it with his lips. Straightening, he said, "It certainly is, but a rather nice one. You're out quite early after our late evening."

"I have to do my errands and get back to the boardinghouse to help with the laundry this morning. Then there's my employment later this afternoon. No rest for the wicked, you know," she said lightly.

"How industrious, I'm impressed. Disappointed, though. I was just about to ask you to join me for some tea before I go to my office." His smile was boyish and appealing.

Camille found him charming, but was not in the mood to be social this morning. "Thank you, Dr. Jarvis, but I really must decline."

"Is something wrong, my dear? Your eyes don't have the sparkle they had last night."

Her attempt at a smile wasn't much of an improvement over the last one. "I'm just a little tired, not being accustomed to long social evenings."

"Please allow me to remedy that situation. I'd very much like to take you to dinner some evening."

Why not? she thought without much enthusiasm. He would be an interesting companion to spend some lonely hours with occasionally. Especially when Cooper and Seth departed . . .

"I think I'd like that. I'm staying at O'Leary's Boarding House on Wilson Street."

"I shall call on you soon." He gave her a slight bow and then held the door for her to exit.

Camille wiped the sweat from her brow on the sleeve of her brown and white gingham dress—the last clean article of clothing she possessed. Her hands were immersed in hot, sudsy water up to her elbows, scrubbing the bloodstain from her bedsheet. It was fortunate for her that the job was a hot one, or Mrs. O'Leary would notice the telltale flush on her face. She was washing away the evidence of the night she'd spent in Seth's arms.

"Give me that sheet, lass, before you scrub a hole through it. I'm thinkin' it's clean now." The older woman took one end of the sheet while Camille took the other, and they twisted out the excess water.

When Mrs. O'Leary had seen the bloodstain and the dark circles around Camille's eyes, she'd made mention of the monthly curse. Camille hadn't corrected her. The stain was gone, but not the memory, she thought sadly.

Dropping the sheet into the tub of rinse water, the older woman suggested, "Why don't you hang that basket of clothes out on the line and get some fresh air? I'll finish rinsing these things, dearie."

Camille nodded, still preoccupied with her thoughts, and made her way to the backyard. Setting the willow basket on the grass, she took a moment to arch her spine while rubbing her aching lower back. A gentle breeze lifted the wispy tendrils of hair from her face and cooled her skin. Straightening, she adjusted her apron and heard the rustle of paper in her dress pocket—Seth's letter. She'd forgotten to remove it when she returned from shopping, but he and Cooper had gone out before she got back. She'd give it to Mrs. O'Leary to pass on to him, she thought, as she began to hang the wet clothes on the line. After what happened the night before, she didn't think she could face him.

Before the thought left her mind, Seth stepped out the back door and crossed the yard to where she stood.

"I knocked on your door this morning, but you'd already left. Are you all right?" His gaze traveled over her body in a slow perusal, from the delicate flush on her face to the curve of her hip in the sedate cotton dress. He felt a decided tightening in his loins. She wasn't looking at him, but had continued with her chore.

The sound of his voice affected her deeply, but she managed to keep her composure. Reaching into the basket, she took the next wet article and shook it out. Her face flamed an even brighter red. It was her lawn nightgown. "I had errands to run," she said, a touch of belligerence in her tone, and then cringed. It was not going to be easy to present a cool facade. Stepping sideways to hang up the wet garment brought her in closer contact with him, and he didn't offer to move out of her way.

"I've been giving our, uh, situation, some thought and—" he began.

"We don't have a situation, Seth. I told you to forget it ever happened, and I would appreciate it if you would honor my wishes," she said, interrupting quickly over her choking, beating heart. Why was he tormenting her?

Seth frowned at her defiant attitude. "I'm just trying to be reasonable about this, Camille. Would you stop for a minute and look at me, please?"

She was bent over, pulling another garment from the basket. She dropped it and straightened. Her blue eyes were glacial as she faced him. "How many ways do I have to say this, Seth? I don't want you in my life. All I'm interested in is saving enough money to get to Oregon and find my brother. Forget about me, all right?"

For a moment, Seth just looked at her. Then a slow smile curved his sensuous mouth. "You are so beautiful when you're mad."

Camille blinked in confusion, and then did something she'd never done in her life. She slapped his face with a resounding smack. "There! Do you find that amusing?"

His eyebrows rose as one hand came up slowly to rub the spot that was turning red. "You're quite a little hellcat, aren't you?" he said softly, surprise and a hint of admiration mingling in his dark gaze.

Realizing what she'd done, Camille promptly burst into tears, dropping her face into her hands and sobbing, "Just go away."

Seth ignored her command and wrapped his arms around her shaking form. He held her fast until she stopped struggling, whispering soothing words in her hair and stroking her back. That he'd caused her this much unhappiness flooded him with more guilt. He couldn't leave her behind when he returned to Oregon. His conscience wouldn't allow it. Extracting a handkerchief from his coat pocket, he pressed it into her hands and said gruffly, "I'm not taking this lightly, I assure you. Everything's going to be fine, Camille. Please stop crying. I think you should marry me. It will solve both our problems."

Her head jerked up, glaring at him. "Don't do me any favors." She wiped her tears and blew her nose. "Since I've been a problem to someone most of my life, I don't intend to be your charity case." Her fierce gaze dared him to say the wrong thing.

He frowned. "I never have and never will think of you that way. I really do need a wife. I'm sick of eating, sleeping and drinking with a bunch of bad-tempered loggers for company. My cabin needs a woman's touch . . . and I get lonely sometimes." The last he added almost as an afterthought, but it had a nice ring to it, he decided.

"Oh-h-h . . . you are such a liar, Seth Braden! Now let me

go before the neighbors start to gossip about us." She pushed against his chest, and he freed her this time.

Seth sighed, pushing his hands into his pockets. "It's the truth, and my offer stands. You think about it."

"I won't, not for one minute," she shot back, stuffing the handkerchief into her pocket. Her fingers touched the envelope and she pulled it out, shoving it at him. "Here."

His fingers deliberately brushed hers as he accepted it. He didn't even glance at it, his eyes holding her gaze instead. "What we did has changed everything," he said with quiet emphasis.

Swift color rose in Camille's cheeks, and she turned back to her clothes basket. "This discussion is over," she said, her voice not quite steady.

Seth started to say something else, but then turned and walked back to the house.

"We're due to leave in four days. Just where'll we find a second cook in that length of time?" Cooper asked, his brows drawing together in a frown.

Seth dropped the letter on the settee beside him. Closing his eyes, he leaned back, resting his head on the plush upholstery. "Why didn't Hallie send a wire instead of writing a damned letter? We'd have known about this a week ago," he said crossly. What else was going to go wrong today? First his disastrous encounter with Camille—and now this.

Cooper eyed his partner speculatively before he turned to pour each of them a shot of whiskey from the decanter on the table. "Why don't we offer the job to Camille? She's anxious to reach Oregon and find her brother," he said.

Seth glanced away. "I don't think that will work," he said, remembering how angry she was with him.

Cooper handed his friend a glass and draped himself over an armchair. "Don't worry. I've given up the idea of matchmaking. You're both as stubborn as mules. I'd really like to help her, though, especially since it's my fault she's stranded here.''

Seth didn't mention he was suddenly feeling a responsibility to Camille that went beyond Cooper's guilty conscience. Half-heartedly, he said, ''But she can't cook. She told me so herself. And if she's stuck back in the woods at our camp, how will she find her brother?''

''Hallie could teach her,'' Cooper pointed out. ''And we can post some notices in Empire City asking about her brother.''

Seth sat up and drank his whiskey in one swallow, feeling the heat of it sear his empty stomach. He was of two minds in this dilemma. The side of him that fought for decency desper-ately wanted to take her with them, to protect and care for her. The other side of him—the hot-blooded male side—knew he'd never be able to leave her alone if she was near. Why was he worrying? he thought suddenly. She'd never agree to this proposition anyway. He looked up at Cooper and nodded. ''Ask her. It's all right with me.''

Cooper grinned. ''It'll work out fine, you'll see.''

''Cook for twenty men? Are you crazy?'' Camille looked at Cooper as if he'd lost his mind.

He was walking with her to work on Monday evening when he brought up his newest plan. ''You'd just be Hallie's helper. She knows how to do everything and would teach you in a flash.''

Camille shook her head. It was impossible. She'd see Seth every day and be reminded of the intimacy they'd shared. ''I'm terrible in the kitchen, Cooper. The poor woman would probably quit if she had to put up with me. No, I just can't do it.''

Bringing out the big guns, he said, ''You'd be closer to finding Forrest, you know. And I'd help you all I could.''

Camille wavered for a moment, thinking about her brother.

Seth's face swam before her eyes, however, and the memory of how she'd made a fool of herself with him more than once. "Forrest will write to me soon, I just know it," she said stubbornly. "But thank you for the offer."

When Seth stopped at the El Dorado for a drink just before midnight, he saw Cooper sitting at a table with three other men. As he made his way purposefully across the crowded room, Seth's mouth was tight and grim. "Doesn't Camille finish work about this time?" he asked without preamble.

Cooper glanced up from his hand. "Oh, hello, Seth. What time is it?"

"You forgot her, didn't you? It's nearly twelve. Don't bother. I'll do it." Without waiting for an answer, he turned and strode from the room. Climbing into one of the carriages for hire outside the saloon, he gave the driver instructions and told him to hurry. Settling back, he ground his teeth in frustration. Most of the time, Cooper could be counted upon. Otherwise, Seth would never have gone into business with him. However, there were times when his friend's easygoing attitude toward life made Seth want to strangle him.

When he arrived at Kelly's, he paid the driver and made his way inside. There were a few sailors drinking quietly at the bar, and a tall, thin man with a short-cropped beard was playing the piano in a desultory fashion. Seth spied Kelly coming out of the kitchen and approached him.

"The lass left not five minutes ago," the big man said, seeing the questioning look on Seth's face. "I tried me best to get her to wait a bit longer, knowin' that you or Mr. Maxwell would come along, but she's a stubborn little mite."

Seth cursed under his breath and turned on his heel.

*   *   *

The evening had been so busy Camille had barely had time to think. She'd served food to at least half the population of San Francisco, or so it seemed. Kelly had even enlisted her help serving drinks for a time.

Why did home have to be up the hill? she wondered tiredly. Pulling her shawl a little tighter against the cool night air, she sighed. Cooper's offer of a job was so enticing, she wished she could accept it. But it would mean seeing Seth every day, and she didn't think it was wise. He'd said they should get to know each other better, but Camille already knew she couldn't resist his charm. She trembled just thinking about their night together. He was an experienced man of the world, while she was naive. Finding her brother was a major consideration, but it would have to wait.

Up ahead, Camille heard the soft whinny of a horse, but couldn't see anyone coming down the street. Perhaps it came from someone's stable, she reasoned. Her gaze swung sharply around, checking the area. A shadow moved next to a shrub on a lawn nearby, but when she got a little closer, she saw it was just a smaller bush moving in the breeze. Her heartbeat had accelerated, but began to slow again as she chided herself. She wished Cooper had shown up to walk her home, but apparently he'd been occupied. In any case, she thought with a grimace, when they went back to Oregon, she'd be on her own. Might as well get used to it.

At the next corner, the three-storied Bowdon Furniture Company loomed dark and silent. Somehow, walking past homes was not quite as sinister as warehouses and factories. Plucking up her courage, Camille walked on. Just as she was congratulating herself on her supreme bravery, a man's figure stepped from the shadows of one of the entryways. "Well, now. Fancy meetin' you here," he said, his hand snaking out to grasp her arm.

Camille gasped and tried to jerk free, but his grip was merciless. "Let me go!" Her voice was a mere whisper, fear having closed her throat.

He pulled her close to his body and stepped back into the alcove. "Now, now, don't fight it, lovey. Jack'll show ya a good time."

He had her arms pinned to her side, but Camille struggled anyway. Her mind told her to scream, but she was lucky to be gasping for air in his tight hold. He smelled of sweat and stale tobacco, and his breath carried the scent of strong garlic. She gagged when his mouth descended to cover hers. A small part of her mind registered the fact he was the sailor who had bothered her the first night at Kelly's. And he'd been there tonight as well. She felt as if she was being suffocated, and her knees began to buckle.

Her attacker broke the kiss and shoved her against the rough wooden door at her back. Camille drew in life-giving drafts of air for a moment as she wiped her mouth with one hand. He moved closer to her, and she pushed ineffectually at his chest, trying to stave him off. When his rough hands grabbed her skirts and yanked them up in front, Camille found her voice. "No! Stop it . . . let me go," she cried, her voice rising in volume.

He clamped one hand over her mouth and continued pawing at the material with the other. Camille scratched his face while trying to tear his arm away from her mouth. If she could just scream, maybe someone would hear her, she thought frantically.

"Bitch," he spat out, grabbing her hand. Taking his hand away from her mouth, he cuffed her on the side of the head.

Camille's world spun for a moment and a mist of darkness threatened. Sagging back against the door, she fought to keep from fainting.

The sailor lifted her skirt and fondled the satiny skin of her inner thighs. "Ah, lovey, you're finer than any ladybird I've ever had in all me travels," he crooned in a raspy, excited voice.

His repulsive touch was more than she could stand, and she felt life and energy flowing back into her limbs. Wait for the right time, she cautioned herself. She let her knees buckle.

"You're gonna like this," he promised, sliding his hands up to her waist to lower her to the ground.

It was so dark, Camille had to go on instinct. Bringing her knee up with all her might, she connected with his groin. As he doubled over, she gave him a mighty shove and sent him sprawling. Without hesitation, she slipped past him and ran full tilt into a hard, warm body. She screamed this time, and pounded with her fists against the solid wall of his chest.

"Camille! It's me, Seth—stop it!"

As soon as her mind registered this fact, she trembled with relief. "He . . . he tried—" she gasped.

He could hear the soft moans coming from the alcove. Grasping her upper arms, he moved her aside and plunged into the dark space. Camille could see two shadows struggling, but couldn't tell who was hitting whom. The scuffle lasted not more than a minute. Then Seth stepped over the body of the other man and took her back into his arms.

For a time, Camille accepted the comfort he gave, holding onto his coat lapels with a fierce grip. As reality set in, she began to shake, while tears slid down her cheeks.

Seth's heartbeat throbbed in his ears and a shiver of desire coursed hotly through his body. Even at a time like this, he couldn't touch her without kindling a fire. His hands caressed her back in a slow, sensuous motion as he said thickly, "I heard your cries when I was running up the street. Don't you ever scare me like that again!"

His hands, his voice, the heat of his body were all having a drugging effect on her senses. "I'm so glad you're here," she breathed, sliding her arms around him and turning her face up to his.

Seth gladly took what was offered. His head dipped and his mouth covered hers hungrily. He crushed her to him, lifting her off the ground. Lord, but he wanted to bury himself deep inside her.

Camille kissed him back, sliding her tongue into his mouth, knowing it pleased him. She was rewarded when he groaned deep in his throat. His hands gripped her buttocks, pulling her against his hard, swollen need. Camille thought she'd die of the wild pleasure it evoked. His mouth left hers to trail kisses down her throat. "Tell me to stop," he commanded hoarsely, dipping his tongue into the little valley where her pulse beat rapidly.

She knew he should stop, but, oh, how she wanted him to continue. Burying her hands in his thick hair, she pulled his head up and placed a lingering kiss on his lips. "What about . . . *him*?" she breathed against his mouth.

He let her slide slowly down his body, and gently smoothed a tendril of hair from her cheek. "Right. We do have to do something about him, don't we?"

Her mouth throbbed from his kisses, and there was a weakness in her limbs. She wanted to be with him so much it hurt. These new feelings frightened her almost as much as her attacker had. Fresh tears slipped down her cheeks. "Damn him! He w-was waiting for me."

Seth reached into his pocket, found a handkerchief and pressed it into her hand. "It's over. Try not to think about it," he advised soothingly. Like her, he didn't comment on what had just happened between them. It was safer. Pulling her gently to him, he let her cry for a short while, and then held her away and smiled. "Better?"

"Yes." Camille glanced at the man on the ground. He looked more like a heap of rubble than a threat. "Thank you."

Seth tipped her chin up with his finger. "No need to thank me, Camille. You'd already felled him like a giant fir before I came on the scene. What did you do to him anyway?"

She hiccuped. "Just something Big Amos taught me—a sharp thrust with the knee between the legs." She blew her nose vigorously and stuffed the linen square into her own pocket.

"Ouch," he said, grinning at her. "I should apologize for doubting you. It seems you can take care of yourself." He moved to hoist the man over his shoulder. "We'd best get him to Kelly's before he wakes up and I have to hurt him a little more. The sheriff can pick him up there."

Camille retrieved her shawl from the ground where it had fallen during the struggle. Wrapping it around her shoulders, she fell into step beside him. "You wouldn't ... kill him, would you?"

Seth glanced at her worried expression. "Worse. I'd turn you loose on him. He'd be damned sorry."

A smile found its way through her mask of uncertainty. "You'd better remember that, mister, the next time you decide to cross me."

There was a trace of laughter in his voice. "Don't worry. I have no desire to be changed from a rooster to a hen."

When they reached the tavern, Seth dumped his burden unceremoniously on the floor and explained the situation to Kelly. "Are you all right, lass?" the older man asked gently, touching her shoulder.

"I'm fine, Kelly. I should have waited, like you said," she said demurely.

"Don't let that sweet, helpless look fool you, Kelly. She had this sorry bastard pleading for mercy when I got there." Seth eyed her with amusement. She constantly amazed him, this slip of a girl with beautiful doe eyes and a soft drawl.

Camille felt warmed by his praise and the tenderness in his gaze. "Why, Seth Braden, what nonsense you talk. A Southern lady does not engage in common brawls," she said with a slow smile.

He chuckled and took her elbow. "Let's go home."

She glanced up at him. "Shouldn't we wait for the sheriff?"

"You've had enough excitement for one night. Tomorrow

will be soon enough to talk to the law. Would you tell him where he can find us?'' Seth asked Kelly.

"I surely will. You'll be takin' care of the lass now, won't ya?'' Kelly's brows rose.

Seth nodded, reading the other man's thoughts. "She won't be without an escort from now on.''

When they were on their way, walking up the quiet street, Seth said, "When I get my hands on Cooper, he'll wish he hadn't gotten so wrapped up in that damned poker game.''

"I wondered what happened to him. But really, Seth, I'm not his responsibility. Or yours,'' she added, glancing up at his handsome profile. Her heart turned over in response and she quickly looked away.

"Of course you are. If it hadn't been for us, you wouldn't be in San Francisco,'' he told her quickly.

"No, I'd be married to a lecherous old goat. And he'd have taken my virginity instead of you,'' she said quietly. "I know what we did wasn't right, but when I think of what it would have been like with him . . .'' She shivered, drawing her shawl closer. "The way he looked at me made my skin crawl.''

"The old bastard,'' Seth muttered. "What in hell was your aunt thinking of?''

"The money, I suppose, and she wanted to be rid of me, I'm sure.''

She said it so matter-of-factly that it twisted Seth's heart. How could anyone mistreat her? She was trusting, sweet and kind. Even when her temper flared, there was a justifiable reason. He quelled the urge to take her in his arms, to love and protect her. "I wish you'd reconsider coming with us to Oregon. We could look out for you,'' he said.

Camille shook her head. "No. I'd be taking the job under false pretenses. You know I can't cook.'' She wished that were the real reason for turning him down, but it wasn't. She just couldn't trust herself with Seth. Right now, with their arms merely brushing as they walked, her heart was pounding, and there was a strange fluttering in her midsection. Her feelings for him were intensifying. She couldn't hope to keep them under control if she was with him constantly.

They'd reached the boardinghouse, and Camille started up the front steps. Seth grabbed her arm, halting her progress. "You've gotta be the most stubborn woman I know. Do you realize that when we're gone, there'll be no one standing between you and scum like that sailor?"

She faced him with more bravado than she felt. "Kelly will escort me home from now on. Please don't worry about me," she said gently. Reaching out, she trailed a finger down his face, tracing his jawline. "I really do appreciate your concern, but it would be best for both of us if I stay." For a long moment, she studied his face, as if committing it to memory. It was a strong face, bronzed by wind and sun, with dark, handsome eyes and a generous mouth. Her gaze lingered on his firm, sensual lips until she could almost feel them on her own.

Seth caught his breath when she touched him. He ached with the need to take her in his arms. She looked ethereal, unreal in the soft moonlight. He could clearly read the awakening desire in her eyes, and knew if he didn't leave her now, he wouldn't be able to. Catching her hand, he grimaced as he dropped it gently back at her side. "Maybe you're right. In all the excitement, I forgot I had a late appointment tonight. I'll see you tomorrow."

Camille nodded, feeling a sense of loss, as if he'd already gone out of her life. She went inside while Seth turned and strode down the street.

Once she was settled in bed, Camille closed her eyes tightly, willing sleep to come. Her body ached with physical tiredness, but her mind raced in circles, like a dog chasing its tail. She didn't want to think about it, but her mind replayed scenes from the attack, vivid and real. The sailor's rough hands on her body and his vile breath came back to haunt her. Pulling up the covers, she huddled under them, drawing comfort from their warmth. She forced her thoughts away from the disturbing encounter, but Seth's face took its place in her mind.

His kiss had been different, more intense. Camille trembled just remembering how she'd felt in his embrace. There had been desire and passion, but there'd been something else as well, something stronger. Or perhaps, she just wanted something more from him?

Where was he now? she wondered. It was too late for a business appointment, so it had to be something personal. Her spirits sank when she thought of him with another woman. Abruptly, she turned over and punched her pillow. She had to forget him. The only reason he pressed her to go with them to Oregon was because he felt duty-bound. She was sick and tired of feeling like a charity case and an obligation. And the next time she promised to marry someone, it would be for love.

Chapter 8

The cool waters of the bay washed over Camille's bare feet as she walked along the shore holding her skirts up. The sun was warm on her head and a light breeze lifted strands of her loose auburn hair to flutter gently. Hearing her name called, she glanced up at the grassy slope above the beach and saw Cooper coming toward her. He was dressed in a blue frock coat, striped trousers and a white ruffled shirt.

Camille waved, noting the frown on his face. He stopped short of the lapping waves. "Seth told me what happened last night, and it's all my fault. I'm sorry. I'd never forgive myself if anything happened to you."

He looked so downcast Camille impulsively put her arms around him. "Don't take on so, Cooper. It wasn't your fault." She leaned back to smile at him. "Everything turned out fine, as you can see. And remember, I told you two hardheaded loggers that I could take care of myself."

Cooper's countenance lightened and he lifted her off her feet, swinging her around. Setting her back down, he said,

"Damned if you didn't. Seth told me what you did to that polecat. I'm proud of you."

"It was nothing more than he deserved. Now, do you feel better?" she asked.

His eyes grew serious for a moment. "Yes, but next time you might not be so lucky. What if there'd been more than one varmint waiting to grab you?"

Her brow furrowed in a frown. "Well, that would have taken a little longer . . ."

"Camille! I do admire your sense of humor, but this is not a laughing matter," he scolded her.

She took his arm and urged him to walk. "I realize that, but it's done. And as I told Seth, I won't walk home without an escort from now on. Satisfied?"

"No. I still think you should come to Oregon with us," he said stubbornly.

Camille chuckled. "You never give up, do you?"

"All right," he said grudgingly, and changed the subject. "I saw Uncle John last night. He was real pleased you came to the party Sunday night."

"I had a lovely time. Your uncle and his . . . wife were very gracious to me."

Cooper's glance was bemused. "Annabelle is only gracious to men. She just tolerates her women guests. His marriage to her was a mistake, but he won't give her a divorce. And she won't leave him and all his money. I don't think she realized what a careful, frugal man my uncle was when she married him. Uncle John swears she'll never get his money, not even when he's dead."

"How awful!" she exclaimed. "If they're both unhappy, why won't he give her a divorce?"

Cooper shrugged. "Pride, stubbornness—not to mention the fact that he's trying to get appointed by the city council to the committee for land development. A divorce would leave a bad impression, he says. Even though he has a mistress and

Annabelle has her quiet affairs, I guess that's more acceptable than divorce in polite society.''

Camille sighed. "It's really a shame when people care more about money than happiness. Aunt Lavinia has always been like that. She envied my father—her stepbrother—the money and plantation my grandfather left him. Papa would have given her the shirt off his back, but she was jealous and bitter. She wouldn't have anything to do with us until Mama and Papa died. I think it gave her great pleasure to sell Sweetwater, even though she had to pay the outstanding debts with most of the money.''

They came to a place on the beach where several boulders blocked the path. They turned to retrace their steps, and Cooper gave her hand a comforting squeeze. "People like that are to be pitied, Camille. They'll never be happy.'' Reaching into his pocket, he took out his watch and flipped open the cover. "Seth and I have an appointment with Sven Lang soon. I'd better get back to the house. Coming?''

Camille shook her head. "I'll be along in a little while.''

He started up the hill, but then turned. "I posted some notices around town asking for a second cook.''

"You'll find someone,'' she said firmly. The faint hope in his eyes died, and she had to bite her tongue to keep from telling him she'd take the job.

Camille and Lucy ate lunch in the kitchen with Mrs. O'Leary that day. All the other boarders were at work or out on one errand or another. The three women talked and laughed easily as they dined on fresh-baked bread, garden tomatoes and cold chicken left over from the day before.

Finishing up, Camille wiped her fingers on a napkin and glanced at Lucy. "I'm going to check on the mail and pick up a few things for Mrs. O'Leary. Would you like to come with me?''

Lucy made a face. "I'd love to, but I'm supposed to meet with a member of the school board at one o'clock. We're going to look over the materials we got in from the East. I can hardly believe school starts in a week."

"Is that the fine-lookin' gentleman who came here lookin' for you two weeks past, lassie?" The older woman's brows rose innocently as she got up to gather the dirty dishes.

Lucy blushed. "Yes. Mr. Gamble is my direct superior."

Camille fixed her with a calculating look. "Would this Mr. Gamble, perhaps, be young and unattached?"

Lucy rose hastily and picked up her dishes, carrying them to the sink. "Why, yes. I believe he is unmarried."

"You told me your social life has been lacking of late, Lucy Grainger," Camille said accusingly.

Lucy defended herself. "He hasn't come courting. The only times I've seen him have been about school business."

"Ah-h-h, a shy lad. I could tell that the moment I met him." Mrs. O'Leary nodded sagely. "All he needs is a push in the right direction, lass. Now, why don't you invite him to supper tonight?"

Lucy looked aghast. "I couldn't! He would think me forward."

"It's a supper invitation, not a marriage proposal," Camille pointed out.

Lucy looked from one to the other and sighed. "I'll think about it." Her cheeks were rosy as she left the room.

Mrs. O'Leary chuckled. "The lass just needs a wee bit of help."

Camille smiled. "Speaking of help, I'll dry the dishes before I leave."

The brass knocker on the front door echoed through the house as they were working, and Camille went to answer it. A stout middle-aged man with a bushy mustache stood on the porch, hat in hand. He wore a tin star on his shirtfront. Nodding politely, he said, "Afternoon, ma'am. I'm Sheriff Moody, and I'm here to talk to Miss Sinclair."

"Come in, please. I'm Camille Sinclair." She ushered him into the parlor and offered him a seat.

"Thank ya, ma'am." He took one of the wing-backed chairs and Camille settled on the edge of the settee. "I'm right sorry about what happened to you last night. Would you like to press charges?"

"Of course I will. He attacked me and I think he should be punished!" Her blue eyes were wide with determination.

He looked down for a moment at the hat he was twisting in his hands. "The man's name is Jack Reed and he's been in trouble before—roughed up one of the girls at the Red Door Saloon. There was a witness that time." He glanced up then to look her in the eye. "When I questioned him this mornin', he said you promised to meet him after you left Kelly's and that you was lyin' about the attack."

It took a moment for his statement to register in her mind. She rose to her feet, her fists clenched angrily at her sides. "That's not true!" she gasped, hardly aware that she'd left her seat.

He stood up, looking pained. "I'm sorry, ma'am. I believe you, but it'll be hard to prove to a judge. It'll be your word against his."

"But Mr. Braden was there. He's a witness."

"Kelly told me that Mr. Braden came along after the fact, so to speak. He didn't actually see the man attack you, did he?" he asked, a faint hope in his voice.

"No, but he knows I'm telling the truth. Are you saying I should just forget it happened?" Camille's eyes were blazing, and she felt as if there was a tight knot in her chest.

"No, ma'am. I just thought you oughta know what you're up against. He'll most likely get off." He took a folded paper from his shirt pocket and opened it. "I brought this warrant for you to sign, just in case you still want to."

Camille took the document from his outstretched hand and glanced over it. She was so angry, however, that the words blurred. Moving over to a small desk in the corner, she took a pen and signed the paper with an unsteady hand.

Sheriff Moody took it from her and put it back in his pocket. Giving her a sympathetic look, he said, "I'll let you know when the case comes up before the judge. Afternoon, ma'am."

Camille saw him out. Leaning back against the door, she closed her eyes. It wasn't fair! That a man could accost a woman, lie about it, and walk away free—it was an abomination! If she hadn't defended herself, he would have raped her. He might possibly have killed her.

She shuddered and pushed away from the door. Making her way back into the parlor, she sat down and absently massaged her temples with her fingertips.

"Camille? What's wrong, honey?"

Startled, she jumped, looking up to find Cooper and Seth staring at her. She hadn't heard the front door or their approach. "The sheriff was here. He says Jack Reed will probably get away with what he did to me." She answered Cooper's question in a dull voice.

"The hell you say!" Seth exploded, crossing the room to her side. "What does that idiot sheriff mean saying Reed will get off?"

Cooper hurried over and laid a restraining hand on his friend's arm. "Calm down and let her talk." He sat beside Camille and took her hand. "Now, what exactly did he say?"

She recounted the conversation. When she finished, her eyes were bright with unshed tears. "It makes me so angry to think he might go free," she said fiercely.

"I'll go to the sheriff and tell him what I know," Seth said, stooping down beside her.

Camille shook her head. "He already knows you came on the scene after the attack. All you can really tell him is what

I told you—that I'd been attacked. Sheriff Moody says it's not the same as an eyewitness account.''

There was a knock on the front door, and Cooper rose to answer it. While he was gone, Seth took Camille's hand in his. ''Don't worry, we'll sort this out. I'll have a little talk with the sheriff anyway. Will you be all right?''

The tender concern in his eyes warmed her like a soft woolen blanket on a cold night. ''Yes,'' she said, attempting a smile. Seth drew her hand up to kiss her fingers gently, holding her gaze with his own. She caught her breath. It was so easy to get lost in the dark depths of his eyes. His tongue flicked out to graze her knuckles and her gaze traveled down to his sensuous mouth. It conjured up the soul-satisfying kiss they'd shared the night before.

Seth swallowed tightly as if he read her thoughts. ''Camille, I—'' he began, but stopped as voices from the foyer reached them. Cursing under his breath, he released her hand and stood up.

When Cooper entered the room, Dr. Paul Jarvis was with him. ''I hope I'm not intruding, Miss Sinclair? You said I might drop by sometime . . . and here I am.'' Jarvis's smile was charming.

Camille barely had time to compose herself. She came to her feet, feeling a distinct tension coming from Seth. ''Of course you're not intruding. Please sit down. You've met Seth Braden?'' She gave Seth a sidelong glance.

Seth stepped forward stiffly, holding out his hand. The two men shook briefly and Dr. Jarvis nodded. ''Yes, of course. At the Maxwell dinner party.''

''If you'll excuse me, I was just leaving,'' Seth said, a frown marking his countenance. He strode out of the room, leaving dead silence.

Cooper smiled. ''He has business with the sheriff, and I need to go with him. Nice to see you again, Paul. Camille, I'll see you later.''

The doctor watched his hasty departure with raised eyebrows. Turning to Camille, he grinned ruefully. "I sure know how to clear a room, don't I?"

Camille relaxed and sat down, nodding toward the nearest chair. "Please, make yourself comfortable. And pay them no mind. They were planning to leave before you got here."

He sat down, resting his hat on his crossed knee. "All the same, Miss Sinclair, I have a feeling I came at a bad time. If you'd like me to go, I'll understand."

Taking a deep breath, Camille shook her head. "No, there's no need. As a matter of fact, I could use some pleasant company." Smiling, she added, "And please, call me Camille."

"All right, Camille. I was hoping you'd come out for a ride with me this afternoon. And perhaps on Friday, you'll consent to have lunch with me?"

She didn't quite know what to say. He was moving a little fast for her, and then there was Seth. "Well, I don't know about Friday yet, but a ride this afternoon would be nice. If you wouldn't mind stopping at Lewis's so I can pick up the mail?"

He grinned engagingly. "My chariot is at your command, m'lady."

Camille rose. "I'll just tell Mrs. O'Leary I'm leaving and freshen up a bit."

He stood up. "Take your time. It'll be my pleasure to wait."

After a side trip to the kitchen, she changed into her yellow and white gingham dress, brushed her hair, letting it fall over her shoulders, and put on her straw hat with the wide brim. Her face was freshly washed and shining when she came back downstairs. Paul came into the foyer to meet her. There was admiration in his eyes as he smiled. "I'll be the envy of every man we see this afternoon."

Camille blushed at his extravagant compliment. "Mind your tongue, Paul, or my head will swell too large for this hat."

He chuckled and offered his arm. After seating her in his

buggy, he urged his team around on the wide street and headed toward town. "I hope Seth's not having any difficulty?"

Camille's brows rose as she glanced at him. "What do you mean?"

"Cooper mentioned a meeting with the sheriff," he explained, keeping his eyes on the road.

"Oh, that. No, no, it was just some personal business he had to take care of," she said, not wanting to discuss the attack. She didn't want to talk about Seth either.

Paul relaxed visibly at her offhand tone. Sometimes he worried about being recognized. Even though he'd changed his name, and his appearance somewhat, there was always a chance. San Francisco was a city teeming with transplanted Easterners. The duel he'd fought with Judge Winslow over Sue Ellen had been a fair one, but the woman's husband had died by his hand and the judge's influential friends had pressed for a murder charge. Anyway, he was safe for now. Stopping the carriage in front of Lewis's General Store, he started to climb down, but Camille stopped him with a hand on his arm. "Please don't bother. I'll just be a moment and then we can be on our way."

In a few moments, she returned, staring woodenly at the envelope in her hand. Paul jumped down and helped her up on the seat. "I hope it's not bad news," he said, noting her downcast expression.

"It's not the news I was hoping for." Disappointment edged her voice. "This is a letter I sent to my brother. He was supposed to be at a logging camp in Oregon. At least that's what his last letter to me said." As Paul urged the team down the street, Camille continued. "According to the notes on the envelope, he wasn't found in Empire City or at four logging camps along the river there. I just don't know what to do now."

"Maybe you could hire a detective to find him," he suggested.

If I had any money, or if I knew of a detective . . . if, if, if! Camille sighed. "Perhaps if I knew where to send him to look.

I thought Forrest was going to a place on the Umpqua River, but obviously he's not there.''

"I hate to be the bearer of bad tidings, but from what I've heard, there are hundreds of logging camps up in Oregon and Washington Territory. Maybe you should sit tight and let him find you.''

"Except that he doesn't know I'm here,'' she pointed out dismally. "He has no way of knowing I've left Charleston.'' The streets were climbing higher as they moved away from the business district going south. Camille barely noticed the run-down buildings that housed the city laborers. "That's why I came out here—to find him. I just didn't realize how big Oregon is. Or Washington, for that matter.''

Paul gave her a sympathetic look before turning his attention back to the road. "I'm sorry. I wish there was something I could do.''

She stuffed the letter into her reticule and sighed. "Thank you, Paul. I'm just lucky I've found such good friends since I've been here.'' Turning to him, she smiled. "That's enough about my problems. Tell me where we're going.''

He pulled hard on the reins, slowing the horses as two, dirty urchins chased each other across the road in front of the carriage. When the danger was past, he replied, "I thought a ride into the country would be nice.''

"It sounds lovely. I have to be back by three o'clock, though. I'm a working girl, you know,'' she reminded him.

"Ah, yes, I remember you saying something about that last time we met. What exactly do you do?''

"I'm a waitress at Kelly's Tavern. It's on the north side of the bay.'' The quick flash of surprise in his eyes amused her. "Are you shocked?''

Recovering himself, he said, "It's just that you look so delicate. I envisioned you as a tutor, or some such. You're obviously educated.''

Camille glanced out at the passing scenery, the carriage

having left the city behind. The rural countryside was beautiful—trees, wildflowers, colorful birds. "While that's true, I've also known hard work most of my life. And I took the first job I could find. It's not so bad." Glancing at him, she gave a careless shrug. The episode with Jack Reed flashed through her mind, but she firmly pushed it away. It was an isolated incident, and would never happen again.

"I'm truly impressed," he said. "Not only are you beautiful, you're honest and hard-working as well." His eyes held a genuine glint of admiration.

She smiled. "Thank you, Paul. You've bolstered my spirits considerably."

"Anytime I can be of service, you need only call on me," he said seriously.

Camille glanced away from the obvious message in his eyes. While flattering, his interest in her as a woman was a bit unsettling. She enjoyed his friendly banter, but she didn't feel romantic about him. Yet when Seth looked at her in that same way, it caused her pulse to race. "As much as I'm enjoying this, I think we'd better start back."

"Of course," he replied easily. Finding a wide place in the road, he turned the carriage around and headed back the way they'd come. Camille asked him about his practice and where his home had been. He gave her the pat answers he gave everyone, which left him free to admire her expressive face and let her soft, sultry voice wash over him like warm ocean waves. There was something about Camille that burrowed under his skin. She seemed fragile, innocent, helpless, yet at the same time seductive and alluring. It was a lethal combination, especially for a man who couldn't resist the challenge of a beautiful woman. He ached with the need to kiss that full mouth and caress those luscious curves. She was skittish, though, he sensed it. With a little time and patience, however, he would have her eating out of his hand like a prized filly.

*   *   *

Annabelle Maxwell arrived at Paul Jarvis's small, elegant house in South Park around two-thirty in the afternoon. As she turned the buggy into his wide driveway, she frowned. His carriage was not in evidence. Mrs. Lake, the nurse he employed at his office, had told her he'd gone home for the day. Pulling the horses to a halt, she climbed down and let herself into the house with the key Paul kept in a flowerpot on the back porch.

She barely gave a glance to the small, immaculate kitchen or the elegant dining room, but moved on to the front parlor. She deposited her bottle-green silk hat and jacket on a gilt, upholstered chair and walked over to the small rosewood desk situated in one corner. Curious, she tried one of the drawers. It slid open and she extracted the loose papers inside. They were receipts and bills—grocer, tailor, livery. Dropping them back inside, she closed it and tried another. It was locked, piquing her curiosity further. She searched the desk thoroughly, but could find no key.

Taking a pin from her upswept hairdo, she worked at the lock until it gave a satisfying click. Inside there was a neat sheaf of papers tied with a faded ribbon, and she carried them to the side window without a qualm. Peering outside to make sure Paul had not arrived, she untied the ribbon and scanned the letters and documents with a feral gleam in her eyes. This was the answer to her problem, she thought. Carefully, she folded the papers back together and retied the ribbon. Her heart fairly sang as she replaced them in the drawer.

For a time, she moved about the house, admiring the wash drawings and oil paintings that were tastefully displayed. The young doctor had expensive tastes, and what she'd found in his papers told her he'd come from a privileged background. She was growing frustrated with the waiting and paced the parlor. When they'd been together the night before, Paul had told her he had only morning hours today. Where was he?

The sound of a carriage rolling past the side of the house drew her to the window. Paul was pulling the team to a halt next to her small buggy. A lustful gleam lit her dark eyes as she undid the buttons down the front of her bodice.

When Paul entered the house, Annabelle met him with a sultry smile. "Where have you been, you naughty boy? I've been waiting a long time."

He tossed his hat onto a chair and removed his jacket, his breath quickening. "Hot little bitch ... you're just what I need." She slid her arms around his neck and he took her mouth with a savage intensity. His hands gathered up the skirt of her dress until he felt the bare satiny skin of her buttocks beneath his fingers. She moaned deep in her throat and pressed against him. When he broke the kiss, he pulled at the shoulders of her dress, trying to remove it.

Annabelle's laugh was husky as she brushed his hands away. "I can't, Paul ... as much as I'd like to. I have to leave. We have guests coming and John's expecting me home soon."

Paul's heavy-lidded gaze flashed. "The hell you say. This won't take long, darlin'."

Annabelle turned away and began fastening her bodice. "If you'd come home when you were supposed to, there would have been time for a delicious romp."

He tried to pull her back against him, but she resisted. His tone was wheedling. "I had an emergency, sweet Annabelle. You know I'm a doctor and can't refuse the sick when they need me."

She knew he was lying. His nurse had said it was a quiet morning. Turning, she buttoned the last button and frowned. "Sorry, love, but I have my responsibilities too."

Paul pulled her roughly to him and kissed her thoroughly. "Why don't you leave that cold bastard and we could play anytime we wanted?"

The time was right. She traced a finger around his full lips. "I couldn't leave all that lovely money behind, and John's already refused to give me a divorce. But I do have a plan, dear Paul. One which would allow me to have it all—my freedom and the money.''

His brows rose. ''Sounds intriguing, love.''

She smiled sweetly, but the warmth failed to reach her exotic eyes. ''We'll kill him, you and I. It's the only way. Once he's gone, I'll be a wealthy widow.''

He laughed. She was trying to shock him. Annabelle was very dramatic, very theatrical . . . leftover playacting from her days on the stage. ''How shall we do it? We can't cut out his heart. He doesn't have one.''

She gave a little shake of her head and said earnestly, ''I thought poison would be a good way to do it—no mess, no fuss. And that's where you come in. I need something that will kill him by degrees, making him think he's sick. Something that can't be detected in case another doctor attends him besides you.''

Paul's eyes widened. Damned if she wasn't serious. ''I'm a doctor. I save lives, I don't take them.''

She chuckled. ''Oh, Paul, that sounded so deliciously righteous. You could have been an actor. I know you killed a judge and you're hiding from the law.'' At his look of surprise, she added, ''I've been reading your private papers—letters from your father, newspaper clippings about the duel and a medical diploma in a different name, Dr. Shelby. You really shouldn't keep incriminating evidence around, silly boy.''

He stepped away from her, shaking his head. ''Obviously not.''

She watched him walk across the room, letting him have a few moments to think.

Finally he turned. ''What's in this for me, besides keeping my secret, that is?''

She gave him a genuine smile this time. ''Money, my sweet, lots of lovely money.''

* * *

Cooper noticed Camille's downcast attitude as they walked home from Kelly's that night. She'd been quiet earlier, and he'd put it down to the ordeal she'd been through the night before. He didn't know if the news he had for her would be good or bad, so he decided to save it. "I'm a good listener if you'd like to talk, honey," he urged.

She tried to smile, but failed miserably. "You must be tired of hearing about my problems."

"Nonsense. It takes my mind off my own. You're really doing me a favor when you weep on my shoulder," he teased, and was rewarded with a smile from her.

"It's not a new problem. I got my letter back from Oregon today—the one I sent to Forrest. Nobody's heard of him up there." Pulling her shawl closer against the damp, cool air, she sighed. Why couldn't life ever be simple?

Cooper slipped a comforting arm around her shoulders. "If you'd like, I'll send out some feelers when I get back to Empire City. I know a steamboat captain who travels as far north as Puget Sound, and he'd put up some notices for me if I asked."

"Thank you, Cooper. I would appreciate that. I just don't know what else to do."

She was trying to be brave, but he detected a thread of desolation in her voice. He bit his tongue to keep from suggesting once more that she accompany them to Oregon. Instead he told her, "Sheriff Moody came by the boardinghouse after supper to let you know about the hearing for Jack Reed. It'll be day after tomorrow."

Camille unconsciously lifted her chin a degree. "Well, that's good news. I don't think I could stand to wait very long. I'd rather know, good or bad, and put it behind me."

"That's my girl," Cooper said in a bracing tone. "You know Seth and I will be there with you."

That thought was the only bright spot in her day.

* * *

When Camille walked into the courtroom, her legs felt shaky.
Flanking her on either side were Seth and Cooper. Sheriff
Moody was there, and rose to show her to a seat at the front
on the right side. A deputy sat beside the accused man to the
left. Jack Reed caught her eye, and without so much as a word
or gesture, he exuded a threatening attitude.

Seth, seeing the direction of her gaze, stepped between them
and ushered her into her seat with a firm, comforting grip on
her arm. "He's like a renegade wolf—don't show him any
fear," he whispered.

Camille gave a brief nod. The judge strode in and took his
place at the high table in front.

As a deputy recited the name of the court, the case number
and charges brought by her against Reed, Camille felt an icy
finger of fear slip down her spine. Reed's look had been venom-
ous, but more than that, his eyes had promised retribution.

The deputy withdrew and Judge Howard called Camille to
the witness stand. After being sworn in, she sat down, her hands
clenched in her lap.

"I've heard the formal charges, young woman, but I'd like
to hear what happened in your own words," the judge said,
peering at her over the top of his spectacles. Camille nodded.
Her throat was dry, but she told her story. When she finished,
the judge's face remained impassive. "You may take your
seat." He then called Jack Reed to the stand, and after he was
sworn in, he took the witness chair.

Reed was dressed in a clean shirt and trousers, his hair slicked
back in place. The look he turned on the judge was one of
pained injury. "I don't like to dispute a lady's word, sir, but
she's lyin' on me. We fixed a time to meet after she finished
work, and she seemed mighty 'appy to see me, she did. The
reason she squawked and got 'oppin mad was because I

wouldn't go the price of a room for us . . . if ye know what I mean, Yer Honor.''

"That's not true! How can you say such a thing?" Camille sprang to her feet, her voice rising in indignation.

Seth tugged gently on her hand, urging, "Sit down, Camille, please."

"You've had your chance to speak, Miss Sinclair. Kindly take your seat and don't interrupt again," Judge Howard cautioned, his brows drawing together in a frown.

Camille expelled her breath in a shaky sigh and sat down, glaring at Jack Reed.

"Do you have any more to add to what you've told us, Mr. Reed?"

He shrugged and gave a knowing smile to the judge, man to man. "She's a willin' wench, Yer Honor, always makin' eyes at me at Kelly's Tavern. Ask any bloke what goes there. 'Ell, look at them two sittin' beside 'er. They're sniffing after 'er all the time."

Tears of anger clouded Camille's eyes as she gripped her chair arms. Seth stood up, his face pasty-white under his tan. A muscle flicked angrily at his jaw, but he restrained himself with great effort. "When Mr. Reed is finished, I'd like to say something, Judge Howard."

The judge looked toward Reed. "I'm done, Yer Honor, sir." He stepped down and resumed his seat. The judge motioned for Seth to come forward.

When Seth was seated in the witness chair, he stated his name. "I came on the scene just moments after Reed assaulted Miss Sinclair. If she hadn't been quick-witted, Your Honor, I would have been too late. Miss Sinclair is a decent young woman, and would never consider associating with scum like Jack Reed. Sheriff Moody will tell you that he was arrested for beating a prostitute not long ago. He's a brutal man."

The judge glanced at the sheriff and received a nod of affirmation from him. Turning back to Seth, he asked, "What is your relationship to Miss Sinclair? Are you her fiancé?"

Seth shook his head. "No, sir. She's a friend. My partner and I are staying at the same boardinghouse, and we've been escorting her back and forth to work each evening so something like this wouldn't happen . . . only we were a little late that night."

"I see." The judge studied Seth's flushed face for a moment and then asked, "So you've never been romantically involved with her?"

Seth felt a sinking in the pit of his stomach. He had sworn an oath to tell the truth, and lying did not come easy to him. Glancing at Camille's stiff posture and frozen expression, he sighed. "For a time we were, but that has nothing to do with this."

"I see," the judge repeated, giving those two little words a wealth of meaning. "How long have you known Miss Sinclair?"

"A few weeks, but I know she wouldn't—" he began, not liking at all the direction the judge was taking.

"So you don't know what sort of profession she might have been engaged in before you met her?"

Seth's face darkened. "She had no profession. She was an innocent young woman living with her aunt."

"You may step down, Mr. Braden." The judge shifted the papers in front of him as Seth walked back to his seat. He wrote a few notes on one page, and then looked up at the assembled court. "We have a case here of one person's word against another—no eyewitness. After hearing both sides, I don't find sufficient evidence to hold this over for trial. Mr. Reed, the charges are dismissed." Judge Howard rapped his gavel. "Next case," he said.

Camille's tears had dried, leaving a burning anger. So this was justice? As they stood up, Seth's fierce gaze locked with Jack Reed's. Cooper reached around Camille to grasp his friend's arm. "Steady, old man. The judge would put you in jail for sure if you lay him low in the courtroom."

Reed swaggered toward the center aisle, smirking. "Yer lucky, mate. I could've 'ad you arrested for assault, but I'm a soft'earted bloke."

Seth jerked free of Cooper's hold with fire in his eyes and took a step forward, but Camille stepped in front of him this time, placing her hands on his chest. "No, Seth. Don't get into trouble for me. He's not worth it."

Reed feigned a look of hurt, placing his hand over his heart. "That cuts deep, m'lady." Laughing at his own joke, he swaggered from the room.

Seth's breathing was harsh as the three of them slowly made their way out. "I'll kill the bastard," he muttered.

"I can't believe he got away with it, even though the sheriff warned me," Camille whispered, the shock of the whole thing settling over her. "The judge thinks I'm a tart! I could see it in his expression."

"That was my fault," Seth growled. "I'm sorry, Camille. I think my testimony hurt you more than helped. I should have my tongue cut out."

Camille gave a heavy sigh. "You told the truth."

Outside, the sun was shining brightly, while a soft breeze lifted the loose tendrils of hair around Camille's face. They stood on the steps in front of the courthouse for a moment as people made their busy way around the three. They were still stunned by what had happened. Finally, Cooper took the initiative. "Neither of you is to blame for anything, so stop bleating like sheep. I've heard it said that justice is blind, and today we've got proof. I'll go get the carriage."

Seth stuffed his hands in his pockets, glaring at the world through narrowed eyes. Cooper was right, of course, but Seth felt as if he'd let Camille down in that courtroom. He was angry that he'd had to tell the truth about his relationship with her, giving all and sundry tantalizing ideas about her virtue.

"Oh, no!" she cried suddenly, and started to turn back toward the front door of the building.

"What is it?" he asked, alarmed.

"I left my shawl. It's the only one I own," she wailed.

Damnation! She was taking on worse about that scrap of wool than she had the verdict. "Stay here. I'll get it," he growled. At least there was something he could do, he thought sourly.

Camille took her handkerchief from her reticule and dabbed at the perspiration on her face. Moving down the steps, she sought shade from a tree near the boardwalk. A carriage was passing on the planked street, but the driver hauled sharply on the reins as the occupant yelled a command. Camille was too distracted to pay much attention until she heard a familiar voice.

"Me luck's runnin' 'igh today, ducky."

Camille stood transfixed as Reed stepped out of the carriage and glanced sharply around. "Where's yer bodyguards?"

A twinge of fear, as well as anger, rose up to stifle her breathing. "I'll scream," she warned in a breathy voice, backing up a step.

His smile was nasty as he lowered his tone so as not to be overheard by the hack driver. "Yer friends won't be around much longer. I checked 'em out. Then we'll see 'ow brave you are."

The veiled threat brought on fragmented memories of the attack. She shivered as he hopped back into his carriage and it moved down the street. The nightmare was not going to end, she thought desperately. Her frustration over the unfair verdict now paled in comparison to this new horror.

When Seth touched her arm, she jumped and let out a yelp. "My God, Camille! What's wrong?" He took one look at her pale face and slipped an arm around her waist for support. "You look like you've seen a ghost."

With an effort, she swallowed past the lump in her throat and willed her limbs to stop shaking. "It was n-nothing, Seth.

Jack Reed stopped to gloat over his victory, that's all.'' She couldn't tell him what the man had said. Seth would go after him, there would be trouble, and Seth would be the one in jail. It was not his problem. She would handle it herself . . . somehow.

"That bastard!'' he growled. "What did he say to you?''

Camille felt the trembling in her limbs again, but forced herself to answer in a level tone. "Just that I should have known better than to tangle with a clever man like him. Just bragging, Seth. That's all it was.''

Seth's grip on her relaxed a bit, but his expression remained grim. "Which way did he go?''

Camille did the only thing she could think of. She sagged against him and let her head fall on his chest. "Oh, please, don't leave me to go after him. I can't take any more. Let's forget this awful business, please?''

Cooper pulled the carriage to a halt beside them just then, and Seth helped her up. "All right—for now,'' he said, glancing at Cooper's questioning look. "That son of a—Reed had the nerve to stop and say something to her when I went inside for her shawl.'' He climbed in and settled himself beside Camille, taking her cold hand in his.

Cooper's brows rose as he looked at her with concern. "He didn't threaten you, did he?''

Camille's eyes dropped to her lap, where she was twisting the strings on her reticule. She hated to tell an outright lie, but it was for the best, she reasoned. "No, nothing like that. He was just bragging about his victory. Could we go now? And please, let's forget about this?''

Seth and Cooper exchanged worried glances, but said no more.

Chapter 9

"Each time I bid ye lads farewell, I feel like I'm sendin' me own sons off. Here's to a safe trip." Mrs. O'Leary raised her glass of wine as she stood at the head of the table. The others followed suit, drinking a toast. Camille, sitting between Seth and Cooper, took a small sip, but had trouble swallowing past the painful lump in her throat. She felt like crying, but wouldn't allow the glistening moisture in her eyes to spill out. Seth and Cooper were leaving for Oregon in the morning. Back to Oregon and out of her life. In just a few short weeks, the two of them had insinuated themselves into her heart, especially Seth.

The spry little Irish lady sat down and passed the bowl of potatoes to her right, signaling the start of the meal. Lucy Grainger spoke up. "Did your contract come through with Mr. Lang's mill?" she asked Cooper.

He nodded. "It sure did. He'll take all the logs we can't handle. We're talking about adding machinery to our mill next year, but for now, we cut more than we can process."

Mrs. Callen, a thin, quiet woman in her middle years, said, "Fascinating business. Since we've been here, I've seen dozens of new buildings going up in the city. Why, our daughter's house was just one of three on her street, and now there's four more being built across from hers."

"If you think there's a building boom here, you should travel through the North. There are gold mining towns scattered through the Washington Territory and up into Canada. Bellingham's become the jumping-off spot to the gold rush on the Frazer River. We sent every board-foot we cut up there last season. Last I heard, the population had grown to fifteen thousand." Cooper smiled at the older lady's look of awe. "Have you folks decided to stay here or go back to Illinois?"

Mr. Callen cleared his throat as he accepted a bowl of greens from his wife. "The wife's dead set on staying near Ellen, so I guess we will. A good tailor can find plenty of work here."

Mrs. Callen smiled happily. "Sally's expecting a baby. We're going to be grandparents in January."

Happy exclamations sounded around the table, and Mrs. O'Leary insisted on filling everyone's glass for another toast.

Camille said very little, concentrating on her food. In reality, every bite she took tasted like sawdust. She was painfully aware of the touch of Seth's arm brushing hers, the heat of his body and the familiar masculine smell of his spicy aftershave. She noticed that he had nothing to contribute to the general conversation, but remained stoically quiet. Was he distressed to be leaving her behind? Of course not, she chided herself. More likely, he was relieved to see the last of her. Since she'd arrived, his life had been turned upside down. She was a constant source of irritation, and he'd made it clear he didn't relish the thought of a commitment.

Between mouthfuls, Cooper dipped his head and whispered, "I'm glad you didn't have to work tonight, Camille. I'll miss you when we leave."

She had to take a firm grip on her emotions to keep from

crying. Giving him a wan smile, she replied, "Mrs. O'Leary said you planned your departure for a Monday on purpose so I could be in on the farewell dinner."

He smiled sheepishly. "She always does this when we leave, and what did it matter if we waited a day or two more before we left?"

Camille dropped her head and nodded. The lump in her throat was growing larger. "Are you sure it won't be too much trouble to get some notices posted asking about Forrest?"

He reached over and took her hand, squeezing it gently. "No trouble at all. I'll write and let you know if we find out anything, all right?"

Two wayward tears slipped down her cheeks, and she hastily brushed them away, trying to smile. "I appreciate that, Coop, and I also want to know how you're doing. I've grown very fond of you and . . ."

"I know," he said, a look of kind understanding in his eyes. "Take a walk on the beach with me after supper?"

She nodded and turned back to her meal. Seth, she noticed, didn't have anything to say to her.

The sun was slipping below the gentle swells on the bay as Camille and Cooper walked along the sandy beach, hand in hand. They talked a little, about his hopes and dreams for his business, she about finding Forrest someday soon, but then they lapsed into a comfortable silence. Neither saw the lone figure that stood atop the dune watching them. Instead, their eyes were cast out on the bay, watching the schooners bob lazily on the tide.

"Will you see us off tomorrow?" Cooper asked suddenly.

Camille shook her head, refusing to look at him. "I don't think I can, Cooper. Please understand."

He heard the break in her voice, and brought her hand up to kiss the back softly. "I suppose I do. Dammit, though, you're like a sister and I hate leaving you behind. Come with us, it's not too late!''

Camille stopped walking to face him. She lifted her free hand and touched his face lovingly. ''Oh, Coop, you're such a dear, but I can't go. I think you know the reason and I'd rather not talk about it.''

''All right,'' he said grudgingly. He pulled her into his arms and held her for a moment. ''If you ever need me, just write . . . or come to me. Promise you'll do that?''

She hugged him tightly. ''Yes,'' she whispered brokenly.

Seth awoke to the grayness of predawn. He lay quietly, staring at the outline of the ceiling, a great weight resting heavily on him. Camille had filled his dreams, she occupied his waking thoughts and she robbed him of the anticipation he usually felt when returning to the deep woods of Oregon. He could hear her moving about in her room. Obviously, sleep was eluding her as well. Rising, he pushed her from his thoughts and splashed water on his face. After shaving, he dressed in a red shirt and brown canvas pants—his traveling clothes.

As he made his way downstairs and out onto the front porch, his countenance was grim. He and Cooper were leaving today— leaving Camille behind. He should feel relieved at the thought, but he didn't. She was like an itch he couldn't reach, and just as irritating. He sat on a wicker chair and stared broodingly into the fog that hung low over the bay.

What he'd seen between Camille and Cooper on the beach disturbed him more than he liked to admit. Coop constantly sang her praises, and he'd been affectionate toward her. But until last night, Seth had reasoned that his partner looked upon her as a friend. Now he wasn't so sure. Their embrace had seemed more than that. Perhaps Cooper was in love with her, and she with him? But then why wouldn't she come to Oregon with them? He knew the answer to that—what had happened between Camille and himself had made things awkward, even impossible for her and his best friend.

Seth ground his teeth in frustration. He wasn't in love with her, but each time she was near, he trembled with need. That wasn't love. He knew what love was—he'd been in love with Patience most of his life . . . hadn't he? They'd played together as children, he'd teased her unmercifully as a young man and then when she'd reached marriageable age, he had begun courting her. That was love. Why, then, did he feel this gut-wrenching pain when he thought of Cooper and Camille together?

The front door creaked. He looked up to see the object of his thoughts standing there, her long auburn tresses floating about her shoulders like a cape.

She noted his presence in a split second and sucked in a startled breath. Turning, she started back through the doorway.

"Camille?" he called before he could stop himself.

She froze, trying to decide whether to ignore his summons, then felt the touch of his hand on her arm. She fought the weakness in her limbs. Swallowing tightly, she lifted wide blue eyes to his. "Good morning, Seth."

"Come, sit with me a few minutes?" he asked, his gaze warily probing hers.

She looked away from the intensity in his dark eyes and drew her shawl closer about the soft gingham dress she wore. "Why don't we go to the kitchen and I'll make coffee?"

He nodded, following her. He sat down on one of the wooden chairs at the table and watched her fill the coffeepot with water from the pump. She had discarded her shawl, and his gaze roamed hungrily over the swells and curves of her slender body. The rich silk of her loose hair beckoned to him. He longed to run his fingers through its length and bury his face in its sweet fragrance. He shook his head to dispel such thoughts. "I wanted to tell you that if you ever need me, us, don't hesitate to write. Or send a wire. You can send it to Empire City. They'll bring it out to our camp." His little speech sounded stilted, even to his own ears. It was not exactly what he wanted to say, but pleading with her to go with them was useless. His pride wouldn't allow it anyway.

Camille felt her heart swell nearly to bursting. She carefully measured the coffee into the pot and placed it on the stove before she answered stiffly. "Thank you, but I'll be fine. You've been very good to me already. And I was nothing but a stranger to you." She couldn't look at him or she would cry, so she busied herself with getting kindling from the wood box to build a fire. Seth was suddenly by her side, brushing her hands away, finishing the chore. She stepped back and gathered her composure while he brought a small blaze to life and then closed the cast-iron door.

He rose and turned to face her. "It was easy to be good to you, Camille." His expression reflected tenderness, concern and a touch of remorse. "I wish I could give back what I took from you . . ."

Reaching out, she placed her fingers on his lips, stilling his speech. "Don't! I gave willingly. Forget it happened." Her tone was sharp, but her eyes bore a trace of pain.

Seth would give anything if he could erase that pain, but he didn't know how. His punishment would be the guilt he carried like a heavy weight on his heart. His hand closed over hers, but she pulled it free. Turning away, she took cups from a shelf and placed them on the table. "What time are you leaving?" she asked calmly, as if they had not shared anything personal.

Seth took his cue from her. "Soon. If you'll excuse me, Camille, I don't want coffee after all." He strode from the room.

She stared at the empty doorway for a moment before her eyes filled with tears and her face crumpled.

A man in sailor's garb with a thin scar marking his left cheek watched as a small launch took Braden and Maxwell across the bay to the schooner *Oriental*. The girl was not with them. Leaving the cluster of crates where he'd been concealed, he made his way to a nearby warehouse to begin his day's work.

Camille spent the morning helping Mrs. O'Leary wash clothes and bed linen. After lunch, the older woman asked her to do some marketing, and then Camille helped prepare supper by peeling vegetables. As she was walking to Kelly's, she realized Mrs. O'Leary had been trying to keep her occupied with enough chores to stave off her misery. Camille had to admit it had helped. Still, there was a great emptiness inside her such as she hadn't felt since Forrest went to sea.

Better to be heartsore now than to have gone with Seth and be heartbroken the rest of her life. He was in love with someone else, and Camille was sick to death of being everyone's charity case. She couldn't bear having Seth pity her. At the tavern, she resolutely tied on an apron and threw herself into work. The sailors, for the most part, were a friendly lot, having grown used to her. They treated her with respect, even gently teased her, but no one stepped out of line as Jack Reed had done. After helping the cook clean up late that night, Kelly sent a trusted friend of his to walk her home. The man had a pistol in his belt, and was alert even though he carried on a conversation with her all the way to her door.

Tuesday, Wednesday, Thursday, Friday—the days ran one into another without mishap. Camille's worry over Reed began to subside. There were dark smudges beneath her eyes, however, from lack of sleep. That, she knew, was not from anxiety, but from the loneliness that gripped her. At times she woke from fitful dreams of Seth and her face would be wet with tears. Time healed all wounds, Big Amos used to tell her, but this slicing pain was as grievous as the death of a loved one.

On Friday afternoon, Camille had Finnigan drive her to Lewis's General Store. She shopped carefully, and finally lined her choices up on the counter, nodding to Mr. Lewis. "That's all, I think."

He figured the price of two jars of lavender bath salts, a bar of lavender soap, some hairpins and a small music box inlaid with jade. When he finished, he gave her the total and smiled as he wrapped her items. "I knew you'd buy that music box sooner or later, Miss Sinclair. I've seen you admiring it often enough. It's a fine piece of work, came all the way from China." Handing her the package, he added, "I checked the mail while you were looking around and there's nothing today."

Somehow, she had known there wouldn't be. "Thank you, Mr. Lewis. Have a nice evening."

When she arrived at the boardinghouse, Camille thanked Finnigan and took her package to her room. Dropping her hat and reticule on the bed, she unwrapped the bundle. Taking a jar of the bath salts and the music box, she made her way downstairs to the kitchen. Mrs. O'Leary was stirring a pot on the stove and turned with a welcoming smile.

"Back from town so soon, lassie? I'll wager you dinna stop on Montgomery Street, or those fine shops woulda held ya longer." Placing a lid on the pot, she turned with a sparkle in her eyes. "Irish stew for supper. I'll fix you a bowl before you leave for Kelly's."

Reaching into her pocket, Camille pulled out some money and handed it to her landlady. "The rent for this week. And I bought bath salts to replace the ones you so kindly left in my room. And this is a gift for you to say thanks for being so good to me." She placed the jar of salts on the table and handed the music box to the older woman.

"Oh, lassie . . . you dinna have to do this at all!" Mrs. O'Leary's gaze rested lovingly on the beautiful trinket. She lifted the lid and the tinkling notes of a sweet ballad drifted out. Her eyes were shiny with moisture as she hugged the younger woman. "You're a dear, sweet colleen, and I'll always treasure this lovely gift."

"I assure you, it was my pleasure," Camille said, growing misty-eyed herself. She stepped back and smiled. "I think I'll go for a walk on the beach, unless you need my help."

Mrs. O'Leary wiped at her eyes with the tail of her apron. "Be off with ya, lass. I've got everything rolling along here."

As she topped the rise that led down to the sand, Camille lifted her hair from her neck to catch the breeze. She loved the view of the bay with the great ships, schooners and smaller boats bobbing on the blue surface. These vessels represented the world, and she often sat watching them, dreaming about where they'd been and where they were going.

Alone, except for a seagull circling overhead, she sat down and peeled off her shoes and stockings to walk barefoot in the sand. When she reached a spot well above the tide line, she dropped her shoes and stockings beside her favorite rock perch and started down the beach.

As she came to the rocky promontory marking the point where she always turned to walk back, she decided to climb over it to explore the beach on the other side. There were hand- and footholds, so she had no trouble. Once on top, she gazed at the untamed beauty of the deserted beach. There were more boulders strewn along the sand, as if scattered by some giant's careless hand. She spotted some shells lying about, and wished she had her sketch pad with her. Tomorrow, she promised herself, she would bring it along and make a drawing of this isolated place.

The lonely solitude seemed to beckon to her and she scrambled down the other side, letting the warm sand soothe her feet, tender from the sharp rock. For a few minutes, she wandered along, picking up shells. Pulling up the hem of her skirt, she created a pouch in which to store her treasures.

"What a pretty picture, ducky."

The oily voice caused Camille's heart to constrict before it began to race violently. She turned, her head jerking up to find

Jack Reed smiling at her. He leaned casually against a boulder, his bold gaze raking her form.

"What do you want?" She felt as if someone was squeezing her chest, robbing her of breath. In a split second, she took in her precarious situation and began to back away. His leering glance at her bare legs caused her to drop her skirt, sending the shells rolling from their nest onto the sand.

Before she could turn and run, he sprinted forward, grasping her arm. "You know what I want, lovey. And you won't get away this time. Ain't no bodyguards to save ya."

Camille jerked, trying to free her arm, but his grip was like steel. She wanted to scream, but her voice came out like the croak of a frog. "Seth will be along any minute. He's meeting me here." She tried to mask the fear in her eyes with defiance.

He laughed, jerking her hard against his body and imprisoning her flailing arms. "Now, now, ducky. It ain't nice to lie to ol' Jack. I saw them two blokes board a ship on Monday. Now it's just you and me."

As Reed's mouth covered hers with a sickening, breath-stealing kiss, Camille fought the blind panic that threatened to overwhelm her. She tried without success to bring her knee up in a repeat performance of the last time. Reed remembered the trick, however, and had his legs braced firmly against hers, affording her little movement. She struggled fiercely, fighting not only for her freedom, but for a breath of air. She felt as if she would gag when he pushed his tongue into her mouth. On pure instinct, she bit down on the offending intruder and instantly the metallic taste of blood spread through her mouth.

Reed's hands moved to her throat to squeeze painfully as his guttural sounds filled the air. Camille held on, knowing that to give up would seal her fate. Her world began to blur and grow dark around the edges. Her lungs felt as if they would explode any minute, but her last coherent thought was she'd rather die than submit to this man's torture.

Miraculously, the darkness began to fade. A faint light filled with bright sparkles danced before her vision and she found herself lying on the sand, free of her attacker. Shaking her head to clear the mist in her mind, she saw Reed kneeling at the edge of the water. He appeared to be drinking from his cupped hands, but a moment later, she saw him spit. This was her chance, she thought, and was galvanized into action. Rising, she started to run for the rock formation, a slight dizziness hampering her speed. She dared not look back, and felt a moment of triumph as her feet found the first niches. Her victory was short-lived when a hand grasped her skirt and dragged her back. "No!" she screamed hoarsely, finding her voice at last.

She turned, her fingers curled into claws, and raked his face before he could grab her arm. A flat-handed blow to the side of her head quickly followed his yelp of pain. "You bloody bitch," he hissed, slapping her again as he pounced on top of her. "You'll pay for that."

The pure venom in his voice gave her one last burst of strength as she rolled to the side, catching him off guard. She ended up on top this time, and tried valiantly to raise her knee for a well-aimed blow, but her full skirts defeated her, tangling her legs hopelessly.

A deafening sound jerked them both to stillness. Reed lifted his head, his face going gray, his eyes filling with fear. Camille looked behind her to see Seth standing atop the rock promontory with a gun leveled in their direction. Her heart sang and relief washed over her in a tremendous wave. If Seth was a mirage, he was certainly a welcome one.

"Let her go," Seth said between clenched teeth.

Reed's instinct for survival came to the fore as he read the message of death in Seth's dark, piercing gaze. With Camille's body shielding his, though, he pressed his edge. His arms loosened around her as if he were going to comply, but when she started to push away, his hands moved suddenly to her throat. "I'll kill 'er—snap 'er pretty neck as quick as a wink, Braden.

Now, throw the gun down 'ere and I'll let 'er go. You get 'er and I get me freedom. Sounds like a fair deal to me."

Seth studied the desperation in the man's eyes for a few moments before he let his gun arm down slowly. "I'm not a fool, Reed. I'll toss the gun away, but not to you. If you let her go, I might just let you live. Otherwise . . ."

Reed's eyes narrowed, and then he nodded. "Do it," he ordered, getting slowly to his feet, dragging Camille up with him. His gaze never left Seth's. "Toss it now!"

Seth's fingers flexed involuntarily on the gun, but he tossed it over his shoulder, out of reach. When he did, Reed shoved Camille away and sprinted down the beach. In the same moment, Seth leaped from the rock and hit the ground in a roll that brought him back up on his feet. He caught up to Reed in a matter of seconds, a growl of fury coming from his throat. "You no-good bastard!"

Camille followed on unsteady legs, picking up a piece of driftwood along the way. If Seth needed her, she wanted to help. It wasn't necessary, though, for Seth was pummeling the man into a bloody mess. The rage on Seth's face was terrifying. Camille saw that he'd lost all reason as he continued to strike Reed's face with his fist. She dropped her weapon and ran to Seth, pulling at his shoulders and calling his name. "Seth, you'll kill him—please stop! Seth!"

Her desperation penetrated the red haze of his rage, for he went lax, his shoulders heaving with his harsh breathing. Camille touched his arm, and he rose, pulling her close to his side. He looked with disgust at the bloody, unconscious face of Reed. "Why did you stop me, Camille? He's nothing but vermin."

She let her head rest on his broad chest, hearing the rapid, strong beat of his heart. "I did it for you," she whispered.

Reason began to return to him and he tipped her chin up to look at her face. Her lip was split and one cheek was swollen. Tenderly, he touched her injuries, his mouth a grim line. "You should have let me kill the bastard." Then, as if realizing there may have been more to the assault than was visible, he asked gently, "Did he—?"

"No . . . he didn't get that far." Her relief was so great, her eyes filled with tears.

Seth let out the breath he'd been holding. No amount of pleading would have stopped him from finishing the job he'd started on Reed had her answer been different. "This time, the sheriff will have enough proof to put this scum in jail. I was a witness."

Camille's gaze devoured his handsome face as if he were some sort of dream she was having in the middle of the day. "How did you get here? You left for Oregon on Monday."

"I left the ship at Bodega Bay, bought a horse and rode like hell to get back here. No matter how hard I tried, I couldn't get past the notion that you needed me."

"I'm so lucky you acted on your feelings," she breathed. Her limbs were trembling now and she felt hot and cold all of a sudden. "I think I'd l-like to go b-back to the boardinghouse now," she said, her teeth chattering. For the life of her, she couldn't stop shaking. Seth swung her up into his arms, and she held onto him fiercely.

"You're a hell of a fighter," he whispered in a soothing tone. "You almost had him whipped when I showed up."

She burst into tears at his gentle praise. He held her, whispering quiet encouragements in her ear. When her sobs changed to sniffles, he set her on her feet. "Better now?"

She nodded and took the handkerchief he pulled from his pocket. She wiped her eyes and blew her nose. "What'll we do with him?"

"I'll have to carry him. That is, if you can walk?"

She nodded. "I'll manage." Glancing up at him, she added grimly, "I hope this is the last time we have to do this."

He hoisted the unconscious man over his shoulder, none too gently. "It will be, I promise you."

Chapter 10

Camille watched as the sun sank toward the horizon, turning the sky a mixture of red, orange and purple. Her favorite chair on the porch was comforting, as was the old brown shawl draped around her shoulders. Her nightmarish afternoon was fading, especially since Sheriff Moody had assured her Reed would go to jail this time. She and Seth had given statements about the attack, and the sheriff had taken note of her bruised face and throat.

Mrs. O'Leary had clucked over her like a mother hen, tending her injuries, helping her bathe and putting her to bed with a shot of brandy. She'd slept for several hours, but had been too restless to stay in bed. When she'd dressed and sought Mrs. O'Leary out, the older woman had told her Seth was out on an errand. His unexpected return had both thrilled and terrified her. This lonely week had seemed endless without him. Was that love? She didn't know, but he was here and she never wanted to lose him again. The terrifying part was that she couldn't control her feelings for him, yet she realized he merely felt responsible for her. Her head ached, and not solely from the blows Reed had delivered.

Something made her look up just then. She saw Seth riding down the street toward her, and a warm sensation curled through her midsection at the sight of him. She fought down the urge to throw herself into his arms. That would never do, she scolded herself. Putting on a calm facade, she gave him a smile as he dismounted and led his horse to the side of the porch. "You're looking better," he commented, his expression neutral.

"I feel much better, thank you," she said. "Did you take care of your business?"

He nodded. "Yes. If you feel up to it, I'd like to talk to you after I put him in the stable."

"I'll be here," she agreed quietly.

He returned shortly and stood at the rail, looking out on the bay. "Camille, you've got to reconsider and come to Oregon with me. Strictly a business arrangement," he hastened to add, and then plunged on. "What happened between us, well, surely we can put it behind us."

He made it sound easy, and Camille knew it wouldn't be. She wanted to say yes anyway, but restrained herself. "I don't understand why you want me to go. I've been nothing but a thorn in your side."

"I—I mean, we did nothing but worry about you from the minute we sailed out of the bay. Don't you see? We've sort of adopted you and if you're with us, we can stop worrying and get on with our work. Coop's miserable, you know. He told me not to come back without you."

Camille's face softened and a smile curved her mouth. "He's such a dear."

Seth's gut twisted painfully. He had been telling the truth about Cooper's anxiety. Now it seemed she had feelings for his friend as well. It didn't matter, he thought resignedly. He couldn't rest unless she went with him. Turning, he faced her. "We do need a cook, and Hallie can teach you." Bringing out his final argument, he added, "And you'll be closer to finding your brother up there. We'll help you."

Camille weighed his arguments against her fears, and found her will crumbling. The pain and loneliness of this week had been unbearable. "You've gone to so much trouble for me, I don't know how I can refuse. I accept the job, but I insist on paying my own passage."

Two days later, Camille stood on the deck of the schooner *California* and watched the city of San Francisco grow smaller as they headed out to sea. She would miss Mrs. O'Leary and Lucy, and even Kelly, whom she'd grown fond of, but today there were no shadows across her heart. Seth stood at her side, his arm a hairsbreadth away from hers, and she found herself extremely conscious of his presence. Being near him day after day was not going to be easy, she thought ruefully.

The scent of lavender surrounded Seth, filling his mind with images of Camille he had sworn to forget. Glancing down on her shiny auburn hair, blowing in the gentle breeze, he had to remind himself of his promise. No intimacy, no romantic interludes—strictly business. He caught himself just short of groaning aloud. He'd made that promise just two days ago, and already he was hard-pressed to keep it. The royal blue traveling dress she wore brought out the blue in her wide, soulful eyes. Standing a head taller than Camille, he had a clear view of her pink-tinted full lips. They were parted as she gazed at the world around her with a sense of awe. He felt a warm surge in his loins, and abruptly turned his gaze away from temptation.

"How long will it take us to reach Coos Bay?" she asked.

"About four days. Cooper will wait for us at Empire City. Hallie will probably still be there as well. She has a son who's a sailor and he tries to take some time off at this time of year to be with her."

"I'm anxious to meet Hallie. The two of you have talked about her so much. Do you think she'll be upset when she finds out I can't cook?"

Seth glanced down at her earnest expression and smiled. "Hallie will love you. She'll take you under her wing and mother you to death if you let her. I'm hoping she'll give me and Coop a rest once you get there."

She laughed. "So that was your real reason for offering me this job."

"Now you know," he teased back. Their eyes locked, and for a moment, he thought there was a flicker of desire in hers, but then she looked away, and he wasn't sure.

"I think I'll go rest for a while," she said, her voice impersonal once again.

In her cabin, Camille opened the small trunk Mrs. O'Leary had given her and began removing the contents. She hadn't really wanted to rest, but the excuse had served her purpose. Perhaps if she stayed out of his way as much as possible, the overwhelming urge to throw herself into his arms would pass.

Lovingly, she smoothed the folds of the yellow lawn day dress she'd purchased for the trip. She also had the royal blue silk she was wearing, two soft wool dresses for winter in blue and green, and the beautiful jade silk gown that was folded carefully at the bottom of the trunk. A trip to Madame Riva's dress shop had nearly depleted her store of money after she'd purchased her passage on the *California*. She smiled remembering Seth's carefully worded offer to pay her way to Oregon. "I would do that for anyone I hired," he'd argued. But in the end, she'd had her way. The clerk at the bank had looked pained as she withdrew the funds she had deposited only the day before.

Her money had stretched to cover some stockings and two silk chemises. As she took them, one by one, out of the trunk to inspect them, she felt a surge of excitement. She hadn't owned so many pretty things since she'd been a little girl at Sweetwater. Her final purchase had been a deep blue velvet mantle to protect her from the chilly winds of winter in Oregon.

Camille had to be truthful with herself. Not only did the new things make her feel good, she liked the admiring glances she'd received from Seth that morning when she'd descended the stairs wearing her new traveling dress. Perhaps in time, she could make him forget Patience. Maybe he could learn to care for her. Sighing, she replaced the garments in the trunk and lay down on the small bunk. The excitement of going to Oregon with Seth had robbed her of sleep the night before, so it wasn't long until she slipped into a dreamless slumber.

For Camille, the next three days passed in a euphoric blur. She stood at the rail a lot watching the gentle swells of the ocean, where dolphins and other exotic fish played, and seagulls drifted on the warm breezes. On this third night, the black velvet sky was studded with stars and the only sound, besides the lap of the waves against the hull of the ship, was the soft strains of a guitar being played by one of the crew—a young Spanish man named Raoul. The tune he'd chosen sounded sad, affecting Camille in a strange way.

Seth had been avoiding her, spending his time with the captain—talking business, he said. And she hadn't cared to strike up a friendship with the two couples who were the only other passengers aboard. Pulling her shawl tighter, she realized she was shivering in the cool night air. She was reluctant to retire to her cabin, though, for it was even more lonely there.

"There's something about sailing at night that's magical somehow," Seth said softly at her elbow.

Camille gave a small start, and looked up as he settled his arms on the wide rail beside her. "That must be true—you appeared out of nowhere," she said crossly.

He chuckled. "I'm sorry I startled you."

"It's just that I've spent so much time alone, the sound of a human voice was peculiar," she told him dryly.

He turned sideways to look at her. "Poor Camille. I've neglected you, haven't I?"

His deep, husky tone caused a wild fluttering in her midsection. "I didn't expect to be mollycoddled," she said defensively, refusing to look at him. He smelled like spice and tobacco and man. The combination caused her heart to pound recklessly.

He slid his arm along the rail to stroke the back of her hand. "What's so interesting out there? You've done nothing but gaze into the distance for days."

Camille could barely breathe, his touch sending shivers of excitement racing up and down her spine. Swallowing tightly, she said, "The ocean . . . the scenery. But I've been doing a lot of thinking too."

His curious fingers traced a pattern along her arm. "About something important?"

"Oh, just wondering where Forrest is, and what a logging camp will be like and how glad I'll be to see Cooper again." He dropped his hand and turned to look out to sea. Camille was sorry and relieved at the same time.

After a small silence, he said, "I suppose I should explain things since you'll be living there. We're on the Umpqua River, almost ten miles inland from the bay. There's a steamboat line that runs every day from Empire City, and stops at all the camps, it's faster than overland. The camp itself is on a gentle rise above the river. Last year we built a new cookhouse and bunkhouse, and the old ones now serve as houses for myself and Coop and Hallie. You'll be bunking with her."

"I can't wait to see it all. Cooper has talked about how beautiful the Oregon country is," she mused.

"It's like nothing you've ever seen before. The trees are enormous and the forest starts at the water's edge and goes on for miles. The deep woods are so thick that midday looks like twilight and midnight is as black as sin. When Coop and I first explored the area, I thought I was dreaming. Everywhere we turned, there was timber—and on such a grand scale, it was unbelievable. And the supply is endless. For a lumberman, it's like the promised land.''

"You make it sound so wonderful, my fingers are itching to sketch.''

"You'll have plenty of time to do that before the men arrive, but after that—well, I hope you won't mind long workdays.''

No, she thought, the long nights will be the difficult part. "I'm used to hard work. Aunt Lavinia believed in it, especially for me.''

"We never work on Sunday, so it's not as bad as I'm making it sound,'' he offered.

She smiled. "And I'm not complaining. What does one do on Sunday in an isolated logging camp?''

"We wash clothes, sharpen axes, mend harnesses.''

She chuckled. "That sounds restful.''

"Well, it's a lot easier than chopping down a giant tree, or slicing two thousand feet of boards a day. And some of the men take their weekly bath, write letters or go visit wives and family.''

Camille wrinkled her nose at the thought of a bath every seven days. "Don't the wives and families live with them?''

"They could. Coop and I would certainly help build cabins for them, but the men prefer to keep them in Empire City and visit as often as they can. It's pretty isolated out there; no schools for the children or medical help.''

"I hadn't thought of that. Those things are important,'' she agreed. "But they must miss their families a lot.'' She was thinking of Forrest. She hadn't seen him in nine years, and still, she felt an empty place in her heart. She could see his face when she closed her eyes, but couldn't remember what his voice sounded like.

"It does get lonely." He had planned to send for Patience, but each year it seemed there was more work to keep him busy, or not enough time to build a house for her. Something had always postponed that decision . . . until it no longer mattered. She had married someone else.

There's more than one kind of loneliness, she thought. "I think I should go to my cabin. It's getting colder," she said. Being this close to him was difficult, and she was tired of fighting the urges of her body.

"Of course," he said. "I'll walk with you." For the most part, the ship's crew was trustworthy, but a woman as beautiful as Camille had drawn their interest. He didn't think putting temptation in a sailor's path was a good idea.

They made their way below, and down a narrow corridor lit at intervals by oil lamps. The close confines of the passageway seemed overwhelmingly intimate. They were alone and sharply aware of each other. Seth walked behind Camille, mesmerized by the provocative sway of her hips, and she, in turn, felt the heat of his gaze. By the time they reached her door, Camille was breathing raggedly, anxious to escape his presence. "Th-thank you. I'll see you in the morning."

Instead of stepping past her, he stopped, their bodies just scant inches from each other. "The captain assured me we would arrive at Coos Bay tomorrow evening."

"I'm looking forward to it," she said, her voice barely a whisper. Her heart was pounding recklessly. He was too close, he smelled too masculine and his dark eyes were intense, mesmerizing. She was reminded of the amazing night he'd spent in her bed, loving her exquisitely and thoroughly. She'd been wanton, totally shameless in his arms, and she could feel that unbearable need rising up inside her now. If he touched her, she would shatter into a million pieces.

He did touch her, but her limbs turned to warm honey. He cupped her chin with his hand and tilted her face up. "It's Coop you're thinking of, isn't it?" he asked, his voice strained.

Camille felt her breath rushing in and out between her barely parted lips as she studied his lean, handsome face. A spark of excitement had jumped inside her at his question. Could he be jealous? she thought wildly. She spoke of Cooper often, and fondly—he was like a brother. Had Seth misconstrued her feelings for his best friend? Camille's tongue slipped out to wet her lips. "I'll be glad to see him. Is that what you mean?" Her answer was deliberately vague, just in case she was reading him wrong. If he didn't have strong feelings for her—the proper and permanent kind of strong feelings, she amended silently—she had no wish to make a fool of herself.

Seth's thumb moved back and forth slowly against her delicate jawbone. At this moment, he wanted to lean down and kiss her ripe mouth more than he wanted to breathe. There was his promise, though—his promise to keep their arrangement strictly business. He sighed and dropped his hand. To touch her and not have her was hellish torture. "I didn't mean anything, I suppose ... just making idle conversation. After all, you accused me of neglecting you the last few days."

For a brief moment, she glimpsed a mixture of desire and resignation in his eyes. She felt him withdrawing, and a sudden panic seized her. "I didn't accuse you of anything. And furthermore, I don't need or want you to keep me company."

"Hey, kitten, pull your claws in. I was just teasing," he chided her.

"And don't patronize me," she said. There was a challenge in her voice, but an invitation in her eyes.

His breathing quickened. Reaching out to tuck a stray lock of hair behind her ear, his fingers lingered to caress its outer shell. "I don't know why you're so riled all of a sudden, but what can I do to make up?"

The devilish gleam in his dark eyes gave her the courage to be bold. "Kiss me," she commanded, her voice husky.

He warned softly, "That could be dangerous." His hand moved

to cup the back of her head. When his lips were almost touching hers, he whispered, "This isn't the business we agreed on."

Camille felt a curling heat start in her belly and spread to the apex of her thighs. She held his eyes, hers sending messages he couldn't possibly mistake. "If you're afraid . . . or if you don't want to . . ." she whispered, her breathing ragged. He smelled spicy, and his breath held a tinge of whiskey.

Seth's body, held in a frustrated state of arousal for weeks, seemed to catch fire and burn out of control. He pulled her close, his lips moving hungrily over hers. When he'd kissed her urgently and thoroughly, he broke free and his lips moved to nuzzle her ear. "Hell, yes, I'm afraid . . . but not scared enough to turn down the invitation," he said in a hoarse whisper.

Camille bit her lip to keep from moaning in anticipation. She'd been dreaming about Seth every night, and during her busy days, her mind had been filled with thoughts of him. But until this moment, she hadn't realized how much she wanted him to make love to her again. Her request was shameless, and her face flamed as she thought about it. However, she was not so embarrassed she wanted to back out of his embrace.

Seth's hand moved to cup the weight of her breast, teasing the nipple through the material of her dress. His mouth came down on hers again and muffled her unrestrained moan of pleasure.

Camille's hands wound themselves in his thick hair, and she arched against him, aching to be touched everywhere.

Abruptly, Seth pulled away from her, his breath rasping painfully in his throat. "We can't do this in the corridor, Camille."

She closed her eyes, her own breathing labored. She wanted him. Taking his hand, she opened her cabin door, and he followed her inside. He closed the portal and leaned against it. "Are you sure about this?" he asked, praying she was.

Camille swallowed tightly and nodded, dropping her shawl to the floor. Seth reached out and began unbuttoning the bodice of her dress with nimble fingers. His eyes glittered in the moon-

light that intruded through a small brass porthole as
Camille helped him remove the dress. He sucked in his breath
when he beheld her in a transparent blue chemise. Her hardened
nipples pressed against the silk while he murmured words she
couldn't understand because of a humming in her ears.

Pressing his palms flat against her breasts, he rubbed in a
sensuous circular motion. Then he bent and took one hard nub
into his mouth, sucking gently through the material. Camille
arched her body toward his torturously sweet ministrations. A
deep moan bubbled up in her throat when his hand moved to
cup the mound between her legs. She gripped his shoulders
fiercely to keep from buckling at the knees.

Gently, he lifted her and laid her on the bunk against the
wall. Then he stripped away his own clothing and joined her
on the bed, covering her body, yet careful not to crush her with
his weight. "I haven't thought about anything but you, like
this, since that night," he murmured against her ear, kissing it
softly, making his way down the slim column of her throat.

"Oh, Seth . . ." she whispered, closing her eyes tightly as
he dipped his head to suckle at first one breast and then the
other. She so wanted to believe him, but she'd smelled cheap
perfume on him on more than one occasion. It was pointless
to debate it now, though, when she had no intention of getting
out of this bed. Her desire for him overrode her pride.
"Oh-h-h," she moaned involuntarily as he moved lower and
lifted her chemise to kiss the bare skin of her flat stomach.
Thoughts of other women, real or imagined, fled from her mind
as Seth shifted her legs, urging them wide apart. When his
mouth covered the most intimate part of her, she writhed with
pleasure, wanting more of what his tongue was giving her, yet
craving the hot, hard length of him inside her. A sweet, awful
joy built in her, reaching for that distant peak, like the first
time, she thought exultantly.

From deep inside, Camille felt the tremors begin, and a low
keening moan escaped her lips as the spasms widened from

the core of her heated body. Seth moved up to lie between her legs, his hand stroking the hair back from her face. Camille opened her eyes, just barely able to make out the angular shape of his face in the darkened cabin. She felt his smile and the warmth in his gaze more than saw them. Slipping her arms around him, she arched upward, brushing the hot, hard length of his arousal. "Oh, Seth, I want to make you as happy as you've made me," she whispered, kissing his lips gently.

He laughed softly. "You think I didn't enjoy that, love?" He took her mouth with a sort of sweet violence that caused Camille's blood to race to her head and then back to her feet in a single wave. "You'll make me happy, Camille . . . don't you worry about that," he breathed harshly against her lips. He guided his erection to her hot, moist opening, and in one smooth stroke, he entered her. Seth swallowed her gasp of pleasure in a deep kiss, his tongue taking her thoroughly, eliciting small whimpers from her throat.

Lifting himself on his forearms, he left her lips and began moving in and out slowly, teasing her flesh with his own. Camille groaned and instinctively arched her hips to meet his thrusts. Her hands grasped his shoulders, urging him to increase his rhythm. She murmured words of encouragement against his sweat-dampened chest, her tongue flicking through the whorls of dark hair.

Her passionate response sent a fire coursing through Seth's veins, and he drove fiercely into her sweetness. He had been without her for so long, he was unable to hold back the great, staggering wave of pleasure that rolled through his body. Just as he felt the final burst of ecstasy explode in his loins, Camille's shuddering climax joined his, her muscles flexing around his shaft, her hoarse cries mingling with his.

Camille lay panting under his weight as her world came back into focus. The spicy musk scent of Seth's body filled her nostrils, surrounding her with a sweet sense of contentment. She would be happy to lie in his arms forever, make a home for him, have his babies . . . she was in love with him. The realization hit her squarely between the eyes, and she moaned inwardly. That was why she'd goaded him into kissing her. That was why she'd so brazenly led him into her cabin and her bed. He had held a fascination for her from the first day they'd met, and her feelings had continued to grow. Yet, while he wanted her body, he held his heart away from any emotional attachment.

Seth stirred after a few moments, placing a gentle kiss on Camille's brow before he rose from the bunk. He lit the brass lantern attached to the wall, casting a warm glow in the small space. Then he extracted a pitcher of water and a basin from her wall cabinet, placing it on the small table next to the porthole. Taking a cloth from the rack beside the table, he wet it and wrung it out.

Camille watched him through new eyes. His body was magnificent, all hard sinewy muscles and flat planes. Even as sated as she was from their fierce coupling, her heart beat faster and a curling warmth trembled between her thighs. When he turned and moved toward her, she dropped her gaze, blushing at her brazen thoughts. She was afraid too that he would read the newfound love in her eyes. That would never do, she thought warily.

He knelt down beside the bunk and gently wiped the perspiration from her face, smiling tenderly at her. "I'm not surprised to see you blush after the way you carried on," he teased softly.

Her eyes flew wide and she raised up on one elbow, mortified. "I did no such thing," she protested, her cheeks flaming brighter.

He eased onto the bed and pulled her against his chest. "Don't get riled. I like it when you carry on."

After a moment of silence, she asked, "Do you think I'm a . . . brazen hussy?"

He smiled. "To tell you the truth, I haven't thought about it one way or the other. But, no, I wouldn't describe you that way. You're a warm, caring woman who's a little stubborn and as independent as a hog on ice.''

Camille laughed at his backhanded compliment. ''You'll turn my head with your pretty speeches.''

He pulled the quilt over them and gathered her closer. ''There's a solution to your worry, love—marry me. I asked you once, and the offer still stands . . .''

Camille's eyes stung with unexpected tears. She wanted to belong to Seth. She couldn't imagine leaving him to start a new life, even if she found Forrest. It would rip her heart from its moorings. He needn't know she was swallowing her pride. ''I won't marry you out of pity, or need, or even for decency's sake. So if you're offering for those reasons, then forget it,'' she whispered fiercely.

Seth felt her determination in every taut muscle of her body. A wild, racing joy filled him, but he carefully masked the emotion in his voice. ''What about a marriage based on friendship and respect? We have that, you know, and it's more than a lot of couples start off with.''

Would that be enough? she wondered. She desperately wanted his love, but in a split second, she decided to take a gamble. ''I can accept that. But if either of us decides it's over for any reason, we'll part with no guilt or blame. Until then, I promise to make you a good wife. I'll learn to cook and darn your socks and—''

Seth's body was responding heatedly to the touch of hers as his head dipped to catch her lips. ''Just warm my bed, Camille, and I'll be a happy man,'' he told her, his voice husky.

She surrendered to his mouth before she could reply, knowing his request would be easy to grant. The lovers sealed their bargain with a deep kiss that led to another fiery mating. When the bonfire of passion tapered once again to smoldering coals, they slept, peaceful and content with their decision.

* * *

"Dearly beloved, we are gathered here to join this man and this woman . . ." The captain's words blurred and faded for Camille. This was her wedding day. It was sunset, a warm breeze lifted the stray tendrils of hair around her face and her heart felt light, as if it could take flight like the seagull soaring overhead. The ship was just an hour away from Coos Bay, and when she stepped ashore, she would be Mrs. Seth Braden. Glancing shyly at her soon-to-be husband, she trembled with love for this man who was handsome, good and kind. He's also in love with another woman, a practical little voice inside her head pointed out. Her eyes traveled hungrily over the square planes and angles of his face. Perhaps that will change, she challenged the small voice.

"Mrs. Braden?" The captain's voice brought Camille back from her musings.

She blinked. "Pardon me?"

Captain Stuart, a burly, older man with a balding pate, smiled at her. "I just gave permission to kiss the bride."

Camille blushed, glancing at Seth's amused gaze. "Oh," she murmured, tilting her head back and closing her eyes. She felt the feather touch of his lips for just an instant before he withdrew and took her hand. The other passengers, who had been curious witnesses to the proceedings, stepped forward to shake Seth's hand and give their best wishes to Camille.

In the soft light of dusk, the *California* docked at Empire City on Coos Bay. Camille stood at the rail beside Seth, anxious to catch her first glimpse of Oregon. From the shore, up a rolling incline, the land was cleared of trees, raw stumps having been left in place of the towering cedar and fir. Wooden houses were scattered over the hillsides surrounding the town proper.

As far as she could make out, there were three laid-out streets.
The air smelled fresher and cleaner than in San Francisco, due
to the fact there were no factories here belching out black
smoke. Instead, pungent wood smoke and the sharp scent of
pine filled her nostrils. She glanced up at Seth's face, catching
an expression of pride and barely concealed excitement there.
He loves this wilderness, she thought. Her gaze moved to the
thickly wooded area beyond the town. She saw what Seth must
see—trees, huge glorious trees—a bonanza of green gold. She
felt a thrill as she caught the excitement of forging a home in
a new land, rich in natural bounty, practically untouched. She'd
heard Seth and Cooper talk about building an empire in the
wilderness, but before now, hadn't understood.

As Camille walked down the gangplank, she saw several
small groups of squatting Indians beyond the wharf and some
curious lumberjacks. The latter were big and brawny for the
most part and seemed singularly unprepossessing. They stood
with their hands in their pockets, chewing tobacco and spitting.

When the couple stepped off the wharf onto the sawdust-
covered street, Seth nodded to several of the big men. They
parted for Camille to pass, tipping their hats respectfully. She
lifted her skirts and watched where she walked, avoiding muddy
spots and horse droppings. "Will Hallie and Cooper be at the
hotel?" she asked when they reached what looked like the
main street. Two-storied buildings, lining both sides, housed
various businesses with painted signs swinging from extended
porch roofs.

"I expect they will." He stepped onto the boardwalk and
turned to help Camille. "The Talbot Hotel is that white-painted
building halfway down the street," he pointed out.

Camille's curious gaze drank in the sights before complete
darkness obscured the town. Most of the buildings were weathered and unpainted, but a small restaurant across the street,
between the general store and a barbershop, sported a nice coat
of sky-blue. The sign in front read, "The Blue Ox," in bold

letters. Lantern light brightened the interior, and she could see people sitting at tables through the large window. It had a cozy, welcoming look to it.

As they approached the door of the hotel, a woman stepped out. "Pardon me."

"Hallie!" Seth said, wrapping his arms around the stout, gray-haired woman in a bear hug. He kissed her soundly on the cheek. "You're a sight for sore eyes."

The older woman laughed. "Put me down, you young scamp! The whole town'll be talkin'."

He set her down and grinned. "You bet they will. Especially when they find out I've brought my wife to meet my best girl." Turning, he drew Camille forward. "Camille, meet Hallie Smith. Hallie, my wife, Camille."

"Wife! Well, it's about time." Hallie's expression was one of surprise and quick appraisal. She smiled, holding out her hand. "Howdy do, Camille. Cooper told me a little about you, but I wasn't expecting to meet you so soon."

Camille returned the smile and the hand. "I'm very happy to meet you, Mrs. Smith. Seth and Cooper have talked about you so much."

Hallie's brows lifted. "It's just plain Hallie. I ain't Mr. Smith's wife no more. He's dead and good riddance, but that's a story for another time. As for what them two's said about me, I wanna caution you about believin' every tall tale a lumber-jack spits out."

Camille chuckled. "It was all good, Hallie."

"Well, in that case, those two are pretty truthful," she said dryly. Glancing beyond the young couple, she said, "Here comes the other scamp now."

Cooper joined them with a whoop of joy and picked Camille up, swinging her around. "I was hoping you'd come," he said, setting her down gently.

"Why didn't you bring home a pretty little wife like Seth did, young man?" Hallie chided, giving him a mock scowl.

Cooper's eyes widened. "You got married? That's great! I knew it would work out." He slapped Seth on the shoulder and leaned over to kiss Camille's cheek.

Hallie spoke up. "I say we go to the Blue Ox for a celebration supper."

"Good idea," Seth said. "I'm starving. Coop and I can get the bags from the dock afterward."

When they entered the restaurant, it proved to be as warm and welcoming as Camille had pictured from the outside. The scattered tables were covered with blue-and-white-checked tablecloths, and a candle enclosed in a globe graced each one, giving a cozy light. Camille felt a welling happiness deep inside as she counted her blessings. She liked Hallie every bit as much as she'd hoped she would. Cooper was a dear friend, and she was married to a man she loved. Given time, there was a good chance he'd return that love. The only thing that would make her happiness complete would be to find her brother.

Once the four of them had given their order to a short Chinese man, Hallie turned the conversation back to their marriage. "Now, how did you two meet? Cooper was mighty mysterious about that."

Seth's brows rose as he directed a pointed look at his partner. "It was Coop's doing."

Cooper grinned. "You know, I don't think either of you thanked me properly for bringing you together."

Camille gave him a droll look. "Be thankful, Coop. We had several discussions about giving you what you deserve."

Seth explained what Cooper had done, and by the time he finished, they were all chuckling. Hallie wagged a finger at Cooper. "You're lucky it turned out good, you scamp. These two could have strung you up to the nearest tree." Hallie turned that same finger to Camille. "And you, young lady, took a mighty big chance. What if you'd got to San Francisco and found an old scoundrel waiting for you?"

Camille grimaced in good humor. "It couldn't have been

worse than what I left behind." After she told Hallie about Josiah Hall, the older woman threw up her hands in defeat.

"I'll never understand you young folks, but I'm glad it worked out." Hallie grinned then, a wicked light in her eyes. "Especially for me. I'll have a helper who knows what she's doin' this season."

When the other three stared at her for a split second and then burst out laughing, she gazed at them in bewilderment.

Chapter 11

Camille stood awkwardly in the middle of the hotel room, looking around at the sparse furnishings. A cedar chest stood against one wall with a pitcher and bowl on top. A wood-framed mirror hung behind it on the wall. A straight-backed pine chair and small table graced the opposite side of the room. The only other piece of furniture was an iron bed covered with a clean patchwork quilt. Seth carried their lantern over to hang on a wall hook beside the bed. It was bedtime and she felt shy. Spying her trunk across the room, Camille let out a sigh of relief. Here was something to do. She moved over to kneel beside it. Undoing the straps, she lifted the lid and searched inside for her nightgown.

"Would you like a bath sent up?" Seth asked behind her. "If you would, I'll go for a drink and give you some privacy."

Without turning, she said, "Thank you, yes."

A young man carried in a wooden tub a short time later, and then made several trips with buckets of hot water. Finally,

Camille latched the door and sank gratefully into the steaming water. The scent of lavender wafted up under her nose from the salts she'd added, and she sighed with pure pleasure. After soaking for a time, she washed her hair, rinsed it with a pitcher of clear water and then washed her body. Her lawn nightgown felt wonderfully cool against her clean skin as she sat in the middle of the bed to comb the tangles from her hair. She'd opened the window to catch a breeze, and the muffled sounds of the town saloon drifted in. The strains of "Clementine," played on an out-of-tune piano, mingled with feminine laughter and a deep male voice singing lustily, if not melodiously.

After a time, Camille put her comb away and unlatched the door. She turned the lamp down and slipped beneath the quilt, but sleep wouldn't come. Her thoughts jumped from the happy prospect of having a home of her own at the logging camp to the possibility of Seth wanting his freedom sometime soon. She tossed and turned and punched her pillow. The sound of booted feet coming down the hall sent her heart fluttering in anticipation, and stilled her movements. Closing her eyes, she pretended sleep as the doorknob turned and Seth entered. He closed the door quietly and started across the room. A loud thump and a muffled curse told her he'd bumped into the bathtub, which still sat in the middle of the floor. She stifled a giggle.

She felt his weight on the other side of the bed as he sat down to pull off his boots. The sound of his belt buckle and the rustle of cloth told her he was undressing. Her amusement evaporated as she thought of his hard, muscled body lying naked next to hers.

When he lifted the quilt to slide in beside her, Camille held her breath. She could feel his warmth and smell the faint scent of whiskey, tobacco and man on him. It was a heady combination.

He turned to face her back, reaching out a hand to stroke her arm. Camille felt a curl of desire in her belly like liquid heat, spreading down to her very core. His wandering hand moved to glide over her hip and around to her stomach.

"Sweet, sweet, Camille," he whispered near her ear, his breath hot against her skin. "I want you so much."

She trembled at his light touch, her body catching fire. Stretching like a feline, Camille turned on her back, gazing into his face in the dark. All she could see was the outline of his head as it moved down to capture her lips. Her feelings were bittersweet. He wanted her, but he didn't love her. *But it's enough for now,* she thought, her mouth hot and hungry under his.

Camille awoke to the sounds of shouted curses outside her open window. Gazing around the unfamiliar hotel room, she took a moment to remember where she was. She started to get out of bed and investigate the noise on the street below, but discovered she was naked. A vivid memory of the brazen way she'd behaved the night before flashed through her mind. A pink blush colored her cheeks, even as a happy glow filled her being. "He's my husband, after all!" she defended herself aloud to no one in particular. The indention where Seth's head had rested was still in the pillow next to hers, but he was gone. The sun was up high, and she figured it must be late morning. She stretched and started to rise, but a knock on the door stopped her. Clutching the quilt up around her chin, she called, "Who is it?"

"Eric, ma'am . . . come to get the tub," he said.

It was the young man who'd brought her bath last night. She wished she had a wrapper to put on, but made do with the quilt. "Come in," she called. The blond-haired boy, who looked to be thirteen or fourteen, glanced at her briefly, blushed and turned his full attention to dragging the tub from the room. "Have you seen my husband this morning?" she asked.

"Yes, ma'am. He's downstairs talkin' to some folks in the

lobby. He's the one told me you'd most likely be up by now so's I could fetch the tub.''

"Thank you, Eric," she said as he pulled the door closed without looking at her again.

She got up and moved to the mirror, looking at her reflection critically. Her thick hair was tousled, her lips were puffy and her eyes were clear blue and contented. She wondered if Eric could tell she'd been thoroughly loved by her husband the long night through, or if she only thought it was plain to see.

Anxious to begin the new day, she poured some water from the pitcher into the basin. She sponged her body and put on a blue calico dress.

At the bottom of the stairs, she paused, looking for Seth. There were two men talking to the desk clerk—huge, hulking men. They both sported black beards, and wore red homespun shirts and heavy canvas pants tucked inside black boots that reached to their knees.

Not seeing her husband, Camille started across the lobby to the front door. The clerk saw her and spoke up. ''Mrs. Braden? Your husband asked me to tell you to meet him at the Blue Ox.''

"Thank you," she said. Her glance caught that of the two men, who turned to look at her. A shiver ran down her spine. The largest of the two had a vacant look in his eyes, and a stream of spittle ran from the corner of his mouth down to his chin. He tried to smile, but it was a twisted effort, one side of his face refusing to cooperate. The other man's expression, however, was not so innocent. His black eyes had the look of a hungry wolf spying its prey. He ran his tongue over thick lips and gave her a smile with yellow, crooked teeth. ''Mrs. Seth Braden?'' he asked, his voice scratchy and deep.

She felt a definite urge to run, but was rooted to the spot by good manners. Inclining her head, she said, ''Yes. Do you know my husband?''

"Ya might say we're neighbors," he replied, his eyes raking

boldly over her. "The name's Slidell—Jake Slidell, and this here's my brother, Owen. He's an idiot. Been that way since birth."

Camille felt a blush stain her cheeks. She ignored his roving eye and the remarks about his brother. "It's nice to make your acquaintance, both of you. Now, if you'll excuse me, I have to be going." Opening the door, she started out.

"I'm sure we'll see more of each other, Mrs. Braden. Matter of fact, I'd almost bet on it," Jake called out.

Crossing the street, Camille felt Slidell's gaze on her back, and it was all she could do not to break into a run. Without looking, she knew he was standing at the hotel window watching her progress.

By the time she entered the restaurant, her heart was pounding. This is just plain silly, she chided herself. They didn't do anything to me, and Lord knows, the simple brother can't help the way he looks. She pasted on a bright smile as she arrived at the table where Seth and the others sat. "Good morning," she said, avoiding Seth's gaze as he rose to seat her.

Cooper snorted. "You mean good afternoon, don't you? It's nearly time for the midday meal, Camille. Didn't you get any sleep last night?"

She blushed profusely as Cooper chuckled. Seth fixed his friend with a dampening look and warned in a soft voice, "Cooper."

Hallie took pity on her. "Don't pay him no mind, honey."

Camille smiled and placed her napkin on her lap as the Chinese waiter appeared at her elbow. Looking around at the others, she asked, "Were you waiting for me, or have you eaten?"

"We waited for you," Seth said, holding his coffee cup for the waiter to refill.

While the waiter took the other's orders, Camille looked Seth directly in the eye for the first time, and saw a warmth in

Here's a special offer for Romance readers!

Get 4 FREE Zebra Splendor Historical Romance Novels!

A $19.96 value absolutely FREE!

Take a trip back in time and experience the passion, adventure and excitement of a Splendor Romance... delivered right to your doorstep!

Take advantage of this offer to enjoy Zebra's newest line of historical romance novels....Splendor Romances (formerly Lovegrams Historical Romances)- Take our introductory shipment of 4 romance novels **-Absolutely Free!** (a $19.96 value)

Now you'll be able to savor today's best romance novels without even leaving your home with our convenient and inexpensive home subscription service. Here's what you get for joining:

- 4 BRAND NEW bestselling Splendor Romances delivered to your doorstep every month
- 20% off every title (or almost $4.00 off) with your home subscription
- A FREE monthly newsletter, *Zebra/Pinnacle Romance News* filled with author interviews, member benefits, book previews and more!
- No risks or obligations...you're free to cancel whenever you wish...no questions asked

To get started with your own home subscription, simply complete and return the card provided. You'll receive your FREE introductory shipment of 4 Splendor Romances and then you'll begin to receive monthly shipments of new Zebra Splendor titles. Each shipment will be yours to examine for 10 days and then if you decide to keep the books, you'll pay the preferred home subscriber's price of just $4.00 per title plus $1.50 shipping and handling. That's $16 for all 4 books plus $1.50 for home delivery! And if you want us to stop sending books, just say the word...it's that simple.

Check out our website at www.kensingtonbooks.com.

4 FREE books are waiting for you!
Just mail in the certificate below!

If the certificate is missing below, write to:
Splendor Romances, Zebra Home Subscription Service, Inc.,
P.O. Box 5214, Clifton, New Jersey 07015-5214
or call TOLL-FREE 1-888-345-BOOK

FREE BOOK CERTIFICATE

Yes! Please send me 4 Splendor Romances (formerly Zebra Lovegram Historical Romances), ABSOLUTELY FREE! After my introductory shipment, I will be able to preview 4 new Splendor Romances each month FREE for 10 days. Then if I decide to keep them, I will pay the money-saving preferred publisher's price of just $4.00 each... a total of $16.00 plus $1.50 shipping and handling. That's 20% off the regular publisher's price plus $1.50 for shipping and handling. I may return any shipment within 10 days and owe nothing, and I may cancel my subscription at any time. The 4 FREE books will be mine to keep in any case.

Name _____

Address _____ Apt. _____

City _____ State _____ Zip _____

Telephone ( ) _____

Signature _____
(If under 18, parent or guardian must sign.)

Terms and prices subject to change. Orders subject to acceptance by Zebra Home Subscription Service, Inc. .
Zebra Home Subscription Service, Inc. reserves the right to reject or cancel any subscription.
Offer valid in U.S. only.

SN010A

SPLENDOR ROMANCES

ZEBRA HOME SUBSCRIPTION SERVICE, INC.

120 BRIGHTON ROAD

P.O. BOX 5214

CLIFTON, NEW JERSEY 07015-5214

AFFIX
STAMP
HERE

his gaze that made her tremble. She took up the smudged menu and studied it until it was her turn.

The conversation turned to the supplies they intended to buy. It wasn't until they'd finished eating and were walking to the general store that Camille mentioned the Slidell brothers.

''I met two men—Jake and Owen Slidell—in the hotel lobby this morning. Jake said he was your neighbor.''

A muscle in Seth's jaw twitched. ''What else did he say?''

''Only that he'd be seeing me again. Is he a friend of yours?'' Camille felt nervous just thinking about another meeting with those two, but kept her fear to herself.

His mouth tightened. ''He owns a logging camp a few miles upriver from ours, but he's not a friend.''

Cooper and Hallie were walking behind them, and Cooper spoke up. ''He's a low-down skunk and as dangerous as a mean snake, Camille. When you see him coming, you go the other way.''

She looked at Seth for further explanation. ''He made my skin crawl, but I didn't know why,'' she said. ''Has he done anything to you and Cooper?''

''Nothing we can prove, but there's been some sabotage around our camp, and a few unexplained accidents,'' Seth said, his face grim. They'd reached the store, and he opened the door for her. ''You'll be fine if you don't go wandering off alone.''

Camille thought about this as she walked around the store while the other three gathered the things on their list. Obviously her instincts had been correct about the Slidell's—about Jake anyway. Seth hadn't said anything about Owen, but he too made her nervous. Shrugging off these unpleasant thoughts, she searched through a rack of ready-made clothes and found a blue cotton wrapper. When she saw Seth go out back with the clerk's young helper to fetch some sacks of oats, she hurriedly approached the balding man behind the counter. ''Excuse me, sir. Do you have any men's pocket watches?''

"Sure do, little lady." He took a wooden box from beneath the counter and opened it for her. Inside, four silver watches lay nestled in red velvet.

Camille chose the one with a raised likeness of a ship on top and touched the small catch on the side. The top flipped up easily and revealed a large, plain watch face. There was a heavy silver chain attached. "How much?" she asked.

"Ten dollars, ma'am. The other ones with trees on 'em are right popular with the lumberjacks here about. I sell them for fifteen."

If she bought the watch and the wrapper, it would take the rest of her money, but she'd have no need for money out in the deep woods, she reasoned. And she wanted to buy something for Seth. The ship reminded her of a happy time they'd spent together. Making up her mind, she handed the watch to the clerk. "I'll take it and this wrapper. Please wrap the watch quickly. It's a surprise for my husband."

The watch was safely hidden in her reticule when Seth returned. He noticed the package in her arm and frowned. "Did you need some things, Camille? I didn't think to ask. Pick out anything you'd like and have Mr. Williams add it to my bill."

She shook her head. "I had enough money."

They stood a few yards away from Hallie and Cooper, who were talking to the clerk. "I can certainly pay for anything my wife needs, Camille. You needn't use your money," Seth insisted quietly, a peevish note in his voice.

Knowing his pride was pricked, she leaned against his chest and smiled up at him. "Then you can pay me back, Mr. Braden, with interest."

The mischievous light dancing in her blue eyes caused his heart to pound as his arm slipped automatically around her waist. "I think I'd rather take it out in trade, Mrs. Braden," he murmured with a devilish smile.

Camille's breath quickened. "Don't you think this is too public for what you have in mind?" she asked with a twinkle in her eye.

He chuckled and let her go. "Then we'll go someplace else," he promised, making his way toward the clerk to pay the bill.

Chapter 12

After explaining abruptly to Cooper and Hallie that he wanted to take Camille for a buggy ride in the country, Seth took his wife's arm and headed for the livery stable. Before Camille could catch her breath, they were bouncing over a log road into the countryside.

Camille concentrated on the scenery as Seth hummed a tuneless melody. They'd left behind the acreage scarred by raw stumps, and now drove through a dense tract of giant fir. When she grew uncomfortable with the silence, she asked, "Why haven't these trees been cut?"

"Somebody'll get to these sooner or later. They're still cutting on the hillsides around town. Most lumbermen, like us, applied for tracts of land upriver. That way, the bay won't be choked with more logs than it can handle," Seth answered, glancing briefly at her cameolike profile. Her satiny skin had turned golden from days in the sun aboard the *California* and the blue flowers on her calico dress brought out the blue in her eyes. The occasional jolt of his thigh against her hip had been driving him wild since they'd left the town behind.

"When will we leave for your camp?" she asked, wanting to talk about anything but what she was feeling.

"Tomorrow morning. There's a boat leaving at seven." Seth turned the horses off onto a side road barely more than a wide path with grass growing tall between the wheel ruts. "There's a lake at the end of this track. I thought you'd enjoy seeing it," he added.

Camille detected a husky note through his nonchalance, and it set her pulse to racing. "I'm sure I will. It's beautiful country," she said, her voice a trifle breathless. Their destination, she thought, was to be a deserted lake off the beaten path. It would be a perfect place for a romantic tryst. Her cheeks colored as heat rose in them. Since she'd met Seth Braden, she'd had the most unladylike thoughts. Aunt Lavinia would be shocked right down to her lace pantalets, Camille thought with a sudden smile.

At that moment, the buggy topped a slight rise and down below, she saw a sparkling, blue lake surrounded on three sides by lush foliage—leafy shade trees, thick grass and a profusion of late summer wildflowers. "Oh, Seth . . ." she breathed. "It's beautiful."

He enjoyed the rapt expression on her face, and would have bent to kiss her parted lips if he hadn't been worried about keeping the horses in line down the steep hill.

When they reached the lake, Seth helped her alight and they walked along the edge of the water. Camille took her straw hat off and carried it by the ribbons, enjoying the breeze as it ruffled her hair. The subtle scent of pine, wild roses and cool water wafted on the breeze, filling her with a wonderful sense of contentment.

"This would be a perfect place for a house, just over there," Camille said, pointing toward the right of the lake. "The view would be lovely, and you could see up the road to the top of the hill when company came callin'."

Seth smiled at her enthusiasm. "I'm sure someone in town has had the same idea, but this tract of land belongs to the government and it's not for sale. Maybe the government surveyor staked this out for himself for the future."

"I wish I had my sketchbook with me. I don't know if I can recapture this from memory," she said, her expression wistful.

She stumbled over a root, and Seth took her arm. "This is a pretty spot, I'll grant you, but wait till you see some of the sights along the river. And the deep wood is the most magical place this side of heaven. So don't worry. There'll be plenty to sketch."

Seth didn't release her arm as they continued to walk, and the warmth and strength of his fingers set her skin to tingling through the material of her sleeve. *Damn him,* she thought with a mixture of irritation and anticipation. *Damn Seth Braden for making me want him so much.* "What about . . . our home? Tell me how it looks," she said, her insides already trembling. It was just a matter of time before he took her in his arms and kissed her. She knew it, felt it.

He stopped beside a dogwood and leaned back against it. His strong brown hands slid down Camille's arms until his fingers linked with hers. "I've already discussed this with Cooper and he's agreed to sleep in the new bunkhouse until a cabin can be built for him. Hallie can have the old cookhouse, and you and I will take the old bunkhouse. It'll do until . . . well, for a while anyway."

Until we have a family? Was that what he'd been about to say? On the heels of that heady thought came the more sensible ones. Until he tires of me . . . or until he no longer feels responsible for my well-being—such as when Forrest is found and can take me off Seth's hands. A knifelike pain twisted in her belly at the thought. She prayed every day he would come to love her, but there was no guarantee. The way his gaze shifted away for a moment when he hesitated over that "until" told the story. She swallowed past the lump in her throat. "I'll do my best to make it presentable, but I fear I don't possess many wifely skills."

"The most important one you possess in abundance, Mrs. Braden," he said in a husky tone. Slowly, he drew her into his arms, and his head dipped to take her mouth.

At the touch of his lips on hers, she was lost. Common sense warned her not to become too emotionally involved with this man, but her traitorous body molded itself to the hard length of him, and her fingers threaded themselves through his thick sable hair. Her toes curled inside her shoes as he kissed her expertly and thoroughly. Before she knew what was happening, the front of her calico dress was unbuttoned, and he cupped the weight of her ripe breasts in both hands. His touch hardened the nipples beneath her chemise, causing them to ache.

Seth broke the kiss to take one of the straining nubs into his mouth, teasing it with his tongue. Camille arched her back and gasped aloud at the sheer pleasure coursing through her. Gripping his shoulders with her hands, she leaned back, allowing him to love her breasts in the way she'd come to expect and savor. When he slipped the dress off her shoulders and down her arms, pulling her chemise with it, Camille's eyes flew open. "Anyone could come along," she protested breathlessly.

Seth continued nuzzling the tender flesh. "We'd hear or see anyone coming over the rise," he rasped. "Let me love you here, sweetheart—we'll make a memory . . ."

Camille groaned as one of his hands slipped under her skirt and caressed her thighs. There was no way she could fight the waves of desire washing over her, especially when his fingers found her most intimate place. The fierce anticipation of the sweetness to come caused Camille to tremble violently, and her knees grew weak.

A flicker of something shiny caught her eye in the distant

trees, causing her to stiffen. "Seth," she whispered hoarsely. "I saw something."

He turned and squinted into the distance. "What was it?"

"A reflection of some kind—something shiny." Both of them scanned the area carefully, but saw nothing suspicious. Camille was mortified to think someone might have been watching them.

"Could have been a bird. Some of them are scavengers; they pick up all sorts of shiny things," he suggested, but pulled the straps of her chemise up and began doing the buttons on her dress. "I think you're just a little nervous."

Camille frowned. Maybe it was her overactive imagination, but she couldn't shake the strange feeling. When her clothes were straightened, he helped her into the buggy and turned the horses in a wide arc, heading them back up the hill.

Before they topped the rise, Camille felt the hairs on the back of her neck raise with gooseflesh. She looked over her shoulder toward the woods, and a small movement caught her eye. She couldn't be sure; it was so far away.

Seth and Cooper stepped inside the sheriff's office, nodding to the tall young man with sandy-brown hair who stood behind a scarred desk. "You the sheriff?" Seth asked.

"Yep. Bob Wyman. What can I do for you fellers?" He dropped the posters in his hand onto the cluttered surface and motioned to the hard-backed chairs in front of him. "Grab a chair." Sheriff Wyman moved to the potbellied stove in the corner and lifted the tinware coffeepot. "Care for some coffee? I just made it."

"No, thanks," Cooper answered for them both. "We won't take up much of your time. I'm Cooper Maxwell, and this is Seth Braden. We own a camp about fifteen miles up the Umpqua."

The sheriff set his cup down on the desk and shook hands

with both men. "I don't recollect ever seein' you two before. I been here two years now."

Seth grinned. "We try to stay out of trouble, Sheriff. There's plenty of work to do in a logging camp."

"I know that for a fact. Worked in one myself for a couple of years up near Portland," he said, an easy smile curving his mouth. "You havin' a problem?"

"Yes, but I don't think you can do anything about it. We want you to know what's happening, though," Seth began. "During the last season, we had equipment stolen, our cook-house was ransacked and a good amount of logs were pirated."

The sheriff nodded and leaned forward in his chair. "I get a stack of complaints every year on pirating, but I just don't have enough men to catch up with 'em. Do you think one of your men was responsible for any of it?"

"No. We're not dead sure, but we had a good crew. We think it was Jake Slidell—or one of his men," Cooper said.

Bob's eyebrows flickered. "I had a complaint about him last year from Crenshaw. He owns a small mill upriver from Slidell where he cuts split-shakes. Him and his men woke up one mornin' and found two weeks' worth of bundled shakes gone. Crenshaw swore it was Slidell 'cause he saw the brother—the one that's addled—sneakin' around the day before."

"Owen. We see him in the deep woods sometimes." Seth stood up and walked to the window to peer out. Shoving his hands in his pockets, he continued. "Not only does Owen skulk around, but Jake has made remarks to us insinuating he knows what's going on. He taunts us, but stays just out of reach."

"That's pretty much what Crenshaw said. You fellers did the right thing by reportin' this, I'll have my deputy make the rounds of all the camps regular-like this year. Maybe Slidell will think twice about pullin' any shenanigans if he knows the law is on to him." Bob stood up and offered his hand to the two men once more.

Cooper rose, and he and his partner shook hands with the

sheriff. "We had some money stolen from our safe too. Just fifty dollars, but a loss. After that, we hired a detective to investigate the Slidells. If he turns anything up, we'll let you know."

"And we'll let you know if anything else happens," Seth promised on the way out.

The earsplitting sound of the whistle sounded twice as the steamboat, *Libby Jane,* left the dock at Empire City and headed toward the mouth of the Umpqua River. Camille gripped the rail and watched the shoreline recede. She was anxious to see her new home, and her stomach churned with excitement. Somehow, she felt her marriage would seem more real there.

"Take a long look. It's the last you'll see of civilization for a while," Seth warned, standing at her side.

She smiled up at him, the breeze lifting her loose auburn curls. "If you wanted to discourage me from going, you should have said something at the dock."

His gaze lingered on her temptingly curved mouth as he answered. "Never. The men will skin me alive if I don't bring back a cook."

Camille glanced away. She knew he was teasing her, but she wanted to hear him say he couldn't bear to leave her behind . . . that he wanted her by his side forever. "They may skin you alive when they sample my cooking," she said dryly.

He chuckled. "They'll be so busy looking at you, they won't know what they're eating."

Instead of feeling flattered, Camille felt her heart sink. He certainly wasn't jealous, she thought with irritation. "Thank heaven I'll be good for something," she said. "I have a headache. I'm going inside to sit with Hallie."

"Would you like—"

"No. I'll be fine," she cut him off, and walked toward the salon.

Seth stared after her, his mouth open. Now what was wrong? Just when he thought he had her figured out, she became a mystery again.

"You look like one of them thunderheads that rolls in and rattles the timber in the spring," Hallie commented as Camille sat down, none too gently, on the bench next to her.

"Are all men pigheaded?"

"I'm afraid so. The only difference is that some are more pigheaded than others," Hallie told her as she resumed her knitting. "Don't you think this red is a purty color? I'm makin' warm socks for Seth and Cooper for Christmas. It gits downright cold in them damp woods in the winter."

"I don't care if he freezes to death," Camille muttered under her breath. In a normal tone, she asked, "Tell me what your day is like when you're cooking for twenty men."

The older woman smiled. "It's more work than any human should have to do, but I wouldn't trade it for anything. Except maybe grandchildren."

"Your son isn't married, is he?"

"Not yet. He's one of them rovin' sailors, but I'm hopin' he'll bring a wife home someday. But that don't have nothin' to do with what you asked me, does it?" She paused to count a few stitches, then resumed. "I git up at four o'clock and start fryin' salt pork, makin' biscuits, gravy and tea. Sometimes if them temper'mental hens is layin' heavy, I fry eggs. After the men go to the woods, I clean up the mess and start a big pot of beans and bake enough bread for at least two meals. Twice a week, I bake pies. Some days I have to carry lunch on my wagon out to the men."

Camille's eyes were round with wonder. "When do you get any time for yourself?"

Hallie smiled. "After the supper cleanup and on Sundays,

we slice a smoked ham and the men make their own sandwiches so I can rest a little too.''

"I should have asked you instead of Seth about the job," Camille said glumly. "It's not that I mind hard work, but I thought I'd have some time to draw. I don't know when I'll have time to see to our cabin either."

Hallie stopped knitting to reach over and pat Camille's hand. "Don't worry, honey. I'll see you have some time for yore new husband."

"He won't even notice if I'm not there." *I'm not a real wife, I'm just a responsibility,* she thought.

Hallie clucked her tongue. "I don't like to dispute nobody's word, but I think yore wrong. Seth Braden looks at you like a starvin' man sittin' down to a feast."

"That's not . . . he doesn't care . . . it's just . . ." Camille finally clamped her mouth shut and blushed to the roots of her red hair.

Chuckling, Hallie said, "You think it's just lust? Honey, he didn't have to marry you to settle a cravin'. There's a little gal at the saloon in town more than willin' to accommodate Seth Braden. And town ain't far away. A man can make the trip once a week if he's a mind to."

Hallie's words had the opposite effect of the one she'd intended. Camille felt a sharp stab of jealousy. Who was this girl . . . and had Seth visited her before they left town? Her pride wouldn't allow her to ask any questions, however.

After stopping at several places along the river to debark passengers or supplies, the *Libby Jane* came abreast of the dock at the Braden-Maxwell camp. Seth carried Camille's small bag and helped her onto the sturdy platform built well out into the water.

The beauty of the small cove impressed Camille. Unlike the other camps along the way, Seth's small settlement was not an ugly scar on the landscape. The only trees taken out of the clearing were the ones used to build the buildings. From the edge of the clearing outward, the forest grew thick, and between the giant trees a jungle of lush growth rose up. A wide path had been cut on the eastern edge of the cove and snaked into the forest. It resembled a shadowed green cave with the huge firs towering on either side. The river road ran along the shore with a side track veering up the hill to the camp buildings.

"It don't look all bare and ugly like them other camps, does it?" Hallie asked, coming up beside them. "Seth and Coop planned this. They git their logs farther back in the woods and skid 'em out."

"It's a lovely place," Camille breathed. It felt like home already, and she had to bite down on her tongue to keep from telling Seth this. He'd think she was silly, or that she expected to stay here forever.

Coop stepped onto the dock with a large crate in his arms. "Can I get some help here, Seth? That is, if you can tear yourself away from your bride for a few minutes."

"I'll take no more nagging from you, Maxwell. That's my wife's job now," Seth said with an exaggerated frown.

"If I were you, mister, I wouldn't insult the woman who'll be cooking your food," Camille declared.

"That's right, honey. You keep that big oaf in line," Hallie encouraged. "Come on. I'll show you where you'll be livin', and we'll let these men unload the supplies."

Camille reached for her bag. Seth winked at her as he handed it over. There was a lightness to her step as she followed Hallie up the gentle rise. For the first time since her parents' deaths, she felt as if she belonged to a family—a happy family, she added silently. A small stream cut a path from the woods down the hill and separated the large new cookhouse and bunkhouse from the two older and smaller buildings on the other side. A quaint little arched bridge had been built over the water, and she and Hallie crossed it. "This here'll be your house, Camille. Mind, it ain't fixed up any, but most new brides like to do their own fixin'."

Camille looked at the square building—the roof and sides covered with cedar shakes—and couldn't have been happier if it had been a brick mansion. "It'll do," she said with an impish smile. "I just hope I have some decent neighbors."

Hallie laughed and wagged a finger at her. "You get too sassy and I won't let you help me in the cookhouse."

Camille giggled. "What a shame that would be."

The two women entered the dim building, and a foul smell made them catch their breath. "Lordy! Something must have died in here," Hallie exclaimed, and moved to throw open the shutters. As the room lightened, Camille looked cautiously around, breathing through her handkerchief. To the right, there were two wooden beds, topped by straw-filled mattresses. One of them had a jagged hole in the corner and the straw was sticking out. Hallie stopped to inspect it. "Dad-blamed mice! That ole tomcat ain't doin' his job."

Camille walked over to the large fireplace. The opening was deep, and held a large kettle on an iron swing-arm. As she pulled it toward her, it creaked with disuse. Seeing what was inside, she gasped, "Oh, Hallie!"

"What is it?" Hallie asked sharply, leaving the bed to have a look. When the older woman saw the orange-striped tomcat, dead and decaying, with a rope tied around its neck. she growled, "That no-account varmint is at it again. Seth and Cooper'll have his hide."

"Who would do this to a poor animal? It's vicious," Camille asked, her voice shaky.

Holding her nose with one hand, Hallie unhooked the kettle with the other and started for the door. "Slidell, honey. We got no proof, but I'm as sure as the day is long, it's him or that brother of his."

Out in the sunshine and fresh air, Camille breathed deeply, but a residue of the rancid smell lingered in her nose.

Placing the kettle on the ground, Hallie cupped her hands around her mouth and called down to the men. In no time, Seth and Cooper were up the hill. "Something wrong?" Seth asked, a frown on his brow.

Hallie pointed to the kettle. The two men looked inside. "Hell's fire!" Cooper growled.

Seth's eyes narrowed. "That bastard."

Camille's hands were clenched together. "Hallie said it was Slidell. But Seth, we saw him in town just yesterday."

"It's not that far to town, Camille. And this was done a few days ago. He could have come out here, and then slipped back to town." Turning to Cooper, he said, "Now I'm worried about Gabe. He's not in camp or he would have come down to the dock the minute he heard the whistle."

"Lordy, I hope nothin's happened to the boy," Hallie put in.

"Who's Gabe?" Camille asked, looking from one to the other.

"He's our camp watcher. We leave a man behind every year in the off-season to look out for things. Gabe hurt his arm at the end of the season and volunteered to stay to make up for the time he lost," Cooper explained.

Seth started back down the hill. "I'll leave one of my pistols for the women, and we'll go in search of Gabe. The supplies can wait."

"If that low-down varmint has the nerve to show up while you and Seth are gone, I'll blow his fool head off," Hallie promised.

"You ever shot a gun, Camille?" Cooper asked.

"No, but I could learn," she said, remembering how Jake Slidell had looked at her. She shivered involuntarily. The thought of Jake or Owen coming near her stiffened her back-bone.

After the men headed into the woods, Hallie took an old rusty bucket from the lean-to shed at the side of the cabin and set it in a clear spot facing the river. She explained to Camille how to cock the Colt .45, aim and squeeze the trigger gently.

After several tries, Camille felt moderately comfortable shooting the weapon. She even hit the bucket one time.

Once that was taken care of, the two women set about putting the cabin to rights. Camille swept the board floor while Hallie took the mattresses outside to beat the dust out of them. Then Camille laid a fire in the fireplace and found another kettle in the lean-to for heating water.

Every now and then, one of them stepped outside to scan the area, but all remained quiet. Camille tried not to worry about Seth and Cooper. They were capable and strong, she chided herself, and had managed to survive without her concern before now.

When Camille's house had been set to rights, they moved to Hallie's new home next door, and repeated the process.

"In that big trunk over there, you'll find clean linen for the beds. I stored it all there before I left, and it's a good thing I did, considering the mice have been livin' it up around here." Hallie dragged a washtub from the corner. "We'll just take this over to your cabin. You'll be wantin' a hot bath tonight after all this scrubbin'."

Her arms loaded with sheets, Camille protested, "What about you? I can't take your tub."

"There's another one in the lean-to I can use. Now, let's quit arguin' and go make up your bed. We gotta see to some supper afore the men come back."

They carried the tub by its handles as they walked back to Camille's house. "What will we fix to eat? There's nothing on the pantry shelves in either house."

"We bought supplies—canned meat, vegetables and fruit— from the store in town. The men sometimes kill game out in the woods when they're workin', but mostly we buy what we need. None of us got any time to tend a garden." They made Camille's big bed in companionable silence, leaving the extra bed unmade. "Coop'll take this bed out of your way once his cabin is built."

"It won't be in my way," Camille said, blushing as she smoothed the sheets and thought about the night to come.

"Now, let's git our supper cooked so we can have them baths instead of talk about 'em," Hallie suggested.

By midafternoon, the fragrant smell of stew and fresh-baked bread filled the clearing. Camille and Hallie had carried all the boxes they could handle from the dock, and left the rest for the men. Hallie left Camille to fuss with her new house while she went to have her bath in her own cabin.

At one end of the large room, there was a screen, and behind it a small chest of drawers. Plain wooden pegs adorned the wall. Camille hung up her dresses and put the rest of her things in the drawers. Finally, she carried more water from the stream to heat for a bath. When she was ready to undress, she placed the thick pine bar across the door, resting it on the iron holders on either side of the facing. Pulling the screen over to the fireplace, she arranged it around the tub. She scrubbed her body, washed her hair, and then rinsed with a bucket of clear water she'd reserved. Once she finished, she dressed quickly in her yellow and white gingham dress and combed her damp hair.

After moving the screen back to the corner, she decided to go see how Hallie was doing. When she stepped out the door, she saw Seth nearing the porch, blood staining his shirt.

Chapter 13

"Dear Lord, you're hurt," Camille exclaimed. She crossed the porch and ran down the steps.

Seth held his hands up and shook his head. "I'm not hurt, darlin', just a mess. It's rabbit blood."

Cooper appeared around the corner of the house looking much the same. Relief, sharp and sweet, swept over her. She launched herself at Seth. "Thank God! I'm so glad you're back," she muttered in a rush.

A look of surprise flashed across Seth's face, but his arms encircled her waist automatically, lifting her off her feet. She smelled of soap and lavender. His loins tightened painfully for a moment. Chuckling, he said, "I guess it's safe to say you missed me?"

"I should have sent off for a bride for myself," Cooper teased. "A welcome like that makes a man feel wanted."

Camille blushed, letting her hands slide from her husband's neck to push at his chest. "Stop making light of the situation;

Hallie and I were worried!'' she exclaimed. "What happened? Did you find Gabe?''

Seth placed her on her feet and grinned. "Yeah. He was out hunting. We helped him skin the rabbits he'd shot. He's in the new bunkhouse washing up.''

Backing up a step, Camille sniffed. "Well, don't just stand there—you'd better clean up too. Supper's ready and has been for a while.''

A short time later, the five of them sat on Hallie's porch and ate big bowls of venison stew and crusty chunks of bread. Camille liked Gabe Alspach immediately. He was shy but friendly, with an engaging grin. He looked to be about twenty years old, had shoulders as broad as an ax handle and carrot-colored hair. As she passed the basket of bread to him, she asked, "Where are you from, Gabe?''

"Ohio, ma'am. My family lives on a farm in the southern part of the state near a little town called Willow Bend.'' Taking the bread, he added, "Thank ya, ma'am.''

"Did you come out to Oregon by yourself?''

"Oh, no. Me and my Uncle Charlie came out West to pan for gold three years ago, but we didn't do no good. Uncle Charlie went back home 'cause Aunt Dessie wrote and said she'd yank a knot in his tail if he didn't. Farmin' ain't for me, though.'' He shrugged and dipped his bread in the stew, taking a big bite.

Cooper chuckled. "I found Gabe in the El Dorado last summer playing the harmonica for his keep. I took one look at this big, strapping boy and offered him a job.''

"Gabe's one of the best ax men they got,'' Hallie said to Camille. "He can purt-near do the work of two.''

Seeing Gabe's ears turn red, Seth scolded, "You're embarrassing the boy, Hallie.''

Hallie snorted. "Pshaw! I thought you loggers loved to compare tall tales.''

"Not in front of the womenfolk,'' Cooper informed her.

The older woman turned to Camille. "Men are awful hard to please, honey. I want you to remember that. If you brag on 'em, they're not happy. If you chew on 'em, they kick. I'll just bet if you was to hang 'em with a brand-new rope, they'd have some complaint."

"Most likely," Camille agreed with a twinkle in her eyes. Seth's thigh brushed against hers as he turned to frown at the older woman.

"Better watch it, Hallie. You'll scare the girl off and then who'll help you cook all those meals?" he cautioned her.

"We'll just have to make sure she's got good reason to stay, now won't we?" Hallie said with a significant lifting of her brows.

A quick glance at Camille's innocent expression eased the sudden anxiety that gripped Seth. For a moment, he was afraid Camille had been talking to Hallie about leaving. His tight look relaxed. "I'll do my part," he promised.

A quiet, fragile happiness unfolded inside Camille as she looked away, blushing at the wanton thoughts his gaze had conjured up.

Cooper gave a hoot of laughter. "Now look who's turning as red as an autumn apple."

"You're not too old to get cuffed on the ears, Coop," Hallie reminded him. "So just quit teasin' the poor girl."

Seth judiciously changed the subject. Hallie brought out coffee. They all enjoyed a cup in lazy contentment before the men finally rose to carry the remainder of the supplies up the hill. Hallie and Camille washed the supper dishes in companionable silence, both tired from the long day.

When Camille retired to her cabin, she lit a lamp on a small table beside the front door. Going behind the screen in the corner, she undressed and put on her nightgown. Seth and the others were still toting the supplies, and she was thankful for that. She still felt self-conscious getting undressed in the same room with him. Cousin Pru had always teased her, saying she was an ugly duckling. Her eyes and her breasts were too big, Pru had said. Men were attracted to tall, willow-slim women with a dainty bustline. Camille wondered anxiously what Seth thought of her. It was true, he enjoyed making love to her, she knew that ... but what about all those other women? There was the exciting saloon girl in Empire City, and then there was always Patience, the true love of his life. How could she, plain little Camille, ever compete with them?

She took a folded quilt from the end of the bed and spread it out over the sheets. The nights were much cooler, and they would need its warmth. Crawling into bed, Camille turned on her side and pulled the covers up to her chin. Her heart began to thump rapidly when she heard footsteps on the porch. Would he make love to her ... or would he be too tired? Did she even want him to? After all, she chided herself bitterly, he wasn't in love with her. Where was her pride?

She closed her eyes when Seth entered and set the bar across the door. He crossed the room to the bed, and she felt his presence beside her. She almost opened her eyes when he caressed her cheek gently, but then he moved away. She heard him putting wood into the fireplace, and then the sound of his boots hitting the floor. Two minutes later there came a soft splash. He was taking a bath in the water she'd left. She smiled. The water was probably ice cold by now. Turning over, she glanced across the room through half-closed lids and felt a curious swooping pull at her innards. The firelight bathed his muscled shoulders in a bronze glow, and outlined his rugged profile sharply. She could even see the shadow of the day's beard on his jaw.

A sense of excitement filled her as she watched him soap his face, hair and shoulders. After he rinsed off, he stood up and began washing the rest of his body. And what a magnificent body it was, she thought, mesmerized. Thick muscles bulged from his chest, arms and legs. Her eyes strayed to his manhood, jutting out of the nest of dark hair. She shivered. He was so handsome and virile, it was no wonder women fell over themselves to please him. She squeezed her eyes shut, aching inside for what she felt she'd never have.

When she heard him rise and step out, she regulated her breathing so he would think she was still asleep, but her heart pounded so loud in her ears, she was afraid he'd hear it. In a matter of minutes, he blew out the lamp and crossed to the bed. The mattress gave under his weight, and she hung on to her side to keep from rolling toward him. He snuggled close to her, his hand trailing slowly down her arm and over her hip. She could feel his warm breath on her neck, and then on her ear as he brushed the hair aside. "I know you're not asleep. I felt you watching me," he murmured, tracing the outer shell of her ear with his tongue.

Her body ached for his touch, but still she held back. When his hand moved around to cup her breast through the thin material, she gasped. Rolling against him, she gazed up into his dark, fathomless eyes, her breathing ragged. "Are married people supposed to do this every night?" she whispered, running her hand over the taut muscles in his upper arm.

There was a smile in his voice "Absolutely. It's a rule." Dipping his head, he captured her lips, and began probing her sweet mouth with his tongue.

Camille groaned deep in her throat as his hand found its way beneath her gown to caress the softness between her legs. When his finger slid inside her moist warmth, she opened up to him like a flower to sunshine.

She arched up to meet his gentle thrusts, and thought she would die of the pleasure. In moments, Camille began to feel the beginnings of release undulate through her belly and down to the very core of her being.

Seth felt it coming and abruptly rose above her, entering her as the first quiver erupted. He rode the crest of her wave, swallowing her mewling cries with a deep kiss. When her last shudder subsided, he held her tenderly, careful not to crush her with his weight. He rained gentle kisses on her face and neck, murmuring sweet words about what a delectable morsel she was, and how he was going to make her body catch fire again and again.

Camille sighed and stroked his broad back with her hands, loving the feel of his taut skin beneath her fingertips. "That's the most wonderful feeling, Seth ... how many times can it happen in one night?" she whispered, emboldened by the fact that the room was dim.

He raised his head to smile into her eyes. "Greedy little thing, aren't you?"

She smiled back, her eyes twinkling. "For that, yes."

A deep laugh rumbled in his chest. "I'll oblige as many times as I'm able, sweetheart. And it'll be my pleasure, I might add." He kissed her then, his swollen staff again moving in and out of her body, filling her completely. Together, they found the rhythm that made them one. A sheen of sweat broke out over their bodies as Seth spilled his seed deep inside her, while at the same time, she reached the summit of her passion. Making good on his promise, Seth loved her again and again until, exhausted, they fell asleep in each other's arms.

Seth woke Camille with a kiss. She opened her eyes and smiled. "Why are you dressed? It can't be time to get up," she murmured sleepily.

Seth caught his breath at the sensuous picture she made lying there, her copper curls tossled, her lips puffy from sleep, and her eyes heavy lidded. He couldn't resist one more kiss, but then backed away from the bed. Cooper was outside having a cup of coffee, and wouldn't appreciate waiting. Smiling, Seth chided her. "What a slugabed you are. If I'd known that, I'd never have married you." He moved to open the door.

Camille sat up abruptly, forgetting she was naked. The pink nipples of her bare breasts peeked at him above the sheet. When

Seth's eyes dropped automatically, Camille hastily drew the cover up. "Where are you going? Wait and I'll fix breakfast for you." She slid her legs over the edge of the bed, wrapping the quilt around her.

He grinned, taking a step toward her. Mentally checking himself, he stopped. "I've already eaten. Hallie was up before the chickens. She said to let you sleep late this morning. Coop and I are going to stake out our first section to be cut this year. We'll be back later."

He was gone before she could reply, but his parting smile warmed her clear down to her toes.

Once she'd made herself presentable and straightened the bed, she hurried over to Hallie's, hoping for a cup of coffee. "Ah-h-h," she sighed, sipping the hot brew that Hallie handed her. "I knew I could count on you."

The older woman replaced the tin pot near the coals in her fireplace to stay warm. "I keep a pot goin' day and night. It was the thing I missed most when we crossed the prairie—I could only make coffee twice a day, and toward the end of the trip we ran out altogether." Moving to the small table, she took a muslin cloth from a basket to reveal biscuits. "Sit yerself down and eat a bite afore we get to work. There's jelly, but no butter yet. Seth'll have to go get Betsey and the girls afore we have proper breakfast food."

Camille sat down at the small wooden table and reached for a golden biscuit. "Betsey and the girls?"

Hallie poured a cup of coffee for herself. "Our milk cow and the hens. Ike Raymond—he's got a cabin way back in the woods bordering our land—he tends the animals while we're gone."

Spreading apple jelly on half of her biscuit, Camille asked, "Is he a logger too?"

"No. He strips chittamwood trees and sells the bark to a ship captain he knows. Down in San Francisco, they use it to make a laxative called cascara. He also grows vegetables and sells them up and down the river to folks like us who don't have time to grow our own.''

Camille washed down a bite of the delectably light bread with a sip of coffee. ''If a man's interested in working, there seems to be plenty to do in the Northwest. Does Ike have a wife?''

''Naw. He's livin' in sin—as Preacher Holbrook would say—with an Indian woman. She's a Klamath. Not a bad-lookin' little thing, if she'd jest take a bath.'' Hallie shook her head regretfully. ''She smells to high heaven. Course, Ike don't smell much better.'' Hallie finished her coffee in one long swig and rose to deposit her cup in a metal washpan sitting on a wide board counter. ''He's a good man, though. I reckon he'd do anything for Seth and Cooper. Thinks the sun rises and sets in them boys.'' Extracting an apron from a peg on the wall, she slipped the neck strap over her head and tied the strings at her waist. ''I'll be over at the new cookhouse gittin' started.''

Camille jumped up and gulped down the remainder of her coffee. ''I'm finished—I'll go with you.'' Grabbing another biscuit, she flipped the cloth over the ones left in the basket and followed the older woman out the door, snatching her apron from the peg.

The cookhouse, built the previous spring, was huge and still smelled new. The roof had been covered with cedar shakes, but the side walls were still bare boards, already weathering to a dull gray. Camille was impressed with the new-looking cooking stove. ''I've never seen one that big,'' she said, running her fingers down the long iron surface. There were six burners, wide-spaced, and two large ovens at the top. A deep reservoir at the side would hold several gallons of water for heating.

Hallie took some pieces of kindling from the wood box against the wall. ''Seth sent all the way to a foundry in New York for this. They built it special. Seth and Coop said I needed something to make my life easier, especially since it's so hard to keep a second cook.''

Camille opened the door on the front of the stove so Hallie could deposit the dried sticks. She smiled to herself. Hallie was as proud of this stove as she would have been of a brilliant child. And Ike Raymond, she decided, wasn't the only one who thought the sun rose and set in Seth and Cooper. "Well, you have a second cook now, Hallie, for as long as all of you want me. I just hope it doesn't wear you out teaching me what I need to know."

Hallie took some matches from a shelf and stooped to light the fire. "Pshaw! A smart girl like you will catch on in no time."

"Aunt Lavinia said I was all thumbs." Camille retrieved two larger sticks of wood from the box and handed them to Hallie.

Closing the firebox door with a bang, the stout, older woman grunted, "Fiddlesticks. You worked like a lumberjack all day yesterday, and did a fine job at everything you turned your hand to. I think yore aunt was wrong."

Unbidden tears sprang into Camille's eyes at the staunch praise. Hazy memories of her own mother's soft-spoken support came back to tug at her heartstrings. She hadn't realized how much she'd missed it till now. Impulsively, she hugged Hallie. "With a teacher like you, I don't doubt I can learn everything!"

For a brief moment, Hallie returned the embrace, then she grumbled, "We won't get nothin' done if we stand around talkin' all day."

Hallie showed Camille where the springhouse was located—up the hill behind the cookhouse, at the mouth of an ice-cold spring. Gabe had stored the cleaned rabbits there to keep them cold. "We'll make rabbit and vegetable pies," Hallie told her.

They spent the morning cleaning the new cookhouse. The long, smooth wooden tables, where the lumberjacks ate, had to be scrubbed, along with Hallie's worktables. The older woman showed Camille how to mix pie crust that would, in her words, melt in your mouth. They opened canned vegetables, made a spicy sauce and put the meat pies into the oven to bake. Since they had enough bread left over from the day before, they sliced a small, smoked ham to make sandwiches for the noonday meal. Camille was doing that very thing when the men returned.

Gabe nodded politely, his face growing pink with pleasure when Camille smiled at him. Cooper grinned behind his back and followed the younger man over to the stove to take a peek at the golden meat pies lining the cooling shelf below the window.

Camille's eyes met Seth's warm gaze when he stopped beside her. Her hands stilled in midmotion at the glittering desire she read there. As color suffused her cheeks, she hastily glanced at the others to see if anyone was watching.

Seth dipped his head and captured her mouth briefly, his tongue slipping between her lips. Camille unconsciously swayed toward him, but caught herself and drew back. "Seth!" she whispered, turning back to her task.

He smiled and leaned a hip against the table, crossing his arms. "Ummm, I'm hungry. This looks good."

Camille's hands were trembling as she cut the thick sandwiches with a butcher knife. She chanced a glance up at him and found him staring at the swell of her bosom above the round neckline of her dress. "You'd better get washed up, Seth Braden, and get your mind on lunch," she chided, waving her knife around.

He chuckled and removed himself as the others approached. The afternoon proved to be as busy as the morning for all of them. Seth and Cooper set out in the small wagon for Ike Raymond's place to retrieve the chickens and Betsey. While Gabe had watched over the eighteen head of oxen during their absence, he wasn't able to milk the cow with a bad arm. So Betsey and the flock of high-strung chickens had been farmed out to Ike.

Gabe took on the chore of cleaning out the huge barn located beyond the sawmill. They were expecting a shipment of hay on the next riverboat to help feed the oxen through the winter.

Hallie and Camille began unloading the food supplies and stocking the larder in the new cookhouse.

By supper time, when the five of them gathered together again, there was a general feeling of accomplishment. Seth and Cooper recounted their visit with the eccentric Ike. It seemed the newest tale Ike had to impart was about the huge half man, half beast who was roaming the deep woods. Cooper rolled his eyes. "Ike swears he saw this creature one day while he was out gathering bark, but he wasn't close enough to see its face clearly. He was scared out of his wits, though."

Seth frowned. "I know Ike's partial to telling stories, but he's not one to tell a barefaced lie. I'm sure he saw something unusual."

An involuntary shiver raced down Camille's spine. Not only did she have to worry about the Slidell brothers, she would probably have nightmares about this frightening creature. Back home, she thought wryly, all she'd had to contend with was snakes, swamp fevers and Aunt Lavinia.

"Speaking of creatures," Seth went on, "we'd like you to take the boat into town tomorrow, Gabe, and report our latest incident to Sheriff Wyman. I know a dead cat is not a big issue, but it was deliberate. The person responsible wanted us to know it was no accident."

Cooper added, "We thought you'd like to see a little civilization after spending two solid months here."

Gabe nodded shyly. "Much obliged, fellers."

"Beverly Jean at the post office was asking after you," Cooper said with an innocent expression.

Gabe grinned and asked, "Should I check the list, or did you take it down before you left?"

"We left it. There were sixteen men signed up, and we're hoping for twenty-five this year. Last season was a little tight," Seth said.

"Tight, hell. We were nearly worked to death," Cooper put in.

Seth grinned. "Are you complaining about our business growing?"

Hallie stood up to refill coffee cups. "It's jest like I said, men are never happy."

On that note, the men took their second cup of coffee and their cigars out on the front porch, and left the women to clear up.

When Camille and Seth reached their cabin a while later, she shivered, not so much from the cool evening air, but from anticipation. Seth made love to her each time they found themselves alone, and she confessed to herself she was as eager as he.

After barring the door, Seth followed her behind the screen and brushed her trembling fingers away from the buttons on the bodice of her dress to finish the task himself. When he took her to bed, she had no need for the nightgown draped over the screen . . . Seth's body kept her warm through the night.

The following morning, an unusually bright sun quickly burned the fog off the water and the mist from the timber to create the perfect day for doing laundry. Camille and Hallie set up their operation in front of the cookhouse. Hallie built a small fire under the iron framework, which held three tubs, while Camille sorted the clothing. The men carried dozens of buckets of water from the stream to fill the tubs.

It wasn't long before the lye soap was melting and bubbling in the hot wash water. This was a job in which Camille felt relatively at ease, since back home she had helped old Sadie with the wash each week. The two women took turns scrubbing the garments on the ribbed washboard. Coop had strung a new line for them from the cookhouse to a tree before he and Seth left for the woods. Before long, dresses, shirts, pants and unmentionables were blowing in the breeze, hanging on for dear life with the help of sturdy clothespins.

Lunch was leftover meat pie and chunks of bread, washed down with cold milk, donated by an obliging Betsey the evening before.

"Would you like to see the sawmill and the rest of camp this afternoon?" Seth asked Camille as they all lingered over coffee.

"Why, yes. I've been curious, but we've been so busy," she answered. Glancing over at Hallie, she asked, "Could you spare me for a while?"

Hallie gave an exaggerated sigh. "I suppose so, but the boss will get mad if he finds out."

Seth winked at Camille. "I know him personally, and if you're really nice to me, I'll square it with him."

"That's mighty kind of you," Camille said dryly, shaking her head at the two of them. Cooper went off to the barn to tend the oxen while Hallie and Camille cleared the table. Seth disappeared for a time, but turned up just as Camille was hanging her wet dish towel on the clothesline. She draped her apron over the hitching rail at the end of the cookhouse and took Seth's proffered arm. "Perhaps if the cooking job doesn't work out, you could put me to work sawing boards," she teased as they walked down the hill and across the little bridge.

Seth's grin was downright devilish. "The men wouldn't get a darned thing done if you worked at the mill . . . and I'd be trying to get you behind the building all the time."

They reached the lower ground surrounding the cove, and followed the well-worn path. It climbed up the hill, on the opposite side of their dwellings, toward the huge open-ended building housing the hungry, sharp-bladed saws. Camille loved the mingled smells in the air of moist woods, drying lumber and wood smoke from a huge sawdust pile. She let his rascally comment go unanswered, but her heartbeat quickened as he led her inside the darkened building and pulled her close for a fierce kiss.

When Seth forced himself to pull back, he stroked her cheek, his dark eyes devouring her flushed face. "I'm tempted to whisk you behind that stack of lumber right now."

Camille's eyes widened in mock surprise. "In the middle of the afternoon? Why, Mr. Braden, I'm truly shocked."

Seth chuckled, and let his hands wander up to lightly cup the weight of her breasts beneath the calico material. "If I wasn't worried about Cooper barging in here, I'd shock the petticoats right off you."

Camille's heartbeat quickened. She could feel her nipples growing hard, and her insides turning warm and quivery. "Perhaps we'd better get on with our tour," she whispered.

Seth's grin was wicked as he reached for her hand. "I can wait till dark."

He led her through the building, pointing out the huge saws run by steam from a boiler. Seth explained how the operation worked, and how on a good day, they could saw forty thousand feet of lumber without hardly breaking a sweat. They left the building on the opposite end and walked a few hundred feet up the skid road. "In Bangor, we had no such thing," Seth reminisced. "There was always snow, and we wrapped chains around the logs and pulled them behind sleighs to the river. Here, the ground is too uneven and soft for sled runners or wheels. Coop and I saw a skid road like this at a camp on the Rogue River when we were scouting this area, looking for land to buy. It was one of the first things we built."

Camille shook her head in wonderment. Every project in this Northwest country was as vast as the giant trees that had enticed the first loggers. She gazed at the unending tunnel cut through the dense woods, where huge trees still hovered and shaded the cleared track. Every few feet, a log, cut free of limbs, lay more than half-buried in the soft ground. "What you've carved out of this wilderness is wondrous. I'll wager your parents are proud of you,'' Camille said.

Seth shrugged. "At first, I wanted to prove to my father I could succeed in life, just as he had. But as time went on, I found myself working to prove it to myself. I do think my folks would be proud if they came out someday.''

"Have you asked them?''

"Why, no. I suppose I haven't thought to do that.'' He took her arm as they turned back toward the mill.

"Will you write and tell them about our marriage?'' Camille asked, giving him a sidelong glance.

Seth met her gaze. "Do you think I should?''

"It depends, I suppose. If we part company in the near future, there's no use telling them. But I've been worrying lately—what if there's a child?'' Camille dropped her eyes, her cheeks growing pink. "After all, we've, uh . . .''

"Been behaving like a married couple,'' he finished for her. Rubbing his chin thoughtfully, he said, "I'll confess, I hadn't thought of that. It would cause problems if you decided to move on, wouldn't it?''

"Or if you wanted to be free—either way.'' Camille felt her heart constrict. His tone was so matter-of-fact it shattered the budding hopes she had for their marriage. Swallowing tightly, she said, "We haven't been too careful in that respect, have we? It wouldn't be fair to bring a child into the world. Maybe we should sleep in separate beds?''

Her soft-spoken suggestion was like a blow to Seth's midsection. Suddenly, the scales fell away from his eyes. The thought of not making love to Camille was a hundred times more painful than the loss of Patience had been. He hadn't been in love with Patience, or else he'd have married her before he left Maine. He was in love with his wife, and she seemed hell-bent on finding her brother and leaving him. For one frantic moment, he thought about throwing her over his shoulder and carrying her deep into the woods where she couldn't find her way out.

Reason, however, reasserted itself. He had to map out a plan of action to win her over, not scare her away.

"If you think that's best," he said quietly, and then took it a step further. "I spoke with Captain Jack this morning when he stopped to pick up Gabe. He told me he'd distributed the posters about Forrest we had made up in Empire City. He also gave a few to a couple of ship captains he knows who make the run to Puget Sound each week."

They reached the bridge over the stream. Camille got a grip on her emotions and remembered her Sinclair pride. Smiling stiffly, she said, "Thank you, Seth. I want to find Forrest more than anything else in this world."

"I'll do my best to help you like I promised. Now, I've got work to finish at the mill," Seth said gruffly, turning to go back down the hill.

Every step up the hill was work. Camille felt as if she had a leaden weight sitting on each shoulder. She couldn't face Hallie just yet, so she decided to go to the springhouse and fetch the leftover venison pies and some eggs for supper.

Once inside the cool, dim building, Camille dabbed at her eyes with the tail of her calico dress. "Damn him," she muttered. When she'd suggested they sleep in separate beds, he hadn't put up a fight. It seemed she was merely a diversion— he was still in love with Patience. Or perhaps he didn't care who warmed his bed. The saloon girl in Empire City would still be available.

Camille picked up the basket of eggs and hooked the handle over her arm. As she reached for the meat pies, a low growl at the back of the building caused the hair on her neck to rise. Her eyes made a wide sweep of the interior, her heart pounding in her chest, but there was no place for a large animal to hide. The growl came again, a little louder this time. She realized it was coming from behind the building. In a swift movement, she slammed the door, shutting herself inside.

Chapter 14

Dear Lord, Camille thought frantically, what if it was the wild creature Ike had seen? Would it be smart enough to find the door? The same door that didn't have so much as a latch to secure it from an intruder? Her heartbeat pulsed in her ears as she tried to be calm and think what she should do next.

She was shaking as she put the basket down and felt her way to the back wall, climbing over sacks of meal and flour. Placing her ear to the wall, she swallowed a whimper of fear when she heard loud, labored breathing on the other side. It was waiting for her . . . She wanted to scream, but her throat constricted. Another deep growl galvanized her into action. She began beating on the wall with both fists, hoping to frighten the beast. When she stopped, she could hear a crunching in the underbrush, and prayed with all her heart it was leaving. Straining to listen, she thought the sound grew fainter. She slipped to the door and opened it a crack, peering out. Nothing moved. Growing braver, she stuck her head out and then her body. At the edge of the building, she chanced a look around and saw a huge, hulking figure loping into the dense woods. From this distance, it looked hairy and was clothed in a rough garment resembling bark. Momentary relief swept through her as she watched it disappear from sight. Not one to press her luck, she picked up her skirts and ran.

"Hallie! I saw it!" she gasped as she burst into the cookhouse. "Ike's creature . . . I saw it!"

The older woman had her arms in floured bread dough up to her elbows. "Great day in the mornin', child! Are ya tryin' to scare an old woman to death?" Hastily, she wiped her hands on a muslin cloth, a frown marring her brow. She crossed the room and led Camille to a chair, pushing her into it. "Catch yer breath, and then tell me what this's all about."

Camille clung to one of Hallie's hands. "I was in the springhouse . . . it growled . . . I beat on the wall . . . it was so big—oh, God, Hallie, I was frightened out of my wits!"

The older woman reached for Camille's other hand and squatted down beside the chair so she could look her in the eye. "Calm down, honey. Yer fine, and there ain't nothin' gonna git ya." She spoke slowly, giving Camille's hands a comforting squeeze. "Now, I'm gonna step out in the yard and yell for Seth. When he gets here, you can tell us what you saw, all right?"

Hallie's strength and firm tone calmed Camille. Her heartbeat slowed and she nodded, letting go of the older woman.

In minutes, Seth was kneeling beside Camille, looking anxiously at her drawn face, pale beneath her tan. Having caught her breath, Camille recounted the story. Hallie pressed a cup of hot coffee into her hands while she talked.

"Are you sure it wasn't a bear? They come out of the deep woods sometimes looking for food," Seth asked.

Camille shook her head. "Absolutely not. It had on a long shirt that looked like tree bark. Animal's don't wear clothes! It was Ike's creature, I know it was." There was an edge of hysteria to her voice.

Seth patted her knee. "I believe you, honey. Coop and I will check it out. Something that big leaves tracks." He rose and turned to Hallie. "Keep your gun handy while we're gone."

Hallie dropped the wooden bar into place across the door when he left, and fussed over Camille, warming her coffee and bringing her a cool cloth to wash her face. Then the older woman finished kneading the bread dough and placed it to rise near the stove, keeping up a general chatter. Gradually, Camille's color returned.

"Why don't I jest go get them eggs and we'll make a cake for supper?" Hallie suggested.

Camille jumped up and put her cup on the worktable. "Not by yourself, you won't," she said firmly. "I know I was beside myself for a little while, but I'm not afraid now. Besides," she said with an impish smile, "one of us will have to carry the gun while the other one totes the food."

Hallie chuckled, tucking the Colt .45 into the waistband of her skirt. "You've been durned good for this dull old logging camp. I swear, we've had more excitement since you came than the Red Door Saloon has on Saturday night."

They arrived back at the cookhouse without a sign of any trouble, although Camille had felt a residue of fear when she glanced into the thick woods beyond the springhouse. She had the feeling someone—or something—was watching her. Shaking off the feeling, she chided herself. The creature wouldn't still be close by, not with Seth and Cooper on its trail.

Two golden yellow cakes were cooling on the shelf under an open window when the men returned. Cooper gave Camille a comforting hug after he stood his rifle next to the door. "Are you all right, honey?"

She smiled and patted his cheek. "Of course I am. It's that hairy creature you should be worried about. I probably scared the living daylights out of him when I beat on the springhouse wall He was running like a scalded cat the last time I saw him.''

Cooper threw back his head and laughed. ''You beat anything I've ever seen. Most females would still be swooning if they'd come that close to a monster.''

Seth felt an unreasonable twinge of jealousy at seeing Camille's and Cooper's closeness. ''Dammit, Coop. Don't go calling it a monster and scaring her again. It was a man—a huge man, but a man nevertheless.''

Hallie spoke up. ''You found somethin'?''

''Tracks. He must have been wearing some kind of soft boots. They looked like the tracks the Umpquas make in winter when they cover their feet with fur.'' Seth busied himself pouring a cup of coffee.

''We lost his trail about a half mile into the woods. It just vanished,'' Cooper put in, shaking his head.

''I think he climbed a tree and hid. It would have been an easy thing to do considering how dense the growth is in there,'' Seth said, shrugging.

''So you think it was an Umpqua Indian?'' Camille asked, fetching a cup of coffee for Cooper.

Seth scowled at her action. ''I don't know, but until we find out who, or what, this thing is, I don't want you women going anywhere without a gun. We'll never get any work done around here if we have to worry about you constantly,'' Seth said irritably.

''Would you like me to give you a few lessons in shooting, Camille?'' Cooper asked.

Before Camille could reply, Seth barked, ''I'll show her how to shoot the damned gun.''

Neither Camille nor Hallie mentioned she'd already had a lesson.

* * *

A few mornings later, Camille sat on the edge of the dock just as the sun was coming up. In a charcoal drawing, she was trying to capture the mist hanging above the river, sending ethereal fingers through the giant trees on the other side. Her concentration was sorely lacking, however. Thoughts of Seth sleeping in the extra bed in their cabin kept intruding. She missed him in her bed. It was small comfort to know he did not sleep soundly at night, but tossed and turned just as she did. Since the morning at the mill, neither of them had spoken about it, but he had taken the other bed, and refrained from touching her in any way.

Abruptly crumpling the paper she was working on, she doggedly began a new drawing. In the distance, she could hear the sound of hammers striking nails. Cooper, Seth and Gabe had been working on Coop's new cabin since the day Gabe returned from Empire City. It was coming along nicely, and soon, Coop would have need of his bed. Camille chewed at her thumbnail, wondering what would happen when there was only one bed left in their cabin.

A steamboat whistle nearby shattered the relative calm of the morning, causing Camille to jump. She nearly dropped her sketch pad into the river, catching it at the last minute. Out of the mist came the white-painted boat, its huge paddle wheel slapping the water with a rhythmic swishing. She scrambled up and waved when she recognized Captain Jack standing in the wheelhouse. From the salon on the port side, several men poured out onto the deck carrying satchels. For the most part, they wore red shirts and canvas pants—the uniform of the logger. Almost to a man, they leaned over the rail, at least fifteen pairs of eyes fixed on her.

Camille backed away, her cheeks turning pink. "How do, ma'am." "Mornin'!" "You the new cook? I hope!" Their good-natured comments, interspersed with whistles, deepened her blush. "Yore a purty little thing," one burly man called out, his white smile flashing across a tanned, rugged face.

It would be childish to turn and run, although she wished she could. The big boat drifted in and bumped gently against the wooden piling, and a sailor jumped down to secure it with a thick coil of rope. "Morning, Mrs. Braden," the young man said, giving her a small salute.

Camille smiled in relief. He was someone she recognized. "Hello, Joe. You're by awfully early this time, aren't you?"

"Yep. We only made two stops between Empire City and here. In another two weeks when the logging season starts, we'll be stopping at every wide spot on the river." He turned and helped his mate lower the gangplank onto the dock. "Got some of your help on board today. Don't mind their bad manners, ma'am—loggers ain't refined like us sailors."

The group of men scrambled down the narrow walkway, shoving and elbowing each other in the process. Camille watched in fascination, marveling that not one of them ended up in the river. They swarmed around her, grinning, and talking all at once. Far from feeling threatened, Camille was reminded of the time Aunt Lavinia's collie had had a litter of ten puppies and every time she'd slipped out to visit them in the stable, they'd all rushed at her, barking and wanting to be noticed. Before the men could smother her with their enthusiasm, however, one logger slipped his brawny arm around her and glared at the rest until they fell back a pace or two. "Don't be afraid, liddle lady. Vladimir Koloffsky will protect you from these rude peasants." Stepping back, he gave a small bow and formally offered his arm.

Smiling at his theatrical manner, Camille laid her hand on his arm. "Thank you, Vladimir." He was quite handsome, with wavy brown hair, combed back and brushing his collar, a thick mustache and a well-kept beard.

The others cleared a path, and then followed the giant logger as he led her across the dock toward the hill. "I'm Camille Braden, Seth's wife," she introduced herself.

His wide grin flashed white against the ruddy tan of his skin.

"Had you been the wife of any other, I would have fought the man to take you for my own. I have much respect for Seth Braden, though. He's king of the hill in these woods—the best bullwhacker, ax-man and white-water man. Throw a piece of soap in the water and Seth Braden vill ride the bubbles to shore. He is the only man better than Vladimir Koloffsky."

Camille smiled sweetly up at him. "Although I thank you for the compliment, Vladimir, I'm not a prize to be won or lost in a barbaric fight. Please remember that."

His blank look testified to the fact it took him a moment to realize her honeyed tone masked a firm rebuke.

Admiration lit his ebony eyes, and the broad smile returned. "A woman with spirit—I love that!"

At that moment, the object of their conversation met them coming down the hill, Cooper and Gabe in his wake. "It's about time you lazy devils showed up to work," Seth growled, a mock frown furrowing his brow.

Vladimir gave Seth a great hug, and Seth pounded the Russian giant on the back. "I've been admiring your beautiful wife, Seth. You are a lucky bastard," Vladimir said, laughing.

Seth's glance strayed to Camille's smiling face, and he felt another twinge of jealousy. "I am a lucky man, my Russian friend. However, brains, more than luck, have gotten me where I am today," he added, turning back to the logger, a devilish light in his dark eyes.

A deep laugh rumbled up from Vladimir's chest. "Are you saying I not only possess the strength of a bull ox, but the brain as well?"

Seth smiled, slipping an arm around Camille's shoulders. "I wouldn't say that to a man as big as you."

"Then I indeed agree you are a smart man."

The men laughed, and one of them thumped the Russian on the shoulder. "If the horseshoe fits . . ."

Cooper spoke up. "I wouldn't let them insult me on an empty stomach, Koloffsky. Hallie's got a pot of coffee brewing strong enough to float an ax handle, and she's started breakfast.''

Anxious to remove Camille from her host of admirers, Seth suggested they head up to the cookhouse As he walked along, his arm still resting on her shoulder, Seth had to agree with Vladimir—Camille was beautiful, so beautiful it made him ache all over.

Aware of Seth's proprietary gesture, Camille supposed the pretense was for the benefit of his men. Whatever the reason, the contact made her warm and tingly.

By the time the women set a breakfast of biscuits, eggs and gravy on the table, the men had gone through two pots of coffee and a dozen bunkhouse stories—whitewashed out of respect for Camille and Hallie—each one taller and more outrageous than the last.

Cooper jumped up and offered his chair to Camille, which put her between Seth and Vladimir. Taking a seat on the other side of the long trestle table, Cooper looked mischievous as he watched Seth and the big Russian vie for her attention.

The men spent the remainder of the day working on Cooper's cabin. By nightfall it was finished, right down to the split-shake roof and wide front porch.

After moving Cooper's bed to his new home, Seth returned to their cabin and dropped the bar into place across the door. The large room was softly lit by two oil lamps and the glow of a small fire in the fireplace.

Camille retired behind the screen to take a sponge bath. She heard the bed creak and his boots hit the floor one at a time. Her heart fluttered. After donning her nightgown, she picked up her comb and began working the tangles from her hair. The vigorous activity relieved some of the tension in her body. It also delayed things. Perhaps if she stayed behind the screen long enough, Seth would go to sleep, and she needn't worry about the awkwardness of this moment.

A sharp tap on the framework of the screen caused her to

jump. "Is there any more water back there? I'd like to wash up when you're finished."

His deep-timbred voice did strange things to her insides. "Yes. Vladimir carried two fresh buckets for me before he went to the bunkhouse." She slipped on her blue wrapper and came around the screen to see him standing a few feet away, arms akimbo, a scowl on his face.

"If you had asked, I would have gotten the water when I got back from Coop's," he said shortly.

Camille's delicate brows rose a notch. "I didn't ask him to do it. He just showed up at the door." She felt a prickle of annoyance when she saw his frown deepen.

Sweeping past him, she moved to the fireplace to warm herself. Seth went behind the screen, and she could hear him mumbling and splashing water. Why was he so angry? It had saved him an extra trip to the stream. Maybe he was tired. Hallie had remarked one day that men were like small children who took their bad tempers out on anyone close by. The older woman also recommended that Camille not let Seth get by with such behavior or else she'd spoil him beyond bearing. "Speak up, Seth I can't hear you," she called out.

"Nothing. I was just thinking out loud," he growled.

Camille decided this was the time to use Hallie's advice. Taking a pillow and the extra blanket from the end of the bed, she dropped them in a heap in front of the fireplace. Shedding her robe, she hopped into bed and covered up to her chin.

When Seth came from behind the screen, his glance softened when he saw she was in bed waiting for him. "I'll get the lights and be right th—" He stopped in midstride when he saw what lay in front of the fire. "What's that?" he asked suspiciously.

"Your bed," Camille said primly. The lamplight cast a golden glow over his bare, muscled shoulders, while droplets of water glistened on the mat of sable hair on his torso. For a brief moment, Camille longed to retract that statement.

"What the hell is wrong with the bed? It's big enough for two," he exploded. Things were definitely not going as he had planned.

"We're not ... sleeping together anymore, remember?" she pointed out defensively, her cheeks growing warm at the implication.

Hands on his hips, Seth ground his teeth in frustration. "We're not making love anymore—sleeping has nothing to do with it. Do you have any idea how hard the floor is?"

"No, but you can let me know in the morning," she said, and turned over, presenting her back to him.

"I'll sleep where I damn well please," he shouted, and stomped to the other side of the bed.

She'd lost the fight, she thought with delicious anticipation. Her eyes were tightly shut, and she expected to feel his weight on the bed any moment. Instead she heard him swear as he stumped his toe on the bedpost. Opening one eye, she saw him bend over and retrieve his boots. "I'll be at Cooper's if you need me," he growled, and slammed out of the cabin.

Sitting up in bed, Camille gaped at the open doorway. "Well! I thought he had more tenacity than that," she muttered, swinging her legs over the side of the bed. Padding barefoot to the door, she closed it and replaced the bar.

During breakfast, Camille refilled coffee cups and replenished breadbaskets and bowls on the table. Seth sat at one end and gave her less attention than if she'd been a waitress at the Blue Ox. The loggers, however, treated her to gentle teasing, and praised every move she made as if the simple pouring of a cup of coffee was a feat worthy of the highest recognition. Seth's bland expression became a black scowl as the meal progressed.

Having missed out on a warm family relationship, Camille blossomed with the harmless attention. She smiled, laughed, and teased in return. During a lull in the conversation, Cooper commented to her, "You're as chipper as a squirrel this morning. Obviously you had a good night's sleep."

She smiled and glanced at Seth briefly. "Oh, my, yes. I slept like a rock. Aunt Lavinia always said peaceful rest was the reward of a clear conscience and an untroubled spirit."

"That only works if you don't have someone snoring in—" Cooper began.

"I hate to break up this delightful conversation," Seth growled, standing up, "but it's time we divide into crews and get to work. There's a smokehouse to be built and brush to be cleared in our first section."

Camille winked at Cooper and began carrying dirty plates to the worktable. Seth took half the men to the woods with him, and Cooper led the remainder to a spot above the stream where the building was to go up.

Hallie gazed out the open window and dried while Camille washed. "Thought I heard a commotion going on in Coop's new cabin late last night. Sounded a lot like Seth's voice, rantin' and ravin'."

"Do tell? Maybe you were dreaming." Camille dropped the last plate into the rinse water and squeezed out her rag to wipe the table. "Think you could teach me how to make pie crust this morning?"

Hallie grinned before she answered. "Sure enough, honey. That man of yours will take to a hot pie a lot quicker than a cold shoulder."

"Why don't you tell her you love her, Seth?" Cooper asked as he baited his hook with a fat earthworm. The two men sat on the bank of a clear stream just north of the camp after supper.

Seth shifted his large bulk to a point where the bark on the red cedar gouged him a little less. "What makes you think I care about her?'' he asked, yanking suddenly on his fishing pole as the line wiggled. It went slack and he didn't bother to check the hook. The way his luck was running lately, the worm was long gone and so was the fish.

''Well-l-l. All I heard last night was how you'd like to pinch her stubborn little head off her unreasonable little shoulders.'' Cooper pulled in a gorgeous salmon and added it to his stringer, where three of its brothers were flopping at the edge of the water.

Seth snorted. ''As always, your logic escapes me.''

Baiting his hook again, Cooper threw out the line and settled back. ''You know insults bounce right off my thick hide, Seth. I'm just trying to help you—and Camille. I like her too, you know. If you don't quit fooling around, you're going to lose her. Do you know how many men would line up if they thought she was free?''

Seth yanked his line in and frowned as he dug around the bucket for a fresh worm. ''Dammit, Coop, you've used all the bait!'' Throwing the bucket down, he got up and took a few steps to the edge of the water, where he stooped and washed his hands. Drying them on his canvas pants, he sighed. ''I can't tell her I care for her. We made a deal. If either of us wants out of the marriage, there'll be no strings. It wouldn't be fair to tie her down with emotional attachments, especially if she finds her brother.''

''You are such a mule-headed idiot,'' Cooper said mildly, shaking his head. ''Don't you know she's in love with you?''

Seth swung around and glared at his friend. He knew it wasn't true, and he wouldn't let Cooper get his hopes up. ''How the hell would you know about such a tender emotion? You let my sister marry that pasty-faced little pencil-pushing clerk. If you're so damned smart, why did you let her get away from you?''

For a brief moment, Cooper's eyes mirrored his painful loss, before a twisted smile appeared. ''That's why I'm telling you this. If I could go back and do it over, I'd marry Phoebe in a minute, money or no money.''

Seth stared at his friend for a long moment, the anger draining away as quickly as it had come. ''Sorry, Coop. I shouldn't have spouted off.''

''Apology accepted. It's true, though ... I was a fool.'' Cooper's pole was nearly yanked out of his hand, but he scrambled to his feet and managed to haul in another large fish.

Rolling his eyes heavenward, Seth added it to the heavy stringer. ''We've got enough here to feed all the townfolk of Bangor for a week. Maybe we should leave some for another day.''

''We?'' Cooper asked, his brow arching mischievously. ''Correct me if I'm wrong, but I believe I caught all those beauties.''

Seth grinned and tossed the smelly, wet string of fish to Cooper, who caught them against his chest with a surprised *woof.* ''You're absolutely right. You caught them, you can carry them and clean them. I wouldn't want to steal any of your thunder.''

Alerted by Seth and Cooper's voices, Camille pretended an intense interest in the charcoal drawing she was working on. When they rounded the corner of her cabin, she didn't want Seth to think she was waiting for him to return.

The likeness of the sawmill was not very good, and she longed to wad the drawing up and start again, but she didn't. Back in Charleston, she'd had no trouble recreating anything she'd put her mind to, even faces. Her concentration, however, was sorely lacking the last few weeks.

Camille simulated a look of pleasant surprise when the men came into view. ''Fish for supper tomorrow night,'' Cooper said, holding up his catch.

Camille smiled. "For loggers, you two are sure great fishermen."

"Cooper is. All I caught was a chill," Seth said mildly. His eyes devoured her face. In the soft light of dusk, it was as delicate as a cameo. Her thick, auburn hair curled softly around her face, and he knew just what it would smell like if he buried his face in it . . . sweet lavender. His groin tightened painfully.

There was a question in her eyes as she looked at him, but her voice was casual. "I have a fresh pot of coffee inside. Would the two of you like a cup?"

Cooper spoke up immediately. "That's the best offer I've had all day. I'll just clean these beauties and be right back."

"I'll help you," Seth offered.

"No, no. Fair is fair. I caught 'em, I'll clean 'em. You and Camille might have a few things to talk about in private." With that, he strode off, whistling a tune.

She looked at Seth for confirmation, and he nodded. "I guess I'll take a cup."

Camille put her sketch pad and charcoal down and stood up. Glancing self-consciously at her blackened fingers, she turned to the door, but Seth caught her elbow. "This might help," he said, offering his handkerchief. When she took it, her fingers brushed his, the contact causing her heart to beat faster.

He reached around her and pushed the door open, allowing her to go inside ahead of him. Camille felt tongue-tied in his presence, and searched frantically for something intelligent to say. Her gaze fell on the stack of clean clothes on the bed. "Hallie and I did the wash today. Do you want to take some clean clothes to Cooper's?" As soon as the words were out, she wanted to snatch them back. "That is, if you're planning to stay there—but you don't have to, this is your house, after all, and I'm more or less a guest. Well, really not a guest exactly. More like an employee . . ."

He gave the door a shove with his boot, closing it. Then he advanced the three steps that put him a hairsbreadth away from her. His eyes were intense, dark and fathomless, causing Camille to wonder what his intentions were. He pulled her into his arms and took her mouth in the most exquisitely gentle kiss she'd ever known. His tongue slipped between her parted lips and caressed hers with erotic strokes. Moments later he drew back far enough to gaze into her sky-blue eyes. "I missed you last night, and the night before, and the night before that," he murmured in a husky voice. "I'd like to come home."

If Camille hadn't been leaning against his strong bulk, she would have been wobbly. She could feel the warmth of his skin through his shirt where her hands gripped the material, and his masculine scent filled her senses to overflowing. The word "yes" fluttered on her lips even while a small voice in her head cautioned her to refuse his request. Having learned the art of sacrificing from living all those years with Aunt Lavinia, she whispered, "We might make a baby."

The genuine concern in her eyes made him feel ashamed for taking advantage of her weakness. He dipped his head and brushed her lips lightly. "You're right, honey. There isn't a way in Hell I can avoid making love to you if I stay the night. I'll just learn to keep my distance."

Her stomach tightened painfully. She wanted to belong to him in every sense, not just in name only. Being his paramour was not enough. "We have to remember it may not last. I mean, either one of us could decide to . . . to . . ."

Seth's hands strayed from her waist to her rounded hips, pulling her a little closer. "I know," he whispered.

Camille sucked in a swift breath at his action. The obvious evidence of his arousal pressed against her softness. Closing her eyes, she breathed deeply, searching for a reserve of strength to resist his magnetism. His mouth found hers again, and she surrendered—for the moment, she told herself—to the kiss. Her arms wound themselves around his neck like the hungry clinging vines of summer. His hands moved restlessly over her body, touching, caressing, pulling her closer to his heat. He ignited a fire inside her that flickered and then roared to life at his skillful touch.

Camille's mind jerked her back to the present when she felt his hands gathering her skirt up around her hips. Pushing at his chest, she gasped. "Seth, stop!"

He immediately dropped his hands and stepped back, his breathing a hoarse rasp in his throat. Desire still smoldered in the dark depths of his eyes. "I don't think I'd better stay for coffee after all." Turning on his heel, he left the cabin.

Camille and Hallie were washing the breakfast dishes when they heard the whistle of Captain Jack's steamboat. He tooted twice, which meant he was stopping with passengers or cargo. Hastily, the two women dried their hands on their aprons and left the cookhouse. The sun was barely up, but it was later than the last time he'd stopped by. She and Hallie were being slugabeds—according to the older woman—compared to the early hour they'd be rising once the logging and mill went into full operation for the season.

As they hurried down the hill and across the bridge over the stream, Camille was grateful for the reprieve. Since Seth had moved out of their cabin, she never fell asleep until the wee hours, despite the cheery impression she tried to present to everyone each morning. She knew the men speculated among themselves about their boss's marital problems. She'd noticed the sidelong glances from them, and heard a few whispers. They didn't, however, have the nerve to openly comment on it.

When Camille and Hallie reached the dock, young Joe Baker was coiling the thick rope around a post. "Mornin', ladies," he called, smiling as he raised up.

The two women returned his greeting, and Camille shaded her eyes, looking up toward the wheelhouse for Captain Jack.

The older gentleman leaned out a window and waved. "Brought you some more hands, Mrs. Braden," he called.

"As if we didn't have enough work to do already," Hallie snorted.

A group of men, some tall, some short, but all muscled, came filing down the gangplank. Camille counted nine. Several of them called Hallie by name, and teased her about her strong coffee or inquired about her feather-light pies. The older woman waited until they all stood on the dock, and then introduced Camille as the boss's wife. Hallie urged all of them to give their names so Camille could start getting to know them. "This little lady will be helping me cook yer grub, so be nice to her. She ain't tough like me, so I'd better not hear one rough word in the dining room, ya hear?"

Camille had to smile at the look on their faces. To a man, their expressions registered shock that any such thing would happen. One man, who looked to be around forty, spoke up. "You know good and well, Hallie Smith, that we don't forget ourselves around womenfolk. Have you ever heard any one of us cuss in the dining room?"

She chuckled. "No, Sam, but I've heard cursing on the skid road that would fair singe your ears."

"That's different," he pointed out.

"I suppose it is," Hallie conceded. "Darned if I didn't have you loggers mixed up with sailors. Can you ever forgive me?"

"Shame on you, Hallie," Camille chided her with a smile. "These men will think I'm a prim little puritan and get right back on the boat."

"Not likely, ma'am," a blond-haired giant spoke up. "Your husband pays better and runs a smoother operation than just about anybody in the territory."

Hallie patted the young man on the arm. "We're just teasin' you boys now. Me and Camille need to talk to Cap'n Jack, so why don't you all go up to the new cookhouse and have some coffee. I left a fresh pot brewin'."

After consulting with the captain about some spices they'd ordered, the two women left the dock.

Over lunch, Seth made a point of telling the newcomers about the man-creature who had frightened Camille. He also cautioned them all to be on the lookout for the Slidell brothers. When the meal was finished, Cooper fetched a ledger book from a shelf beside the door. "I need to add the new men to the book."

Hallie provided him with a quill pen and an ink pot. With little regard for legibility, Cooper began writing each man's name on a new page. Seth was standing over his shoulder scowling. "Dammit, Coop, take a little more care, will you? How do you expect us to read those hen scratches later?"

Cooper looked up and pointed out mildly, "The reason I took over the job was because we couldn't read your scrawl."

"Why not let Camille keep the books?" Hallie suggested, her arms in dishwater up to her elbows. "She's got the purtiest handwrite you ever seen."

All the men favored Camille with a look that plainly said, "Smart as well as beautiful."

Camille's cheeks turned pink as twenty-seven pairs of male eyes rested on her. She turned back to the worktable and picked up a plate to dry. "I'm sure Seth and Coop don't want me interfering with their business," she protested.

Seth's gaze was speculative for a moment. "You would be doing us a favor . . . if you wouldn't mind, that is."

"Of course I wouldn't mind, if you think I could help . . ." She dried her hands and came over to the table.

Cooper stood up and handed her the quill with a flourish. "I gladly hand over this job, madam. Seth has chewed my bones about the books since the first year we went into business."

"How can I refuse when you make it sound so appealing," she said dryly, sitting down.

Seth shook his head in puzzlement. "He makes me sound like an ogre. Lord knows where he gets his crazy ideas."

The men who knew the partners gave a hoot of laughter.

Camille carefully put each man's name on a separate page. She had a smile and a word for each one, making him feel special. When she finished with the new men, Vladimir lounged against the table. "I vill be looking out for the creature that bothered you, so don't have any more fear," he said, his accent rolling the words out in a peculiar way.

Camille gave him a fond smile. "Thank you, Vladimir. That makes me feel better." She had no doubt he could give the creature a good fight. He was every bit as big.

"I don't want any man going to the woods without a weapon until this man is caught," Seth spoke up, his voice carrying throughout the cookhouse. "Some of you know from last season about the problems we had—accidents that were not accidents. I can't prove anything, but I believe it's the Slidell brothers. Cooper and I have talked about this, and we've decided we need a camp guard at night. Coop and I will be taking a turn, and we'd appreciate some volunteers, but you don't have to. When a man pulls this duty, he won't be expected to work in the woods the next day. In that way, the women will have a man near the cookhouse every day, even if he's sleeping, in case there's trouble." He laid his hand on Camille's shoulder. "And if you need help, just ring the dinner bell. That would wake the dead, as well as bring the men from the sawmill."

When the men were leaving to go back to work, Camille asked Seth for a private word. Her hands were clasped tightly together to prevent their trembling. The idea came to her like a bolt of lightning. She followed him out the door to stand on the porch. Hallie was inside, out of earshot, and the men were already halfway down the hill. "Would you consider moving back in with me?"

Chapter 15

Camille's expression was wide-eyed and innocent, yet her words set his pulse racing. He had lain awake nights trying to figure out how to achieve that very thing. However he felt vaguely suspicious. "What changed your mind?"

She couldn't hold his gaze with a lie on her lips, so she glanced down at her white knuckles. "I've been . . . nervous, what with the creature and all, and I've barely slept since you went to stay at Cooper's." Raising her eyes, she squeezed out a tear. "I'm sorry to be such a baby about this, but I hear noises in the night and . . ."

Seth took her into his arms, holding her close, stroking her back comfortingly. "Sh-h-h, love. Don't apologize. I should be horsewhipped for leaving you in the first place. Of course I'll come home," he said with tenderness. Maybe it wasn't the reason he longed to hear, but he decided to worry about that later.

Camille felt the steady thumping rhythm of Seth's heartbeat beneath her ear as she rested her head on his chest. She knew it was sinful to lie, but she'd missed him so much, and somehow, pride and noble self-sacrifice offered little comfort in her cold bed. Half a loaf was better than none, she decided, loving the feel of his solid strength. An impish smile curved her lips as she murmured, "Thank you, Seth."

"Maybe now the men will stop gossiping about our living arrangements." He kissed the top of her head and gave her a quick hug. "I've got to get going. See you at supper."

So much for absence making the heart grow fonder, Camille thought. She stopped patting herself on the back as she watched Seth lope down the hill after his crew. He had jumped at the chance to save face with his men.

Her feelings were getting so mixed up, she didn't know what to do. First she didn't want him to touch her if he didn't love her. But she wanted him so much, she decided friendship was enough. Then she didn't want to tie him to her with a child, but now she'd just asked him to come back to her bed— more or less—and to hell with any accident that might happen. Perhaps she should discuss the situation with Hallie. After all, the woman was older and had been married. She should know a little something about men, Camille surmised.

Hallie was cutting a chunk of salt pork into a pot of beans sitting on the stove. Camille got out the biggest crockery bowl they had and began measuring flour into it to make bread. After a couple of false starts, Camille explained her feelings to the older woman and begged for advice.

Hallie smoothed a stray wisp of hair into the neat bun at the back of her head, her eyes narrowing. "My ma always said out of all her kids, I had the most common sense, and I'd have to say I seen a lot of life go by already. Now, in my opinion, this business arrangement thing you and Seth got going should be tossed out the door with the dirty dishwater. Jest say what ya feel and devil take the hindmost."

"But what if Seth tells me something I don't want to hear? He might not care a fig for me! And what about the lie I told him about being nervous?'' Camille measured some lard and milk into the bowl and began to work it into a batter.

Hallie watched Camille's quick, capable movements for a moment. ''I think yer worryin' too much, but think about it. For the time bein', movin' back in together is a good start.''

''Do you really think so?'' Camille asked hopefully, looking up from her work.

Hallie pulled two buckets down from a shelf. ''When you got a good man, you should hang onto 'im. I had a bad one, honey, so I know what I'm talkin' about. Mr. Smith was sour at the best of times, but when he got to drinkin', he was meaner than a snake. And he got to where he drank all the time.'' Hallie put the buckets on the end of the worktable and sat down on a stool, gazing out the window as if her past was drifting by.

''That must have been terrible for you. I'm sorry,'' Camille said gently.

''It was like livin' in Hell, for me and my boy. He used to hit me, and little Frank would try to git between us. He'd beg his pa to stop. Mr. Smith wanted to come West on a wagon train to the gold fields, so we did, but that didn't make 'im happy either. Before we got halfway to Californy, he was back to drinkin' and knockin' me around.''

The older woman paused, still staring out the window. Camille put down her spoon and pulled a stool close to Hallie's. She sat down and took one of her work-roughened hands, giving it a comforting squeeze. ''You don't have to talk about this if you don't want to. I'm sure it's painful.''

Hallie glanced at Camille and smiled sadly. ''Yer a sweet girl, and if I'd had a daughter, I'd want her to be just like you.'' Glancing back to the window, she sighed. ''I ain't never talked about this to nobody, and I shouldn't burden you with it now.''

''You talk all you want, Hallie. I'm your friend, and if I can help by listening, that's little enough.''

Two tears slipped down Hallie's cheeks. "I killed Mr. Smith one night when we was camped on the trail. He beat Frank real bad and I couldn't stop 'im. When he passed out in the wagon, I drove a nail into his skull and then covered it with his hair so's it didn't show. Next mornin', I told everybody he died of the fever. We'd had an outbreak of cholera on the train, you know, so nobody asked no questions. I couldn't take 'im hurting my boy."

Hallie's sad voice was little more than a whisper. Camille put her arms around the older woman and held her for a long time without saying a word. Finally, she drew back and stood up. "I'd better get that bread to rising or we won't have any for supper."

Hallie glanced up, catching Camille's eye for a long moment as acceptance and understanding passed between the two women. "I'll help. Then we'll move Seth's things back to your cabin and go berry pickin'."

When those chores were finished, Hallie double-checked their pistol to make sure it was loaded, and they headed west along the riverbank to where blackberries grew profusely. In no time at all, their buckets were full. They worked in companionable silence, neither woman mentioning Hallie's confession, but Camille felt closer to her friend, and felt a deep compassion for what Hallie had endured.

On the way back to the cookhouse, Camille began feeling a strange tingling sensation in her arms and her face. She decided it was too much sun.

Camille washed the fruit while Hallie built up the fire in the stove and stirred up pie crust By the time the two women had four large cobblers ready to put in the oven, Camille was feeling ill. "You look plumb puny, girl. Why don't you go lay down till supper time. Just about everything's done already." Hallie pushed her toward the door. Camille was feeling much too sick to argue.

Her sleep was fitful with bizarre dreams intruding. She saw

Aunt Lavinia and Prudence sitting on a wide stump down by the river, and they were eating blackberry cobbler. Her aunt spoke up, saying, "Well, I see that stupid girl learned to cook something after all. Of course, it's not as good as Sadie would have made, but she married a common man, after all, so it won't matter."

Prudence, her nose in the air, remarked, "I'll swear, Mama, I don't know what that handsome man saw in our ugly Camille. He must have been desperate for a wife out there in the wilderness."

When the next dream came into focus, fear clawed at Camille's insides with hot talons. The creature she'd seen in the woods was now standing at her window peering inside at her. She opened her mouth to scream, but she couldn't get her breath. Its face was no longer shadowed by distance, but clear. It was the face of Jake Slidell. He smiled an evil yellow smile, and his eyes were deadly, like those of a reptile just before it strikes. As in the way of dreams, when he spoke, it was as if he was beside her. "I was waiting for you . . . why did you run away? I'm back . . ."

Camille's heart began to pound erratically at the threat in his deep voice. She felt rooted to the bed. His face disappeared, but her feeling of relief was short-lived when the door began to slowly swing inward. Her breath solidified in her throat as the creature's huge, hairy body came into view. She shook with a chill, but at the same time her skin burned like fire. Closer and closer, he moved toward her, and she struggled in vain to climb off the bed and run, but her legs wouldn't move. Her heartbeat thundered in her ears when she woke up panting in terror.

Sitting up abruptly, she scanned the room quickly, even though she realized she'd been dreaming. Still, she needed the reassurance. Taking several deep breaths, she began to calm down until she caught a glimpse of her hands and arms. Holding them out in front of her, she experienced a returning twinge of fear when she saw they were mottled, swelled and scratched. There was a throbbing, stinging pain in her hands, arms and face. "Dear Lord!" she gasped, her hands flying to her face to find it was swollen and lumpy. Frightened now, almost more than she had been in the dream, she slid off the bed and ran to the mirror behind the screen. "Dear Lord," she repeated in a whisper, her voice choked. Her face was misshapen with lumps and an angry red rash. Not bothering to put on her shoes, she fled the cabin and ran all the way to the cookhouse.

Flinging open the door, she gasped in a winded voice, "Dear God, Hallie, it's cholera! I'm dying—no—don't come near me!"

The older woman was filling a cup with coffee at the work-table, but set the pot down and started forward, the alarm on her face changing to confusion. "Camille, honey! What's this all about? You look funny, but how do you know it's cholera?"

Camille leaned against the doorjamb, her knees suddenly weak. "I've seen it before . . . seen people die of it. You swell up, there's fever, rash . . ." To prove it, she flung out her arms.

Hallie frowned and stared at the younger woman for a moment before she came forward. "If you ever scare me like that again, Camille Braden, I'll take you over my knee."

Camille was shaking her head vehemently and backing up. "It's contagious, Hallie! Please don't get too close."

"A poison sumac rash is contagious, but not deadly," Hallie said drily, grasping Camille's hand and examining the rash up close. "Yep, that's what it is. Between the rash, the sunburn and them scratches from thorny berry vines, you look like sin that's been dipped in misery. But I expect you'll live."

Camille stared at her friend for a moment, trying to absorb the good news. She leaned weakly against the doorframe again, this time with relief. A hysterical giggle escaped her lips. "What a ninny I am! Thank heaven the men were not here to witness my—"

Hallie cleared her throat loudly and drew Camille forward

into the room. "We have company, honey. I nearly forgot 'em when you scared me so bad."

Camille was trying to hang back, suddenly embarrassed by the way she looked as well as the scene she'd just made. "Oh, dear . . . I didn't realize. I'll just go on back to my cab—" Too late. Hallie stepped aside. Sitting on a bench at one of the tables to their left, Camille saw two pretty young women. They were dressed in stylish traveling gowns, the matching hats resting sedately on the table. One had honey-blond hair and the other, dark sable.

"Don't be bashful, honey—they're kinfolk," Hallie chided, taking her by the arm and leading her to their guests. "This here is yer sister-in-law, Phoebe Hart." Hallie stopped beside the dark-haired girl, and Camille tried to smile, but her face felt stiff with the swelling.

The young woman resembled Seth a great deal, with his coloring and dark hair and eyes. Her smile was sympathetic. "I must say I'm very happy your problem turned out to be sumac instead of cholera. I'd hate to lose my new sister-in-law before I've even gotten a chance to know her." Phoebe glanced quickly at her blond companion before she added, "In his usual careless fashion, Seth forgot to let us know he'd gotten married, but let me say welcome to the family."

Camille felt a little more at ease with Phoebe's warm manner. "Thank you. I've heard a lot about you from Seth and Cooper." Her gaze turned to the petite blonde. Hallie had said they were kinfolk. "And you are . . . ?"

A look of uncertainty flashed in the young woman's green eyes. "Patience Runako. You may have heard of me— depending on how mad Seth was. I used to be engaged to your husband."

For a few moments there was an uncomfortable silence as Camille digested this bit of information.

"You coulda knocked me over with a feather too," Hallie said, stepping into the breach. The older woman gave Camille's shoulder a comforting squeeze. "I was just makin' us a cup of coffee when you came in, Camille. Why don't we set a spell and git acquainted before we start supper?"

Camille simply couldn't get over how beautiful Patience was. There was a sick feeling in the pit of her stomach as she thought of how much Seth had loved this girl . . . and perhaps still did. Pulling herself together, she nodded. "Yes, Hallie. That's a good idea. I take it you ladies arrived on the afternoon boat?" Camille moved around the end of the table to sit across from them. She tried not to think about how bad she looked compared to their sophisticated city appearance.

Phoebe spoke up. "Yes. And I must apologize for the way we've just shown up. I was afraid if I wrote to Seth, he would forbid us to come." She glanced down at her folded hands. "My husband died a few months ago . . . lung fever. Anyway, I needed to get away from Bangor for a while."

Camille's eyes widened. "Oh, dear. I'm so sorry."

Hallie arrived with a tray, and Phoebe looked up with a sad smile. "Thank you. I'd rather not talk about it if you don't mind. This trip has been a time of healing and a godsend for me. I just want to get on with my life now." Turning to Patience, she added. "And my dear friend here has lent moral support when I needed it the most, even though she's had a loss of her own."

Camille's stomach lurched. What sort of loss? she wondered, a sudden fear crowding her throat. "Your husband?" she asked, her voice faint.

Patience dropped her gaze and nodded. "Yes. He's . . . gone."

While Hallie passed the cream and sugar around, Camille was sure she murmured the correct sympathetic phrase, but for the life of her, she couldn't remember saying a word. She felt as if she was in a daze where rational thought processes refused to enter. Hallie, bless her, carried the conversation, and then sent Camille to show the two women where her cabin was so they might freshen up. Once that was done, Camille hurried to her own house. When she looked into the mirror, she promptly burst into tears. She looked every bit as bad as she remembered—worse. When she ran out of the house in a panic, she hadn't even brushed her hair or smoothed her clothes. Wishing she could crawl in a hole and hide, she nevertheless began doing what she could with her appearance. Her personal humiliation would just have to take a backseat to her duty. Hallie needed her help.

When she finished, Camille calmed herself with the thought that she looked more presentable. She'd put cold compresses on the swelling on her face and hands. With a clean gingham dress and fresh apron, her hair combed into place, she felt somewhat better. That lasted until she reached the cookhouse. Phoebe and Patience were there already helping Hallie. The long tables were set, and the venison stew was bubbling on the stove. Loaves of fresh-baked bread and cobblers lined the cooling board below the window.

Camille's gaze strayed to Patience, and she felt her heart sink anew. The girl looked pretty as a picture in her green sprigged calico dress and white apron. Her blond hair was secured in a bun on top of her head, but several wisps floated around her flushed face. Camille felt like an ugly cow next to a dainty kitten. Sighing, she reached for her apron. "I'll do the dishes, Hallie. It looks like everything else is done," she said.

Hallie looked up from the coffee she was making. "No, ma'am. You're gonna take it easy for the next few days. Phoebe and Patience offered to take up the slack so the rash can heal. You don't wanna get it infected now."

"But they're our guests!" Camille protested. "And I'm not an invalid."

Phoebe wiped her hands and came around the worktable. Putting her arm around Camille, she led her to a bench. "Of course you're not an invalid, dear. But neither are we guests. We fully expect to do our share of the work while we're here and I won't hear another word on the subject. If we aren't allowed to help, we'll go back to Maine.''

Camille sat down and glanced up into Phoebe's kind brown eyes. ''I certainly don't want to start off on the wrong foot with my in-laws,'' she said, a flash of humor crossing her face.

Phoebe laughed. ''Smart girl. I can see why my brother married you.''

Camille glanced quickly at Patience, but the girl was busy slicing a loaf of bread, and seemed unaffected by Phoebe's comment.

Dusk was settling over the camp when Camille went out onto the porch and rang the dinner bell. She saw lights in the bunkhouse window. Leaning over the rail, she looked the other direction, across the stream, and saw lights in her own cabin. Seth would be here soon, she thought with anxiety twisting her insides. How would he react to Patience? Would he regret he hadn't married the pretty blonde? ''Damnation!'' Camille whispered. ''Why do I have to look like death warmed over tonight of all nights?'' The crickets and tree frogs were tuning up for their nightly concert, but provided no answer to her question, so she went back inside.

As it happened, Seth and Cooper were the last to arrive in the dining room. Hallie had introduced the two women to the loggers already, explaining that Patience was an old friend of the family, and that Seth and Coop were not yet aware of their arrival. The men fell silent when their bosses walked into the room, waiting anxiously for the reunion.

Camille watched Seth's face from behind the worktable. He saw Phoebe first. He frowned, as if his eyes were deceiving him. Then surprise followed by pleasure raced rapidly across his face. ''Seth!'' she breathed, running to meet him.

He scooped her up into his arms and swung her around. ''Phoebe Braden! Where did you come from?''

She laughed in sheer joy. ''Bangor, Maine, you mule-headed dolt. That's where you came from too, don't you remember?''

He chuckled with happy memory. "I've missed that sharp little tongue of yours." He set her on her feet and held her away so he could look at her. "You're prettier than when I left. Where's your husband?" He glanced around, expecting to see his dandified brother-in-law lurking behind her.

Phoebe placed her hand on his arm just about the time he saw Patience standing at the end of a trestle table. "I'm a widow now," she said quietly.

Phoebe's words struck him in a delayed reaction, and he pulled her close again. "I'm sorry, sis. What happened?"

She drew back and patted his cheek. "Could we talk about it later?"

"Sure, honey." Distracted, he glanced over her head. Phoebe's eyes followed his, and she sought to lighten the strain of the moment. "You remember Patience, of course. She accompanied me on the trip."

Seth nodded, his hands falling away from his sister's arms. "Hello, Patience."

For a brief moment, Patience looked at Seth with deep longing before she masked the emotion. Seth's expression was guarded. Camille's gaze went back and forth between the two of them, and her heart twisted painfully.

Patience nodded politely. "Seth. It's good to see you. I understand congratulations are in order."

Seth's expression was blank for a moment before it registered with him what she was referring to. "Oh, yes, my marriage." He glanced around until he found Camille. Alarm flashed through him when he saw the puffiness of her features and the red rash on her skin. He hardly noticed that Cooper had stepped around him to take Phoebe's hands. Seth made his way to Camille's side, concern wrinkling his brow. The men, tiring of the reunion scene, went back to talking and passing the steaming bowls of stew.

Seth tipped her chin up. "Camille, honey, what's wrong?" His voice was full of tender concern. Camille burst into tears and fled the cookhouse. The cool evening breeze soothed her hot cheeks somewhat. Hearing the door open behind her, Camille stiffened. "Please, go back and visit with your guests," she urged, her voice shaky with tears.

Seth's hands rested lightly on her shoulders, and he gently massaged her tense muscles. "Tell me what's wrong, honey."

"Nothing! I'm just feeling a little low because I got this horrible poison sumac, and a sunburn, and my hands look raw and ugly from being scratched by blackberry vines," her voice ended on a wail. She fished a handkerchief from the pocket of her dress and blew her nose loudly. "I look worse than the monster." She couldn't prevent the tears from starting again.

He turned her in his arms and held her close, rubbing her back soothingly. "Sh-h-h, love, don't cry. I think you're beautiful, rash and all."

She cried harder.

Seth didn't quite know what to do, but he decided she probably wouldn't want to go back inside, so he swung her up into his arms and carried her to their cabin. He pushed the door open with his boot and stepped inside. A single lamp burned on the fireplace mantel, giving a gentle light. Her sobs had dwindled to hiccups. He set her on her feet. "Put on your nightgown, honey. I'll get some medicine for your rash and then bring your supper." Bending, he brushed the top of her head with his lips.

He was gone before she could reply. Going behind the screen, she removed her dress and slipped the lawn nightgown over her head, tying the ribbon at her throat. Glancing into the mirror brought fresh tears. Now her eyes were swollen and splotchy from crying—she was a mess. And Patience was fair, and sweet and beautiful, an impish voice taunted inside her head. Camille climbed into bed and buried her face in the pillow. Tonight was to have been a happy reunion with Seth . . . now it was a nightmare. Sure, he was being kind, but she'd seen the way he looked at Patience. There was no mistaking the fact he was hiding something.

When Seth returned with a tray of food, Camille had dried her eyes. "Thank you. I'm sorry I caused this trouble when you've hardly gotten to speak to your sister and . . . and . . ."

Glancing away from her, Seth cleared his throat. "Forget it. Phoebe and I will have lots of time to talk." He placed the tray on their table. Picking up a bottle, he flipped the cork from the top. "Coop got this from one of those traveling peddlers last year, and it works. One of the men had a brush with poison sumac and we tried it out on him." He smiled a lopsided smile, "Since he didn't die, I figure it's safe for you to use."

Camille was not in the mood to be teased. "If I died, it would solve a lot of problems."

Seth had sat down on the edge of the bed. His brows rose at her bald statement. "Feeling sorry for yourself, are you?"

Camille bristled. "No. It's true. The woman you've been in love with for years is here. I'm sure she came all this way to see you and not just to accompany your sister! Anyway—"

Seth held up his hand. "Whoa! Aren't you getting a little carried away? Patience is married, and although I don't understand why she left her husband to come here with Phoebe, it doesn't change—"

Camille glared at him. "She's a widow too—she told us this afternoon."

Seth couldn't have looked more surprised if she had slapped him. "A widow?" he echoed.

Was that hope she saw flickering in his eyes? she wondered dismally. Throwing back the covers, Camille climbed out of bed and moved to the table. "Yes. And here you are stuck with me," she said in a flat voice. It hadn't been a marriage based on love, she reminded herself, but it might have worked out if Patience hadn't shown up.

"I don't think of it as 'stuck,' Camille," he chided gently.

Her rigid back kept him from moving across the room to touch her.

The kindness in his tone told her more than if he'd tried to deny his affection for Patience. His innate gentleness beneath a strong, rough exterior was one of the things she loved best about him. She could feel her heart breaking, but pride came to her rescue. "We're friends, Seth, remember? We don't have to lie to each other. Whenever it's convenient, we'll end the marriage."

Frowning, Seth asked, "Is that what you really want?"

Camille's hands were gripping the edge of the table so hard her knuckles were white. It was the least she could do for him. "I think it will be the best thing for both of us."

Seth carefully set the bottle of lotion on the night table, and made his way to the door. Without turning, he said, "I'll ask Phoebe to stay with you so you won't be alone, and I'll go back to Cooper's."

Camille didn't trust her voice. After a moment, she turned and found him gone. Was he on his way to tell Patience the good news?

Chapter 16

Phoebe and Patience had been at the camp for ten days when a traveling preacher showed up on a Sunday morning to hold services. Everyone was eating a breakfast of biscuits and salt pork when the cookhouse door opened and a tall, thin man dressed in a black suit stepped inside. He carried a worn Bible in one hand and with the other, swept off his black, flat-topped hat. "God hath made this wondrous Sabbath day," he said, his deep voice ringing with conviction.

Cooper, who was sitting at the end of the closest table, stood up and extended his hand. "Glad to see you, Reverend Holbrook. Why not have a bite of breakfast with us and then if you have a sermon, we'll be happy to hear it."

The preacher's eyes strayed to the mound of golden biscuits on the platter, and he nodded. Camille got up and fetched a plate, silverware and a cup of coffee for him. When he'd taken the edge off his hunger with several biscuits, Camille, sitting across from him, said, "I suppose you get around to a lot of camps in these parts?"

"Yes, ma'am," he said.

"I'm trying to locate my brother and I have reason to believe he's working in the territory. His name is Forrest Sinclair."

The preacher wrinkled his brow, but then shook his head. "I don't recollect that name, ma'am. But I'll be on the lookout for him from now on."

Disappointed, Camille thanked him. Later, Reverend Holbrook preached a sermon on the Ten Commandments. When he got to the one about adultery, Camille couldn't resist a glance in Seth's direction. He was looking at her with a scowl on his face. He should be happy, Camille thought indignantly. I've all but given him his freedom and shoved him into Patience's arms. And still, he acts like a bear with a sore toe. The man is never satisfied. In a childish gesture, she wrinkled her nose and turned her head.

After Reverend Holbrook got on his horse and rode away, camp life returned to normal. Several men lugged their laundry down to the river, while some less fastidious loggers decided to wear their dirty clothes for one more week and settled to letter writing, whittling or storytelling.

Hallie was having a bad spell of gout in her foot, and Camille ordered her to bed. That meant Camille had to do all the wash by herself, but she didn't mind. She needed something to keep her busy and take her mind off Seth and Patience. In the past week, she'd seen the two of them talking privately several times, and each time his dark head leaned toward her blond one, Camille felt a knifelike pain in her chest.

As she carried the basketful of dirty clothes out to the yard, she saw Vladimir heading her way. He waved and a huge grin spread across his face. "Put that down, my lovely. I vill carry it for you," he called.

Camille smiled in spite of her somber mood. There was no use arguing with the Russian, so she put the basket down and walked on to the three tubs set up near the stream. The small fires she'd laid a while ago were burning just right, and the water was warm. Fishing a chunk of soap and a paring knife from her apron pocket, she cut slivers of it into one of the tubs. "Thank you, Vladimir. I don't know what I'd do without you when it comes to heavy lifting."

"You are delicate, like porcelain figurine. You should have servants for this peasant labor. Bah! I vill take it up with Seth myself when he returns from Empire City." Vladimir set the basket near her and then rested his fists on his hips.

Camille glanced up from separating the clothes. "Seth's gone? When did he leave?"

"A short vhile ago." He scowled. "You did not know?"

Camille hastily went back to her sorting, a blush stealing across her cheeks. "No," she said shortly.

"He said he vill be back in day or two."

Camille felt foolish. She was Seth's wife and yet he'd told her nothing. Even though they weren't living together, he could at least show her some common courtesy. Chances were, Patience knew he was going to town, and why, Camille thought with irritation. "Where he goes and what he does makes no difference to me," she lied. Dropping the underclothing into the tub first, she took her stick and began to stir them. If she hadn't been so angry, she would have found Vladimir's presence embarrassing while she washed her chemises and petticoats.

"I know there is trouble, and is none of my business, but I am sad to see you unhappy," he said gently.

Camille began to scrub a chemise on the washboard, rubbing hard enough to wear a hole through the material. "I'm not unhappy, Vladimir. And there is no trouble. Seth and I have a business deal, nothing more."

"Ah-h-h . . . a marriage of convenience. In my family, there were many such alliances." He nodded sagely. "Once I was betrothed to the Countess Anya Riasanovskaya, distant cousin to the Czar Nicholas, though we had never met. A marriage

between us would have been socially and economically benefi-
cial to both our families.''

Camille dropped the clean chemise into the rinse tub and
reached in the water for another soiled article. ''I take it something happened and you didn't marry?'' she said, forgetting
for the moment her anger and humiliation.

''The year of the wedding, my family fled Russia to make
new life in this country. My father was intellectual man, and
he disagreed with Czar Nicholas about many government poli-
cies. We left under cover of darkness. It was twelve years ago.''
The gentle giant shrugged and grinned. ''That is why I am
common logger and not Count Vladimir Koloffsky.''

Fascinated by the story, Camille had forgotten the wash.
When he finished, she reluctantly went back to scrubbing. ''I
don't think there's anything common about you, Vladimir,''
she assured him, and then asked, ''You haven't met a woman
in this country to take Anya's place?''

''It is strange you mention this, because I am in love for
first time in my life. She is beautiful beyond compare, and
sweet and kind. But there is a sadness in her soul. She needs
Vladimir to take care of her . . . I vill heal her spirit.''

Camille dropped another clean chemise into the rinse water,
her interest piqued. ''Does she live in Empire City?''

He laughed. ''No, no! She is here . . . my beautiful Patience
is a stone's throw away.''

Patience? Camille's mind raced with the possibilities.
Patience had only been here for a little over a week. ''Have
you told her how you feel?'' she asked, cautious jubilation
starting to bubble in her.

''Not yet—but I vill tell her soon.''

Camille sighed. So much for hopes and dreams, she thought.
A movement across the stream caught her eye. It was Cooper
and Phoebe coming up the path. He was leaning toward her,
and she was laughing up at him. Something about the familiar
way his arm slipped around her waist told Camille they were

more than friends. Before she had time to speculate further, they looked up and moved self-consciously apart.

"Oh, Camille, honey! I'm sorry," Phoebe called as they reached the bridge. "If I'd known you were doing the wash, I would have stayed to help."

Camille made a face at her. "Don't fret. There's plenty left to do."

Phoebe hurried toward the cabin she'd been sharing with Camille, and called over her shoulder, "I'll be back as soon as I change."

Cooper stopped to lean both arms on the handrail of the bridge. He grinned. "I've been giving Phoebe the grand tour this afternoon."

Camille frowned. "I thought you did that last Sunday."

"There were a few things I hadn't shown her," he said innocently.

Camille knew he was up to something, but for the moment, Vladimir was starting to look downcast for all his bravado. "I meant to ask Patience if she'd like to use the wash water to do some of her clothes. Would you mind asking her, Vladimir? And find out if Hallie is feeling better?"

A huge grin lit his handsome face. "Anything for you, Camille."

She smiled as he headed toward Hallie's cabin. Turning toward Cooper, she startled him with a swift change of tone. "And just why didn't you, or Seth, or somebody tell me my husband was leaving? And why did he go to Empire City? I'm sure you know, Cooper Maxwell. The two of you are as thick as thieves."

Cooper's eyes widened and he backed up a step. "Now, now, honey. Don't get your feathers ruffled. Seth told me to watch out for you while he's gone, but he figured you were still mad at him."

"And now I'm even angrier. Most likely everybody in camp knew he was leaving but me. He doesn't care a fig for my feelings!'' She threw a balled-up petticoat in the rinse tub, causing the water to slop over the sides.

Cooper backed up a step. ''That's not true. Why, you're the very reason he's gone to Empire City. It'll put everything to rights, he said, once he talks to . . . that person he's going to talk to. He told me he's doing this for you.''

A chill finger slid down her spine. ''And who is this person?'' she asked. A lawyer, a judge?

''Can't tell you. Seth would skin me alive. But he does care for you. I know it for a fact.''

Camille dropped her gaze, her face growing pale. Cooper was sweet to try to cheer her up, but she couldn't afford false hope. She didn't want Cooper to see her chagrin. He would tell Seth she was upset, and she didn't want that. If Seth wanted to be rid of her, she would let him go. Poor Vladimir would be hurt for a while when Patience married Seth, but he would surely get over it. She, on the other hand, would grieve until her dying day . . . but Seth would never know, she vowed fiercely.

''Did you hear me, Camille?'' Cooper asked. He moved to her side and touched her shoulder. ''He loves you, really.''

''We'll see,'' she said, swallowing past the lump in her throat. She looked up at him and forced a smile. ''I appreciate your concern.''

''Everything will turn out fine, you'll see.'' Cooper patted her shoulder and took himself off to the bunkhouse, where a poker game was always in progress on Sunday afternoon.

Camille took a deep breath. ''I have to concentrate on finding Forrest. I won't think about Seth,'' she muttered to herself as she attacked another piece of clothing.

''Did you say something?'' Phoebe asked at her sister-in-law's elbow.

Camille jumped and gave a startled yelp. She hadn't heard the woman approach. ''Heavens above, Phoebe! Has my hair gone white?'' she asked with mock horror.

Phoebe laughed. "I'm sorry. Mother always said I was more Indian than Yankee the way I could sneak up on a body."

"This is my last white piece, and then you can do yours before we switch to colored things," Camille told her.

Phoebe began sorting her clothes on the ground. "Did Cooper say something to upset you?"

Camille gave the task at hand more concentration than it deserved. "He didn't mean to. I didn't know Seth was going to Empire City."

Phoebe brought her white clothes and dropped them into the tub as Camille finished. "You know I haven't asked any questions since I've been here—because it's none of my business—but I can tell you're in love with my brother. He cares about you as well, so I don't really understand why the two of you are living apart."

Phoebe took over the washboard and Camille stepped back, drying her hands on her skirt. "Our marriage is one of convenience, a sort of business arrangement."

Phoebe's brows rose. "Coop told me it started out that way, but I think it could be a real marriage if the two of you tried."

Her sister-in-law was being kind, but Camille wondered if Phoebe hadn't had high hopes of a reconciliation between her brother and Patience. Hearing soft laughter behind her, Camille turned and saw Patience coming down the path, her arm linked through Vladimir's. "You and Cooper are being too sentimental and someday you'll have to face the truth," Camille said, keeping her voice light. "We did try and it didn't work out."

Phoebe sighed, but dropped the subject. She gave the approaching couple a mischievous smile. "Wouldn't you like to do your washing, Patience? Camille has done all the hard work already, getting everything ready."

Patience blushed and shook her head. "Thank you, Phoebe, but Vladimir has kindly offered to take me for a walk. What with that creature running loose, we don't get to venture away from camp very often."

The Russian promised solemnly, "Vladimir vill protect you." Glancing toward Camille, he added, "Hallie said to tell you she vill not lay for long in that cursed bed."

Camille smiled. "She sounds better."

"If you'll get your things, I'll do them for you," Phoebe offered.

"Oh, Phoebe, thank you, but I'll just do it another day," Patience said.

Vladimir spoke up. "I vill carry water and build the fires for you any day you say."

Patience blushed again and murmured her thanks. When the couple moved across the bridge and down the path, Phoebe nodded with satisfaction. "I knew it would do her a world of good to come with me."

Camille was wringing out her underthings and dropping them into a basket. "Patience didn't want to come?" She assumed the girl had wanted to resume her relationship with Seth.

"She fought tooth and nail, but I finally won her over. It's good to see her coming out of that shell she was in."

"I suppose she took her husband's death pretty hard," Camille said.

Phoebe looked uncomfortable. "Well . . . the situation did upset her. But she was afraid Seth wouldn't want her here after what happened between the two of them. I convinced her to come, though, and it's working out nicely."

"I hope Patience realizes what a good friend she has in you," Camille said, feeling an unaccustomed prick of envy. Aunt Lavinia and Prudence had seen to it that she had little time for friends. Big Amos and a few others around the docks had been good to her, but it wasn't the same as having another female to confide in, someone who could share your hopes and dreams and secrets. She couldn't blame Phoebe for wanting her best friend to marry her brother. It would be an ideal arrangement.

"It works both ways, you know. Patience helped me through

several rough spots in my life.'' Phoebe stopped scrubbing a chemise to help Camille finish squeezing out her clean clothes. ''We'd better get these hung up to dry. It's starting to look cloudy to the north.''

Camille sensed Phoebe wanted to change the subject. Her grief was obviously still too raw to talk about.

The rain held off until after midnight. Camille was awake when she heard it pelting the roof. She snuggled down into the covers and wondered what Seth was doing in Empire City. Was he visiting his lady friend at the saloon? Or was he contemplating how his life would be once he married Patience?

Seth returned from town on Monday afternoon. The women were in the cookhouse preparing supper when he walked through the door. His eyes sought and found Camille's before he spoke. ''Any coffee?'' he asked casually, moving to lean on the worktable where Hallie and Patience were rolling out pie crust. Camille turned back to the pot of stew she was stirring on the stove, her heart pounding. His eyes said he was glad to see her. Despite the fact she too was happy to see him, he would have to come up with a solid explanation for his mysterious visit to Empire City.

In the next instant, Camille began to doubt she knew anything about this man. She heard him asking Patience if she could give him a few minutes in private. He said he had something important to discuss with her. Patience murmured her consent and the two of them left the cookhouse. Camille stood ramrod straight, stirring very carefully, as if one too many cycles with the wooden spoon would spoil the stew. The line of her mouth tightened. So her fear had been valid, she thought grimly. It was obvious he wasn't even going to wait for the divorce before he spoke to Patience about marriage. Never again would she trust a man with her heart . . . never again . . .

After supper, Seth caught Camille's arm as she walked beside his place at the table. "When you're finished here, I'd like to walk you to your cabin. There's a few things we need to talk about."

With her hands full of serving bowls, Camille couldn't shake him off, but she glared at him. "I'm tired. Maybe I'll feel like talking tomorrow night, or next week."

His brow rose at her sharp tone. "What's wrong with you?"

She tipped the bowl of stew over his head, and although it had very little left in it, there was enough brown gravy to soak his hair and dribble down his face. "Nothing, dear." Setting the bowl on the table, she took the dish towel that was tucked into the pocket of her apron and dropped it into his lap.

The few loggers who still remained snickered on their way out the door. Seth glared at them as he wiped the mess from his head and face. "I don't know what's gotten into you, woman, but—"

"Don't call me 'woman,' you skunk! My name is Camille—Camille Braden, in case you've forgotten," she snapped. Stomping over to the worktable, she slammed the bowls down.

Hastily, Phoebe slipped an arm around her sister-in-law. "Camille, honey, the three of us will take care of this. Why don't you go have a little rest?"

Angry tears stung her eyes. "I can't leave all this work—"

"Yes, you can. I'm the boss and I say so," Hallie said, siding with Phoebe.

Nodding, Camille took herself out the door, refusing to look at Seth, or anybody else for that matter. The cool evening air felt heavenly on her flushed cheeks. The stars and a sliver of moon lit the path to her cabin. As she crossed the bridge, the stream gurgled beneath her in a comforting way. Why in the world had she embarrassed herself like that? Her anger had spilled out so fast, she couldn't control it.

By the time she reached her cabin, she was angry again, this time at herself. She stripped down to her chemise and washed in cold water. She didn't know how she was going to face Seth and the others—especially Patience.

A knock on the door brought her thoughts up short. She put on her wrapper and belted it around the waist, thinking it was most likely Phoebe. Before she lifted the bar from the door, however, she asked who it was just to be on the safe side.

"It's your husband, Camille," came the dry reply from outside.

She crossed her arms over her chest and sniffed. "You don't act much like a husband."

"Let me in and I'll remedy that," he coaxed.

"Husbands tell their wives when they're going on trips," she persisted.

"Dammit, Camille, you weren't speaking to me."

She sighed. Sooner or later, she'd have to hear what he had to say. Lifting the bar from the door, she pulled it open. He moved to stand beside the fireplace. His hair was still damp from being washed, and he wore a clean red shirt. In his wake, he left a spicy, masculine scent in the air.

Camille sat down at the table. She wished she had a cup of coffee to hold in her trembling hands. Instead, she laced her fingers together in her lap. "I see you got the gravy out of your hair," she said.

"Had to soap it twice. I'll wager you'll have a hell of a time getting the grease out of that shirt come wash day," he said, a flicker of amusement in his gaze.

Camille stared at her hands. "I may not be here next wash day. I could get some word on Forrest, you know."

"I think I've located him," Seth said shortly.

Her head jerked up. "You've found him?" For some reason, she hadn't been expecting this. Not that she wasn't happy about it—she was. But all the same, her heart felt heavy and a dull ache was starting at the base of her skull.

Seth jammed his hands in his pockets and walked over to stand across from her, putting one booted foot on a chair. "A friend of Captain Jack's who runs a steamship in the Puget Sound area saw the poster and thought he might know a man fitting your brother's description. Captain Jack stopped on Friday to let me know his friend was supposed to be in Empire City this morning, but he never showed up."

The constriction in her chest eased. "So that's why you went to town. But we still don't know if it's him?" Restless all of a sudden, Camille got up and moved to stand in the place Seth had vacated beside the fire.

"No, but Captain Jack said his friend was pretty sure the fellow's name is Sinclair."

"So, what do we do now?" she asked in a small voice.

Seth came up behind her and lightly rested his hands on her shoulders. "We could make the trip up to Puget Sound to talk to this man, or wait for Captain Jack to carry messages back and forth whenever he gets a chance. If we decide to make the trip, however, I can't get away until December. The orders we've promised Sven Lang will take a while."

Camille wanted to lean back against the strength of his broad chest, but she hadn't yet asked the question that had been burning in her brain since yesterday. "I have work to do too. I've waited this many years, a few more months won't make any difference. Could you send a message with Captain Jack?"

Seth's hands had slid down to encircle her waist. His head dipped to nuzzle her neck and breathe deeply of her sweet-scented hair. "I took the liberty of doing it while I was in town," he said, gently drawing her back against him.

Camille closed her eyes and tried to resist the pull of his magnetism. "In the meantime, we wait . . ." she whispered, her mind on what he was doing rather than saying.

Seth brushed a warm kiss on her skin. "Uh-huh." He turned her in his arms, holding her against him with one strong arm, while the other hand slid inside her wrapper to cup a plump breast.

Camille trembled with a keen pleasure at his touch. Her

eyelids fluttered closed again. It seemed so terribly long since they'd made love, and she'd missed him so much. Seth's mouth descended to hers, his tongue prodding her lips apart and then plundering the sweet warm cavern of her mouth. Anger and worry were driven from her mind as she gave herself up to Seth's tender lovemaking. She moaned deep in her throat when his hand parted her robe and slid between her legs to stoke a fire there.

Camille felt as if her bones had turned to liquid, and her blood to fire. Her fingers entwined in his hair, fiercely holding him to her. She barely noticed when he picked her up and carried her to the bed. He laid her down and followed, loosening the belt of her wrapper. Pulling her chemise up, he gazed lovingly at her bare breasts. The nipples hardened before he even touched them with his mouth. "Oh, Camille, I've missed you," he said hoarsely. His hot, wet mouth made a blazing trail down her stomach to the juncture of her thighs.

Camille's breath came in fast, hard gasps. Her fingers gripped the sheet as if she would fly right up off the bed unless she held on. What his mouth was doing to her was exquisite, but she yearned to feel the hard length of him inside her. "Please, please . . . oh, Seth," she murmured.

Pulling back, he looked at her with glittering passion in his dark eyes. "I'll do my damnedest to please you," he whispered, working at the buttons of his pants.

A sound outside the door froze them both in a tableau of frustrated passion. The sound came again. It was Cooper's hearty laugh. Cursing roundly, Seth rebuttoned his pants while Camille jumped to her feet and closed her wrapper, hastily tying it. Seth moved to stand facing the fire to hide the obvious bulge in his pants. Camille sat down in a chair at the table just as the door swung open to admit Phoebe and Cooper.

The newcomers glanced from one to the other, and then at each other. Camille's cheeks were fiery and her hair disheveled. Seth's shirt was pulled loose from his pants on one side and he refused to face them. Clearing her throat, Phoebe said, "Oh, I'm sorry, Camille. We came to cheer you up, but since Seth is here—well, we'll just take a little walk while you two talk . . ."

Camille dipped her head. "Thanks, Phoebe," she said, blessing the other girl's thoughtfulness.

For once, Cooper didn't say a word, but followed Phoebe back out the door, closing it behind him. Seth turned. "I should have bolted the damned thing, Camille. I'm sorry."

Camille gave him a sad smile. "Don't apologize. It's for the best, I'm sure. We almost . . ."

"Made love? We are married, you know," he pointed out.

"But for how long?" She watched his face and waited almost breathlessly for his answer.

Chapter 17

Seth knew from the start if they found Forrest too soon, he might lose her. Why had this news come so quickly? He felt torn between his promise to let her go and his need to keep her. Regret etched sharp lines in his expression. "Maybe we could give it another try? I'd be willing if you would?"

Camille saw the uncertainty in his eyes. He was in love with Patience, but was willing to stay married out of duty, or honor, or worse—out of pity for her. She knew he was physically attracted to her, but he had a history with Patience, a strong bond, and they had probably shared passion as well. No, she wouldn't bind him to her with false strings. Summoning a brighter smile, she said lightly, "You're just afraid the quality of the meals will go down if I leave."

Seth didn't smile at her jest. "So your answer is no." He moved toward the door. "I have guard duty tonight, so I'd better get going."

Camille swallowed past the lump in her throat. "You'll be careful . . . won't you?"

He nodded and let himself out.

Camille and Phoebe were on their way to the cookhouse a few mornings later when they met Vladimir on the bridge. He paused for only a moment. "Gabe is sick. I must get Seth."

"What's wrong with him?" they asked in unison, but the Russian was well past them and headed for Cooper's cabin.

"Let's go see what we can do," Camille suggested.

"You go ahead. I'll go back and alert Hallie. I saw a light in her cabin when we started out. She may have more knowledge of doctoring than Seth does," Phoebe said.

When Camille got to the new bunkhouse, she knocked on the door. With twenty-some men living there, she didn't know what she would find. A logger she knew as Daniel answered the door. "Ma'am," he said, nodding politely.

"Vladimir said Gabe is sick. Could I . . . is everyone dressed?"

"Yes, ma'am, come on in." He stepped back. "We been up for a good half hour, all except Gabe. Nobody noticed him for a while."

He led her to a bunk at one end of the long room. Gabe had thrashed about until his covers were tangled hopelessly around his body. She placed her hand on his forehead. It was clammy with sweat, his skin hot.

"Miz Braden . . . I tried to get up . . ." he mumbled, his eyes glassy.

"Don't worry about getting up, Gabe, you're sick. How long have you felt bad?" She stooped down beside him.

He closed his eyes for a moment and tried to swallow. It seemed to be a painful process. Camille called for one of the men to bring a cup of water. When she'd raised his head and fed him a few swallows, he opened his eyes again. "A few days, I guess. Nothing real bad, except today."

His voice was weak, and she noticed something strange as she smoothed his hair back. There were bare, patchy spots. "How long has your hair been coming out, Gabe?"

"Few days. Since I been feelin' sick." He closed his eyes and seemed to drift off to sleep. Camille got to her feet just as the door opened and Seth and Cooper came in.

While Seth looked Gabe over, Camille told him what the young man had said. He nodded thoughtfully when she mentioned the hair loss. Turning to the others, who were gathered around the cast-iron stove in the middle of the room, Seth asked, "Anyone else been feeling sick lately?"

A young man with prematurely white hair named Jim Kalal spoke up. "Joshua Pepper's been lookin' mighty peaked this week. He was on guard duty last night."

Cooper looked at Seth. "Joshua usually helps Gabe with the oxen at night, doesn't he?"

"Yes. Anybody else, Jim?" Seth asked.

"No, sir. Not that I know of," he replied.

"All right, men. I'll send for the doctor, but in the meantime, I don't think there's anything to worry about. If this was contagious, there'd be more sick than two since you all sleep and eat in the same place," Seth told them, and then added, "Hallie's getting everything organized in the cookhouse before she has a look at Gabe, so you can all go over there now."

The men left, and Seth turned to Camille. "When you get to the cookhouse, tell Hallie to bring her medicine bag and cloths for bathing Gabe. His fever is pretty high."

His tone was sharp, and Camille wasn't sure if he was angry with her, or just worried about the patient. She nodded and walked away.

When she reached the door, Cooper caught up with her. Slipping an arm around her bent shoulders, he whispered, "Don't mind Seth, honey."

She gave him a wan smile. "I'm used to it, Coop. I'm just worried about Gabe. I truly hope it's not contagious like Seth said. I've seen fever sweep though Charleston before, killing young and old alike."

As they walked away from the building toward the cookhouse, Cooper assured her, "Try not to worry. I'm sending one of the men for the doctor."

"We'll make some soup today. Sick folks seem to be able to keep that down better—and plenty of hot tea," she offered.

"That'll help," he said, leaving her at the door of the cookhouse.

Before breakfast was half over, all hell broke loose. Cooper found Joshua Pepper dead in the barn, along with three oxen. There was no doubt the other oxen were sick as well. They were lying in their stalls, unable to get up. Seth sent a second man to town for the sheriff, the first man having left just thirty minutes before to bring back the doctor for Gabe. Since the rest of the men seemed to feel fit, they were sent to the woods to work. Seth and Cooper stayed in camp to bury the dead animals and help Hallie prepare Joshua for burial. After performing these tasks, the two men returned to the cookhouse for coffee.

"We'll have the funeral in the morning," Seth said, warming his hands around his cup.

Camille laid a comforting hand on his shoulder as she paused behind him to top off his cup from the large granite coffeepot. "Does he have any family?"

"Nobody around here. I believe he has a sister in Pennsylvania. There should be a letter or two in his things that'll tell us something." Seth put his hand over hers for a moment.

Hallie and Phoebe were busy with a mountain of bread dough at the worktable, and Patience was taking a turn sitting with Gabe in the bunkhouse.

Cooper threaded his fingers through his blond hair in a gesture of frustration. "When I pack up his things I'll look for a letter."

Camille moved around the table and refilled his cup. "I'll help after we get lunch out of the way."

"Sure. Maybe when it's your turn to sit with Gabe we could do it," he suggested.

Camille bit her lip and looked at Seth. "You don't think Gabe will . . ."

"No, honey. He'll be all right," Seth said with more assurance than he felt. "I think his fever's down a little from this morning, and with any luck, the doctor will be here before nightfall."

"I've never seen anything quite like this," Cooper said, raising his worried gaze to Phoebe, who was working quietly beside Hallie across the room. "I just hope to God it's not contagious because everybody in this camp will have been exposed to it."

Seth's brow creased in a frown. "What's strange about the animals is that the mules seem fine. Just the oxen are sick."

Camille went back to work on the vegetable soup she was making. Ike Raymond had brought potatoes, tomatoes, carrots and onions from his garden just the day before. Ike hadn't mentioned any trouble at his place, Camille mused to herself. It was frightening to realize there was something going on they knew little about, and it was deadly enough to kill.

Seth hooked the mules to one of the wagons and helped the women load a huge pot of beans, several loaves of fresh-baked bread and a bucket of coffee to take to the men in the woods. Cooper stayed behind to sit with Gabe. Seth drove the wagon over the skid road to the section where the men were working.

When everyone's appetite had been slaked and the coffee bucket emptied, Seth drove the women back to camp so they could begin supper preparations.

A venison stew was soon simmering in a big pot on the stove, and Hallie was baking an apple cake to tempt Gabe's appetite. Just after they'd returned from the woods, a gentle rain had begun to come down, dropping a misty gray curtain over their world.

At midafternoon, Camille slipped her brown shawl over her shoulders and took the cloth-covered plate Hallie pressed into her hands. "Tell the boy I'll be by to see him before supper time," Hallie urged, and then eyed Camille's light wool shawl. "Land sakes, girl, yer gonna get wet. I hope you brought a canvas mackinaw."

Camille shook her head. "I'll be fine." Making her way outside, she hadn't gone five yards when she met Seth coming around the building carrying a load of firewood.

When he saw her, he frowned. "You'll catch your death in this rain. Where's your mackinaw?" Even as he asked, he was dropping the wood and pulling off his canvas coat to drape over her shoulders. Taking off his wide-brimmed hat, he plopped it on her head.

One minute he snapped her head off, the next he fretted over her well-being. She hardly knew how to gauge his moods anymore. "Thank you, but you'll get wet now."

"I get wet every day in the woods, but you're not used to it," he said sternly. His coat nearly swallowed her, and all he could see beneath the hat brim were those big blue eyes. He had the strongest urge to kiss her senseless.

"The only thing I have is my blue velvet mantle for the cold, but this rain would simply ruin it," she protested, and then continued on to the bunkhouse.

He rolled his eyes heavenward and then called out, "I'll get you a canvas coat from the supply room."

Camille was still smiling as she hung up the coat and hat on a peg in the bunkhouse. Cooper was halfway down the long room standing beside a bunk. Camille made her way to him, glancing toward Gabe's bed. He was asleep and seemed to be resting comfortably. "How's his fever?" she whispered.

Cooper nodded. "It's down. I think he's getting better." He handed an envelope to her. "Josh's sister wrote him this summer. Could you write to her, Camille? I know I should do it, or Seth, but she probably couldn't read our hen scratches. And besides, you'll be able to say the right things to her, being a woman.''

Camille took the letter and slipped it in the pocket of her gingham dress. ''I didn't know Josh that well, but I'll try. Maybe you or Seth could help me with it?''

''Sure. What's under that napkin? It smells mighty good.'' He reached for the plate, but she slapped his hand away.

''It's apple cake. Hallie made it especially for Gabe. If you're nice to her, though, she'll give you a slice with a cup of coffee.'' Putting the plate down on the bunk, Camille asked, ''Anything I can do here?''

''Not really. Josh had very little, and I've got it all packed up in his bag. I'll send it to his sister the first chance I get.''

Camille looked at the small leather bag that was only half filled and felt sad. There were a few articles of clothing, a pipe, a pouch of tobacco, and a daguerreotype. She picked up the picture and recognized the man as being Josh, a younger Josh. There was a plain-looking woman with a nice smile standing beside him, and a boy who looked to be about fifteen. They were posed in front of a small farmhouse. ''Josh's wife and son?'' she asked.

''Yes. They died about ten years ago in a freak snowstorm. Josh didn't talk about them much, but once he told me what happened. He sold his farm and came West. He just couldn't live in Pennsylvania anymore, he said, too many memories.'' Cooper sighed and rubbed his chin. ''The longer I live, the less I understand about life. Like why did the Good Lord take Josh's wife and son away when they were a happy family? And then there's my Uncle John and Annabelle, who are miserable, yet they stay together because of money and political power. It's a puzzle.''

Camille touched his arm. ''I've never known life to be fair, but in this case, Josh is with his wife and son now. They're a family again.''

Cooper leaned down and kissed the top of her head. ''You're sweet. I wonder if Seth realizes how lucky he is to have you.''

Camille placed the picture back in the bag and retrieved the covered plate from the bed. ''Seth seems a little confused at the moment. But I suppose time will take care of it.''

Turning away, she started toward her patient. ''You'd better get over to the cookhouse for that apple cake before the men get back from the woods,'' she advised.

Sheriff Wyman and Dr. Grammet arrived on horseback that evening with the two men who had been sent to fetch them. The doctor examined Gabe and then took a look at Joshua's body.

Seth and Cooper brought the doctor and the sheriff back to the cookhouse where the women were waiting to feed them a late supper.

After his first few bites, the young sheriff smiled at Hallie, who was sitting across the table from him. ''This is the best venison stew I ever tasted, ma'am. If I wasn't committed to the law, I believe I'd ask for a job here just to eat your cooking every day.''

Hallie grinned. ''Are you flirtin' with me, young man? 'Cause if you are, I have to be truthful and tell you I'm old enough to be yer older sister.''

The doctor, an older man with a bushy mustache and a balding pate, spoke up. ''No use buttering her up, Bob. I've been trying to get her to marry me since the first summer she spent in Empire City. She won't budge.''

Hallie got up to get the coffeepot from the stove, and snorted in an unladylike way. ''What an offer! Doc's just tryin' to git my cookin' and nursin' services free of charge. At least workin' here, Seth and Coop pay me good and I get all the free compliments I can use from the loggers."

"A small-town doctor doesn't make much money, but I'd make up for that in love and devotion," he insisted with a grin.

"Love for my pies and devotion to my venison stew," Hallie clarified. Everyone at the table laughed.

Camille took advantage of a lull in the conversation to ask the doctor, "Is Gabe going to be all right? What do you think is wrong with him?"

"The boy seems to be coming along fine. In my opinion, I would say he'll be all right in a few days. As to what's wrong with him, and what killed Mr. Pepper, it's mercury poisoning. Before I came to Oregon, I lived in a mining town in California. The mining company was dumping their waste in the river that was the main water source for the town. Needless to say, everyone began to get sick, and a few died before I figured out what was wrong and persuaded the company to stop poisoning the drinking supply."

"But, Dr. Grammet, there are no mining operations around here. How could they have been poisoned by mercury?" Phoebe asked.

"It could be that someone deliberately poisoned the pond with the stuff," Cooper said grimly. "Since several of the oxen died, as well as Josh, we figured it had to be something they all came in contact with. The only thing would be the pond water."

"That's a fair guess, but we'll know for sure when I test the sample I took," the doctor added.

Seth held out his cup for more coffee and Hallie filled it. "Going on this theory," he said, "we figure Joshua used pond water to make coffee at the barn all the time, so he would get a greater concentration of the mercury in his body than Gabe, who said he drank a cup of Josh's coffee only occasionally. Which is why Gabe is sick, but not dead."

Patience asked, "Why did the oxen die and not the mules? Don't they all drink from the pond?"

"Mules are much smarter than oxen. They sensed something was wrong with the pond and found their drinking water elsewhere. With as much rain as we get, there are puddles and streams everywhere," Seth explained.

"I'll bet a dollar to a doughnut it was them Slidell brothers," Hallie said, pushing the sliced apple cake toward their two guests. "Help yerself, boys."

"We don't have any proof, and without something solid, Sheriff Wyman can't do anything to them," Seth pointed out, his voice bitter.

"But a man died . . . that's murder," Camille exclaimed.

The sheriff nodded regretfully. "I'm going over to question them, but they'll lie to protect each other. And I doubt their men would tell me anything, even if they knew for sure. Some would be too scared, and some are as rotten as the Slidell brothers."

Silence reigned for a few minutes as the reality of the situation bore down on them. Finally, Hallie rose and began collecting the dirty plates. The other three women got up to help. Camille shivered as she thought of how easy it was for Jake and Owen to slip through the night to their camp and perform their deadly tricks. And there was nothing Seth and Cooper could do about it unless they caught them red-handed. What would they do next? she wondered.

There were no more accidents or suspicious happenings in the Braden-Maxwell camp for the next two weeks. There was, however, a great deal of work going on. Seth immediately put some men to building a fence around the polluted pond and digging another one near the barn. The rest of the loggers went to the woods before daybreak, and didn't return until dark. The Lang order had to be filled, as well as orders Seth had procured from two of the mining towns in the territory. With the discovery of gold in several places, towns were springing up overnight, and turning into large rowdy cities. The demand for lumber was enormous, the prices going up every day.

Joshua Pepper had been laid to rest under a giant fir tree at the northern edge of the camp, and Gabe had recovered in a week. Seth made a trip to town to purchase more oxen, and Cooper spent long hours at the sawmill, overseeing its operation.

For the women, the days ran together with hardly a break to let them know there was more to life than cooking, dirty dishes and laundry.

Camille began to live for Sunday, her only day of rest. When it arrived, she took her sketch pad and charcoal and headed to the dock to sit in the weak sunshine. She couldn't believe her luck. It had rained every day for two weeks, but this morning, she'd opened her eyes to a world that was light and dry. She slipped out, leaving Phoebe to some well-deserved sleep. Hallie always made the coffee and sliced the ham and bread for the Sunday morning breakfast, leaving the other three women to do as they pleased. It was wonderful to have the break, Camille thought, sitting down on the weathered dock. She hugged the canvas coat closer to her wool dress as a brisk breeze blew across the water, lifting her loose auburn hair off the collar.

The whole left side of the cove was filled with giant logs, roped loosely together, awaiting a ship to carry them to San Francisco to Sven Lang's sawmill. Despite the problems in camp, the work had progressed at a feverish pace. The men had rallied to help get the orders out on time. Usually there was a high-pitched whining in the air, coming from the big, hungry saws in the mill, but today, they were resting, silent.

Camille made a quick sketch of the sawmill and the skid road beside it, stretching from the water's edge to deep into the woods. She was pleased with it, and decided it might make a nice gift for Cooper for Christmas if she framed it. The sawmill was essentially his domain, while Seth ran the logging operation in the woods. The sight of the log-filled cove was so awe-inspiring, she decided to make a sketch of it also. Moving back up the incline for a better view, she perched on a stump and began working. She had almost finished when a lump of debris floated to the surface between two of the huge logs and caught her eye. The river traffic was brisk, not to mention the waterway fed into the Pacific Ocean. Camille was used to seeing all sorts of flotsam drifting by.

Placing her things on the stump, she moved around the incline until she had a better view of the object. Gooseflesh rose on her skin and her scalp prickled when she saw an arm extended from the lump. Walking cautiously down the hill, she circled a bit further and saw what looked like a lump of matted hair connected to the object. Her heart thumped harder as she backed away. She knew what it was, but prayed she was wrong. As she turned, the reflection of something shiny flashed in her eyes and she jerked her gaze toward the woods, catching a glimpse of another flash. Gathering her wide skirt in her hands, she raced up the hill. She couldn't shake the feeling someone was watching her from the woods, making her a moving target.

Reaching the cookhouse porch, she rang the dinner bell vigorously, wanting every soul in camp to come running. She didn't care if it was Sunday and the men were sleeping.

"Land sakes! What's all the commotion about?" Hallie demanded, throwing open the door.

Camille seized the older woman's arm and gasped, "Oh, Hallie! I think there's a body in the cove . . . and somebody was watching me from the woods."

By then, the men were at the cookhouse in various stages of dress—some slipping into shirts, others pulling suspenders up and most carrying their caulked boots, not having had time to put them on. Vladimir leaped up on the porch and drew a trembling Camille under the protection of his arm. "Somebody is bothering you? Tell Vladimir what's going on."

"Please, see if there's somebody in the woods beyond the sawmill. I saw something there," she begged, afraid if they didn't hurry, the intruder would get away.

"Camille?" Seth's voice held a hint of alarm. He and Cooper were approaching at a run from the direction of their cabin. Phoebe and Patience were following, wearing wrappers and looking sleepy and disheveled.

The sound of Seth's voice brought soothing relief to Camille's spirit. She flung herself into his arms when he reached the porch and repeated her story. He held her tightly for a moment before lifting her back onto the porch. "Most of you men come with me to search the woods. A couple of you go with Coop to see what's in the cove." Turning, he urged, "You ladies keep the gun handy."

Phoebe put her arm around Camille. "How awful for you, honey."

"I just hope I'm wrong, and it's not a body in the water," Camille said, unable to take her eyes off Seth as he and the men moved toward the wooded area across the cove. Who was there? Did they have a gun? she wondered, growing alarmed again. What if something happened to Seth? Her teeth began to chatter uncontrollably.

"Let's go inside and have a cup of coffee," Hallie said, "I think we need it and it won't do no good to stand here and watch." Hallie left them to follow her, and was pouring the coffee when they made their way to the worktable.

Camille felt a little better as the strong brew warmed her inside and out. She stopped shaking and began helping Hallie slice bread, needing something to occupy her hands.

Cooper and Gabe returned twenty minutes later, their faces grim. "It was Ned Johnson. He and Roy Ellis had guard duty last night. Roy said when he got to the bunkhouse at daybreak and didn't see Ned, he thought he was over here in the cookhouse getting a cup of coffee."

Camille swallowed tightly. "He's . . . dead?"

Cooper accepted a cup of coffee from Hallie and nodded. "His neck's been broken and it doesn't look like an accident."

Phoebe's face went pale. "Where's Seth? Are he and the others back?"

Cooper moved to slip an arm around her shoulders. "He'll be fine. He has a gun and knows the woods like the back of his hand."

Camille was not comforted by Cooper's words. Whoever killed Ned and Joshua could very easily kill again. She knew deep down the killer was in the woods beyond the sawmill this morning . . . and he'd been watching her.

"Calm down, Annabelle!" Paul hissed, looking up and down the second-floor hallway before jerking her inside and shutting the bedroom door. "Are you crazy? Do you want the servants to become suspicious now, after we've been so careful?"

She clutched the lapels of his coat, her eyes wild. "You don't understand!" she wailed.

Paul slapped her face smartly, startling her to a stunned silence. "Lower your voice," he ordered.

Annabelle whimpered and collapsed against his chest, tears flowing now. He rubbed her back soothingly and held her. "Now, what's this all about? I've never seen you lose control before."

She wiped her eyes with the handkerchief he pressed in her hand. "The bastard made a new will and didn't tell me. I found it in his drawer a little while ago when I was choosing clothes for him to be buried in."

Alarm flickered in Paul's eyes, and his fingers tightened on her arms. "I take it he doesn't name you the beneficiary?"

"You're hurting me," she snapped, keeping her voice low this time. When he eased the pressure, she continued. "One dollar and a run-down shack on State Street is what he left me.

The rest, which is considerably more than I'd even realized, goes to his nephew, Cooper.''

Letting her go, Paul locked the door and strode over to a table that held a bottle of brandy and some tumblers. Pouring a liberal amount in one, he stared out the window at the manicured back lawn of the mansion. ''Do you think the lawyer has seen it, or could it have perhaps been a last-minute thought of John's?''

''It's a copy . . . with John's and his lawyer's signatures on it. Why it wasn't in his safe, I don't know!'' she said, following him to the table and helping herself to the brandy.

''Either John was too sick to get down to his study with it, or maybe he knew you had the combination and didn't want you to see it,'' Paul said, taking a large, fortifying swallow of the amber liquid.

''The date on it was Tuesday of last week. That was the only day I left the house in the last three weeks. I've been trying to play the devoted wife. He must have sent one of the servants for his lawyer the minute I left,'' she said, her voice bitter.

Paul took her arm and led her to one of the overstuffed chairs near the bed. ''Just be calm and drink your brandy. I've got to think. There has to be some way around this.''

Paul paced for a while, then stopped to gaze out the window again. Turning abruptly, he asked, ''Will Hanover be reading the will soon?''

Annabelle blinked. ''Well, no, I think he said the reading would take place when all the parties involved were present. What difference does it make?''

''All the difference in the world,'' he said, a smile curving his mouth. ''I'm going to persuade Hanover to let me carry the message personally to Cooper in Oregon. When I get there, I'll see he has a fatal accident.''

Annabelle sat up straighter. ''Won't it look suspicious? What excuse will you use for going there?''

Finishing off his brandy, he placed the glass on the lace-covered table. "I'll be going to see the woman I'm in love with. She wrote me that she was very unhappy. I, of course, will race to rescue her. Plausible story, don't you think? Anyway, it's what I'll tell the lawyer."

"You're talking about that Sinclair creature, aren't you?" Annabelle's eyes lit with admiration. "It might just work. That is, if Hanover hasn't sent a telegram to Cooper yet. You know, they do have some modern conveniences in the wilderness."

"I don't think he would have. You just sent a message to him after I signed the death certificate this morning. He'll probably show up this afternoon to pay his respects to you and discuss some business. I'll come back this afternoon to check on you—you did get hysterical this morning, the servants can vouch for that—and I'll have a little talk with Hanover."

Annabelle smiled and clapped her hands. "Bravo, Paul, bravo! Had you been my leading man on the stage, we would have had the theatrical world at our feet."

He gave a rakish grin and bowed at the waist with a sweeping gesture. "Thank you, m'lady."

Chapter 18

"Oh, Seth, I made such a mistake by marrying Antonio, I know that now," Patience wailed softly, her tears wetting the front of his shirt. He held her and stroked her hair in a soothing way.

"We all make mistakes, honey. What counts is how we live with them and go on with our lives."

"Can you forgive me for hurting you?" she asked in a tremulous voice.

"There's nothing to forgive. I left you dangling for six years, and there's no excuse for that. If anyone is to blame for what happened, it's me. Let's forget about the past. We've got a bright future ahead of us. With the word you got from Mr. Roman, there's nothing stopping you from marrying again— to the right man this time."

Camille felt as if someone had just twisted a knife in her heart. She stood in the shadow of a tall stack of sawed lumber, and had a clear view inside the office in the sawmill. She'd done the supper dishes and decided to get caught up on the ledger books. She hadn't realized anyone was in the office until she heard Seth and Patience talking. Before she could either leave or make her presence known, her attention was caught by their conversation. Somehow, she'd held onto a slim hope her marriage could be salvaged. Turning away, she fled the building, running up the skid road. She couldn't face anyone at the moment . . . solitude was what she needed, and time to pull herself back together.

"She has to be somewhere in camp. Camille knows it's dangerous to wander off, especially with what's been happening lately," Seth growled. He refused to acknowledge the sharp taste of fear in his mouth.

"Phoebe's looked everywhere for her. When she couldn't find her, she came to get me," Cooper insisted, worry lines creasing his brow.

Seth's heart thumped against his ribs. "Did you try the bunkhouse? She might have gone there to tend to an injury, or—"

Phoebe laid her hand on his arm. "I checked there, and the cookhouse, the springhouse and Hallie's cabin. We were on our way to the sawmill."

"We just came from there," Patience said, her eyes wide.

Seth's face darkened. "Ring the dinner bell, Coop. I want every man in camp looking for her."

"But it's getting dark, Seth. We'll never find her—"

"I don't give a damn how dark it is, we're going into the woods. We'll take torches," Seth growled. "I'll get more ammunition. Tell the men to bring their guns."

Phoebe, Hallie and Patience gathered in the cookhouse, made a large pot of coffee and began making bread dough. Hallie said it would give them something to do with their hands while they worried. The men took torches and guns and fanned out into the woods.

* * *

Camille felt the warmth of the fire on her skin and the flicker of light behind her eyelids before she came fully awake. As she struggled to get beyond the edge of sleep, she stretched her limbs, and encountered something very soft against her skin. Maybe she was dreaming, she thought. Blankets were not that soft, not like the fluff of a cloud on a summer day, or what she imagined it would feel like. A rank smell drifted under her nose. It was a mixture of body odor, decay and rotting wood. If she was dreaming, could she separate and identify smells like that? she wondered.

A low grunt sounded near her ear, causing her to start. Her eyes fluttered open, and panic closed her throat off before she could utter a sound. Owen Slidell's dirty, bearded face was just inches from hers.

Camille jerked back, pressing herself against the wall. He gave another grunt, cocking his head to the side, as if he'd asked some sort of question and was waiting for an answer. Camille's heart was slamming against her ribs so hard, she found it difficult to breathe. When he reached out a big, dirty hand toward her, she gasped and pushed herself up into a sitting position. "No! Don't touch me."

Obediently, he rose and moved away from the bed to stand across the room. Relief washed over Camille in waves. She eyed him warily for a minute before deciding he would stay there. Owen was the creature she'd seen running away from the springhouse. No wonder she hadn't recognized him! The first time she'd seen Owen, he'd been reasonably clean, his long hair pulled back with a rawhide string, and he'd been dressed like a lumberjack. Now, like the day at the springhouse, his hair was loose, dirty and wild. His strange garment was made of bark and canvas, while fur boots encased his feet.

A quick glance around the room told her there was no avenue of escape. Owen was standing near the only door, and the only window was also on his side of the room. Where were they? She'd never seen this place before. It consisted of one room, crudely built and weathered with age. There was a fire in the fireplace and a rough table and two chairs.

How had she gotten here? she wondered. Her head was throbbing, and she raised a hand to her temple to massage it, only to find her hair matted and stuck to the skin. Examining the rest of the area, she found sore spots, more matted hair and what she could only surmise was dried blood. What in heaven's name had happened? Had Owen attacked her?

She must have made an involuntary sound because Owen started forward. The sheer size of him, not to mention his frightening appearance, was enough to send her cowering to the corner. But she summoned some Sinclair courage and held up her hand. "Stop!"

Again, he obeyed. Camille decided she'd try something. "I want to go home, Owen . . . Could you take me to the logging camp?"

Immediately, he shook his head, several grunts passing his twisted lips, but nothing she could understand. Except for the fact he was saying no. He tried to smile, one side of his face cooperating, but not the other. The effort was grotesque. He didn't seem to notice the spittle that dribbled into his beard. When his grunting speech came to an end, he turned and let himself out the door. Camille heard an ominous sound, but refused to acknowledge it until she climbed off the bed and tried the door for herself. It had been barricaded from the outside. She moved to the window and pulled the wooden shutter open. On the outside was another shutter that refused to budge.

She shivered, from uncertainty as much as from the chilly night air. Feeling a bit dizzy, she moved back to the bed and pulled the cover off. It was the soft pelt of a bear. She hadn't been dreaming after all, she thought wryly. The fur was black, soft and beautiful, but it smelled rank. The cabin was filthy,

Owen was filthy, so it was no wonder his bedding was not exactly fresh.

It was warm, though, and she wrapped it around her shoulders and sat down in front of the fire. Memory of what happened came back to her in a flash. She'd run away from the sawmill, from the hurtful things Seth and Patience were saying. When her side began to ache, she'd stopped, looked around and realized it was almost dark. Reason seeped in, leaving her apprehensive of the predicament she found herself in. The silence in the deep woods was deafening . . . and frightening. There were no birds, or squirrels, harmless comforting little creatures. However, deer and bear inhabited this land of the lumberjack, and occasionally a mountain cat.

Turning back, she began retracing her steps along the skid road. That was when it happened. In the profound silence, with only her hammering heartbeat for company, she remembered a sudden, loud crack, a splintering of wood. Looking up, she caught a glimpse of the dead limb falling toward her. Then the world had gone completely black.

Seth had told her about this hazard of the woods; he'd called them widow makers because they'd killed more men than anything else. She had been lucky. As dubious as she was about Owen, she shuddered to think about what would have happened to her if he hadn't found her. Where had he gone and what did he have planned? Would anyone be able to find her? She shivered and moved closer to the fire. Even a small amount of warmth and light was comforting.

The sound of a creaking door brought Camille awake in an instant. She rose hastily from the floor in front of the fireplace and stared apprehensively at Owen as he lumbered inside with a bucket in one hand and a skinned rabbit in the other. She backed away when he moved toward the fireplace. He grunted, putting the bucket down at her feet. She inched toward the open doorway while he built up the fire and set the rabbit to roasting above it on a stick.

Leaning on the doorframe, Camille glanced out. She could make a run for it, but he would catch her before she cleared the yard. It helped, though, just to see the outside world, even if the sun was a little weak. At least it was not raining ... at the moment. A few clouds floated by in the small patch of sky she could see from the clearing where the cabin stood. At the edge, however, the fir trees grew thick, blotting out the rest of the world. Turning, she caught Owen watching her, a look of adoration in his eyes. Swallowing her apprehension, she said, "I need to ... go outside, Owen. Do you understand what I mean?"

He cocked his head to one side and then the other, like an inquisitive bird.

"Is there a necessary house out back? An outhouse?" She was mortified to have to ask for this privilege, but he might decide to lock her up again and there'd be no chance.

A spark of understanding flickered in his eyes. When he reached her side, he took her arm and pulled her along after him. After the dirty cabin, she didn't know what to expect, but was relieved and then dismayed to find he was leaving her at the edge of the woods to complete her business. She was self-conscious to be doing private things in the open with only a tree for cover, but at the same time it was most likely a cleaner place than a privy would have been.

When she finished, she walked back to Owen, who had waited with his back turned at the edge of the clearing. Inside the cabin, she found a dusty dishpan on a shelf and poured water into it from the bucket. After she washed her hands and face and dried them on the tail of her skirt, she threw the dirty water out the front door. Sitting down on the bed in the corner, she wished she had a clean cloth to tend the wound on her head, and a hairbrush, but at the moment, she thought it would be better to leave her wound alone. Her eyes were drawn to the rabbit sizzling on the spit over the fire. Her stomach rumbled hungrily and she yearned for a cup of hot coffee. Owen turned the rabbit and left the cabin without looking at her. He barred the door, leaving her to wonder where his business took him, and when he'd return.

Camille got up and walked around the room, looking into every nook and cranny she could find. She didn't know what she was looking for, but she had to do something. Without finding anything but dirt and cobwebs, she moved back to her seat on the bed once more. She had barely settled herself when Owen returned. He was carrying another wooden bucket, and plunked it down on the table. Taking the spit from the fire, he dropped the charred rabbit on the table.

Gathering her courage, Camille moved to sit in one of the chairs. "What do you plan to do with me, Owen? There will be people out looking for me, and they might be angry if they find out you wouldn't let me go."

He moved to her side, and she couldn't tell if he had understood her. His eyes were strangely vacant, but he lifted a big hand and stroked the back of her head as if she were a treasured pet.

It took all her willpower to hold still and not jerk away from his touch. "You can't keep me here forever, Owen. Don't you see that? If you take me back, I'll tell Seth how you helped me when I was hurt."

This time he grunted, and it didn't sound like an agreeable answer to her question. His hand dropped away abruptly and he began to pull the rabbit apart, leaving part of it on the table for her while he carried a haunch to the corner, where he hunkered down and ate noisily.

Camille tried not to think of how dirty his hands were as she ate her portion of the meat. She was too hungry to worry about it, and heaven only knows when she'd get to eat again. He ambled over after a few minutes, dropping his bones on the floor, and turned the bucket upside down on the tabletop.

It was half filled with blackberries. By the time he ate his fill, there was a dark blue stain on his face and hands.

Camille ate some of the juicy berries and then poured more water in the pan to wash up, wondering what was to come next. Did he plan to keep her a prisoner in this hovel? She couldn't bear to be locked up day after day. Turning abruptly, she said, "Please, Owen, take me back to where you found me and I'll find my own way to camp."

His eyes grew fierce, and she knew he understood what she was saying. A low growl rose up out of his throat, causing Camille to take a step back. He reached out and with very little effort, knocked the table end over end. It landed sideways against the wall.

Frightened by this unexpected violence, Camille ran out the open doorway and started across the clearing, but before she got very far, a huge hand caught her by the shoulder and yanked her to a stop. She clawed at his hand, but he swung her up into his arms and carried her back to the cabin. He set her on her feet and gave her a push toward the bed, grunting and gesturing with his hands.

"Stay away from me," she cried, a horrible vision crowding into her mind of what might come next.

Owen pushed her down on the bed and stepped back, grunting something. He turned and moved toward the door.

Although relieved, she grew frantic thinking about being locked up again . . . and for how long? "Where are you going—don't do this!" He kept going, and she threw out one last shot. "Does Jake know you have me here?" She didn't quite understand why she asked it, except she was hoping deep down that Owen was afraid of his brother and would let her go.

Abruptly, Owen turned and his eyes had gone from angry to guarded. He made a growling sound.

"If he knew, would he punish you?" she persisted.

Owen's mouth opened and closed, his face contorting with

effort. "Jake . . . hurt . . . you." With that grim pronouncement, he went out, slamming the door.

Camille wrapped her arms around her waist and rocked back and forth. For Owen to make the effort to speak words instead of unintelligible grunts was serious. There was no doubt he was telling the truth. He knew his brother better than she did. And even though she had been afraid of Jake the first time she met him, Owen's warning sounded ominous.

She simply had to get away. The thought of Jake showing up was more than she could handle. Getting off the bed, she gazed slowly around the room again, searching for anything that might help her escape. Despair washed over her when she came up with nothing. Without some sort of tool, how could she ever hope to break through the heavy wooden door or window? Unable to be still, she paced. On her tenth trip past the fireplace, she noticed how one stick of wood protruded from the fire. The other end of it was burning brightly. It could work, she thought with guarded excitement.

She ran to the window and opened the inside shutter, and then dashed back for the stick of burning wood. She laid it against the outside shutter and thanked the Good Lord above that the shutter was dry and would burn. Her stomach knotted as she watched.

Several things could go wrong. Owen could come back and catch her, or the room could fill with smoke before she secured an opening to escape, or the fire could blaze up, causing the roof to collapse . . .

Standing back, she watched the flames lick around the shutter and then catch hold. One way or the other, she would be free soon.

Seth returned to camp with the search party at daybreak only because Cooper had pressured him into doing so. Seth wanted to remain in the woods, cover more territory; anything but return empty-handed.

While the men fortified themselves with strong coffee and breakfast, Seth and Cooper hitched four mules to the small wagon. "You don't need to come with me, Coop."

"Yes, I do. You'll kill Slidell and then Sheriff Wyman will have to put you in jail and I'll have to look for a new partner. Frankly, it would be too much trouble to find someone who'll do all the work and put up with me too."

Seth swung up onto the wagon seat. A ghost of a smile curved his lips as he waited for Cooper to climb up beside him. "I'll agree," Seth said. "But seriously, I don't want you to get between me and Slidell. You know as well as I do he's behind everything that's been going on here."

Cooper took his seat. "Yeah, I know, but I can't let my best friend get into trouble over scum like Slidell."

Seth released the brake lever with his boot heel and flicked the reins, setting the mules in motion. "If Slidell doesn't tell me where Camille is, I'll beat him within an inch of his life."

Cooper nodded, bracing himself with one leg. "That sounds fair to me."

Seth drove the mules as hard as they could travel over the river road. In little more than a half hour, they arrived at the Slidell camp. The ax men had gone to the woods long before, but the whine of the saws indicated life inside the sawmill.

Seth left the wagon alongside the loading dock and they entered the building at the south end. The interior was dim, but Seth unerringly made his way between stacks of fresh-cut boards and past curious mill workers. Cooper stayed right behind him. In the center of the building, Seth found what he was looking for—Slidell's office.

The door was open and the burly, bearded man sat behind a rough-hewn desk. Without warning, Seth reached across the span and grabbed Jake by the shirtfront, pulling him hard against the edge.

Jake's initial smirk fell away and his face flushed an angry red. "Wha . . . what in hell do you think you're doing, Braden?" His big, meaty hands automatically came up to clamp onto Seth's wrists, but before he could loosen the grip, Seth hauled him across the desktop.

"Something I should have done a long time ago," Seth growled as a surprised Slidell struggled to gain his balance and papers flew in every direction.

One of Slidell's henchmen had followed the two men through the building and when he saw Seth's action, he reached for his gun. Cooper pointed his .45 at the man's midsection. "Take it easy, fella. We just want a word or two with your boss. If he cooperates, we won't hurt him." The husky, middle-aged man with stringy blond hair lifted both hands in front of him in surrender.

Seth gave Slidell a shove and stepped back. "Where's Camille?"

Jake got slowly to his feet, his eyes glacial. "I'll kill you for this, Braden."

"You mean like you did Ned Johnson?"

"That was clean and painless. I wanna see you suffer," Jake spat out, his hands fisted at his sides.

Seth's brows rose. "Careful, Jake. There are witnesses here."

"My man won't tell—will ya, Shorty? See there, Shorty never heard nothin'. As for Maxwell here . . ." Slidell turned his head slowly, fixing Cooper with a cold look. "He's a dead man just like you, Braden. Dead men don't tell tales."

Seth wanted to beat Slidell to a pulp, but he got an iron grip on his temper. "I asked you where my wife is, you no-good bastard."

"I hear tell she don't share your bed. Maybe she left you for a man who could give her what you ain't." Slidell watched Seth's expression as he threw out the insult, and lunged to the left as Braden came after him.

There wasn't enough room for Jake to move out of range

completely, for the desk stood in the way. Seth landed on top of Slidell, his fist smashing into the heavier man's face. "You dirty scum," Seth growled, drawing back his fist for another blow.

Using the desk for leverage, Jake grabbed Seth's shirtfront and pushed with all his strength. Cooper kept one eye on the two combatants and one eye on Slidell's men, who had been gathering outside the office.

Jake followed Seth as he fell backward, and drove a fist into Seth's gut. For a few seconds, Seth felt as if his stomach had been turned inside out, and before he could block the blow, Jake's fist smashed into his jaw. With a strength born of desperation, Seth shoved Jake off and scrambled to his knees. Bringing his fist up with all his might, Seth landed a blow to Jake's jaw that rolled the man's eyes back in his head. He tumbled over like a mighty fir.

Cooper lifted an eyebrow. "Good work, but now how will we get any information out of him?"

Seth hauled himself to his feet and winced at the throbbing places on his body. A trickle of blood ran from the corner of his split mouth. "He doesn't intend to tell us anything, or if he did, it would be a lie." Wiping his mouth on the back of his hand, he glanced at Slidell's man, who stood just outside the doorway. "You, come in here." When the man stepped inside, Seth said, "Tell the others to get back to work unless they'd like some trouble."

Cooper gave the order instead, and they moved away without any argument. He stepped inside and grinned at Seth. "Nothing like absolute loyalty to the boss, now is there?"

Slidell's man glanced down at Jake's unconscious form, and then back up at Seth. "He ain't payin' us enough to git killed over a woman."

Seth's eyes narrowed. "Then I suggest you give me the information I want."

"I ain't seen or heard of no woman around here, and that's the truth," the man said, keeping a wary eye on his boss.

"Where's Owen?" Cooper asked.

"The idiot ain't been around for a few days, but I heard the boss tell him to keep an eye on your camp. Can I go now? I don't know nothin' else, I swear. If the boss knew I told you this much, he'd gut me like a salmon."

"You'd better be telling the truth, Shorty, or there won't be any place for you to hide," Cooper said. The man gave another furtive glance at the huge man on the floor, who was beginning to stir.

Seth nodded and drew his gun. "You're going to walk with us out to the wagon, Shorty. And then you're going to come back in and tell the men to keep on working, right?"

Shorty nodded, eager to get out of the office before Slidell woke up.

As the room filled with smoke, Camille ripped a layer from her petticoat, dipped it in the water bucket, and pressed it against her nose. The wooden shutter at the window blazed, but as yet, the opening was not large enough to climb through. *Patience,* she told herself. She must have patience.

She stood in the middle of the room, one of the chairs beside her ready to use as a battering ram. Her eyes and throat began to burn, and she buried her face in the wet cloth, counting aloud slowly to keep the panic at bay. She thought about Seth and the others back in camp . . . they had become her family. They must have been out of their minds with worry when they discovered her missing. How foolish she'd been to go off on her own, especially at night. But she'd been so hurt, common sense had flown right out of her head.

A fitful spell of coughing seized her, and when she got her breath back, she drank from the bucket beside her on the floor and dipped her cloth once more. The smoke grew thicker and she could feel the fingers of heat from the blaze touching her. It was now or never, she decided, fear clogging her throat.

Taking the handle of the bucket in one hand and the chair in the other, she moved forward. Gathering her courage, she threw the last of the water directly on the blazing shutter. It sputtered and hissed, but gave her a brief, clear view of what she needed to do. Taking the chair, she swung with all her might and connected with the charred wood. It didn't budge. Another fit of coughing overcame her as panic welled up in her throat thicker than the smoke swirling around her body. An inner voice urged her to try again before it was too late.

Raising the chair, she swung it against the shutter. This time a cracking sound rewarded her, but her lungs felt as if they might burst for want of clear air. She used her last bit of strength to land another blow. The boards gave this time, opening a ragged hole in the wall. Fresh air rushed in, causing the surrounding flames to burn hotter, but Camille gulped the hot air gratefully.

Now came the hardest part—escaping through the hole she'd made. Tearing off her petticoat, she flipped the back of her skirt over her head like a hood and dashed forward. A stinging pain ripped at her arm, but she kept going, suddenly finding herself outside. A small flame licked up the front of her skirt. She dropped to the ground, rolled over and quickly snuffed it out.

For a few moments, she lay there panting, taking in fresh, cool air. Her heart thundered against her rib cage, and she shivered with shock, but her mind swelled with the knowledge that she was alive . . . she'd escaped!

When the world stopped spinning, she got to her feet and looked for a direction to go. Thank goodness it wasn't raining and cloudy today, she thought. The sun was directly overhead, which told her it was midday. When Owen had let her out earlier that morning, however, the sun was on the back side of the cabin, she remembered, which meant it was east. South was the direction she needed to go, she felt sure, so she started off and prayed she was right.

A thin spiral of smoke rose from the chimney of the small cabin. Camille chewed on her lower lip, trying to decide what to do. She wanted to knock on the door, but was afraid of who might live there. She'd been walking for about two hours, she guessed, and was still in the deep woods. For most of the way, however, she'd stayed on a trail of sorts. It gave her hope she was going in the right direction. If a pathway had been worn, it must lead to something important . . . hopefully the river.

Before she could make up her mind, the door opened and an Indian woman stepped out. She threw a pan of water into the yard and went back inside. Camille breathed a sigh of pure relief. This was Ike Raymond's cabin; the woman was his companion. Camille had seen her once when Ike delivered vegetables. Making her way toward the yard, Camille didn't even flinch when two dogs ran out barking ferociously.

Hallie stood in front of the cookhouse and fired the pistol four times into the air. It was the signal they'd agreed upon if Camille was found. The men would return from the woods when they heard it. Turning back to the porch, Hallie put the gun in her pocket and slapped Ike Raymond on the back. "Thanks again, Ike. Everybody's mighty grateful you brung Camille home."

"I don't deserve no thanks, Hallie. She saved herself. All I did was give 'er a ride." He dipped his head, hiding a dirty, whiskered face in embarrassment.

"Well, come on in and have some coffee and fresh-baked bread. I got some of them pear preserves you like," she offered, opening the door for him. "I'm so happy I ain't even gonna make ya wash yer hands."

Inside, Phoebe fussed over Camille. "Drink that tea right down, honey. It'll soothe your nerves. Are you sure you won't eat something? We've got supper ready."

She shook her head. "I'm not hungry. Do you think Seth will be angry when he gets back?" she asked, her brow furrowing. Obediently, she sipped the tea.

"Of course he won't be mad. Just the opposite would be my guess. He's been very worried about you."

Phoebe's reassurance made her feel a little better.

Patience appeared at her side and placed a pan of warm water and clean cloths on the table. "I have some headache powders, Camille. Would you like some?" she asked.

Camille wanted to hate the quiet, lovely girl who was taking her husband away, but she couldn't. Patience had been kindness itself since her arrival. She had made several attempts to befriend Camille, but Camille, in her jealousy, had shied away. And it wasn't Patience's fault that Seth and Camille had agreed on a business arrangement. Glancing up, Camille forced a smile. "I do believe that would help, thank you."

The pretty blonde left them to fetch the powders, and Hallie took her place, having served Ike his refreshment. "The men'll get back here as quick as you please, honey." Hallie scowled, shaking her head. "I don't know why we didn't suspect Owen was the creature you and Ike saw. He's always been a strange one, kinda like a wild animal. If he'd a been wearin' caulked boots instead of them fur things, Seth woulda looked to the Slidell camp when he found them strange footprints up by the springhouse. Owen sure better find a place to hide when Seth finds out what he did," she said.

Phoebe was gently blotting the dried wound on Camille's head with a wet cloth, and spoke up before Camille could answer. "Maybe the sheriff can do something this time. After all, holding you against your will in that awful cabin is serious business."

Camille winced at the stinging pain, but held still. "I know, but Owen may have saved my life."

"Are you defendin' that monster?" Hallie crossed her arms over her ample bosom and clucked her tongue. "Them Slidell boys are no good. Maybe Owen don't always know what he's doin', but he can't be kidnappin' people and gettin' away with it."

"I know, but there's something pitiful about him. And he didn't try to hurt me." Camille flinched as Phoebe extracted a small piece of bark from the wound.

"I'm sorry, honey, but there's dirt and bark and blood all matted together here. I think we should put you in a tub of water and rinse this wound thoroughly. We can tend all your scrapes and burns at the same time, and I think you'll feel better once you're clean," Phoebe suggested, looking to Hallie for agreement.

The older woman nodded. "Good idea. Do you feel up to it, Camille?"

"It sounds heavenly, but I hate to be such a bother. It seems like I'm always causing work and worry of some sort."

"Pshaw! It ain't been yer fault, and besides, Phoebe and Patience have been a big help. They're more than willin' to take up the slack. Now, I'll get some hot water ready while Phoebe goes with you to the cabin. By the time it's heated, some of the men should be back to carry it up to you."

Patience returned and mixed the white powders in a cup of water. Passing Camille the concoction, Patience laid a comforting hand on her shoulder. "I'm glad you're back safe," Patience said.

"Thank you," Camille replied, blinking back a sudden rush of tears. She drank the mixture and rose to her feet.

"Lean on me, honey," Phoebe offered.

In no time at all, Camille was soaking in soothing warm water while Phoebe cleaned her head wound and washed her hair. When it was finished, Phoebe handed her a towel for her head and reached for another. "Do you need help getting up?"

Camille shook her head and stood on her own. "I can manage. Actually, I'm feeling much stronger now." She smiled as Phoebe draped the cloth around her. She stepped out and moved closer to the fireplace, where the warmth of a small blaze beckoned. She dried herself while Phoebe fetched a clean nightgown and her comb. After slipping the garment carefully over her head, Camille sat down.

"I'll be careful not to hurt the cut, but I think we should get some of these tangles out, don't you?" Phoebe said.

"You're the doctor," Camille told her with a wistful smile. "It's been nice having a sister. I'll miss you when I'm gone."

Phoebe stopped combing and leaned around to look at Camille's face. "Gone? Whatever are you talking about?"

Camille swallowed a lump in her throat and said lightly, "When I find my brother, I'll be leaving to go to him. Hasn't Seth told you about our . . . arrangement?"

"Seth never tells me anything," she said dryly. "If we women waited for vital information from men, we'd be in trouble. Now, what is this nonsense?"

Camille didn't mention what she'd overheard between Seth and Patience. After all, Patience was Phoebe's friend. Instead, she told her sister-in-law about their original deal to stay married until one or the other wanted out.

"Of all the harebrained things I've ever heard, this takes the cake! I know you two care about each other, even if you have been living apart. And I haven't meddled into your business before, but I can't stand by and watch the two of you do this." Before Phoebe could catch her breath and continue her tirade, the door opened and Seth stood on the threshold.

Chapter 19

Seth looked haggard and disheveled. "Camille? Are you all right?"

Just the sight of him was a balm to her spirit. She wanted to fly into the security of his arms, but stifled the urge. Giving him a wan smile, she said, "I'm fine. Phoebe has taken wonderful care of me." She fell silent, and the the tension in the room grew thick.

Phoebe placed the comb on the mantel. "I think I'll go get Camille something to eat."

Camille bit her lip to keep from calling her sister-in-law back. She didn't want to be alone with Seth. What if she gave her feelings away? She couldn't bear his pity.

When Phoebe closed the door behind her, Seth advanced to kneel down beside Camille's chair. "Hallie told me Owen did this. I swear, I'll kill him."

Camille shivered at the quiet determination in his voice. She wouldn't have been nearly so worried had he ranted and raved. If something happened to him it would be her fault. Reaching out, she smoothed the frown lines on his brow with her finger-tips. "Please don't, Seth. Owen wouldn't let me go, it's true, but he didn't try to hurt me. He's not right in the head, you know, but I don't really think he's vicious."

Seth caught her hand and held it in both of his, his expression earnest. "I didn't tell you this before, but when we searched the area after you found Ned Johnson in the cove, there were footprints everywhere—big prints—of a man the size of Owen."

"Maybe it was Jake. It could have been any number of men. Loggers tend to be big men," she pointed out, hoping to keep Seth from doing something rash.

"I'm sure Jake had something to do with it, but my point is that Owen did the killing. Those footprints had been made by a smooth-soled boot, not a caulked one like loggers wear. Until Hallie told me just now that Owen is the creature you saw, I had no clues, only suspicions." Seth tried to be calm, but he wanted her to realize the danger lurking around the camp. She looked so pale beneath the gold of her skin, he wanted to kiss away the worry and keep her safe.

"Owen killed Ned . . . just snapped his neck?" She said the words aloud, trying not to think about what Owen could have done to her if he'd wanted. She shivered again, and this time she couldn't stop.

Seth stood up and gathered her into his arms, holding her like a baby. He spoke in a soothing voice, telling her everything would be all right, that she had nothing to fear.

For a blissful moment, Camille drew strength from Seth, clinging to him. Finally, though, she lifted her head. "Promise me you won't go after him, Seth? Let the sheriff take care of it . . . please?"

Seth carried her to the bed. "I'm sending word by Captain Jack to the sheriff, but I've got to do something about Owen. All I can promise is I'll be careful."

Camille closed her eyes for a moment, a sinking feeling in

her stomach. "I shouldn't have been in the woods alone, and especially after dark. It's my fault this happened."

"Granted, you shouldn't have wandered away from camp, but the Slidell brothers are responsible for their own deeds." He leaned over and kissed her brow. "Now, you get some rest and I'll see you in the morning."

Her eyes flew open and she clutched his sleeve. "Promise you won't go to the woods without seeing me?"

The deep worry lines between her eyes pleased him. "I promise," he murmured, and dropped a light kiss on her mouth. "Sleep well."

A few minutes after he'd gone, Phoebe returned with a tray. Placing it on the bed beside Camille, she urged her to sit up and eat. Complying, she nibbled on a piece of bread spread with pear preserves and sipped the tea.

Phoebe lifted the hair from Camille's wound and looked it over carefully. "It looks clean now. I'm going to put some salve on it." She reached for the tin she'd brought. "You're very lucky you weren't burned worse, or that all your hair wasn't singed. That was a brave thing you did."

Camille slid her gown up to her thighs so Phoebe could minister to a burn on her calf. "Or incredibly stupid," Camille said. "I could have died."

"You had no choice as I see it. Lord knows what Owen would have done to you if you hadn't escaped. Coop says he's unbalanced and dangerous."

Camille held out her arm, and Phoebe smeared some salve on the scrape. She was tired of talking about Owen. Looking at her sister-in-law speculatively, she said, "I think there's something going on between you and Cooper."

Phoebe's eyes flew up in surprise, and a faint blush colored her cheeks. "Is it obvious?"

"Well, I don't know about everyone else, but I've seen the looks that pass between the two of you. I think it's wonderful. You and Cooper are dear people, and deserve some happiness."

Impulsively, Phoebe hugged her. "Thank you, Camille. I feel the same way about you and Seth. I wish you could work out your differences."

Camille smiled. "Let's talk about you."

Phoebe put the lid on the tin of salve and sat down on the end of the bed. "We're in love. We always have been. When Coop and Seth left Bangor six years ago, I thought my heart would break. Coop and I had talked about getting married, but he insisted he had nothing to offer me. He said when he struck it rich in the gold fields, he'd send for me, but two years later, I got a letter from him saying he was releasing me from my promise to wait. He said there was a big chance they'd never hit it lucky, and he couldn't in good conscience keep me waiting."

Phoebe sighed as she pleated the material of her gingham skirt between her fingers. "I waited another year anyway, hoping he'd come to his senses. I didn't care if he wasn't wealthy, but he did. Anyway, my mother gave me a lecture one day about wasting my life waiting for something that might never happen. So, when Malcolm began to pay attention to me, I returned his interest. We were married a year later.

"It was the biggest mistake of my life, Camille. I didn't love him. He had none of Cooper's spirit and ambition, nor did he have a sense of humor. Too late, I realized I should have followed Cooper out here and made him see reason. I was quite miserable. And I'm a little ashamed to say when Malcolm died, I was secretly relieved."

Camille leaned over and laid a comforting hand on Phoebe's shoulder. "Cooper may have some wonderful qualities, but he was definitely a fool for letting you go. I'm glad to see he's come to his senses."

Phoebe gave her a grateful smile. "He's asked me to marry him, and I said yes. We're just waiting for the proper mourning time to pass before we tell everyone."

Camille hugged her. "I'm very happy for both of you, and I won't say a word."

* * *

The noonday meal was progressing noisily as the loggers discussed the murders, Camille's kidnapping and her harrowing brush with a fiery death. The camp fairly buzzed with tales of her bravery as the story was told and retold. Camille chuckled as she sliced peach pies at the worktable when she heard herself described as a female David, outsmarting her Goliath. When the door opened and closed, she didn't bother to look up, thinking it was Patience, who had gone to the springhouse to fetch a jug of cream.

A silence fell over the room, prompting Camille to look up. Bearing down on her was Paul Jarvis. A small frown knitted her brow as her brain tried to register why he was here. Before she could open her mouth, he had skirted the worktable and grasped her hands in his. "Camille! It's so good to see you again," he said, a broad smile lighting his face.

"Dr. Jarvis," she gasped. "What ... where ... what are you doing here?" The first shock of surprise faded, and she smiled in return.

He let go of her hands and removed his hat. "Well, to tell you the truth, I came to see you."

Now she was even more puzzled. "Me? I'm afraid I don't understand."

She glanced over at Seth's place at the head of the nearest table. He, along with everyone else in the room, was staring at the two of them. His expression was grim, however. Clearing her throat, she asked, "Seth, you remember Dr. Jarvis, don't you?"

Her husband rose and walked over to them. After a brief hesitation, he extended his hand. "Hello, Paul. Welcome to the Braden-Maxwell camp."

Paul noticed the cold light in Seth's eyes, and tried not to flinch at the iron grip of his handshake. Summoning a polite smile, he said, "Thank you, Seth. It's good to see you again.

I apologize for arriving unannounced, but I wanted to surprise Camille.''

Seth slipped his arm around her shoulders. ''I believe the surprise is on you. Camille is my wife. We were married just after leaving San Francisco.''

Paul looked nonplussed for a moment, and then slapped his silk hat against his leg. ''It looks like I've made a complete ass of myself here. I apologize again ... to you and Mrs. Braden. And please, let me offer my sincere best wishes.'' He looked contrite and embarrassed at the same time.

Camille felt Seth relax, and she breathed a sigh of relief. Even though he was not in love with her, he wouldn't want to look foolish in front of everyone. ''Have you eaten, Paul? Please join us,'' she offered politely.

Hallie stepped into the breach. ''I'll just fix you a plate, Doctor. Set down next to Seth there and make yerself at home.''

Paul followed Seth to the table while Camille went back to cutting the pie she'd left. She glanced at Phoebe across the worktable, and her sister-in-law surprised her by grinning mischievously. Camille frowned, thinking it certainly wasn't funny. The whole scene had been embarrassing and uncomfortable.

Camille sat alone on the little bridge, dangling her legs over the side and watching the stream rushing beneath her slipper-clad feet. The midday meal was over, a big pot of beans was on the stove and there were enough pies and loaves left over from yesterday to feed the men for supper.

She touched the bandage on her temple, remembering how Seth had inspected it before he left for the woods that morning. She had waited for him to say something about Paul's unexpected visit the day before, but he'd been unexpectedly silent on the subject.

It had been three days since Ike had returned her to camp. Each day when Seth went into the woods, worry gnawed at her insides until he returned at lunch or sometimes not until supper. She knew he was out scouring the area for Owen, but he never mentioned it. Two days before, the sheriff and a deputy had stopped in to question her on their way to look for Owen.

Hearing voices in the distance, she glanced up and saw Paul talking to one of the guards. Seth now posted two guards during the day and four at night around the camp. The doctor broke off his conversation and came toward Camille.

"Beautiful day, isn't it," he remarked, settling himself beside her on the bridge. He had exchanged his pinstriped trousers and frock coat for canvas pants and a red flannel shirt.

Camille smiled and agreed. "We're lucky it's sunny and mild this time of year. By now, they tell me, it's usually getting cooler and raining almost every day. Did you sleep well in the bunkhouse?"

He rolled his eyes heavenward. "I thought it was thundering most of the night. Did you ever hear a roomful of men snoring at once?"

Camille laughed at his look of comic desperation. "I'm sorry, but we have no place else to put you."

"That's all right. I won't be staying long. I would, however, like to take a look at the logging operation and the workings of the sawmill before I go. The trees here are so enormous, it would be fascinating to watch the men bring one down."

"You better watch it or they'll put you to work. You're dressed for the part."

He fell silent for a moment, looking off into the distance. "Camille, I'd like to apologize again for showing up here without an invitation, and taking something for granted I shouldn't have."

"I'm sorry if I led you to believe—"

He held up one hand and shook his head. "It wasn't your fault. After you left, I couldn't stop thinking about you, and I suppose I romanticized our friendship. It was a shock to find you married."

Camille brushed at some imaginary lint on the sleeve of her calico dress. "It was a sudden decision."

"I hope it was a happy one." Getting to his feet, he added, "I'll speak to Seth about staying until Saturday. That's only two more days, and I won't get in anyone's way."

Just before supper time, Sheriff Bob Wyman and one of his deputies rode into camp with Owen. Seth crossed the small bridge and headed for the cookhouse when he spotted the trio. Anger, swift and sharp, cut through him at the sight of Slidell. If Owen hadn't been trussed up like a Christmas turkey, Seth would have jumped him. "Where in hell did you find him, Bob? I've been scouring the woods for days."

Sheriff Wyman and the deputy dismounted and wound their reins around the hitching post in front of the cookhouse. "We staked out their camp and caught him sneaking in from the woods this afternoon. We got the drop on him and Jake in the sawmill. Jake didn't give us any trouble." Cocking his head toward the young man beside him, he asked, "You know my deputy, Hutson Keithley?"

Seth nodded to the young man. "We met once."

"How do, Mr. Braden. This varmint won't be botherin' your wife anymore, or anybody else for that matter." Hutson stepped back to check the knot on the leading strings of Slidell's horse.

The door opened, and the women came out onto the porch, having seen the new arrivals through the window. Camille hung back, bracing herself against the wall, her eyes on Owen. He, in turn, seemed to come out of his vacant state when he saw her. Making a grunting noise, he began to squirm in his saddle, trying to get loose.

"Take it easy, Slidell. You keep it up and you'll hit the ground, and it's right hard," the deputy cautioned.

"You ain't thinkin' of bringin' him in my cookhouse, are

ye?'' Hallie said, hands on her hips. ''After what he put Camille through, he don't deserve our hospitality.''

Seth, seeing the fear in Camille's eyes, stepped up on the porch and slipped a comforting arm around her shoulders. ''Why don't you go on back inside? There's no need for you to face him,'' he suggested in a low tone.

''What about Jake? Why didn't they arrest him too?'' she asked, leaning against the solid strength of Seth's body.

Sheriff Wyman tipped his hat back on his head and sighed. ''I'd like to do that, ma'am, but we don't have any hard evidence against him. We did give him a warning, though, so I don't think he'll be trying anything knowing we're on to him.'' Casting his eyes toward Hallie, he added, ''Don't you worry, Miss Hallie. I wouldn't dream of bringing the likes of him into your dining room. Matter of fact, we're going to be moving on. There's another hour or so of daylight.''

''I'll jest go pack a lunch for you boys.'' The older woman turned on her heel and went inside. Camille wanted to remain within the security of Seth's arm, but said, ''I'll go help.''

Friday evening, Seth returned to the cookhouse in search of Camille long after supper was over. He found her sitting alone at one of the trestle tables, warming her hands around a cup of coffee. Only one lamp was lit, leaving the large room in deep shadow. He stood in the doorway watching her for a few moments. Deep in thought, she didn't realize she had company. She was so beautiful, her shiny auburn curls brushing her collar, her sky-blue eyes framed by soot-black lashes.

Her expression was downcast, and Seth wondered if she was sad because Paul was leaving the next day. Perhaps she cared more for the doctor than she'd let on. Once he'd been almost sure she and Coop were attracted to each other, but now he realized it had been his fertile imagination. And then there was Vladimir. Seth realized with disgust that his jealousy knew no bounds. The shoe had always been on the other foot through the years; women had flocked to him, fought over him and bared their claws in jealousy instead of the other way around. He had finally found the one woman he couldn't live without and he was about to lose her. Squaring his shoulders, he started across the wooden floor in his caulked boots.

Camille's head jerked up, fear flickering in her eyes before she realized it was Seth. "You startled me," she scolded him lightly. "Want a cup of coffee?"

"I'll get it," he said. When he sat down beside her, a steaming cup in his hands, she gave him a wan smile. "What are you doing in here all by yourself?"

She shrugged, letting her gaze slide back to her cup. "Oh, I suppose I wasn't fit company for anybody tonight. I've been thinking about everything that's happened since I stepped off the stage in San Francisco."

"It hasn't been dull," he said, his lips curving upward.

"No, but you could have done without the kind of excitement I've brought into your life. If I was superstitious, I'd say I'd been marked by a bad-luck gris-gris." She sighed, taking a sip of her coffee.

"Take a look in your mirror, Camille. It's not bad luck that draws trouble to you like flies to honey—it's those big blue eyes and beautiful smile. The bad luck is it attracts bad men as well as the good," he pointed out.

She glanced up to see if he was teasing, but his expression was serious. "I didn't mean to invite trouble," she said earnestly, a warm feeling inside her expanding at his praise.

He reached over and took one of her hands, giving it a gentle squeeze. "Don't apologize for something that's not your fault. I don't regret your coming into my life one bit. As a matter of fact, you've helped me put everything into perspective. I should be thanking you."

Camille swallowed a lump in her throat. His kindness was unbearable when she realized he was talking about his feelings for Patience. When he'd had a chance to compare the two, Camille knew he'd found he still loved the young woman he'd left behind. She closed her eyes and savored the warmth of his touch. Before long, she would have only memories to sustain her. "You were there when I needed you, so I suppose we're even," she said.

"The reason I was looking for you is to let you know some of us are going into Empire City tomorrow. Would you like to go?" The surprise he had for her could turn out to be bittersweet if things didn't go as he planned, but he had to take the chance anyway. Above all, he wanted to make her happy.

Her eyebrows rose. "You're not working in the woods tomorrow? And what about the meals?"

"This is a special occasion. I can't tell you what just yet. Most of the men will be working, and Hallie and Phoebe will be cooking, so you wouldn't be missed."

"Patience is going?" She was afraid to ask more.

"Yes, and Vladimir, and of course, Paul Jarvis. He's going back to San Francisco soon."

"I didn't invite him to come, you know, but I'm sorry if his arrival caused you embarrassment," she said quietly.

"It was a surprise, and not exactly a pleasant one, but let's forget him. Will you come with us?"

Camille thought about spending the day watching Seth and Patience make an effort not to show their feelings, and a weight settled on her shoulders. She was sure he'd asked her because he felt obligated. "I don't think so, Seth. Thank you for asking, but I still don't feel as strong as I should and the trip would tire me."

He released her hand and touched her cheek, concern marking his expression. "Is there something you're not telling me, honey? Maybe I shouldn't leave you."

"No, no," she said hastily. "I'm just not in the mood to go to town."

He sighed. The surprise would have to wait until he returned.

"Coop will be here, and we've decided to continue posting two guards at night. With Owen in jail and Jake knowing the sheriff is on to him, I don't think you have anything to worry about."

Camille nodded and rose. "I'm not afraid."

"I'll walk you to your cabin," he offered, rising.

A soft rain had fallen most of the day, but had stopped just before supper. Their footsteps were muffled as they walked on a soggy bed of fallen leaves. When they arrived at her cabin, he reached out and caught her arm before she could open the door. "Whatever happens between us, Camille, I want you to know I'm sorry I hurt you."

Camille trembled with the emotions that roiled within her. "There's pain in life. I don't think any of us can escape it."

Seth slid his hand up her arm and around to the nape of her neck, his fingers caressing the tender skin beneath her thick hair. "I hate it that you know so much about pain, Camille. And what's more, I hate it because I've caused some of it," he murmured as he leaned forward to touch his lips to hers.

Camille stood perfectly still, letting him kiss her, even returning the kiss. Common sense told her to back away, but her heart refused. After a few heart-stopping moments, Seth groaned and drew her close, his hands touching, caressing. Finally breaking the kiss, Seth whispered hoarsely, "When I get back, we'll talk. I want everything settled one way or the other before I go completely mad."

Abruptly, Seth let her go and melted into the surrounding darkness. Camille wanted to weep for what she knew was coming.

"Would you please just try some soda crackers?" Camille wheedled.

Paul closed his eyes and turned his head away on the pillow. "I can't eat anything, I'll be sick," he mumbled.

Camille touched his forehead, but found it cool. "How about a sip of tea? It's Hallie's special blend."

He sighed and turned back. "You won't be happy until I have something, will you?"

"Starve a cold and feed a fever, old Sadie used to say." She smiled when he sat up on the bunk and reached for the cup in her hand.

"Did old Sadie go to Harvard Medical School? I don't recall seeing her there."

"Mind your tongue, young man," she said sternly.

He chuckled and took a sip, then another. "Very good."

Camille settled herself on a stool and watched him. "It's a shame you couldn't go with the others into town, but you can go on Captain Jack's boat when you feel better."

Shaking his head, he gave a wry smile. "This old stomach complaint flares up every few years, and I never have a clue as to when it's going to happen." He handed the cup back to her and sank wearily back onto the pillow. Closing his eyes, he sighed as if worn out.

Camille pulled the quilt up over his arms. "Well, don't worry about a thing, just rest. When you feel strong enough to get up, it'll be time enough to think about leaving."

She hurried from Coop's cabin, where they'd moved the sick man. The smell of hot biscuits, gravy and coffee greeted her as she stepped inside the cookhouse and closed the door on the chill morning air. Hanging her brown shawl up on a peg, she crossed the room to the work area. The men would be finished eating shortly and going to the woods and the sawmill, leaving a pile of dirty dishes to be dealt with by the three women. "How's the doctor?" Phoebe asked, stirring another pan of gravy on the wood stove.

Camille put Paul's cup in the wash pan. "He's as weak as a kitten. I can see why he couldn't go to town with the others. He can hardly lift his head." She fetched the large bowl from a shelf and began to dip flour in it. "I'll start the bread, Hallie, unless you need something else?"

"Go right ahead, honey. The men are startin' to like your bread better than mine, so that'll be yer job from now on." Hallie chuckled at her own cleverness.

Camille had mixed feelings about Hallie's compliment. On the one hand, her confidence had been growing by leaps and bounds since she arrived. Hallie had taught her so much, and no one had belittled her efforts, or made her feel ugly or unwanted. On the other hand, when she thought about leaving Seth and the others, her heart felt as if it was going to break.

At midday, Phoebe carried some broth to Paul and fed him while Hallie and Camille fed the lumberjacks. Cooper stopped by the worktable on his way out. "Seth told me to ask you ladies if you'd mind making some cakes for tonight's supper. Said he'd like some baked ham too."

Hallie's brows rose. "Sounds like a party or somethin'."

"Could be," Coop said, grinning mischievously. "I'll check on Paul this afternoon so you ladies can get your cooking done."

Camille's spirits sank. It was most likely a celebration, she thought miserably. He would probably come back from town with a divorce paper from the judge.

Hallie and Phoebe speculated as they worked about why Seth had gone to town on a workday, and why he had asked for a special meal. Neither knew what was going on, and Camille assured them she was in the dark. By midafternoon, two large hams had been brought from the smokehouse and were baking in one side of the oven. Camille volunteered to go to the springhouse to get the cream and eggs for the cakes. A light mist fell from a leaden sky as she made her way up the hill.

Taking what she needed, Camille started back. A movement to her right flickered in her peripheral vision. For a moment, she stared, not quite believing what she saw. She ducked quickly behind a fir tree and peered around. Cooper was almost at the edge of the woods beyond his cabin. Paul Jarvis was behind him with a pistol pointed at Coop's back. It didn't make sense. She decided it would take too long to run to the sawmill for help. There was a Colt .45 in her pocket, loaded and ready. She never ventured to the secluded springhouse without it anymore. Placing the cream jug and the bowl of eggs on the ground, she grabbed a stick lying close by and drew an arrow in the mud in the direction she was taking. She hoped someone would find it when they came looking for her.

She followed at a safe distance and ducked behind trees for cover. The ground was so wet, there were thankfully no crunching noises to betray her. She could hear Paul's voice, raised every now and then, telling Cooper to keep moving. They headed toward the bluffs overlooking the river above the camp. What Paul's purpose was, Camille was afraid to speculate on. After ten minutes or so of following them, Paul stopped, pointing with his gun for Cooper to move to the edge of the cliff. Camille's heart jumped up in her throat as she realized what he intended. She crept closer, hoping to get within a reasonable range to fire her gun. She was not an expert shot. She prayed she could hold the weapon steady and have the courage to shoot another human being. By the time she managed to work her way from tree to tree to where she could see and hear them clearly, she was shaking like a leaf. "This is insane, Jarvis. You'll never get away with it," Cooper growled. Camille could hear a note of desperation beneath his bravado. She took the gun from her pocket and ran through the procedure in her mind—take off the safety, pull the hammer back, aim, squeeze the trigger gently. Her heart thumped wildly in her chest as she pushed the safety off.

"A little risky maybe, but not insane," Paul corrected him in a casual tone. He glanced at the overcast sky. "If only the storm would break, the thunder would muffle my shots and no one would be alerted for a long while."

A chill finger traced down Camille's spine. He was speaking of killing Cooper as if it were no more than swatting a fly. When she pulled the hammer back, the clicking noise seemed to reverberate through the woods. She plastered herself against the tree, her heart pounding in her ears. "Who's there?" Paul called, his keen eyes scanning the wooded area at his back.

Camille froze. After a moment, she cautiously peered from her hiding place. Paul was waving the gun at Cooper.

"This way, Maxwell," he ordered curtly, keeping one eye on the woods and one on his captive. Cooper moved to obey, making his way toward Jarvis. "There . . . stop there." Cooper stopped between the doctor and the woods. "Now, come out or I'll blow his head off his shoulders."

Tears of frustration stung Camille's eyes. Damnation! Why hadn't she realized the hammer would make a noise? Why had it been so quiet at that precise moment? She slipped the gun in her pocket and swiped at her eyes. She couldn't leave her friend to this madman. If she ran and he shot Cooper, she'd never forgive herself. Taking a deep breath, she stepped out into the open and faced Paul.

"Camille!" Paul and Cooper spoke in unison, surprise flashing across both masculine faces. Paul recovered first. "What the hell are you doing here?"

"I saw you going into the woods and followed." Even though her insides trembled, her voice sounded normal.

"I wish you hadn't," he said, genuine regret marking his expression.

Chapter 20

"Why are you doing this awful thing, Paul? What could you possibly have against Cooper?"

"I have to do it, Camille. I'm tired of being poor, slaving every day like a common laborer. I'm used to the finer things in life, and living this way has been a slow death for me."

There was almost a pleading tone in his voice, as if he truly cared if she understood his plight. "Why don't you tell me what you're talking about and maybe I can understand," she said in an earnest tone.

He stared at her for a long moment, a flicker of indecision in his eyes. "Toss the gun to me first," he ordered.

Her heart sank, but she retrieved the pistol from her pocket. Her glance strayed to Cooper. He frowned and gave an imperceptible shake of his head.

Paul put his hand on Cooper's shoulder and shoved him down. "Sit . . . and don't try anything, Maxwell." Paul moved toward her. "All right, toss it gently. That's a good girl." He caught it and slipped it in the pocket of his coat.

"Do you plan to shoot me too?" she asked, hugging her shawl against her body.

Stepping closer, he caressed her cheek with his thumb, his expression softening. "I don't want to. When I came up here to do this job, I had planned to take you back with me. But then I found you'd married Braden."

Camille willed herself not to flinch. She glanced down, letting her dark lashes veil her expression. "I didn't tell you before, but our marriage is just a business arrangement," she said. "As a matter of fact, Seth is in Empire City right now getting divorce papers from the judge."

He tipped her chin up with his index finger and looked into her eyes. "You wouldn't lie to me, would you?"

Camille's expression was grim. "It's true. Ask Cooper."

Paul looked down at the man sitting on the ground. "Well, Maxwell?"

Cooper glared. "Yeah, it's true. Seth promised to find her brother if she'd marry him and help run the camp. When his old sweetheart showed up, free to marry again, he decided to accept Camille's offer of a divorce."

Paul considered the explanation for a moment, looking from one to the other. "It has to be true. You're not clever enough to make up such a bizarre story on the spur of the moment, Maxwell."

Hearing the stark truth from Cooper broke her heart. Deep down she'd known it, but had entertained a small hope anyway. She forced her thoughts away from the pain. "You haven't told me what this is about," she reminded him.

Paul let his hand stray to the back of her head, stroking her hair. "I suppose I should tell Maxwell why he's going to die. It's only fair." His voice was matter-of-fact as he wound his fingers in her hair and gave a gentle tug as if to remind her who was in control. "Annabelle and I poisoned your Uncle John. His funeral was over a week ago. You, young man, are your uncle's heir."

Cooper's stunned expression quickly changed to one of fury as he launched himself at Paul's legs. "You bastard!"

Jarvis, however, seemed to expect something of the sort and cracked Cooper's skull with the butt of his gun, knocking him back to the ground in a daze.

"Coop!" Camille cried, reaching for him. Paul's sudden yank on her hair sent needles of pain through her head.

"Now, now. You mustn't get so emotional, sweetheart, or I'll be forced to hurt you."

Camille beat on his chest with her fists. "You're a monster, and I don't know how I could have ever thought otherwise."

Jarvis caught her arms in a firm grip. "It's a shame things have worked out this way. I really wanted you, Camille. You're so beautiful. We would have made a handsome couple." His mouth took on an unpleasant twist. "This was a little test, and you failed miserably. It's as I suspected—you have morals." He stepped back and waved the gun at the two of them. "Let's get this over with. I've got to return to bed and carry on with my pretense of being sick before anyone else discovers me gone."

Cooper struggled to his feet and slipped an arm around Camille's shoulders. A thin stream of blood trickled from a cut on the side of his head. "You may kill us, but you won't get away with it," Cooper promised. "Seth won't let it rest until he finds out who did it."

Paul laughed. "I've heard the talk. He'll go looking for Jake Slidell. A neat and tidy package, don't you think?" He waved his gun, urging them toward the cliff.

Cooper spoke in a whisper. "I'm going to try something. When I do, you drop to the ground."

The pressure of her fingers on his arm tightened. "No, Coop, he'll shoot you!"

"Dammit, Camille, he's going to kill us anyway," he hissed. "We could leap together into the river before he has a chance to shoot," she persisted as they passed beneath a large madrona tree, just yards away from the edge of the cliff.

"It's ill-mannered to whisper," Paul chided them. "Make one wrong move, Maxwell, and I'll shoot Camille right before your eyes."

Camille spared a moment for regret that she'd never told Seth she loved him. She had braced herself for what was coming when she heard a loud thud and a grunt behind her. She and Cooper jerked around. Owen Slidell had Paul pinned to the ground. He wrenched the gun from Paul's hand and slung it away. Grabbing Paul's throat with both hands, Owen gave it a vicious twist.

Camille flinched when she heard the decided snap of the bones. It happened so fast, neither she nor Cooper had time to move.

Owen rose and looked at Camille for a moment, an expression of longing in his eyes. Then he sprinted away into the woods.

Cooper found his voice first. "My God! He came out of nowhere!"

Camille sagged against him to steady her wobbly knees. "And saved our lives." Her emotions raced from fear to relief to jubilance in a matter of moments, leaving her dizzy.

Cooper held her tightly. "We're all right, honey. It's all over now." Cooper glanced down at Paul Jarvis's still form. "I can hardly believe Uncle John is gone. Or that they murdered him."

Camille turned her face away from the dead man. "I'm so sorry, Coop. He was a good man."

"If he had just given Annabelle some money, she would have left quietly. As it is, he's dead and his fortune can't bring him back. What a terrible waste." Cooper sighed, leading her away from the body. "Let's get back. I don't know how Owen can be running loose, but we need to report this."

"They'll hunt him down again, won't they?"

"I'm afraid so. Just because he saved our lives doesn't mean he didn't commit other crimes. Although I'd bet Jake was behind them.''

Owen was a pawn in his brother's unscrupulous games, and yet twice he had saved her life. Camille couldn't help but feel pity for him.

Three men on horseback galloped along the river road, heading east from Empire City. When they reached the Braden-Maxwell camp, they reined in.

Seth dismounted and tossed his reins over the hitching rail outside the cookhouse. The sheriff and his deputy followed suit. When they entered the dining room, they found Cooper seated at the worktable with Phoebe placing a bandage on the side of his head.

Seth began to breathe easier when he spotted Camille standing next to Hallie at the stove. Sweeping his hat off, he tossed it on one of the trestle tables as he strode by. ''Jake broke Owen out of jail around noon today,'' he said, and then frowned at Cooper. ''What happened to you?''

Cooper looked grim. ''Paul Jarvis tried to kill me—us, I should say.'' He glanced over at Camille briefly. ''Your wife saved my life.''

''Owen saved both of us, you mean,'' Camille said, gripping her cup of tea to steady her hands. ''He broke Paul's neck . . . just . . . just snapped it like a twig.''

Hallie patted her shoulder. ''Try not to think about it. It's over and yer both safe, thank goodness.''

Seth made his way straight to Camille and took her in his arms, crushing her to his chest. ''Are you all right?'' he demanded, his voice harsh.

Camille drew on his strength, loving the feel of his arms around her. This could be the last time, she thought sadly. ''Paul hit Cooper with the butt of his gun, but he didn't hurt me.''

"How long ago did this happen?" Sheriff Wyman asked.

"About an hour," Cooper told him. "Owen took off toward the north, but it doesn't mean anything. He knows the woods like the back of his hand."

"He could be anywhere," the sheriff agreed. "But we have to start somewhere. You know the way to Ike Raymond's place, don't you, Braden?"

When Seth nodded, the sheriff continued. "Ike can show us where Owen's cabin used to be—the one Mrs. Braden set afire. He could still be hanging around the area."

"Our men will be glad to help search. Until Jake and Owen are caught, none of us will rest easy." Seth's expression was like granite. "We can cover more area if we split up. We'll go in pairs and fan out over our land and Slidell's."

Cooper stood up. "I'll go talk to the men at the sawmill while Hallie packs food and coffee."

"I'll get some extra guns and ammunition," Seth said, glancing at Hallie. "We'll leave two men here, and I don't want any of you to so much as stick your head out the door till we come back."

Camille began to shake as fearful images built in her mind. "Don't you think they'll be clear out of the territory by now? Surely they won't hang around after what happened. Do you have to go?" This last came out with a hysterical edge.

Seth tipped her chin up and looked tenderly into her eyes. "Don't be afraid, honey. You'll be protected."

She gripped his shirtfront and held back the tears. "I'm not worried about myself, you thick-headed mule. I'm scared for you and Coop and the others."

Seth's expression softened. "We have to get them, Camille. Dangerous animals like Jake and Owen can't go free. Nobody will be safe until they're caught."

When Seth returned to the cookhouse with more guns and ammunition, Hallie gave him a quick rundown on what happened with Jarvis. Glancing across the room to where Camille and Phoebe were packing sandwiches in saddlebags, he shook his head. "I sure didn't see that one coming. I was so jealous of his attentions to Camille, I didn't smell him for the skunk he was. Damned if I wouldn't like to take her over my knee for risking her life."

Hallie chuckled. "You'd better watch tanglin' with a wildcat like her," she warned. Changing the subject, she asked, "What happened to Patience and Vladimir?"

"They'll be back tomorrow. I was supposed to meet Camille's brother in town. He was coming from Seattle, but hadn't arrived when I got the news about Owen's escape. Patience and Vladimir offered to meet his stage and bring him out tomorrow. Don't tell her, though, in case he doesn't arrive. But if he does, I want it to be a surprise."

Hallie gave him a hug. "Yer a good man, Seth. Watch out for yerself and Coop too, ya hear? We'll be fine."

"Don't let her out of your sight," he said, glancing at his wife.

Bob Wyman and Hutson Keithley came in. "Ready?" the sheriff asked.

Seth nodded and picked up two rifles from the table. When he reached the porch, Camille caught up with him. She clutched a saddlebag in her hands, her expression full of anxiety. "Don't forget the food," she whispered.

He stood the rifles against the wall and reached for the saddlebag, catching her hand as well. "Keep your head down and stay out of trouble. I'll be back soon." Slinging the bag over his shoulder, he picked up the guns and strode to the horses.

It wasn't until after they'd gone that Camille realized he hadn't mentioned why he'd gone to town. It was a short reprieve at best.

* * *

Ike Raymond and his Indian woman led Seth and Cooper to the burned-out shell where Owen's cabin had stood. Seth didn't expect to find him there, but they did find fresh tracks around the place. They led in the direction of Slidell's mill. Cooper and Seth rode on alone. "They can't be stupid enough to go back to their camp," Seth said, his gaze sharply assessing the surrounding area.

"Jake is crazy like a fox. If he goes back there, he'll probably wait until dark and sneak in. Some of the low-life scum working for him would cover his movements."

They followed an old Indian trail through the deep woods, keeping a sharp eye for an ambush, but the journey to Slidell's camp was eerily quiet. They left the marked path when they spotted spirals of smoke in the distance, marking the camp. They skirted the area as dusk fell over the woods, giving them subtle cover while they settled into a hiding place to the east of the sawmill. Cooper pulled out two sandwiches and the canteen of coffee from the saddlebag. The coffee had grown tepid, but revived them. "The sheriff and Keithley will have come and gone by now, don't you reckon?" Cooper said.

"Yeah. The men know something's up, or they wouldn't be standing around. They'd be in the bunkhouse getting ready for supper right about now."

"We might be wasting our time here. They could be clear up to the Columbia River by now, or deep in the mountains," Cooper pointed out.

"It's possible, but Jake Slidell strikes me as a man who likes to push his luck. If he's left anything of value here, he'll be back for it."

"Well, Braden, I didn't know you was so smart."

Seth and Cooper scrambled to their feet, turning to find Jake and Owen standing a few yards away. Jake waved his pistol.

"Just drop them guns on the ground and I won't have to kill you . . . yet."

Seth did as he was told. "All you're facing right now is a charge for breaking Owen out of jail. Do you really want to add murder?"

Jake grinned. "I've done murder, Braden. And Owen's killed a few men in his time too. Our record between Minnesota and here ain't none too good. Owen, here, even killed our own daddy. He was a mean old bastard who beat us every time he took a notion. Anyway, it ain't gonna be murder, it'll be a fair fight. I heard some tall stories 'bout how good you are with an ax. We're gonna see." He nodded to Owen, who turned and trotted away, returning shortly with two axes. Jake took them and motioned toward Cooper. Owen obediently moved to grasp Cooper's arms from behind.

Jake tossed one of the axes to Seth. "When I'm done with you, I'll give your partner a chance to best me. Course, I know he can't, but I try to be a fair man."

Seth spat on the ground as he took a firm grasp on the butt of the ax handle with both hands. "You're neither fair, nor are you a man, Slidell. More like a slimy snake who walks on two feet instead of crawling on your belly like the rest of your kind."

Jake's eyes flashed in anger just before he swung the ax wide at Seth's head. Seth jumped back, having expected Jake to try for the advantage, and delivered a glancing blow to his opponent's midsection with the flat side of the ax head.

Jake let out a loud "woof" and scrambled back, a flicker of admiration in his eyes. "Not bad, Braden. There might just be somethin' to all the talk. Too bad you won't live to brag about this fight."

Seth circled Jake slowly. "You've confused the two of us, Slidell. Bragging is how you got your reputation."

Jake laughed, but his narrowed eyes gave away his mood. "I was bull of the woods in Minnesota, and I'll be king here after you're dead. When I add your land to mine, it'll be the biggest operation south of Puget Sound.''

Stepping in close enough to swing, Seth caught his blade on Jake's canvas pants and sliced through them. A thin line of red appeared on the tan material. Dodging Jake's retaliating swing, he blocked the blow with his ax handle. He felt the jarring force all the way up to his teeth. ''You're forgetting a few things, aren't you?'' Seth said. ''Even if you manage to kill Coop and me, you still won't own our operation. And you're wanted by the law.''

''I'll buy a judge. I owned one back in Minnesota. And I'll get your property too, 'cause I'm gonna take your wife. The minute I laid eyes on her in the Talbot Hotel, I decided she'd be mine.'' With that boast, Jake swung twice in rapid succession, his ax head meeting Seth's.

Seth's hands and arms were nearly numb from the blows, but fury, hot and intense, gave him strength. He countered Jake's blows with two of his own, his breath coming in harsh gasps. ''She knows what you are, Slidell. Camille would never accept you.'' Seth narrowed his eyes in the growing darkness. If the fight didn't end soon, it would become even more dangerous.

Jake grinned, stepping in with a quick swing and slicing Seth's arm. ''I don't intend to ask her, Braden. You just don't know how to handle women like I do. You tell 'em what to do, and if they don't mind, you hurt 'em a little. It shows 'em who's boss.''

''You bastard!'' Seth spat out, his controlled anger boiling over. He charged Slidell and swung viciously with the strength of two men. Jake parried his blows with defensive moves. Seth was well aware Jake was watching for an opening.

Both men were panting heavily, their breath forming little wisps of fog in the cool night air. The continuous clash of wood and steel rent the silence for several minutes. Seth could see Jake tiring, but he too was almost spent.

"I'll be between her legs before this night is over, Braden, and she'll forget your name once she's had a real man."

The blood pounded in Seth's head as he lost all sense of time and place. His only focus was to best Jake Slidell; he had to. Their axes connected more than once, slicing through skin, muscle and tissue. Their clothing became saturated with blood, clinging wet and clammy to skin that was hot and sweaty. In one last attempt to fell his opponent, Jake rushed forward, bellowing like an enraged bull. Seth stood his ground and glared into the eyes of death. He knew this would be the final clash. Instead of feigning to the right at the last minute, as Jake would expect, Seth jumped to the left, bringing his ax around in an arc as his feet found solid purchase on the damp ground. This time, the sharp edge of the ax buried itself deep in Jake's side, felling him like a giant fir.

Seth released the handle, and dropped to his knees. He had no strength to remove the weapon, nor did he want to. Panting for breath, he raised his eyes and looked straight into Owen's. The man still held fast to Cooper, and Seth prayed he wouldn't take revenge for his brother's death. Owen's gaze moved to Jake's body, and he stared for a moment. Then he gave Cooper a shove, and ran into the woods.

Cooper rushed to Seth's side and helped him up. "Dammit, Seth, you're a bloody mess. How bad is it, partner? I couldn't tell how deep he was cutting you."

Seth leaned on his friend as they made their way slowly to where they'd left their horses. "I'm sure it looks worse than it is."

"Yeah, right. You'll be as weak as a kitten if you keep bleeding like this. I'll check your injuries before we head home. Your wife'll kill me if I let you die for lack of care."

As Cooper tied a handkerchief tourniquet around the arm with the deepest wound, Seth mused, "I wonder why Owen didn't take up the fight when I killed Jake. Not that I wanted him to, mind you, but it's strange."

"Not so strange," Cooper contradicted. "When Jake was talking about what he would do to Camille, Owen got very agitated. His whole body was shaking. I think he's sweet on her, and he obviously didn't know what Jake had planned for her."

"Maybe you're right, Coop. He never tried to harm her." Seth rose with Cooper's help. "Thanks. I think I can make it back now."

"I don't need to stay in bed, I feel as strong as an ox." Seth's frown was mutinous. He pulled on his right boot, a grimace of pain on his face. Walking slowly, he made his way across the cabin to the fireplace, where he took a cheroot from a box on the mantel and struck a match to it.

Camille stood just inside the doorway with a tray in her hands. Catching the door with her foot, she shoved it closed, and moved to the table to put down her burden. "I guess I should be thankful it's Sunday, or you'd be on your way to the woods to chop down the biggest tree you could find just to prove how tough you are."

"Nag, nag, nag," he muttered under his breath, trying to ignore the throbbing ache in his arm where Jake's ax had cut deep the night before. Phoebe had carefully stitched it at Camille's request since her own sewing skills were lacking. His wife, however, had insisted on caring for his other needs. Her tender ministrations had nearly driven him out of his mind. He loved her deeply, so much so that he was willing to let her go, but the prospect ripped through him like the slash of a knife.

Camille ignored his bad humor as she unrolled the strips of cloth bandages and opened the tin of salve. "The least you can do is let me look at your wounds and change the dressing. I brought some strong coffee and Hallie made your favorite cinnamon rolls."

He tossed his cheroot into the fire and took a seat at the table with a sigh. As he unbuttoned his shirt, his eyes roamed over her enticing curves outlined by a soft, green wool dress. He caught the faint scent of lavender and cinnamon that clung to her. The ache in his loins bothered him more than the one in his arm. Slipping the shirt off, he held out his arm, and she began unwrapping the bandage with gentle hands.

An anxious frown marred her brow as she lifted the material away from the wound. Taking a clean cloth from the bowl of water, she squeezed it out and began cleansing the wide, ugly gash. Tears filled her eyes, and she blinked them away. "What an awful fight it must have been," she whispered, horrific visions filling her mind.

"Don't cry, sweetheart." He reached up with his free hand and wiped a tear from her cheek. "I was lucky he gave me the chance to fight. He could have killed Coop and me in cold blood."

She savored his touch, her heart pounding. "We can be thankful for that at least." Finished with the clean dressing, she stepped back, her eyes avoiding the mat of dark hair furring his muscled chest. Needing to put some distance between them, she said, "I'll let you eat before I take a look at the other wounds." She wandered over to the window and pushed open the wooden shutter to gaze out at the misting rain.

"Did you take care of your business in town?" she asked casually.

"It was interrupted when I learned of Owen's escape. I was worried about all of you here, so I returned with the sheriff."

A vague answer, she thought, and she could guess at the reason. Until he was definite about the divorce, he wouldn't say anything. Her throat tightened as hot tears stung her eyes. "Hallie's been cooking all day," she managed to say. "She said you ordered a celebration supper, but wouldn't say what it's about." She forced herself to turn and look at him.

He glanced up, his expression carefully blank. "I'd rather not talk about it until it's final."

"You can tell me, Seth. It's about a divorce, isn't it? Did you think I wouldn't guess?" she asked quietly.

Chapter 21

Seth's eyes widened in surprise. "A divorce? I don't know what you're talking about."

A slow anger dulled the edge of her pain. "Do you think I'm stupid? Patience is a widow, free to marry, but you married me and feel responsible for my welfare. I won't try to hold onto you if you want to marry her. You should know that." She expected to see guilt in his eyes, but found he looked even more perplexed.

"Marry Patience?" he said, and rose from his chair. He moved toward her, shaking his head. "Maybe we do need to talk."

From outside came the sound of the dinner bell being rung repeatedly. Camille stuck her head out the window and saw a wagon coming up the hill from the river road. Vladimir and Patience sat on the high seat. Her heart sank.

Seth peered out from behind her. "Come on, Camille. Let's go see if there's any news from town."

She resisted the hand he placed on her arm. "No! We haven't had our talk yet."

"It can wait until later. I promise we'll clear this up," he insisted, and pulled her along after him. When they reached the cookhouse, there was a crowd of loggers around the wagon, but they parted to let Seth and Camille through. A young stranger, yet not a stranger, stood beside the wagon wearing canvas pants and a red flannel shirt. His hair was dark auburn, his eyes a clear, sky blue.

Camille stared at the man, and the years fell away as if by magic. It could have been yesterday when he stood on the deck of the ship, tall and handsome, waving good-bye.

His gaze devoured her. "You don't look like that little girl with pink ribbons in her braids, but I'd know that brave smile anywhere." Tentatively, he held out his hand to her.

She took it and let him pull her close. Squeezing her eyes shut to hold back the tears, she savored the feel of his embrace. "Oh, Forrest . . ."

There was loud applause and whistles from the men before they drifted into the cookhouse to give the brother and sister some privacy for their reunion.

Camille could feel the love pouring from him, and she soaked it up like a healing balm to her torn spirit. "I wanted to believe I'd find you, but I was so frightened I wouldn't," she murmured, the tears thick in her throat. Pulling back, she gazed up into his dear face, assuring herself he was truly there. A wild bubble of joy burst inside her, and she laughed and cried at the same time.

"My baby sister," he breathed, his own eyes glistening with unshed tears. "You've grown so beautiful, but then I knew you would. You always had the look of Mama about you. My God, I've missed you." He pulled her close again.

After a few minutes, they were able to let go. He gave her his handkerchief, and she wiped her eyes and blew her nose. Ignoring the soft mist falling out of the evening sky, she took his hand and led him toward the little bridge as the muted sound of voices from the cookhouse faded away. "Why didn't you write to me?" he asked solemnly.

She shook her head sadly. "I didn't hear from you. Aunt Lavinia got your letters and destroyed them."

He closed his eyes a moment and sighed. "I'm so sorry, Camille. I shouldn't have left you." They stopped on the bridge and sat down.

"I was so afraid something had happened to you, but in my heart, I knew you were alive. After a while, though, I began to believe you had forgotten about me—Aunt Lavinia said you had."

"I've thought of you every single day since I left, honey. And I deeply regretted leaving you to that old woman's mercy." He slipped an arm around her shoulders and drew her close. "Two years after I signed up on that merchant ship, I decided to come back for you. I hadn't made the fortune I'd planned on, and realized I probably wouldn't. We were docked in London, and due to sail back to Charleston when I got impressed into the British Navy. I was drinking one night in a dockside tavern, and when I woke up the next morning, I was aboard a British man-of-war heading for the African coast."

"But you're an American!"

His laugh was harsh. "They don't care who you are, just that you can work. The only other alternative they give you is death. It was five long years before I could escape."

"How terrible for you."

"It was Hell, but I survived, and even made it back to Charleston. I went straightaway to Aunt Lavinia's to get you, but she told me you weren't there. She said she'd sent you to some fancy school in Virginia so you could be educated properly. She said you were happy, and I would spoil your chances for a good life if I interfered."

Camille shook her head and whispered, "I never knew you came for me."

"I know now I shouldn't have believed her, but she was convincing. I took a long look at myself and realized I had nothing to give you but a hard life. For your sake, I decided to leave things as they were."

"There wasn't any school in Virginia or any advantages for me. The reason I'm here is because she was going to marry me off to a man old enough to be my grandfather, and so I ran away."

"May she rot in Hell," he muttered. He kissed the top of her head and said, "You obviously got the letter I sent telling you about Oregon."

"It was by accident. I ran into a sailor friend of yours one day on the docks. He was on his way to Aunt Lavinia's to deliver a letter from you. If fate hadn't stepped in, we might never have found each other."

"But we did, and we never have to think about Aunt Lavinia again," he promised. Tipping her chin up with his finger, he smiled at her. "Tell me what's been happening to you. We've got a lot to catch up on."

The painful situation with Seth returned to the forefront of her mind. Blinking back the tears, Camille's voice was shaky. "Oh, my ... there's been so much, I don't know where to start."

"Well, how about your husband? Are you happy?"

"Seth is ... wonderful, and yes, I've been happier with him than I can say, but he's not in love with me."

Forrest frowned. "Vladimir and Patience said the two of you were having some difficulty, but they assured me you were the perfect couple. What gives you the idea he doesn't care?"

She explained briefly the circumstances surrounding her arrival in San Francisco and their marriage. "I can't understand why Patience led you to believe we have a good marriage. She and Seth used to be sweethearts, and if I wasn't around they would resume their courtship, I believe."

Forrest drew his lips in thoughtfully. "You might be wrong, little sister," he suggested, a mysterious twinkle in his eyes.

She shook her head. "I don't think so."

"One thing I've learned is things are not always what they seem," he cautioned. "As a matter of fact, I wasn't sure you'd want me around after all these years."

Camille pinched his cheek. "Just try to get away again, big brother."

He laughed and stood up, pulling her with him. "I'm as hungry as a bear. Think we could have some supper?"

"Men! All they ever think about is their stomachs," she grumbled, holding tightly to his hand as they walked to the cookhouse.

Camille reveled in having her brother by her side throughout the evening. She introduced him to the others and felt as if she were uniting two families, adopted and related. She was happy, yet there was still the discussion with Seth to be faced. Whatever the outcome, though, she would always be grateful to him for reuniting her with her brother.

Seth's eyes followed Camille all evening, a secret smile curving his lips. The conversation seesawed between the incident with Paul Jarvis, Owen's escape and the confrontation between Seth and Jake. Forrest chided Camille in a brotherly fashion for her reckless behavior, but she merely smiled. Hallie brought out the cakes Seth had requested and he sent two men to fetch a barrel of whiskey. Toasts were drunk in celebration, and the men were still singing and toasting when the dishes were done. Camille felt the effects of her unsettling day, and finally said good night to her brother and left the cookhouse with Phoebe.

"Are you all right, honey?" Phoebe asked as they walked along. "I don't know how you've held up these last two weeks."

Camille smiled wryly. "I'm starting to get used to the excitement. I count it a dull day if I don't get kidnapped, shot at or bushwhacked."

Phoebe clucked her tongue. "And through it all, she has a sense of humor. I want you to know I appreciate what you did for Cooper. If you hadn't followed them, it could have turned out very different."

"For a while there, I thought we were lost." Camille shuddered and pulled her shawl tighter despite the warmth of the night.

Someone called her name, and Camille turned to find Seth bearing down on them. They were at the bridge when he caught up. "Could I talk to you a minute, Camille?"

She nodded and turned to Phoebe. "I'll be along shortly."

When Phoebe left them, Seth frowned. "There's a lot we need to discuss, but first, I didn't get a chance to speak to you about what you did yesterday. What in hell were you thinking of when you followed Jarvis and Cooper into the woods?" he asked.

Camille blinked. "I . . . I don't think I like your tone," she said, her chin coming up.

"And I don't like it when you put yourself in danger. I can't leave you alone for a minute, can I? You draw trouble like a magnet."

Her eyes shot blue fire. "Well, mister, you won't have to worry about it much longer, now will you? Why don't you tell me about our divorce and get it over with. Do you have to get mad before you can tell me the truth?"

He looked at her with mingled exasperation and tenderness. "I'm not angry, Camille. I suppose I've just been worrying about the crazy things you do." He reached for her arms, drawing her resisting body toward him. "In the first place, I haven't looked at another woman since the day we got married, much less planned to marry one. And in the second place I love you and I'm tired of waiting for you to realize it."

Camille felt the painful weight lift from her heart as his words soaked in. The tenseness between them melted away. "You love me?" she asked, her voice barely a whisper. "You don't want a divorce?"

He bent his head and took her mouth tenderly, tracing her lips with his tongue, and then exploring its warmth with her full cooperation. After a minute, he raised his head. "Do I need to say more?" he asked, a twinkle in his dark eyes.

She grinned. "Yes . . . but not right now." Taking his face in her hands, she drew him down for another heart-stopping kiss. His arms moved around her, strong and solid, holding her fiercely. After a time, he pulled away and picked her up. Striding toward their cabin, he chided her gently. "You haven't said how you feel about me, Mrs. Braden?"

"Seth! Put me down, you'll open that wound," she protested, but he ignored her. She wound her arms around his neck a little tighter, and complied. "I'll love you till the day I die. There, are you satisfied?"

He grinned. "That's better. I'm moving back into my house, woman, and I'm not moving out again until we build a bigger one. Understand?"

She giggled. "Cooper will be so lonesome."

"No, he won't. My little sister's got a ring through his nose already, and it won't be long before he puts one on her finger." Seth kicked the door open and strode in.

Phoebe glanced up with a start from turning the covers down. Seeing Camille in his arms with a smile on her face, Phoebe grinned. "My goodness, Camille, did you sprain your ankle or something?"

Seth made a face at her. "Don't take this the wrong way, sis, but get the hell out. Hallie would love to have you over at her place, I'm sure." He set Camille on her feet and let his hands rest lightly on her shoulders.

Camille's cheeks turned a rosy hue. "Seth! That's not very mannerly," she chided.

Phoebe chuckled. "It's all right, Camille. I'm more than happy to move to Hallie's." As she walked around them, she winked at Camille. Taking her shawl from a peg by the door, she said over her shoulder, "It's about time."

When they were alone, Seth barred the door and blew out one of the lamps, leaving the room in semidarkness. He placed another log on the fire and then moved to Camille's side. Sliding his arms around her waist, he pulled her close and nuzzled her neck, breathing deeply of her womanly scent. "I've dreamed about you every night, all warm and soft and naked in my bed."

Camille moaned as his hands cupped her buttocks and pulled her close to his burgeoning erection. "Oh, Seth," she breathed, "I thought you were still in love with Patience. I felt like I would die of the pain."

He trailed kisses up the slim column of her throat and paused at her ear. "Once I met you, I realized I was never in love with her. We were always friends, nothing more." He raised his head to look at her. "That's why I spent some time with her. I was lending moral support because she found out her husband was already married. He was a smooth-talking scoundrel who took off with the money from her dowry, leaving her pregnant."

"Oh, dear, how awful for her," she said, feeling guilty for all the bad things she'd thought about the girl. "What about the baby?"

"She miscarried. Phoebe was so worried about her mental state she brought her out here to recuperate."

"No wonder she looked so unhappy when she arrived. I thought she was upset to find the two of us married."

"Patience knew long before I did we were not suited for marriage."

She smiled. "Did you know Vladimir is smitten with Patience?"

He chuckled. "I'd have to be blind not to notice. I think

they'll find their way to each other. For a while, I was jealous of Vladimir. Hell, I was jealous of Paul Jarvis and Coop. I had to fight the urge to smash some faces.''

Her brows rose. ''You were jealous of Coop?''

He sighed. ''I know it's silly, but I thought the two of you were attracted to each other.''

''And all the time, I thought you were acting funny because you didn't want to look foolish in front of your men.'' She reached up and brushed a lock of his dark hair away from his brow.

''You've led me a merry dance, Camille Sinclair Braden, but now you've got to settle down and be a proper wife. No more running away and no more dangerous escapades. Life wouldn't be worth living without you.'' His teasing tone turned serious as he made the last statement. He let her go for a moment and fished in his pants pocket. Picking up her left hand, he slipped a plain gold wedding band on her third finger. ''I bought this the day after we landed in Empire City. I've been saving it for the right time.''

Camille felt her heart swell with love. He had always intended to stay with her. Somehow, it made all the uncertainty seem trivial. She smiled. ''I have something for you too.'' Going to the chest of drawers behind the screen, she took out the watch. When she placed it in his hands, he caressed the embossed top with his thumb. ''It's a handsome gift, my love.''

''I got it the day we were shopping in the general store. The ship reminded me of our wedding trip.''

He slipped the timepiece in his pocket as she held up her ring to the firelight and admired it. Finally, she turned mischievous eyes on him. ''You said something about a proper wife. What do you mean by that?''

Gathering her close to him again, he dropped a kiss on her lips. ''I mean you'll have to learn to sew my shirts.''

''And?''

"And knit socks like the ones my mother used to make."
His mouth dipped and took another, longer kiss.

"And?"

"And cook all my favorite foods."

Her brows rose. "Anything else, my lord and master?"

His eyes lit up. "Oh, yes, that reminds me, you'll have to obey my every command."

Her eyes widened in mock innocence. "You mean like I have in the past?"

He gave her a smile that sent her pulse racing. "Exactly, my love," he murmured, his voice growing husky with desire. "And one more thing—love me more than anything." This time, he kissed her deeply, caressing her curves with impatient hands.

When he drew back, she whispered, "That's a pretty tall order, Mr. Braden. Perhaps you'd better send for another mail-order bride—a woman with all those wifely qualities?"

He swept her up into his arms and started toward the bed. "Not on your life, Camille. I'll just lower my standards and hire a maid to do the chores."

Epilogue

Owen Slidell disappeared into the Cascade Mountains eluding lawmen and bounty hunters alike. From that day on, there were sightings in the hills and mountains once or twice a year of a huge, hairy creature, half man, half beast, all the way from California to the northern Washington border. Some remembered the story of Owen Slidell, and swore it was him, but most folks who glimpsed the creature maintained that the thing they saw couldn't be a man.

Annabelle Maxwell was charged with the murder of her husband, but disappeared before the trial began. There were no clues as to her whereabouts.

Forrest Sinclair stayed on and eventually helped his brother-in-law manage the vast business interests they acquired. While on a business trip to the Orient, he saved the life of a beautiful Chinese girl, brought her home to Oregon and married her.

Cooper and Phoebe decided not to wait, and were united in a simple ceremony by the traveling preacher, Reverend Holbrook, when he made his next visit. Once the logging season was finished, they took a honeymoon trip to San Francisco and stayed in their new home on Rincon Hill, the one Cooper had inherited from his uncle. John Maxwell's fortune could have afforded Cooper retirement and a life of ease, but he and Phoebe decided they had the deep woods of Oregon in their blood and would continue in business with Seth. With a generous spirit, Cooper had two large Victorian houses built atop a hill over-looking the Braden-Maxwell cove—one for him and Phoebe and one for Seth and Camille. Eventually, a small town grew up around the sawmill.

As for Seth and Camille, they had two boys and two girls, all healthy and strong. They grew up fascinated by the romantic story their father told of how once upon a time, a beautiful orphan girl came West to be a mail-order bride.

ABOUT THE AUTHOR

Always a voracious reader, Sandra discovered at a very early age that she also wanted to be a writer. She combined her love of history and romance and sold four Heartfire Historicals to Zebra: *Deception's Fire, Rapture's Reward, Restless Passions,* and *Silver Seduction.*

She enjoys hearing from readers. Write to Sandra at, P.O. Box 230104, St. Louis, MO 63123.

Put a Little Romance in Your Life With
Fern Michaels

__Dear Emily	0-8217-5676-1	$6.99US/$8.50CAN
__Sara's Song	0-8217-5856-X	$6.99US/$8.50CAN
__Wish List	0-8217-5228-6	$6.99US/$7.99CAN
__Vegas Rich	0-8217-5594-3	$6.99US/$8.50CAN
__Vegas Heat	0-8217-5758-X	$6.99US/$8.50CAN
__Vegas Sunrise	1-55817-5983-3	$6.99US/$8.50CAN
__Whitefire	0-8217-5638-9	$6.99US/$8.50CAN